Praise for *Ivory*

"Another enjoyable Resnick yarn in which the inventive, colorful storyteller sustains a romantic vision of human destiny."
—*Publishers Weekly*

"Mike Resnick's new book *Ivory: A Legend of Past and Future* is a winner. Resnick is an excellent storyteller, and *Ivory* is thoroughly entertaining."
—*Cincinnati Post*

"Resnick captures the thrill of the 'hunt.' Highly recommended."
—*Library Journal*

"A lively tale."
—*Locus*

"Trust Mike Resnick to find a moral in this tale, and to make of that moral a marvelously satisfying SF novel ... A definite 'Don't miss!'"
—*Analog*

"Resnick is thought-provoking, imaginative, mordantly funny, and—above all—galactically grand."
—*L.A. Times*

Books by Mike Resnick

MIKE RESNICK
IVORY

**A
LEGEND
OF PAST
AND
FUTURE**

A TOM DOHERTY ASSOCIATES BOOK
NEW YORK

Copyright © 1988 by Mike Resnick

A TOR Book
Published by Tom Doherty Associates, Inc.
49 West 24 Street
New York, NY 10010

Cover art by Michael Whelan

ISBN: 0-812-50042-3   Can. ISBN: 0-812-50043-1

Library of Congress Catalog Card Number: 87-51405

First edition: September 1988
First mass market edition: August 1989

Printed in the United States of America

0 9 8 7 6 5 4 3 2 1

To Carol, as always

And to Perry Mason,
the best damned guide in East Africa

Acknowledgments

The author wishes to express his gratitude to the following people:

Dr. Juliet Jewell of the British Museum of Natural History's Department of Zoology, for allowing me into the museum's security storage area to examine the tusks of the Kilimanjaro Elephant;

Peter Capstick, white hunter and literary *raconteur*, for pointing out a couple of sources that I had overlooked;

The directors of the East African Wildlife Society, and especially Shereen Karmali, editor of *Swara*, for their encouragement;

Stephen Kimmel and Dr. Dean R. Lambe, for the use of their *World Builder* computer program;

Beth Meacham, my editor, for her enthusiasm and support from the very first moment I mentioned this project;

And, most of all, my good friend Perry Mason, for sharing his time, his knowledge, and his country with me, and helping me retrace Jumbo's last journey from the banks of the Tana River to the slopes of Kilimanjaro.

Contents

The ivory of the Kilimanjaro Elephant, photographed at Zanzibar in 1898. PHOTO COURTESY OF CAMERAPIX, NAIROBI

1

The Gambler
(3042 G.E.)

I had many names.

The Samburu called me Malima Temboz, *The Mountain That Walks, for I towered above all others of my kind, and always I would climb the next hill or cross the next valley to see what lay beyond.*

To the Kikuyu I was Mrefu Kulika Twiga, *Taller Than Giraffes, for I could pick succulent delicacies that were beyond the reach of the largest of animals, and no shadow was as long as mine.*

The Makonde knew me as Bwana Mutaro, *Master Furrow, for wherever I went my tusks would plow up twin furrows in the hard African earth, and my spoor could be mistaken for no other.*

In Maasailand I was Fezi Nyupi, *White Gold, for a veritable fortune protruded from my mouth, a fortune such as no other member of my race had ever carried.*

And now I am known only as the Kilimanjaro Elephant, my true name lost on the winds, my body decayed, my bones turned to dust. Only my spirit remains, restless and incomplete.

It was a typical night on Athenia.

The storm had reached gale force. Dark clouds of methane swirled about the sky while tidal waves of ammonia raced across the oceans and crashed resoundingly against the jagged cliffs. Bolts of blue lightning gave the clouds an eerie glow, and the endless claps of thunder seemed to herald an imminent and unpleasant Day of Reckoning.

Once, many centuries ago, the Democracy had possessed a mining colony on Athenia, and the tallest of the planet's mountains, which had been given the less than original name of Mount Olympus, was still honeycombed with hundreds of miles of tunnels and shafts as testimony to that bygone era. Then other worlds had been opened up, richer worlds whose resources were easier to plunder, and the miners had moved on, leaving the mountain—and the planet—completely deserted.

It had remained deserted for almost a millennium, until the day that Tembo Laibon claimed it as his own, erected a dome at the very apex of the mountain, and called it the House of Blue Lights, in acknowledgment of the eternal storm that raged overhead. The House of Blue Lights was ostensibly a tavern, but of course nobody came to the ninth planet of distant Beta Greco merely to drink. In fact, it was precisely because Athenia was so far out on the Galactic Rim and so far from humanity's seats of power that the House of Blue Lights flourished, not so much as a bar but as a meeting place for outlaws and fugitives of all races. The many-limbed Kreboi, who inhabited Beta Greco III and had no love for the Democracy, gave Tembo Laibon permission to operate and extended their protection to include his world.

And now some two dozen humans and nine non-humans sat in the main room of the tavern, ignoring the brilliant blue explosions that illuminated the atmosphere outside the dome. Two men sat huddled with a trio of elongated, crimson-skinned, narrow-eyed Canphorites, negotiating the price for a secret cache of laser weapons; a flashily-dressed silver-haired man was telling two slightly bored companions fantastic tales of the Dreamwish Beast and other myths of the spaceways; a delicate, crystalline being from the Atrian system, his body enclosed in a suit designed to muffle potentially dangerous sounds, sat motionless in a corner, staring balefully at the airlock for no discernable reason; a pair of elegant women, exquisitely coiffured, were bartering their services to a quartet of men who obviously had no need to haggle but seemed to enjoy it anyway; two furry, tripodal Lodinites were arguing with a corpulent and obviously unsympathetic man over the price of a rare Doradusian carving that sat on the table before him.

In a corner four men, another Canphorite, and a Kreboi were playing *jabob*, a card game that had been invented half a galaxy away. The game was entering its seventh month and had had a total of 403 participants. When a player was broke, or tired, or hungry, or decided that he had business elsewhere, he turned his seat over to the next in line. Three men currently sat at an adjacent table, each waiting their turn to join the game.

But despite all this activity, everyone knew that there was another game going on behind locked doors in Tembo Laibon's back room—*the* game.

The room itself had always been the subject of much speculation, for it was here that Tembo Laibon kept his storehouse of personal treasures. Above the hand-carved bar were four mounted heads of hideous, flesh-eating beasts from Earth itself, while pelts of still other animals covered the entire back wall. There were a score of long metal spears on display, as well as a number of small wood carvings locked inside a glass case. And, finally, there were the twin pillars of gently curved ivory that dominated the room, towering above everyone, man and alien alike, who was permitted to see them.

Tembo Laibon himself was there, all six foot nine inches of him, his black skin shining like polished ebony, clad as always in the pelts of alien animals. He sipped a green concoction from a tall glass, wiped his lips, and looked around the table as he began shuffling the cards.

To his immediate left was the alien known only as the Gorgon, a huge, purple-skinned monstrosity who claimed to be from the New Roanoke system. Everyone knew that the New Roanoke system was uninhabited, but one look at his bulging muscles and protruding fangs was sufficient to convince them to suspend their disbelief and inquire no further into his origins or past. Nobody knew how many sentient beings the Gorgon had killed, but rumor had the total well above one hundred.

The Gorgon had been losing heavily for the past two hours, and, not much of a talker to begin with, he had grown increasingly sullen.

Not so the Iron Duchess. More machine than woman, her metal hands were busy putting her winnings into tidy little piles, her titanium teeth reflected the lightning as she smiled, her artificial heart pumped chemically-enriched blood through plastic veins, and her mechanical voice filled the room with the strange melody of her happy chatter. Tembo Laibon studied her out of the corner of his eye, and wondered how much of her was actually alive.

One who was unquestionably alive, and reveling in it, was the creature that sat to Tembo Laibon's right. Nobody knew what it had been originally, but somehow, somewhere, as it wandered down the highways and byways of its life, it had decided that it wanted to be on the winning side for a change, and had undergone a series of surgical alterations that left it looking like a misshapen human. Its eyes were orange, its nostrils were too far apart, its ears were too flat against its head, one could still see where extra fingers and opposing thumbs had been removed from each hand, and it continually shifted its position on its chair, for it had not yet adjusted to the way its new body bent.

It spoke in exquisite Terran, as if it had spent its formative years in an exclusive school on Deluros VIII or even Earth itself, it brushed its locks of false hair back from its reconstructed forehead, it drank dry martinis and tried to hide its expression of distaste, and, when it felt no one was watching, it turned to admire its reflection in the glass of the reinforced viewport that Tembo Laibon had inserted on one wall of the room.

It called itself Son-of-Man, and thus far this evening it was playing as if a more revered Son of Man were standing by its shoulder and bringing it luck.

Sitting directly across from Tembo Laibon was Buko, the red alien from Sigma Silani IV. His lizardlike skin looked slick and moist, and glistened in the dim light of the viewport, and his face, which was incapable of expression, bore a striking resemblance to the dragons Tembo Laibon had read about when he was a small child. Buko was totally naked, and his skin exuded a too-sweet odor of alien oils. Perched motionless between his shoulder blades, its transparent claws and long beak buried deep in his flesh, was a tiny featherless birdlike creature that lived in some bizarre kind of symbiosis with him.

Finally Tembo Laibon put the cards down on the table and shifted his weight on his chair, which hovered a few inches above the floor. The ship carrying the last two players had just docked, and he had suspended the game until they arrived at the table.

"I'd like a drink, please," said Son-of-Man, flashing him

a smile that displayed a mouthful of carefully-chiseled purple teeth.

"Same as last time?" asked Tembo Laibon.

"But of course," replied the thing that looked like a man. "Alien drinks are so . . . so *gauche*." It wrinkled its artificial nose distastefully.

"Anyone else?" asked Tembo Laibon, watching an exceptionally violent blue explosion through the viewport. He wondered idly if the lightning above the sprawling Serengeti Plains was as foreboding, and decided that it couldn't be.

"Last call for drinks."

There was no response, and Tembo Laibon tapped out an order on the panel in front of him. A moment later a robot entered the room, bearing a single glass on a polished silver tray.

"Thank you," said Son-of-Man as the robot placed the drink on the table.

"You are welcome, Honored Sir," replied the robot in a grating monotone.

"He looks so ludicrous!" tittered Son-of-Man as the robot walked away. "A metal monstrosity shaped like a man!"

"What's wrong with metal?" asked the Iron Duchess, as the reflected glow of a blue lightning bolt illuminated her platinum nails and titanium teeth. "It wears a lot longer than flesh."

"Oh, my dear lady!" said Son-of-Man. "I meant no disrespect, truly I did not. Please believe me."

She stared at him coldly, her pupils contracting slightly as tiny microchips within each eye made instant adjustments to the light of the explosions just beyond the viewport.

"I forgive you," she said at last.

"Thank you. I assure you that—"

"I forgive you," she repeated. "That does not mean I believe you."

"Enough talk," rumbled the Gorgon. "It is time to play."

"In a minute," said Tembo Laibon, calling his consciousness back from the green African savannah where it spent most of its time. "Two more participants have arrived."

"Can they afford the game?"

"Nobody gets into this room without an invitation," Tembo Laibon assured him. "They can afford it."

There was a momentary silence, and then the panel in front of Tembo Laibon flashed a silent message. He frowned and looked up.

"My robots tell me there are *three* of them out there."

"Who is the third?" asked the Iron Duchess.

"They're not sure. She looks likes a human female, but the readings are all wrong."

"I hope she's pretty," said Son-of-Man with what it thought was rugged masculine enthusiasm.

Tembo Laibon tapped a message on his panel. "Let's let them in and find out."

A moment later the door slid back, and two men and a woman stepped into the room. One of the men was powerfully built, broad and burly, with curly black hair and small dark eyes; he was Ajax the First, the brawn of the pair. The brain was small and wiry, and sported a bushy red beard; he was Ajax the Second. More than twenty outpost worlds had posted rewards for their capture, and yet they moved freely across the Outer Frontier and the Rim, and more than one bounty hunter who had tracked them down had wished he had gone after easier prey.

The woman, dressed in a glittering metallic blue gown, had long blonde hair piled high on her head, and wore a necklace of gleaming bloodstones from the mines of Altair III.

"Gentlemen, please introduce your companion," said Tembo Laibon, frowning.

"I am Helen," volunteered the blonde woman.

"She's our wife," explained Ajax the Second.

"*Our* wife?" repeated the Iron Duchess, arching an artificial eyebrow.

"His and mine."

"She's married to both of you?"

"That's right."

"She was not invited to participate," said Tembo Laibon. "She must leave the room."

"She's only an android," explained Ajax the First. "She won't bother anybody."

"Please deactivate her," said Tembo Laibon.

"I'd like to watch," said Helen.

Tembo Laibon looked at her. "Because of the stakes involved in this game, there must be no hint of impropriety," he explained. "You must be deactivated."

"How can there be any impropriety if she sits behind me and watches?" asked Ajax the First.

"I have no idea," replied Tembo Laibon. "Perhaps she can see through the backs of the cards. Perhaps she will compute the odds and find some way to relay them to you. It makes no difference. Tempers can run high in a game like this, and for your own sake I would not want it said that you took unfair advantage of your fellow participants."

"What about the little animal on *his* back?" demanded Ajax the First, pointing to Buko. "How do I know that *it* isn't helping him?"

"It is a symbiotic life form that oxygenates my blood when I am on low-gravity worlds," replied Buko.

"This isn't a low gravity world."

"It is to *me*."

"If you are through arguing," said Tembo Laibon patiently, "you may deactivate the android."

Ajax the First shrugged, then looked directly at the android.

"Go to the corner, Helen," he ordered, and she promptly walked to the farthest corner of the room. He then uttered a brief command in a tongue that was unfamiliar to Tembo Laibon. Helen's eyes closed and her head sagged on her chest.

"Satisfied?" said Ajax the First, turning back to the table.

"How do we know she is not still operative?" asked the Gorgon suspiciously.

"Devise any test you wish and apply it," said Ajax the Second.

"That will not be necessary," said Tembo Laibon. "The house rules that she has been deactivated." He turned to Ajax the Second. "She is new," he noted.

"We commissioned her about a year ago. She was completed last month, and she's been with us ever since."

"Why would anyone want to marry an android?" asked Son-of-Man curiously.

"Why not?" responded Ajax the Second. "We like a little pomp and ceremony from time to time."

"How very interesting," said the thing that looked like a man. "By the way, we haven't been introduced. I am Son-of-Man."

"We are the Aiantes," said Ajax the Second.

"I beg your pardon?" said Son-of-Man.

Ajax the Second smiled. "You haven't read your Homer, have you?"

"Who is Homer?"

"*I've* read him," interjected the Iron Duchess. "And to the best of my memory, there was only one Ajax in the Trojan War."

"Then your memory deceives you," replied Ajax the

Second. "There was Ajax, son of Telamonian, a giant warrior who fought shoulder-to-shoulder with Odysseus. That's *him*. But there was also Ajax, son of Oileus, who was small, slight, and the most accurate of spearthrowers. That's *me*. Together, they were known as the Aiantes."

"I'm absolutely fascinated by names," said Son-of-Man enthusiastically. "How did you happen to choose yours?"

"Athenia offers us a safe haven, so whenever we're in this sector, we take Athenian names in gratitude," said Ajax the Second.

"But why the same name twice?"

"Why not?"

"It is very confusing."

"Not to us, it isn't," replied Ajax the Second.

"What names do you use in other sectors of the galaxy?" asked Son-of-Man.

"That's none of your business."

"I was just making conversation," said Son-of-Man petulantly. "There's no need to be rude."

"I wasn't being rude, just cautious," responded Ajax the Second. "If you're so interested in the genesis of names, why not ask the others?"

"There's no need to," replied Son-of-Man. "Buko and Tembo Laibon are proper names, and the origins of the other two are obvious."

Ajax the Second smiled. "Out here no human uses his own name."

Son-of-Man turned to Tembo Laibon. "Is that true?"

"Yes."

"Then what does Tembo Laibon mean?" asked Son-of-Man.

"In an ancient dialect called Swahili, it means Elephant Chief."

"What is an elephant?" asked Son-of-Man.

Tembo Laibon smiled. "Do you see those two pillars of white?" he said, pointing to the ivory.

"What is their relationship to you?" asked Son-of-Man.

"They belonged to the greatest elephant of all," said Tembo Laibon. "I am descended from a race called the Maasai. They used to hunt elephants with spears such as you see on the back wall." He paused. "The last elephant was killed four millennia ago."

Son-of-Man got to its feet and walked over to the ivory.

"They look like wood," it said at last.

"Once they were white, and gleamed like silver in bright light."

"This must have been a very large animal," continued Son-of-Man, obviously impressed. "Are these its ribs?"

"They are its teeth."

Son-of-Man threw back its head and laughed. "You have a remarkable sense of humor!"

"They are its teeth," repeated Tembo Laibon.

"No animal that ever lived had teeth half so large," retorted Son-of-Man. "You are making fun of my ignorance."

"I am enjoying your ignorance," replied Tembo Laibon. "But I am telling you the truth."

"Ridiculous!" muttered Son-of-Man, returning to its seat. It focused its orange eyes on Tembo Laibon for a long moment. "Why are you the Elephant Chief? Your teeth are no longer than mine."

"I am the Elephant Chief because I say I am," answered Tembo Laibon with some annoyance. "Do you plan to spend the rest of the night disputing my right to call myself what I wish, or are you ready to play cards?"

"Cards, by all means," said Son-of-Man. "I have better luck with them than with getting you to answer a civil question."

"Same rules as always?" asked Ajax the Second.

Tembo Laibon nodded. "No currency presently in use in the Democracy will be accepted."

"Not even Stalin rubles?"

"None."

"You let us use them last time," complained Ajax the Second.

"They were all you had last time," replied Tembo Laibon. "And I told you then that they would not be acceptable again."

Ajax the Second frowned. "What about Maria Theresa dollars?"

"Only for the amount of gold they contain."

Ajax the Second muttered something under his breath. "This could be a short night," he said more audibly.

"Since I do not wager, but only deal the cards," said Tembo Laibon, "I will relent if your opponents will accept your currency." He looked around the table.

"Not a chance," said the Iron Duchess. "I spend most of my time *avoiding* the Democracy."

"We all do," chimed in Buko.

"And some of us," rumbled the Gorgon in his deep, growling voice, "have very little confidence in the Democracy's longevity, and hence in the value of its currency."

"I hate to vote against my fellow man," said Son-of-Man with false regret, "but currency is too easily traced."

Tembo Laibon looked at Ajax the Second. "There you have it," he said.

The small man nodded his head. "All right," he said. "You've made your point."

"Buko," said Tembo Laibon. "Your game, your ante."

Buko snaked a hand into a pouch that was made of a pelt which bore a striking resemblance to human skin and withdrew a small sparkling gemstone. He stared at it for a moment, then shoved it to the center of the table. "*Krinjaat*," he announced.

"Please refresh my memory," requested the Iron Duchess, and Buko launched into a brief explanation of the rules of *krinjaat*, a card game that traced its origins to Binder X on the Inner Frontier, deep at the core of the galaxy. When he had finished speaking, she looked totally confused and decided not to pay the ante.

Son-of-Man sorted through his pile of winnings and finally withdrew an exquisite gold figurine. He held it up for Buko to see, then pushed it next to the gemstone after the red alien nodded his acquiescence. The Gorgon and the Aiantes followed suit, the former with an uncut diamond, the latter with a delicate crystalline sculpture, and finally Tembo Laibon dealt each player six cards, three face up and three face down. Bets and card exchanges ensued, and finally the Gorgon claimed the pot.

Tembo Laibon took a small crystalline pendant from the pot, held it up for the Gorgon's approval, and appropriated it for the house's commission. He then looked across the table at the Iron Duchess.

"Your game, your ante," he announced.

"Draw poker," she said, tossing a diamond bracelet onto the table.

The game proceeded for another ninety minutes, with Son-of-Man and the Gorgon doing most of the winning, the Iron Duchess breaking even, and the Aiantes losing so heavily that toward the end they paid the ante only for card games of human origin.

Then, as the storm continued to pound against the viewport, illuminating it with a series of ghostly blue lights, Tembo Laibon declared a ten-minute break.

The Gorgon immediately stood up and lumbered through the door and out to the main section of the tavern.

"But we just got here," complained Ajax the First.

"Some of us have been sitting at this table for four hours," said Buko, getting up and stretching his reptilian arms.

"Right," chimed in the Iron Duchess. "If Tembo Laibon hadn't called a break, I would have done so myself." She began flexing her fingers one by one, studying them with the interest of a master mechanic.

"I could use a drink myself," said Ajax the Second. "I think I'll pay a visit to the bar."

"What the hell," said his partner. "I might as well join you."

The Aiantes walked to the door, which slid open long enough for them to pass through.

"They haven't gotten any better since the last time," remarked Buko with a smile.

"You've played against them before?" asked the Iron Duchess.

"Twice," said Buko. "You'd think they'd have learned their limitations by now."

"The larger Ajax is the poorer player of the pair," added Son-of-Man. "He bluffs when he should fold, and folds when he should bluff."

"Perhaps I should only invite card players who are better than you," suggested Tembo Laibon wryly.

"That's not necessary," said the Iron Duchess. "Just keep 'em dumb and rich and we'll get along fine."

"If they lose two or three more hands they'll be destitute," observed Son-of-Man, getting up and walking over to examine the ivory more closely.

"Then they will rob another bank to replenish their funds," said Buko.

"Is that what they do?" asked Son-of-Man.

"When they're not losing at cards," replied Tembo Laibon.

"I suppose there's no immutable law that says a com-

petent criminal must necessarily be a competent gambler,"
said Son-of-Man thoughtfully. It turned to Tembo Laibon.
"Is that why you only deal and never become an active
participant?"

"I take ten percent of every pot," responded Tembo
Laibon. "Why should I gamble?"

"For the thrill, of course," said Son-of-Man.

"I find other things more thrilling."

Son-of-Man gestured to the four mounted heads. "Such
as killing animals?"

"If it's done honorably," replied Tembo Laibon.

"I trust that the killing involves more honor than your
obviously exaggerated recounting of it," said Son-of-Man.
"Imagine hunting something with teeth like *this*"—he laid
a hand on the ivory—"armed with only a spear!"

"You'd be surprised at the damage a spear can do," said
Tembo Laibon calmly.

"Have you ever hunted with a spear?"

"No."

"Then how do you know?" demanded Son-of-Man.

"It is my heritage."

"I suppose these tusks are part of your heritage too?"

"They are."

Son-of-Man stared at the ivory. "Where were these elephants found?"

"In Africa," said Tembo Laibon.

"Ah, Africa!" said Son-of-Man with an expansive smile.
"The mysterious Dark Continent, covering twenty percent
of the Earth's surface. Home of Mount Kilimanjaro and the
Sahara Desert."

"You've done your homework well," remarked Tembo
Laibon.

"But of course," agreed Son-of-Man. "It's *my* heritage,
too."

"Africa?"

"Earth."

"Have you been there?" asked Tembo Laibon.

"Certainly," said Son-of-Man. "Haven't you?"

Tembo Laibon shook his head. "Not much to see."

"My dear fellow, you're absolutely wrong! Earth is a veritable paradise!"

"Then why has almost everyone left it?" asked Tembo Laibon sardonically.

"Because Man always rises to challenges," replied Son-of-Man. "I wouldn't be anything else."

"So I gather."

"Really, you must go there sometime."

"I don't think so," replied Tembo Laibon. "They've built a city where my people used to live."

"Where was that?"

"At the foot of Kilimanjaro."

"Ah, yes," said Son-of-Man, happy to display its knowledge. "The city of Nyerere, climbing halfway up the side of the mountain: population two million, four airports, one spaceport, and home of the remarkable Waycross Sculpture." It paused. "Surely you would enjoy seeing such a wonder!"

"No."

"But why not?"

Tembo Laibon's dark eyes suddenly flashed with the fire of an ancient hatred. "Because Julius Nyerere was a Zanake, and the city bearing his name was built on Maasai land."

"The city of Nyerere was built more than three thousand years ago," pointed out Son-of-Man. "What possible difference can it make at this late date, especially to someone who has never even been to Earth?"

"I am a Maasai," said Tembo Laibon firmly. "It makes a difference."

"You are a Man, and all men are brothers," said Son-of-Man. "It is the aliens we must worry about, not each other."

"Spoken like one who knows," replied Tembo Laibon with a touch of irony.

The Gorgon reentered the room and plodded over to his chair, and a moment later the two Aiantes, fortified by alcohol, also returned.

"Are we ready?" asked the Iron Duchess, who had finally finished checking every artificial bone and mechanical joint.

Tembo Laibon nodded and took his seat.

"We are ready," he agreed, turning to Ajax the First. "Your game, your ante."

"Five-card stud poker," declared Ajax the First, taking a diamond ring from his finger and putting it in the center of the table.

Tembo Laibon dealt out the hands, then settled back to watch the players.

The Gorgon, he decided, was like the extinct rhinoceros: huge, hot-tempered, subject to sudden rages, but too stupid to survive against such warriors as Son-of-Man and the Iron Duchess. He was a holdover from the bygone days when a direct approach was the only effective one: he never bluffed, never tried to cut his losses, but simply bulled ahead. If luck was on his side, if the sun was in the warriors' eyes or they could not sidestep him in the tall grass, he would carry the day and win the battle, as the Gorgon had done earlier this evening—but he would never win the war.

Ajax the Second studied his cards, then shook his head and withdrew from the play. He is the silver-backed jackal, thought Tembo Laibon; confrontation simply isn't in his arsenal. He circles, he hides, he beguiles, he cajoles, but he never looks the larger predators in the eye as he waits for his turn at the kill. Still, sometimes cunning isn't enough, and tonight the jackal will go hungry.

Son-of-Man could scarcely conceal the smirk on its almost human face as it pushed a large sapphire to the middle of the table. Tembo Laibon looked at the huge pile of booty in front of it, and decided that it was the hyena of the House of Blue Lights' little menagerie: a grinning, cackling repository of the spirits of the dead, he was the most efficient of predators. But the hyena's shrill, irritating laugh and his hideously misshapen body made him shunned and hated above all other animals, as Son-of-Man was shunned and hated in all human and alien societies. The thing that looked like a man chuckled happily when Buko matched its bet, then turned and winked at Tembo Laibon. Yes, thought Tembo Laibon distastefully; definitely a hyena.

He turned his gaze next to the reptilian Buko. A snake, perhaps a mamba? No, the snake was too cunning and devious. Buko was the crocodile, swift and agile, his scaly skin glistening in the sunlight as Buko's shone beneath the blue explosions in Athenia's atmosphere. Hidden beneath the murky surface, the crocodile approached unseen and then struck, just as Buko had been doing all evening to the Aiantes, holding back, never raising, drawing them deeper and deeper into his river of destruction, then opening his fearsome maw when they were too far from shore to retreat.

Ajax the First looked at his cards again, frowned, then removed a jewel-studded platinum locket from his neck and tossed it onto the growing pile in the middle of the table. Tembo Laibon studied him carefully. A lion, he decided. Not a huge black-maned patriarch, such as the Maasai *elmoran*, armed only with spears and shields, would face in mortal combat as their rite of passage into manhood, but a young male who had not yet mastered the hunt, who stood upwind of his prey, stepped on dry branches, allowed a growl of anticipation to pass his lips. It was he who had lost most of the Aiantes' limited supply of treasure, he who had made the hunt doubly hard for Ajax the Second, he who had always given his prey a chance to escape by displaying his strength too soon. Yes, decided Tembo Laibon, a young lion—and, like the jackal, another who was destined to go hungry this evening.

Finally his eyes came to rest on the Iron Duchess. Here was a leopard, small, sleek, savage, intelligent, far more dangerous than animals twice her size. And, like the leopard, she adapted to all terrains. She would bluff the suggestible Son-of-Man and the cautious Ajax the Second; she would back down from the straightforward Gorgon and the hungry Ajax the First. She wasn't holding good cards this evening—even leopards didn't always kill fat, succulent antelope—but even so, she was ahead of the game, as leopards were always ahead of *their* game.

Tembo Laibon sighed and leaned back on his chair, looking at his reflection amid the flashing blue explosions in the viewport.

And what animal are you, King of the Elephants who has never been within fifty thousand light-years of the savannah that gave your people birth? Are you truly your namesake, the strongest and wisest of all living things?

Tembo Laibon stared at himself for a long moment. No, he decided, I am neither the elephant nor any other animal. I am the caretaker of the Maasai, he who tends the twin flames of our former greatness, who keeps them against the day when prophecies shall be fulfilled and gods shall walk the Earth and the withered tree of the Maasai shall bloom once more. We grew up naked and wild on the plains of the vast Serengeti, swarmed like locusts to the stars, and will follow destiny's spoor wherever it may lead us—and eventually it must lead us home.

In the meantime, it is very pleasant to sit here, safe and secure from the raging storms of Athenia, to grow rich from other people's follies, and to dream of the hot African sun on my back and the acrid scent of game in my nostrils.

He looked once again at the ivory. I must polish and clean you, turn you into white gold once more, prepare you for the day that lies ahead, though how far ahead I do not know. I will start tomorrow.

But then Tembo Laibon remembered that he could not start tomorrow, for tomorrow there would be another game, and the day after that yet another. So he would deal the cards and close his mind to the sights and odors of the players, and continue stockpiling his share of each pot against that day that he would truly be the Tembo Laibon of the Maasai.

"Are you going to deal, or are you going to sit there all night staring off into space?" asked Ajax the First, and Tembo Laibon realized with a start that the hand was over. He immediately gathered in the cards and began shuffling.

Tembo Laibon turned to Ajax the Second. "Your deal, your ante."

"Draw poker," announced Ajax the Second. He fished through his pockets, frowning, and finally withdrew a gold timepiece.

"Not enough," rumbled the Gorgon.

"Let me see it," said Tembo Laibon. He examined the timepiece for a moment, then pushed it back. "The house rules that it is insufficient."

"Then you're going to have to accept these," said Ajax the Second, tossing a handful of gold coins onto the table.

Tembo Laibon looked around the table, then nodded.

"The house will accept them for this hand only."

Ajax the First was about to add an uncut diamond to the pot when Ajax the Second grabbed his hand.

"Sit this one out," he said.

"Why?" asked Ajax the First, confused.

"I'll need it if I have to bet."

"Why can't *you* sit it out and let *me* play?" demanded Ajax the First.

"House rules," interjected Tembo Laibon. "If you name the game, you play the game."

"Do what I tell you," ordered Ajax the Second, and finally his partner shrugged and put the diamond back into a pocket.

Buko, the Gorgon, Son-of-Man and the Iron Duchess all placed their antes in the center of the table, and Tembo Laibon began dealing the cards.

"Openers?" he asked when each of the players had had a chance to evaluate their hands.

"Toss the diamond in," said Ajax the Second, and Ajax the First put the uncut diamond on the table. "What else have you got?"

Ajax the First rummaged through his pockets, and came up with another diamond, also uncut.

"Put it in," said Ajax the Second.

Buko studied his cards, then shook his head and tossed them down on the table. The other three matched the bet.

"Cards?" asked Tembo Laibon.

"Three," rumbled the Gorgon.

"Two," said the Iron Duchess.

"None," replied Son-of-Man.

Everyone paused to stare at Son-of-Man for a moment. It smiled smugly back at them.

"None," echoed Ajax the Second.

Tembo Laibon accepted the discards, then dealt out three cards to the Gorgon and two to the Iron Duchess.

"Bids?" asked Tembo Laibon.

"What have we got left?" asked the smaller Ajax.

"Nothing." Suddenly Ajax the First turned to the deactivated android. "Just a minute! We've still got her necklace."

"Get it and put it in."

"You're sure?" asked Ajax the First.

"I'm sure."

The larger Ajax got up, removed Helen's necklace, and placed it in the center of the table.

The Gorgon growled and declined to match the bid.

The Iron Duchess held up a large ruby, surrounded by emeralds and star sapphires in an exquisitely detailed platinum setting, Ajax the Second nodded, and she added it to the growing pile.

"I'll see your bet," said Son-of-Man, casually rolling a large emerald across the table, "and I'll raise you." It rummaged through its winnings, withdrew a delicate crystalline sculpture from the Atrian system, and gently placed it next to the emerald.

"I have nothing left," said Ajax the Second.

"Find something," said Tembo Laibon.

"You have your wife," noted Son-of-Man casually.

"And I'm keeping her!" snapped Ajax the Second.

"You must match his bet or forfeit the hand," said Tembo Laibon.

"I'm not forfeiting *this* hand! Give me a minute to come up with something." He gestured to Ajax the First, who walked around the table, took the cards from him, fanned them out just enough to see them, and then returned them. The two conversed in low whispers for a moment, and then Ajax the First nodded. "All right," said Ajax the Second. "I'll see your bet and raise you."

"With what?" asked Son-of-Man.

"Our ship. If I lose, we'll turn over the registration papers to you."

"How will you leave Athenia?" asked Tembo Laibon.

"I don't plan to lose."

"What's the book value of the ship?" asked the Iron Duchess.

"I'd say it's about eight hundred thousand credits."

The Iron Duchess smiled. "I'm afraid we can't accept the owner's evaluation."

Tembo Laibon activated his panel and posed the question. The answer appeared on a small screen a few seconds later.

"Five hundred and fifty thousand credits," he announced.

"Your machine's crazy!" snapped Ajax the Second. "It's worth an absolute minimum of seven hundred thousand!"

"Not in this game, it isn't," replied Tembo Laibon calmly. He paused. "Do you bet or do you fold?"

"I bet," growled Ajax the Second, glaring at him.

The Iron Duchess pushed three gems across the table.

"More," ruled Tembo Laibon after he had examined them.

She sighed, pressed a small gold figurine to her lips, and added it to the gems.

"I'll match your bet," said Son-of-Man, shoving a substantial portion of its winnings into the pot, "and raise you again."

"Damn it!" shouted Ajax the Second. "You know I haven't got anything left!"

"That's hardly my problem, is it?" said Son-of-Man superciliously.

Tembo Laibon waited for Ajax the Second to calm down. "Do you bet or fold?" he asked at last.

"I'm not folding. You'll have to take an IOU."

"IOU's are not permitted."

"We're good for it," said Ajax the Second. "You know that."

Tembo Laibon turned to the Iron Duchess. "Will you accept his IOU?"

"I don't even know him," she replied.

"And you?" he asked of Son-of-Man.

"I don't mean to be unnecessarily pessimistic," it replied, "but what good is an IOU if the author of it is apprehended by the police before he has a chance to pay it off?"

Tembo Laibon turned back to Ajax the Second. "There you have it."

Ajax the Second studied his cards. "You mentioned Helen," he said at last.

"That was a joke, my good man," said Son-of-Man.

"And *I* didn't mention her," added the Iron Duchess distastefully.

"I'm *not* folding," said Ajax the Second firmly. "How long have I got to raise some capital?"

"You may not leave this room," said Tembo Laibon. "That is the house rule, which I have already bent by allowing you to wager your ship when the registration papers are not on your person. You bet what you entered this room with, and when you have nothing left, you are through playing."

Ajax the Second stared at him for a moment. "You've been accumulating a tidy little pile. I want a loan."

"I am not in the business of making loans."

"You've known me for eight years," said Ajax the Second. "You know I'm good for it."

"Nevertheless."

"I want it for ten minutes, and I'll pay you twenty percent interest."

"You have no collateral," said Tembo Laibon.

Ajax the Second passed his cards to Tembo Laibon. "*This* is my collateral."

"I object!" said Son-of-Man.

"No one gives me orders in my own establishment," said Tembo Laibon, picking up the cards and examining them.

Ajax the Second had a straight flush in hearts, the seven through the jack.

"Well?" said Ajax the Second.

Tembo Laibon stared thoughtfully at the smaller Ajax, and made up his mind. The Maasai, after all, do not reach an accommodation with the jackal; they kill him, or, if they feel charitable, they throw him a bone.

"I will not lend you the money," said Tembo Laibon.

"But—"

"I am not through," said Tembo Laibon. "I will not lend you the money—but I will buy your hand from you."

"For how much?"

"Half of what I have before me."

"You'd better take it," urged Ajax the First. "It looks like the best offer we're going to get."

"And what about my ship?"

"If I win, I will sell it back to you."

"At book value?"

Tembo Laibon nodded.

"All right," said Ajax the Second bitterly. "It's a deal."

"I object!" said Son-of-Man.

"On what grounds?" asked Tembo Laibon.

"You yourself ruled that the one who named the game had to play the game."

"And he has played it as far as he can," answered Tembo Laibon. "If I don't buy his hand, he is through playing anyway."

"What do *you* say?" Son-of-Man asked the Iron Duchess.

"It makes no difference to me," she replied with a shrug. "Only the players will change—not the cards."

Son-of-Man considered her answer for a moment, then nodded its agreement. "I withdraw my objection," it said.

Tembo Laibon divided his pile of treasure in half, and

pushed one of the two new piles over to Ajax the Second. "You are finished playing for tonight," he said. "Your money and your treasure is no longer acceptable at this table until you replenish it."

"That's fine by me," said Ajax the Second. "Just finish the hand so we can leave."

Tembo Laibon estimated how much he owed to match Son-of-Man's bet and placed a number of jewels, pendants and carvings in the center of the table. "I call your bet," he announced.

And then the leopardess struck.

"And I raise it," said the Iron Duchess, as Son-of-Man looked its surprise and Tembo Laibon tried to remember how many cards she had drawn.

Son-of-Man raised again, and Tembo Laibon, after appraising the two bets, pushed the remainder of his treasure into the pot.

"And raise again," said the Iron Duchess, adding a perfect blue-white diamond.

Son-of-Man, seeming a little less sure of itself, merely matched the bet, and then turned expectantly to Tembo Laibon.

"I will see the bet," announced Tembo Laibon.

"With what?" asked the Iron Duchess.

He waved his hand around the walls. "Every artifact here is a rare and valuable collector's item, worth hundreds of thousands of credits on the open market. Choose any two, except for the ivory."

"I choose the ivory," said the Iron Duchess, looking more mechanical and less human with each passing second.

Tembo Laibon shook his head. "Other items are more valuable."

"Not to you," she said. "I want the ivory."

"I am its keeper. I cannot part with it."

"I am the keeper of the Blue Diamond," replied the Iron Duchess. "I choose the ivory, Tembo Laibon."

"You cannot even lift it. What would you do with it?"

"I'll think of something."

"Choose any other three artifacts," offered Tembo Laibon.

She shook her head. "If you're willing to part with them, they're no match for my diamond."

"I rule that they are."

"You abrogated your right to make such rulings when you purchased Ajax the Second's hand. And," she added, "by your prior ruling, you are forbidden to leave the room to bring back more treasure."

"I hate to vote against my host," said Son-of-Man pleasantly, "but she's quite right, you know."

Tembo Laibon leaned back and studied his cards again, lost in thought. Finally he nodded his acquiescence; the Maasai do not retreat in the face of danger.

"The ivory," he agreed.

"That's it," said Ajax the Second. "Let's see some cards."

Son-of-Man laid down its hand first: four aces and the three of clubs.

"Not good enough," said Tembo Laibon, laying down his straight flush.

All eyes turned to the Iron Duchess. Her plastic lips parted in a smile, showing her titanium teeth, as she placed her cards down on the table one at a time: nine of spades, ten of spades, jack of spades, queen of spades, king of spades.

Tembo Laibon sat in stunned silence for a full minute, while the Iron Duchess gathered in her winnings.

"I will buy the tusks back from you," he said.

"They're not for sale," she replied.

"You have no use for them."

"They will make a lovely trophy."

"What need have you for a trophy?" demanded Tembo Laibon. "You have never stalked the elephant across the African plains."

"But I *have* tracked Tembo Laibon to his own lair, and defeated him in fair and honorable battle," she replied with a smile. "Whenever I look at *them*, I will be reminded of *this*." She got to her feet. "I'll be back tomorrow with two of my assistants. Please have the ivory ready and waiting."

"What about my ship?" demanded Ajax the Second.

"I'll be happy to sell it to you," said the Iron Duchess.

"For book value?"

"*Plus* fifty thousand credits," she replied with a smile.

"That's robbery!" snapped Ajax the Second.

"No," she corrected him. "That's business."

"You know I don't have the money with me."

"For another fifty thousand credits, I will take you to wherever your money is kept, and then return you to your ship."

He muttered something under his breath, then turned to Tembo Laibon. "Lend me six hundred thousand credits. I'll have it back to you in twenty-four hours."

"Go away," said Tembo Laibon.

"I *can't* go away!" said Ajax the Second in exasperation. "I need my ship."

"Go away," repeated Tembo Laibon tonelessly. "I have lost far more than a ship."

Eventually the Aiantes agreed to the Iron Duchess' terms and left with her. True to her word, she returned the next morning, and for the first time in more than a millennium the ivory passed from the possession of the Maasai.

Fourteen days later an enormous meteorite broke through

the force field that surrounded Mount Olympus and pierced the House of Blue Lights, killing everyone within it. Tembo Laibon was surprised that it had taken the god of his ancestors two whole weeks to find him.

First Interlude (6303 G.E.)

I was sitting at my desk, examining some authenticating hologram of a near-record Horndemon from Ansard IV, when I suddenly realized that I was no longer alone.

A large man, tall and well-muscled, stood in the doorway, staring at me. His skin was black, his hair close-cropped, his clothing stylish and well-tailored. Since I am almost never visited by anyone except senior editors, I assumed that he had chanced upon the wrong office.

"Good afternoon," I said. "Are you lost?"

"I don't believe so," he replied in a rich, deep voice. "This is the Research Department, is it not?"

"Yes."

"And you are Duncan Rojas?"

"That is correct," I replied, staring curiously at him. "Do I know you?"

"Not yet, Mr. Rojas—but you will. My name is Bukoba Mandaka."

He extended his hand and I took it. His grip was strong and firm.

"I am pleased to meet you, Mr. Mandaka," I said. "How may I help you?"

"They told me at Reception that you are in charge of research. Is that correct?"

"Research and authentication," I replied.

"Then you are the man I want to see. May I sit down?"

"Please do," I said, gesturing toward a chair that rested just beneath an ancient hologram of the legendary hunter, Nicobar Lane, posing beside an enormous Bafflediver he had just slain.

He ordered the chair to approach him, waited until it had floated over to him, turned it so that it faced me, and seated himself.

"I need your help, Mr. Rojas," he said quietly, "and I am prepared to pay handsomely for it."

"I am quite content with my job here at Wilford Braxton's, Mr. Mandaka," I said.

"I know. That is precisely why I have sought you out."

"I don't believe I made myself clear," I said. "I am very happy with my work and my position; I have no intention of leaving."

"You would be worth nothing to me if you left," he assured me. "It is essential that you have access to all of Braxton's data." He leaned forward intently. "I want you to work for me, right here in your office, during your free time and days off. With luck, it may require no more than a couple of evenings."

"I couldn't possibly consider it without first attaining the company's permission."

"I have already obtained it," said Mandaka.

"You have?" I said, surprised.

"Yes."

"What is it that you wish me to do?"

"I want you to find something for me, Mr. Rojas," he replied seriously. "Something that has been lost for a very long time."

"How long?" I asked.

"More than three thousand years."

"Three thousand years?" I repeated incredulously. "Is

this some kind of joke? Because if it is, I am a very busy man, and—"

He placed a holographic voucher for twenty thousand credits on my desk.

"It is made out in your name, and can be withdrawn from any branch of my bank once your retinagram, bone structure, and thumbprint have been confirmed," he said. "Does that seem like a joke, Mr. Rojas?"

I picked up the voucher and examined it. It looked authentic.

"No," I admitted. "It does not. Please continue."

"This is merely a down payment," he said. "When you locate what I am after, I will deposit another thirty thousand credits in any account of your choosing."

I tried to hide my surprise, stared thoughtfully at my interlaced fingers for a long moment, and found myself wondering what service I could possibly render in two or three evenings that was worth that much money.

"What are you looking for, Mr. Mandaka," I asked at last, "and how do you think I can help you?"

"I seek the tusks of the Kilimanjaro Elephant," he replied.

"I have seen photographs of elephants in books and museums," I said. "But I have no knowledge whatsoever of any particular animal known as the Kilimanjaro Elephant."

"Yes, you do."

"I do?" I said, surprised.

"Let me say, rather, that the Wilford Braxton's *Records of Big Game* does," he amended. "You have published four hundred and nine Terran editions—eighty-two under the imprimatur of Rowland Ward, and three hundred and twenty-seven since Braxton's acquired Ward—and every one of them since the third edition has listed the Kilimanjaro Elephant."

"Well, there you have the problem, Mr. Mandaka," I

said. "Our last Terran edition was published almost seven centuries ago, when the last bird was killed. With no possibility of surpassing the various records, there has been no need to come out with a new edition. Our main work these days is in the Quinellus and Albion Clusters."

"But museums and collectors from all across the Commonwealth use Braxton's for authentication of their exhibits, do they not?"

"Yes," I acknowledged. "But our information on these tusks will be seven centuries out of date."

"In point of fact, Wilford Braxton's information is more than three millennia out of date," he said. "If there were any current information, I would not be offering you fifty thousand credits to help me locate them." He paused and stared intently at me. "Will you accept my commission? I will, of course, pay for all computer time and access fees."

"Let us discuss exactly what is involved, and see if we're both still interested," I suggested cautiously.

"That is acceptable," he said. "But I must tell you that if you do not agree to work for me, I will hire one of your assistants." Suddenly his eyes seemed to glow with an unholy fire. "I will not be thwarted, Mr. Rojas."

"I understand," I said, though in truth I did not. "I will need some basic information," I added soothingly. "To begin with, we list the two hundred best trophies of each species. How will I know which of them is your Kilimanjaro Elephant?"

"He was the greatest of them all."

"You mean the largest trophy?"

Mandaka nodded.

"As I recall, there were two separate and distinct subspecies of elephant. Which was yours?"

"African."

"Just a moment," I said, turning to the small glowing crystal on my desk. "Computer?"

"Waiting . . ." replied the crystal.

"Check the 409th Terran edition, under the heading *Elephant*, sub-heading *African*."

"Done."

"What is the data on the largest trophy?"

"Left tusk, two hundred and twenty-six pounds; right tusk, two hundred and fourteen pounds." It went on to list the length and circumference of each.

"Is that your elephant, Mr. Mandaka?" I asked.

"Yes," he replied.

"Computer, who possessed the trophy at the time of the 409th Terran edition?"

"Unknown," answered the computer.

"Have any collectors or museums asked us to authenticate trophies of identical, or even similar, size and weight to these tusks since the 409th Terran edition was published?"

"Checking . . . no."

"Check through previous editions for the most recent listed owner of the tusks."

"Checking. . . The most recent listed owner was Tembo Laibon of Beta Greco IX, also known as Athenia. The listing appears in the 322nd edition, which was published in 3042 G.E. The 323rd edition, published in 3057 G.E., lists no owner."

"Thank you. Deactivate." I turned back to Mandaka. "I appreciate your offer, Mr. Mandaka," I said. "However, I would be taking your money under false pretenses if I didn't tell you that there is only a minimal chance of success. After all, we are talking about a pair of tusks that disappeared more than three thousand two hundred years ago."

"I have exhausted all other possibilities," he replied. "Somewhere in your files or your computer's memory banks or your correspondence there *must* be a clue, a spoor that you can follow until you find the tusks."

"Let me make sure that I understand you correctly," I said. "You have offered me twenty thousand credits to attempt to locate the tusks. If I do not succeed, am I expected to return the money?"

"Not if you have made an honest effort."

"And I am to receive another thirty thousand credits if indeed I do find them?"

He nodded.

"You understand that I will work on this project only at nights and during my spare time?"

"Yes."

"Then," I said, leaning back on my chair, "I agree to work for you. I'll need any information you can supply me with. Computer, record this portion of the conversation."

"Recording . . ." said the computer.

"Well, Mr. Mandaka," I said, "what can you tell me about them?"

"Very little more than your computer," he replied. "I know that Tembo Laibon lost them in a card game to a cyborg known only as the Iron Duchess, and she in turn seems to have vanished from human sight and history in the year 3043 G.E."

"There is no record of what happened to her?"

"She was a criminal," said Mandaka with a shrug. "Doubtless she had enemies." He paused. "If the tusks are not in a museum, and your computer implies as much, they may have changed hands hundreds of times since the Iron Duchess obtained them. I think trying to find out what happened to every owner is fruitless, especially since many of them lived on the Inner and Outer Frontiers, where records are at best incomplete. Besides," he added, "they are all dead; the tusks still exist. Tracing the ivory itself is the only viable course of action."

"What makes you so certain that the tusks still exist?"

"I would know if they did not," he said with absolute certainty.

"How?"

"I would know," he repeated in a manner that precluded further discussion of the subject.

"My next question has nothing to do with my investigation, but I can't help being curious: what do you propose to do should I find the tusks?"

"Purchase them," he said promptly.

"And if the owner will not sell?"

"He will sell," said Mandaka with such assurance that I thought it best not to ask why he thought so.

"What is their approximate value?" I asked.

"I thought you were the expert."

"Wilford Braxton's is merely a registry body for trophies, not a buyer or seller of them," I explained.

"I have no idea what they might be worth to a museum or collector—but I personally am prepared to pay two million credits for them."

"That's a lot of money," I said, impressed.

"They are very important to me," he replied.

"That is my final question," I said. "The elephant itself has been dead for almost seven thousand years. The tusks have been missing for almost three thousand. Why are you so interested in them? What is it about them that makes you willing to part with a veritable fortune to acquire them?"

"I don't think you would believe me if I told you," said Mandaka.

"That is quite possible," I replied. "But why don't you tell me and let me decide for myself?"

"When we know each other better, Mr. Rojas."

"Is that the only answer I am to be given?" I asked.

"For the moment," he said, rising to his feet and directing the chair back to its original resting place. "I don't wish to keep you from your work any longer, Mr. Rojas. I want you to be fresh when you begin tracing the tusks this evening."

"How will I contact you if I find them?" I asked.

"*I* will contact *you*," he replied. He walked to the door, then turned to me. "I cannot stress too greatly the importance of finding them, Mr. Rojas. You may well be the last hope for the future of my race."

"Your race?" I repeated, puzzled. "But you are a Man."

"I am also a Maasai," he replied with both pride and sorrow. "More to the point, I am the *last* Maasai."

Then he was gone.

It was many minutes before I went back to examining the holograms of the Horndemon.

I returned to my office after dinner, closed my door, ordered the couch to take the shape of a contour chair, and sprawled back on it.

"A gentle vibration, please," I said.

"Done," replied the couch, as a pleasant tingle went through my body.

"And a little heat in the small of my back."

"Done."

"And I think I would like a view."

The wall of my office suddenly became transparent, and the lights of the city flooded the room. My clothing instantly adjusted its color, abandoning its bright indoor hues and becoming a sedate brown.

"Thank you," I said. "Computer?"

The crystal on my desk glowed brightly. "Ready," it replied.

"Please recall to memory my conversation this afternoon with Bukoba Mandaka."

"Recalled."

"Do you understand what I have been hired to do?"

"You have been hired to locate the tusks of the animal known as the Kilimanjaro Elephant."

"That is correct. To help me, you will have to access a secondary source, since your own records stop with the 409th edition. Based on your knowledge of the problem, which source would you suggest?"

"If the tusks are currently recorded, they will be registered with the Master Property Tax File on Deluros VIII," answered the computer.

"Even if they're owned by a tax-free institution such as a museum?"

"Even tax-free institutions are required by law to list their property."

I considered it for a moment, then shook my head. "Mandaka said I was his last resort. If locating them was that easy, he'd have found them already."

"It will take me less than two minutes to verify your conclusion," said the computer.

"Go ahead, but I think it's a waste of time."

"Checking . . ."

"In the meantime, I think I'd better find out exactly what these tusks look like, so I'll know them if I see them. Have you any holograms on file?"

"No. But I do possess two photographs, both taken prior to the Galactic Era."

"Let me see them."

The image of a small black-and-white photograph suddenly appeared in the air just in front of me.

"Adjust my angle, please," I said.

My contour chair gradually became straight-backed.

"I need a larger image, please."

The photograph tripled in size. It was a picture of two white-clad men, each one supporting one of the tusks, which

towered far above them. The photograph faded, to be replaced by another one showing them on display in a museum.

"He must have been a monster," I said, awestruck by
the proportions of the ivory.

"He was an elephant," replied my very literal computer.

"I meant that he must have been enormous," I explained.

"Unknown."

"Unknown?" I repeated, puzzled. "How can that be
unknown?"

"The records are incomplete," replied the computer.
The second photograph vanished, to be replaced by the
Elephants, African page from the 409th Terran edition of
Records of Big Game. "Please note," it continued, "that
neither the date of death nor the identity of the hunter is
recorded. Furthermore, every other elephant listed was
measured for height at the shoulder and body length from
tip of trunk to tip of tail, but no measurements exist for
the Kilimanjaro Elephant."

"What about earlier editions?" I asked.

"The data is missing from all editions."

"Including the one that was contemporaneous with the
elephant?"

"That is correct."

I pondered the computer's remarks for a moment. "So
nobody knew anything about the elephant even when we
were still Earthbound, and the ivory completely disappeared three thousand years ago," I said with a sigh. "I
hope I'm being paid enough for this job."

"Reporting . . . The Master Personal Property Tax file
on Deluros VIII has no listing for the Kilimanjaro Elephant's tusks."

"I didn't think it would," I said. A private aircar shone

its lights into the office, practically blinding me, and the wall immediately changed from transparent to translucent, while the color of my clothing adjusted accordingly. "All right," I said at last. "Let's start with what we know about the ivory. Please give me its history since its first appearance."

"The tusks were purchased by an American company at an auction on an island called Zanzibar in 1898 A.D. They were shipped to England, where the British Museum purchased the larger one in 1899 A.D. The smaller was sold and resold many times before the British Museum acquired it in 1932 A.D. They remained in the British Museum until 2057 A.D., when they were donated to the Republic of Kenya and placed in the National Museum at Nairobi. In 2845 A.D. they were removed from Earth and transferred to the Natural History Museum on New Kenya. They disappeared in 16 G.E., appeared briefly on Alpha Bednari in 882 G.E., disappeared for another eight centuries, and then reappeared on the Outer Frontier in 1701 G.E., in the personal collection of Maasai Laibon. They remained the property of Maasai Laibon's descendants until 3042 G.E., when Tembo Laibon lost possession of them and our records cease. According to Bukoba Mandaka, Tembo Laibon lost them in a card game to a woman known as the Iron Duchess, but I cannot verify this."

"That's very curious," I mused. "I wonder if there's a connection?"

"I do not understand," said the computer.

"Didn't Bukoba Mandaka say that he was a Maasai?"

"Checking . . . Verified."

"And one of the owners of the tusks was Maasai Laibon. Could they be related?"

"I must use a secondary source to verify that."

"Please do. And while you're at it, find out exactly what a Maasai is."

"Checking . . ." There was a pause of almost two minutes. "Due to incomplete records, I cannot definitely verify the connection. However, there is a 98.37% probability that Bukoba Mandaka is a descendant of Maasai Laibon."

"Please explain."

"There were less than two thousand five hundred Maasai extant during Maasai Laibon's lifetime, and their numbers have decreased drastically during the past four millennia. Since it is a rigid Maasai social custom to procreate only with other Maasai, the probability of a hereditary relationship between Maasai Laibon and Bukoba Mandaka is 98.37%."

"What *is* a Maasai?" I asked.

"Before the advent of the Galactic Era, humanity was divided into numerous social or political groups, each with its own customs and identity. The Maasai were one of two thousand one hundred and three such groups inhabiting the continent of Africa."

"I also notice that Maasai Laibon and Tembo Laibon bear the same family name, but that Bukoba Mandaka does not," I remarked.

"Laibon is not a name, but rather a title. In the extinct Terran dialect of Swahili, Maasai Laibon means King or Chief of the Maasai, and Tembo Laibon means King or Chief of the Elephants."

"Does Bukoba Mandaka mean anything in Swahili?"

"No."

I pondered the information I had been given.

"So," I said, "if Bukoba Mandaka is a descendant of Maasai Laibon and Tembo Laibon, can we safely conclude that the Maasai have been interested in the ivory for more than four thousand five hundred years?"

"No," answered the computer. "You can draw such a conclusion only of those Maasai who actually possessed the ivory between 1701 G.E. and 3042 G.E."

"But you noted the paucity of their numbers. Doesn't it seem meaningful that the Maasai are so intimately connected with the ivory's history?"

"Not necessarily. We do not know how or why Maasai Laibon obtained possession of it, but it is worth a great deal of money. It is possible that the family retained possession of it only to increase its market value."

"I disagree," I said. "Mandaka doesn't want to sell it; he wants to *buy* it." I paused and frowned. "I wish I knew why."

"I possess insufficient data to offer an answer."

"I know," I said with a sigh. "Oh, well, this is all very interesting, but it's not getting us any closer to the ivory. I think we'd better get to work. Let me have some music, please; perhaps it will help me to think."

"Have you a preference?"

"Greddharrz, please."

The room was suddenly filled with the atonal rhythms and intricate light patterns of Greddharrz's misnamed Fourteenth Symphony—her first twelve had never been performed—and I ordered my chair to conform to the contours of my body once more. Ordinarily I don't like alien music, especially from the Canphor system, but this piece was an exception. The incessant percussion and carefully controlled dissonances always seemed to stimulate my adrenaline, and it was the piece I invariably chose when I was plotting a plan of attack for a unique research problem.

I sat motionless for perhaps five minutes, sorting out all the probable approaches, then ordered the chair to come to rest on the gently undulating carpet.

"Stop," I said, and the music and light patterns immediately ceased. "How much of your total capacity is under my control until the morning?"

"As of this moment, 83.97%. When I finish verifying data for the 36th Sigma Draconis edition, which will take another fifty-three minutes, 85.22% of my capacity will be at your disposal until nine o'clock tomorrow morning."

"Good," I said. "We're going to need every bit of it. First of all, I want you to access the Master Library Computer at Deluros VIII."

"There are one hundred and twenty-seven billion volumes on file in the Main Library Computer," it noted. "It will take seventeen days for me to scan the entire collection."

"I know," I replied. "But we don't have any leads, so we need a very general source. There could be a reference to the ivory in a personal memoir, an auction catalog, a museum brochure, a—"

"I ascertained this afternoon that no museum has asked us to authenticate the tusks since the appearance of the 409th edition," interrupted the computer.

"Not every museum asks us to authenticate its exhibits," I pointed out. "Nor do all alien worlds register their possessions with the Master Property Tax File. In fact, the Bureau of Property Tax has been centralized on Deluros VIII for only four centuries, so even human museums wouldn't have reported ownership of the ivory there prior to 5900 G.E."

"Noted."

"I want you to begin by accessing all listings of art and biological collections for the past millennium, and then, in order, all auction catalogs, all histories and studies of the Maasai, of Africa, and of Terran fauna. If you don't find what we're looking for, then access each of those subjects in five-hundred-year increments back to 3042 G.E. I also want you simultaneously to search for any mention of Tembo Laibon and the Iron Duchess, which means you must scan all accounts of the Outer Frontier beginning at—let me think—oh, I imagine about 3030 G.E. If you finish accessing all of these subjects without success, then begin a more general search through all non-fiction volumes in the Master Library Computer." I paused. "I also want you to scan all recent newstapes and electronic media for any mention or hologram of the ivory."

"Please define 'recent'."

"Within the past three years," I said. "Anything older than that is already on file in the Master Library Computer."

"Have you any further instructions, or shall I begin?"

"Not just yet," I said. "We've only covered the broad-based approach. Now let's see if we can't get a little more specific." I paused to clarify my thoughts. "We know that the ivory was on the Outer Frontier in 3042 G.E. We have no idea how many people have owned it in the intervening three millennia, but I think we can safely assume that sooner or later it must have come into the possession of someone who understood its true value. Therefore, I want you to scan all insurance records since 3042 G.E.; someone, somewhere, *had* to insure the tusks. Now," I added, "the ivory is a unique property, so begin your search with those insurance companies that were most likely to cover such an item. If you are unsuccessful, then scan the records of all the remaining insurance companies."

"Not all insurance records are accessible to me," said the computer.

"Everything during the Democracy and the Oligarchy should be a matter of public record," I replied. "If you reach the Monarchy without any success, let me know and I'll try to arrange access."

"Correction."

"Yes? What is it?"

"You used the word Monarchy. The proper term is Commonwealth."

"I stand corrected," I said. "However, I should alert you to the fact that Monarchy is a term that is used quite frequently in the electronic media, and is for all practical purposes synonymous with Commonwealth."

"Registered."

"That's all. Please access and scan all these sources simultaneously."

"Doing so will add considerably to the time it takes me to complete any of them," noted the computer.

"It can't be helped," I said. "Proceed."

"Working . . ."

The crystal darkened as the computer busied itself accessing various sources, and I left the office and went down the hall to the commissary, where I had a cup of tea and scanned the evening newstapes. I returned almost two hours later, found that the crystal was still dark, and decided to take a nap.

The computer woke me at five o'clock in the morning.

"Duncan Rojas," it repeated over and over, less gently each time.

I sat up, rubbed my eyes, and saw that the crystal was glowing again.

"Yes?"

"I have located the ivory, circa 4375 G.E."

"Which source?" I asked, curious.

"It was listed on an insurance premium, paid to the Blessbull Agency by Euphrates Pym of Szandor II."

"Szandor II? That's on the Inner Frontier, isn't it?"

"Yes."

"How did the ivory get all the way from the Rim to the Core?"

"I possess insufficient data to answer that question."

"Then bring up all the data that the Main Library Computer possesses on Euphrates Pym," I instructed it. "I want to know who he was, what he did, where he lived, and how he came into possession of the ivory."

"Working . . ."

2

The Graverobber
(4375 G.E.)

I had been many places and done many things in my long life. I had seen the Victoria Falls, which men called Mosi-o-Tunya, The Smoke That Thunders, and I had grazed on the slopes of Mount Kenya, where God lives. I had descended into the Ngorongoro Crater, and I had crossed the Mountains of the Moon. Always I stayed away from the places were men dwelled, and rarely did I hunger for food or thirst for water.

I had lived through six droughts, and when the long rains did not come I tested the wind for ten days in a row and could find no moisture in it. I knew, as the other animals did not, that the grass would shrivel and die and the Uaso Nyiro River would run dry before the rains came again, and so I turned my head to the south and began my trek to stay ahead of the wrath of the high African sun.

The holographic screen flickered to life.

"Sir," said Fletcher, "are you quite certain that you want to watch this?"

"I'm quite certain that I *don't*," growled Boris Jablonski irritably.

"Then—"

"I've got to know what he's working on, don't I?"

"We have three spies in his employ," Fletcher pointed out patiently. "We know everything he's doing and everything he's planning to do."

"But I don't know what he's going to say about me in front of two hundred million people."

"Why should you care?"

"Damn it!" snapped Jablonski. "If you can't be quiet and let me listen, then leave the room!"

Fletcher sighed and concentrated on the image hovering in front of them.

A small, dapper man, sporting a neatly-trimmed beard and a thick shock of gray hair, sat comfortably on a shining chair, facing an earnest-looking young woman.

"And now," said the voice of an unseen announcer, "for the science section of our broadcast, our own Elizabeth Keene has traveled all the way to Bellini VI to bring you an exclusive interview with the famed Armchair Archaeologist, Euphrates Pym."

"This is indeed a rare pleasure, Dr. Pym," gushed Elizabeth Keene. "I know how infrequently you consent to speak with the press."

"No more than once a week," muttered Jablonski, glaring at the image before him.

"It's true that I'm a very busy man," said Pym easily, "but since I am working on mankind's behalf, I realize my obligation to keep the public informed of my progress."

"You are still involved with the exploration of the Rhise Empire, are you not?"

He nodded. "That is correct. It's a fascinating culture. We're just now starting to comprehend it, and I feel we may be on the verge of some major breakthroughs."

"Have you been to their home planet?" she asked.

"Rhise Prime? Of course. In fact, I've just returned from there."

"I meant no offense," said Elizabeth Keene hastily. "It's just that almost everyone is aware of the way in which you discovered it."

"In which he *stole* it!" growled Jablonski.

"I was very fortunate," said Pym. "A lot of the ground-work had been done for me."

"Still, it was you who put everything together and made what may be the most important archaeological discovery since the dawn of the Galactic Era," said Elizabeth Keene, as Jablonski muttered an obscenity.

"Well, how important it is remains to be seen," protested Pym, though his expression left no doubt in the viewers' minds that he fully agreed with her.

"Perhaps you would tell our viewers exactly how you deduced the existence and location of Rhise Prime?"

"Gladly," said Pym with a smile. "About ten years ago I read a paper that piqued my curiosity. It seems that Professor Boris Jablonski of Spectra III had spent about a quarter of a century examining various cultures on that Spiral Arm of the galaxy which includes Earth, and he had made some curious, if tentative and fragmentary, findings."

"There was nothing *tentative* about them!" snapped Jablonski at Pym's image.

"He had discovered that eight different planetary cultures on the Arm possessed some fifteen words in common," continued Pym. "Not all fifteen words appeared on each of the planets, but every planet had at least four of these words in common with six or more of the other planets."

"You mean that the words sounded alike?"

"Within the limitations of each race to produce similar sounds. More to the point, they *meant* the same thing on each planet. It was an excellent piece of preliminary work, and I commend Professor Jablonski for it."

"Thanks for nothing!" muttered Jablonski.

"I had been totally unaware of Professor Jablonski's work until I read his paper. In it, he stated that these words, these concoctions of sound, had arisen simultaneously, and that there may well be some instinctive reaction to various objects that causes sentient life to come up with approximately the same sounds when describing it."

"It was only a suggestion!" yelled Jablonski. "I mentioned it as one of *many* possibilities!"

"Well," continued Pym, "I was familiar with one of the cultures he mentioned, the Boroni of Beta Kamos IV, and I knew that their vocal mechanisms were so different from the more humanoid races that Professor Jablonski had mentioned that it would literally be painful for them to voice some of the sounds that were listed."

"*I* pointed that out!" snarled Jablonski, jerking his arm free from Fletcher's gently restraining grasp.

"The more I thought about it," said Pym, "the more I became convinced that these words had originated *outside* the Boroni's culture. This led me to examine the other races, and a number of exobiologists concurred that the lips of the Ptree of Phoenix II were structured in such a manner that at least one of these sounds probably hadn't evolved in their culture, and must have been introduced. Armed with this information, I met with Boris Jablonski on his home world, and we issued a joint paper in which we concluded that a race about which we as yet knew nothing had once established an empire out on the Spiral Arm, and that *that* was how these words happened to be in use on so many worlds."

"And you were roundly castigated by your colleagues for leaping to such a conclusion," noted Elizabeth Keene.

"People will tell you that scientists are the first to accept new ideas," said Pym with a superior smile. "Don't you believe it."

"What happened next?"

"Professor Jablonski continued his field work, and I went home and thought about it."

"And came up with the right answer," said Elizabeth Keene.

"Let's not belittle Professor Jablonski's contribution," said Pym. "He was following the accepted procedure."

"Condescension!" snapped Jablonski. "What I hate most about that man is his condescension!"

"I elected not to join Professor Jablonski. I felt that we had already proven the existence of a star-faring race on the Arm, and—"

"Though not to your colleagues' satisfaction," she interrupted.

"To *my* satisfaction," replied Pym. "One must please oneself first."

"Goddamned egomaniac!" muttered Jablonski.

"Anyway, I went home, had my computer project a map of the Arm, marked those planets where the common words had appeared, and tried to draw some conclusions." He paused for dramatic effect. "And the more I studied it, the more I became convinced, based on the lines of expansion, the necessary supply lines if they had received any military opposition, the fact that they had to be an oxygen-breathing race since all the planets in question were inhabited by carbon-based oxygen-breathers, that something was very wrong." He paused. "You see, you require a certain type of star to produce an oxygen planet capable of supporting carbon-based life—but I couldn't find the right type of star anywhere near where it logically should have been. The nearest oxygen planet had too high a radiation level to support *any* form of life, and the nearest life-supporting planet was more than eight hundred light-years away."

"That was Principia, wasn't it?" she asked.

"Yes."

"And the general assumption among those few scientists who supported your views was that Principia was the logical home planet of the star-faring race that you sought."

"Yes, especially after the discovery of the ruins of a sentient civilization there, a humanoid race that had exterminated itself in a series of devastating wars almost sixty millennia ago." He shrugged. "I rejected it almost immediately."

"Why?"

"First, because there were six inhabited oxygen worlds within two hundred light-years of Principia. If the Principians sought after empire, why did they ignore these worlds and expand in a direction that would be much more difficult for them? Even if they eventually planned to control the entire Spiral Arm, simple logic decreed that they would conquer and consolidate those worlds that were closest to home before expanding eight hundred, and eventually fourteen hundred, light-years into the Arm." He paused. "The second reason was even more basic: there were no traces of the Principian civilization on any of Professor Jablonski's worlds. Surely they couldn't all have rushed home to die in a hideous war."

"But there are no remnants of *any* alien race on any of the worlds," she pointed out.

"That's the primary reason most of our colleagues rejected our hypothesis," he replied. "Yet it became the key to the puzzle."

"How?"

"I kept studying that map, trying to reason things out. I had my computer work out a number of military simulations, and I finally decided that the only way I could accept Principia as the origin of the race we sought would be if the planet existed in the vicinity of Adhara, which of course was not the case. Adhara is a very young, very large blue star, which will eventually die as a black hole. It has only one planet, a world with an atmosphere that is almost 85% helium: the planet couldn't possibly support carbon-based life, or even chlorine- or methane-breathers. In fact, it was too young to have evolved any form of life with which we are acquainted." He stared thoughtfully at the camera, as if he was once again considering all the diverse elements of the problem.

"He always pauses here," complained Jablonski, "so his audience has time to appreciate the magnitude of his piddling little breakthrough."

"So I spent another month trying to make some sense out of the data," Pym continued at last, "and the more I studied it, the more I kept coming back to Adhara. Logistically, it was far and away the most likely home for a race which had conquered those planets—and suddenly I realized why we hadn't found any remnants of that race. If they weren't oxygen-breathers, then Jablonski's planets were probably mere outposts, convenient refueling depots and the like, and their major expansion would be among other helium worlds. They probably stationed only a very small number of technicians on the oxygen worlds, and as their empire began contracting or collapsing for whatever reason, these would be the first worlds to be abandoned."

Pym smiled wryly. "You must realize that up to that

moment we had never encountered a race that evolved on a helium planet, nor a life-bearing planet of *any* type orbiting a blue giant. Both were considered beyond the realm of possibility." He paused. "I was removed from my position at the university when I published this hypothesis."

"And then what happened?"

"I had only one course open to me. I took my savings, plus every credit I could beg or borrow, and sent an expedition to Adhara's planet. I only had enough money to equip a six-man team for twenty-three days—and since I had recently fractured a leg, I myself remained at home. I suggested the most likely places to look, kept in constant contact via subspace tightbeam—and the rest is history. Nineteen days later they came upon the first artifacts of the Rhise civilization, and the planet officially became Rhise Prime." He smiled modestly. "They wanted to name it after me, but I wouldn't allow it." He paused. "As I had deduced, their empire consisted primarily of helium planets. The planets Professor Jablonski had linked together were merely logistical conveniences, nothing more."

"And that's how you became the Armchair Archaeologist," she concluded admiringly.

"That's how he used my work and took all the credit for it!" muttered Jablonski.

"That's a title the press has given me," he replied. "Actually, I get out in the field whenever I can."

"Since you are the acknowledged authority on Rhise Prime and the Rhise Empire, perhaps you can tell us what has been learned thus far about the Rhise people?"

"We still don't know very much about them," admitted Pym. "They were a very unusual life form, of course, and now that we've been able to reconstruct their line of expansion, we've determined that there were at least three other helium-breathing races; my own guess is that we will eventually discover upwards of a dozen just within the Spiral Arm." He paused. "Unfortunately, there are no survivors of any of these races, and since the Rhise people seemed to fight wars of extermination rather than conquest, we've been able to learn almost nothing about their victims. My own guess is that the Rhise people, realizing that Adhara would soon go supernova and destroy their planet, sought living space rather than empire in the more traditional sense of the word, and simply eliminated any race they found on those planets they wished to colonize. It's probably also the reason they did not destroy the populations of the oxygen worlds they conquered; they had no use for such worlds."

"Elementary," said Jablonski. "I pointed that out five years ago."

"Whatever became of the Rhise people?" asked Elizabeth Keene.

"We don't know," admitted Pym. "But since all the helium planets they colonized have since been abandoned, there is every possibility that they have finally found their utopia, and are still out there somewhere waiting for us to discover them."

"Is that really possible?" she asked.

"Certainly. Man has always expanded toward the core of the galaxy, continuously pushing back the Inner Frontier. We've actually done relatively little exploration among the worlds of the Spiral Arm."

"And that's all we've learned about the Rhise civilization?"

"You must remember that I only deduced their existence five years ago," said Pym with a modest smile. "We were fortunate enough to discover what has come to be called the Rhise Document two years ago."

"The Rhise Document?" she repeated.

"You might say that it is the Rhise equivalent to the

Rosetta Stone, but," he added unhappily, "our linguistics experts have made very little progress on it thus far."

"Word has it that you will shortly be making a major announcement of even greater import than the discovery of the Rhise Document," said Elizabeth Keene. "Can you give our audience a hint of what it is?"

"I believe that there is an excellent chance that the Rhise people visited the Earth some millennia before Man achieved space flight."

"You've found traces of the Rhise Empire on Earth?" she asked excitedly. "Were they the ancient astronauts that still exist in some legends?"

He smiled and shook his head. "No to both questions. We've found no evidence, as yet, of a visitation to Earth by the Rhise people or any other aliens."

"Then why do you feel that we were visited by them?"

"There are certain areas in Earth's past—certain incidents, certain artifacts—that could best be explained by an alien visitation. And Earth was directly in the Rhise Empire's line of expansion."

"And this is what you hope to announce?" she said triumphantly. "It seems to me that you've just announced it, Dr. Pym."

"There is a difference between expressing a hope and presenting irrefutable evidence," he replied. "As I mentioned, we've made very little progress translating the Rhise Document, but what little we *have* learned leads me to believe that the remains of a large structure we recently discovered on Rhise Prime may have once been a museum. If this is indeed the case, and if we can find any artifacts that originated on Earth, we will have proven my theory just as surely as if we found a Rhise artifact on Earth."

"And the Armchair Archaeologist will have added yet another brilliant triumph to his career," she said admiringly.

"If so, it's a triumph I must share with my field workers,"

said Pym magnanimously. "And let's not forget Professor Jablonski, whose initial work set the entire process in motion."

"God!" muttered Jablonski. "I think I hate him most when he thanks me!"

"And what advice have you for any young people in our audience who may hope for a career in—"

"Enough!" bellowed Jablonski, and Fletcher deactivated the computer.

Jablonski jumped to his feet and began stalking furiously around his office.

"The gall of that man!" he fumed. "Sitting in the Chair of Archaeology on Selica II, the chair that should have been *mine!* Convincing the foundations that had always funded me to become *his* benefactors instead! And why? All because of one lucky guess!"

"You're getting too excited, sir," said Fletcher gently. "Why not sit down and try to relax?"

"Sit down where?" thundered Jablonski. "He's the Armchair Archaeologist, not me!"

"Please, Professor."

"That smug, pompous son of a bitch!" continued Jablonski. "He can't even write a proper scientific paper."

"I know, sir."

"So what happens? Some publisher pays him five million credits for a totally inaccurate, totally unscientific account of the Rhise civilization, and the works of better, more thorough men languish unread in computer libraries!"

"It happened a long time ago, sir," said Fletcher. "And you've gone on from triumph to triumph."

"All eclipsed by one lucky guess!" snapped Jablonski. "And he's still cashing in on it! Look at what happens when they run a science segment for the public. Do they ask Wanamaker, whose work on the Rim has even surpassed Rosenschweig's? Do they ask Hayakawa, who is working on Earth itself, and has discovered a virtually intact Incan temple? Do they ask me? No! They ask the mad guesser!"

Suddenly breathless, he walked over to his chair, which rose up to meet him, collapsed on it, and glared sullenly at the spot where Pym's image had been.

"Please, sir," said Fletcher. "You can't keep torturing yourself like this. You know what your doctor told you."

"My doctor doesn't have to see the man who destroyed his career on the holo every week."

"Now, that's simply not an accurate statement, sir," said Fletcher. "You've had a very successful career. You are one of the most respected archaeologists in the Oligarchy. Your works are standard reading in almost every academic institution."

Jablonski shook his head. "It doesn't matter. That man has destroyed me. I spent eighteen years on the Arm, making the initial discoveries, correlating my data, testing my conclusions. I was no more than five years away from proving that the Rhise people were helium breathers—*proving* it with rigorous scientific logic, not guessing at it because I was too lazy and too vain to dirty my hands in the field —and then *he* came along. He forced me to publish before I was ready and made us both laughingstocks among our peers—and then, when he made his guess, when we were actually proved right, only *his* reputation was restored." Jablonski paused for breath. "If I hadn't discovered the remains of the Korbb culture in the Wisna system, I'd *still* be looking for a college that would trust me to head its Archaeology Department."

"But you *did* discover it," said Fletcher soothingly. "So why do you let Euphrates Pym upset you like this?"

"Because they still think he knows what he's doing!"

snapped Jablonski. "They still think intuition is an acceptable substitute for hard work!"

"Not everyone thinks so, sir."

Jablonski got to his feet again and walked to a crystal shelf that hovered above the floor just beside his desk.

"Look at these!" he said, gesturing to the eight thick leather-bound books that rested upon the shelf. "They constitute forty-three years of careful, methodical work. They are the result of going out into the field and examining things for myself, not sitting at home and theorizing. They are the sum total of my life." He paused. "Pym sells more books and disks in a week than I have sold in almost half a century."

"Popularity isn't necessarily a barometer of merit," Fletcher pointed out. "Dr. Pym knows how to manipulate the media, so of course his sales reflect his publicity. That doesn't necessarily mean that he's made any lasting contribution to the field of archaeology."

"Fool!" muttered Jablonski. He walked to a viewing bubble that overlooked the steel-and-glass enclosed campus and stared down at the passing students. "You don't understand at all."

"I beg your pardon, sir?"

"He *has* made a contribution!" said Jablonski in exasperation. "The discovery of Rhise Prime and the Rhise Document were the most important archaeological events of the century. *That's* why the man is so dangerous!"

"I don't think I follow you, sir."

"He has virtually discredited the scientific method," explained Jablonski as he turned back to face his assistant. "We are in danger of being overrun by a veritable hoard of self-proclaimed Intuitive Archaeologists." He made a disgusted face. "It's so much *cleaner* than digging through the muck of a chlorine world, so much *easier* than spending years analyzing and reassembling a single alien artifact. Pym does it that way, and he discovered Rhise Prime, so it must be the most effective method." His face became a mask of unreasoning fury. "We *must* discredit this man before it is too late!"

"I really think you are overestimating his importance, sir," said Fletcher.

"I am not!" screamed Jablonski. His face turned red, his breathing became harsh and labored, and Fletcher helped him back to his chair.

"Are you all right, sir?"

"I'll be fine," said Jablonski weakly. "You see, Fletcher? He's not only destroyed my reputation; he's even ruined my health."

"Shall I call your doctor?"

Jablonski shook his head. "I just need to calm down for a moment." He took a deep breath and exhaled it slowly. "I know that you feel this is a personal vendetta," he said at last, "but it's much more than that. If Euphrates Pym is not discredited, he will by implication discredit everything the rest of us are attempting to do."

"He will be discredited when the Rhise museum turns out not to have any human artifacts," predicted Fletcher.

"No," said Jablonski. "He worded that statement very carefully. He *hoped* to be able to prove that the Rhise people had visited Earth; he never said he had proof positive."

"Still, it will be the first time he's guessed wrong about them," said Fletcher. "Perhaps that will tarnish his image."

"*If* he's wrong."

"I ran all the data through the computer this morning, just as you instructed me to, and the computer gives him only a 2.3% chance of being correct."

"It would have given him less chance than that about the location of Rhise Prime," said Jablonski.

"Surely you haven't changed your opinion!"

"About Earth never having been visited? Certainly not. Five thousand years of research would have turned up *something* if Earth had been a Rhise outpost."

"Then he'll be proven wrong," said Fletcher with conviction.

"He'll wriggle out of it somehow," replied Jablonski with equal conviction. "He'll smile, point out the fallacy of groundless theorizing, and then come up with a brand new groundless theory about why the Rhise people never bothered landing on Earth. And they'll heap more honors on him, and he'll get the Menesco grant that I've been promised, and he'll use it to hire away my expedition leader." Jablonski snorted contemptuously. "He'll probably be making an offer to *you* before much longer."

"You have my complete loyalty, sir," said Fletcher promptly.

"As long as I make you my successor," said Jablonski. "No, don't bother to deny it. A man's got to look out for himself—and you're the best assistant I've ever had. You deserve to succeed me."

"Thank you, sir. I'm most flattered that you think so."

"I just hope this damned department is worth having by the time you get control of it. There's only so much money to be spent in our field, and the more Pym gets his hands on, the less there is for the rest of us." He paused. "Damn! If only I could be sure!"

"Sure of what, sir?"

"Sure that he's wrong about Earth."

"But as you pointed out, it doesn't make any difference. He hasn't actually *stated* that the Rhise people visited the Earth; he merely suggested it."

"But if I *knew*, knew for sure . . ." Jablonski's voice trailed off, while Fletcher merely stared at him, unable to follow his train of thought.

Suddenly Jablonski sat upright, seemingly energized by some inner hatred of his rival. "Tell Modell that I want to speak to him."

"He may be unavailable," suggested Fletcher.

"I don't pay him to be unavailable!" snapped Jablonski.

"Shall I scramble the message?"

"I don't care what you do. Just put me in touch with him."

Fletcher activated one of the computers. "Code Blue-Four," he said. "Have Modell contact Home Base."

"Spy stuff!" snorted Jablonski. "Just tell him I want to talk to him."

"It's spy stuff precisely because he *is* a spy," replied Fletcher patiently. "And if our message is intercepted, we don't want the Pym expedition to know who sent it."

"They'll know."

"Nevertheless, it seems a reasonable precaution."

Jablonski muttered something beneath his breath and settled back to await the transmission. Twenty minutes later the image of a craggy, unshaven face appeared in the air above the computer.

"Modell here."

"This is—" began Jablonski, but stopped short as Fletcher made a frantic gesture. "You know who this is."

"Please increase your gain," said Modell. "I'm in a module about fifty feet below the ground. There's a hell of a storm whipping across the surface, and it's creating a lot of static."

"How far along are you?" asked Jablonski, after instructing the computer to boost its signal.

"We're probably a week to ten days from entering the building."

"How many doors?"

"Six, all sealed—and the seals aren't like anything I've

ever seen before. It could take an extra week just to break one of them."

Jablonski frowned. "Are the walls all intact?"

Modell shook his head. "It doesn't have walls in the normal sense of the word, sir."

"What *does* it have?"

Modell looked uneasy. "I'm not sure I can explain it, sir."

"Make the effort. That's what I'm paying you for."

"It looks like a tesseract, if that makes any sense."

"A tesseract?" repeated Jablonski.

"A hypothetical four-dimensional structure."

"I know what it is," snapped Jablonski. "I'm just trying to envision it."

"It's pretty strange," offered Modell.

"Is the building intact?" asked Jablonski.

"Yes."

"And it's definitely a museum?"

"It seems just about certain."

"I assume Pym will be there with the press when you finally break the seals."

"That's what I'm told."

"And nobody goes in ahead of him?"

"It's his expedition," replied Modell with a shrug.

"Is there any way in other than through the doors?"

"There are no other openings, if that's what you mean. No windows, no loading docks, nothing like that." He paused. "A couple of the people here think there might be a way around breaking the door seals by using the structure of the tesseract itself, but they haven't figured out how."

"Why don't they ask their computer?"

"For all I know they have," answered Modell. "Either it couldn't come up with an answer, or they didn't like the answer they got." He paused. "It doesn't make any difference, anyway. The word is that Pym plans to break the seal and go through the door; I guess they're making a documentary holo out of it."

"I want you to transmit a hologram of the structure to me immediately," said Jablonski. "Can you do it?"

"Yes."

"Good," said Jablonski. He broke the connection and turned to Fletcher. "Can you be ready to leave tomorrow?"

"For where?"

"Rhise Prime, of course."

"I suppose so," replied Fletcher, puzzled.

"Good."

"Can you tell me what this is all about?" asked Fletcher.

"Discrediting that pompous ass!" snapped Jablonski. "Haven't you listened to what I've been saying? Computer!" he rasped.

"Yes?" said the computer.

"This morning, based on the data Fletcher gave you, you estimated that the likelihood of the Rhise people ever having visited the Earth was 2.3%, is that correct?"

"2.302%, to be precise."

"What does that figure become if the Rhise Prime museum has no mention of Earth and no Terran artifacts of any kind?"

"The figure becomes 0.738%," responded the computer.

"Good. Have you received a transmission of a hologram from Rhise Prime in the past sixty seconds?"

"I am just receiving one now."

"Access the math department's library."

"Accessing . . . done."

"Does the hologram depict a building in the form of a tesseract?"

"That is correct."

"I want you to find out from our library what institution

is doing the most advanced theoretical work on tesseracts. Then access *its* math and physics libraries, plus all unclassified research material, and determine whether or not there is a way of entering the building in the hologram without breaking the seals on the doors."

"Working . . . Accessing . . ." The computer fell silent for almost ninety seconds. "There is a theoretical means of ingress."

"Please explain the word theoretical as used in this context."

"It means that, in theory, ingress is possible. However, in practice, I cannot certify that such ingress would not be fatal to living tissue, dealing as it does with inter-dimensional transit."

"Could a robot gain ingress and remain in working order?"

"Working . . . probably."

"What is the likelihood of such a robot continuing to function?"

"86.241%."

"And the likelihood of its returning unharmed?"

"86.241%," repeated the computer. "If entering the building does not disable it, leaving by the same means will not disable it."

"Deactivate," said Jablonski. He turned to Fletcher, his eyes wild with excitement. "By God, I've got him! I've finally got the son of a bitch!"

Jablonski and Fletcher entered the museum's complex of storerooms, all of which displayed their usual flurry of energy and activity. The older man led his assistant past those rooms that were devoted to the cultures of the Inner and Outer Frontiers, circled around the complicated maze of interconnected cubicles that had been set aside for the study of the more heavily populated areas of the galaxy, and finally came to the large room that housed the most recently arrived items from the Spiral Arm.

Jablonski immediately began walking up and down the long aisles of the storeroom, nodding an occasional greeting to the staff members who were busily brushing, cleaning, reconstructing, and otherwise working on literally hundreds of items that the university had not yet cataloged.

They passed the Mystic Vase of Valerium VII, which had been the direct cause of three major wars in the dim antiquity of that distant planet, and skirted around the five stones the museum had acquired from New Paraguay's Mosque of the Honored Dead. Jablonski stopped to examine a minute piece of pottery, then held it to his nostrils and inhaled deeply. He loved the smell and the feel of antiquity, the thrill of reconstructing the comprehensive whole of a civilization from the tiniest fragments, the sight of stray bits and pieces sitting on tables awaiting classification. He took a certain justifiable pride in the museum's public displays, but it was here, where the *real* work was done, that he was truly in his element.

"Exactly what are we looking for?" asked Fletcher, as Jablonski paused to look into a small cylindrical sculpture from Aldebaran XIII.

"Something from Earth," replied Jablonski.

"We have a gas mask from World War I on display in the East Wing," volunteered Fletcher. "And we also have a matched pair of Amerind headdresses, as well as—"

Jablonski shook his head. "I *know* what we have!" he said gruffly.

"Then I must ask you to be more explicit, sir," said Fletcher.

"I want something from *here*," said Jablonski.

"From here?" repeated Fletcher, gesturing about the room.

"Something that hasn't been cataloged yet."

"What did you have in mind?"

"I don't care, as long as it's from Earth and the museum's computer doesn't have a record of it."

Suddenly Fletcher's eyes widened. "Now I understand!" he exclaimed.

"It certainly took you long enough," said Jablonski irritably. "Now, please try to keep your voice down."

"You're going to salt Rhise Prime!" whispered Fletcher excitedly.

"Not the planet," answered Jablonski. "Just the museum."

"You'll never get away with it!"

"No—but *you* will."

"Me?" said Fletcher, surprised.

"That's right," said Jablonski impatiently. "Now let's get back to work. You're leaving tomorrow."

Without waiting for a reply, Jablonski once again began walking up and down the aisles, rummaging through containers, searching for his artifact. After half an hour he still hadn't found it.

"Damn!" he muttered. "I *know* we picked up an Aztec carving two weeks ago."

"It went on display earlier this week," said Fletcher.

Jablonski emitted a bitterly ironic laugh. "If I'd *wanted* them to rush it through, it would still be back here gathering dust!" He snorted contemptuously. "Well, there doesn't seem to be anything up here. Let's check the basement."

He walked over to the descent shaft, activated the air cushion, stepped out into the center of it, waited for Fletcher to join him, and then ordered the mechanism to lower them to the basement level. They descended gently as the invisible cushion slowly collapsed into itself, and finally found themselves in the enormous storage basement that ran beneath the entire museum.

The basement was illuminated by a diffused light that emanated from an unseen source, and the elongated shadows it created gave the place a faintly sinister air. Alien ghosts seemed to hide behind every artifact, ready to pounce upon those who had desecrated their ancient homelands, and while the maintenance staff kept the huge room spotless, it *felt* like it possessed layer upon layer of eons-old dust and debris.

Taking up fully a quarter of the room was an almost-complete Korbb chapel that Jablonski had brought back from the Wisna system. Dominating the farthest wall was the Great Serpent of Dorillion, a ninety-foot-long sculpture in the form of a snake, upon which the entire history of the ancient Dorillion race had been carved in tableaus so small that many of them could not be seen without artificial magnification and enhancement.

There were statues and other artifacts that would take up too much space in the restoration complex above, and hence were stored here until such time as students and staff members could prepare them for public exhibition.

Jablonski moved from statue to statue, display case to display case, table to table, in search of his Terran artifact. Finally he came to an abrupt stop in front of a long table.

"What are these?" he asked. "I don't remember them."

Fletcher looked at the twin pillars of ivory.

"I'm not quite sure, sir. They were discovered by Bromheld Sherrinford out on the Rim. They arrived here less than a week ago."

"Sherrinford?" mused Jablonski. "The name's not familiar to me."

"His expedition was jointly funded by twenty academic institutions, including ours," explained Fletcher. "He had been exploring the Guavere culture on Melima IV when he came upon what seems to have been the cache of some

outlaw who lived more than a millennium ago, out on the
Rim." He paused. "According to some legends that Sherrinford was able to piece together, the outlaw was an enormous cyborg who was called either the Iron Duke or the
Iron Prince. Anyway, this was peripheral to Sherrinford's
main field of interest, so once he determined there was
nothing in the cache from the Guaveres, he arbitrarily divided the find into twenty sections of equal value and sent
one to each of the institutions." He gestured to the ivory.
"These are ours."

"What are they?"

Fletcher shrugged. "I have no idea."

"Then have someone run a molecular scope over them
and find out what they are and where they come from,"
said Jablonski irritably.

Fletcher left the basement and returned a few moments
later, carrying a highly complex instrument under his arm.

"I thought it would be better if I did it myself, sir," he
explained. "There's no reason to take anyone else into our
confidence, and several excellent reasons not to."

"Good thinking," said Jablonski gruffly. "Now get to work."

Fletcher activated the scope, attached it to the larger
tusk, and analyzed the readings.

"I believe we're in luck, sir!" he announced after a moment. "It seems to be Terran in origin."

"Organic?"

Fletcher peered at his readings and nodded. "It's definitely carbon-based."

"Take a scraping and give it a more thorough analysis,"
ordered Jablonski. "I've got to be sure."

Fletcher did as he was told, and five minutes later the
scope gave him a complete molecular readout.

"Definitely Terran," reaffirmed Fletcher. "There's no
question about it."

"Now run the DNA pattern through the biolab computer and see what it is."

Fletcher activated a nearby terminal, fed the data into it, instructed it to access the computer in the biology laboratory, and waited for the result.

"They seem to be the tusks of an elephant, sir," said Fletcher when the biolab computer had reported back to him.

"An elephant?" repeated Jablonski. "Isn't that an extinct land animal?"

"Yes, sir," said Fletcher. He stared thoughtfully at the ivory. "I wonder how they ever got out on the Rim?"

"The only important thing is that they're here," said Jablonski. He glanced into the shadows of the empty basement and lowered his voice conspiratorially. "This afternoon, have the computer program one of our AG-203 robots so that it can enter and leave the tesseract. Then, late tonight, I want you to come back here and take the tusks to your ship."

"But I can't just land on Rhise Prime!" protested Fletcher.

"Be quiet and listen!" snapped Jablonski. "I'll instruct Modell to find some pretext for leaving the planet for a couple of days. You'll arrange to dock with him in the Peritane system and transfer the tusks and robot to his ship. Tell him to make sure the robot plants the tusks properly; they can't be found lying, all white and gleaming, on top of the ground if everything else is buried. He'll know what to do."

"And then I return here?"

"That's right."

"What about the robot?" asked Fletcher. "We can't leave it wandering around Rhise Prime."

"Have Modell order it to walk five hundred miles away and self-destruct."

"It will be found sooner or later."

"I don't care about later!" growled Jablonski. "My mission is to discredit Pym. That is the only thing that counts!"

Four months had elapsed. Euphrates Pym had been holographed, photographed, filmed and recorded opening the doors of the Rhise museum. He had emerged a week later, and immediately gone into seclusion to analyze his data and consider his conclusions.

Finally he had called a press conference, and Jablonski had eagerly paid the holo access fee to observe it for himself, rather than wait for an edited version to be broadcast later in the day.

Now Pym, as dapper and self-assured as ever, stood before a veritable army of cameras, cleared his throat, and began to speak.

"Ladies and gentlemen, I wish to make a very brief statement, and then I will entertain your questions." He looked directly into the largest of the holographic cameras. "Those of you who have been following our progress deciphering the Rhise civilization know that I recently suggested that the Earth may very well have been an outpost of the Rhise Empire at some point in the distant past. This theory," he added, "has caused what may justly be called a furor among my colleagues, most of whom have violently disagreed with me."

He paused for a moment, and then continued. "I must report to you that in this instance my colleagues were correct. Based on my discoveries at the museum on Rhise Prime, I can categorically state that the Earth was *not* an outpost of the Rhise Empire."

"What?" bellowed Jablonski.

"Scientists seek only the truth, and thus I am delighted that my work has been able to end all conjecture on this subject and replace it with fact." Pym paused as a round of spontaneous applause broke out, then continued. "As for the ongoing study of the Rhise civilization, I am content to leave it in the capable hands of Hilbert Nieswand, my chief assistant. I plan to take a few months off to recuperate from my efforts, and then I will accept the very generous offer made to me by the Molton Foundation and spend the next few years on Szandor II, heading up their team of experts and trying to make some sense out of the remains of a very bizarre civilization. I look forward to the challenge with great anticipation. And now, are there any questions?"

"What happened?" muttered Jablonski uncomprehendingly. "I *know* you found the tusks, you bastard!"

Suddenly Pym's image began blinking.

"What is it?" asked Jablonski.

"You have just received a private transmission from Euphrates Pym," announced the computer. "Shall I cast it holographically, or would you prefer to wait until the broadcast is finished?"

"It's finished!" snapped Jablonski. "Let me see the message."

Pym's face reappeared, but this time he was wearing different clothing and sitting in a plushly-furnished office.

"Hello, Boris," he said. "This is prerecorded, so don't try to engage me in a dialogue. Just sit back and listen."

He paused long enough to light a large Antarrean cigar.

"I am truly grateful to you, my old friend. You saved me *years* of tedious field work." He allowed himself the luxury of a small, triumphant smile. "You didn't mean to, of course, but this isn't just *anyone* you've tried to dupe. I'm Euphrates Pym!"

Jablonski uttered an obscenity as Pym's image looked smugly out at him.

"I don't know where you got the tusks, Boris, but as

always your methodology was superior to your intuition. You managed to plant them in the museum despite our security, and I congratulate you for that. But I suspect that once you realized that they were from Earth, you didn't complete the analysis." He paused, obviously amused by Jablonski's predictability. "We ran them through a sub-nuclear analyzer. They only date back to the 19th century A.D., and it's inconceivable that the Rhise people could have landed on Earth at that late date without being observed and reported."

Pym drew deeply on his cigar, then exhaled a cloud of blue smoke that hovered just above his head.

"The entire operation reflected your distinctive touch, Boris," he continued. "The careful planning, the methodical execution, the total lack of foresight and imagination. I knew that you were responsible the moment I dated the ivory, but, since I've learned a little of the scientific method from you, I decided to produce proof positive before I confronted you. Therefore, I insisted that every member of the expedition answer my questions while tied in to the Neverlie Machine." He paused, obviously enjoying himself. "Evidently your man Modell has seen what happens when you lie to the machine; he admitted his complicity before we even hooked him up." A smug smile. "Oh, by the way, he is now *my* man Modell."

Another puff, another cloud of smoke.

"At any rate, if you were willing to part with such valuable artifacts merely to convince me that the Earth had been an outpost of the Rhise Empire, that's proof enough for me that the Rhise Empire never reached our mother planet. You may not be brilliant or intuitive, Boris, but you're thorough—so I'm more than happy to reject my original supposition." Suddenly he laughed. "An amusing thought just struck me. Wouldn't it be funny if we were to find a legitimate artifact from Earth now that I've told the public that the two races never met?" He paused. "I suppose I'd simply have to tell them that based on new evidence I had unearthed, poor Boris Jablonski was wrong again."

He chuckled for another moment, then continued.

"Finally, my old friend, I want to thank you for the gift of the ivory. I intend to take it with me to Szandor II, where it will be given a place of honor among my collection of Terran artifacts. And by the way, don't worry about my exposing your little scheme to your university. I'll get much more pleasure from it as an after-dinner anecdote."

The transmission ended, and Boris Jablonski slowly rose to his feet, walked into the lavatory, and opened the veins in both his wrists.

He had been dead for two hours when Fletcher found him.

Second Interlude (6303 G.E.)

I slept in my office, and when I awoke the next morning, I immediately checked to see if the computer had made any further progress locating the ivory. It had not, and as it would be devoting very little of its capacity to the problem until much later in the day, I decided not to waste my time pressing it for answers. I instructed it to produce hard copies of the two known photographs, and spent the next few minutes staring idly at them, trying to fully comprehend the size of the creature from which they had been taken, before finally putting them aside to return, somewhat halfheartedly, to my morning's work, which was the certification of a Horndemon from Ansard IV. The spread of horns was 108.3 centimeters—a measurement that would have placed it 193rd on the list—but there was some dispute over the method of taxidermy used, which may well have added four to five centimeters to the dimensions, and unfortunately the only on-the-spot hologram was somewhat blurred.

I subjected the hologram to computer analysis, but it proved inconclusive, as I had expected that it would. I then examined the sworn statements of both the hunter and the taxidermist, tried in vain to contact the expedition's guide—he was currently leading a party in search of Bell-ringers on Daedalus VII—and finally decided to route the problem to our own taxidermy expert in the Ansard system, leaving a memo on his computer that I needed a decision by the end of the week.

I checked my timepiece, saw that I had less than an hour until my appointment at the Natural History Museum, and rather than start another assignment, I picked up the two photographs once more and studied them, marveling at the size of the ivory and wondering how one killed the possessor of such teeth, back in the days before hunters had access to laser or sonic weapons or molecular imploders.

I don't know how long I had been examining the photos when the crystal began glowing, and suddenly a hologram of Hilda Dorian's face flickered into existence.

"It looks like a busy afternoon," she said. "Can we move lunch ahead by an hour?"

"I beg your pardon?" I replied distractedly.

"Lunch, Duncan," she explained patiently. "You know—it comes between breakfast and dinner. We've been having it together every Wednesday for nine years."

"What about it?"

"Oh, Lord, it's happening again, isn't it?"

"What is?"

"You're hooked again," she said grimly.

"I don't know what you're talking about."

"That's one of the symptoms," she replied. "Now I suppose I can look forward to a month of blank stares, sentences that trail off somewhere in the middle, and broken lunch appointments." She paused. "The last time you were like this was two years ago, when you spent a couple of months proving that Skystalkers were extinct and that that hunter out on the Rim had made a fraudulent claim." She sighed. "And now someone's given you a new puzzle, and you're going to be impossible to talk to until you solve it."

"Nonsense," I said uncomfortably, trying to concentrate on the image before me.

"Just what kind of challenge did the mysterious Mr. Mandaka set for you?" she persisted.

"What do you know about Mandaka?" I asked.

"I *am* in charge of security, Duncan. That means I know who comes and goes around here, and who they visit. It also means I know you spent the night in the office, and that you had the computer working for you all night long." She smiled. "And that you were playing that awful alien music you play whenever you're engrossed in a problem."

"You didn't answer my question."

"What question?"

"What do you know about Mandaka?" I repeated.

"I know that he came to visit you yesterday, and that after he left, word came down that you had permission to use the computer at nights and on weekends."

I shrugged. "Well, I don't suppose it's any great secret, since Mandaka cleared it with the company. He's looking for a record set of elephant tusks."

"You mean from *Earth*?"

"That's right."

"He's going to be disappointed."

"No, he's not," I answered firmly. "I'm going to find them for him."

"Correct me if I'm wrong," said Hilda, "but didn't the last elephant die while we were still Earthbound?"

"He's looking for a particular set that already exists."

"I see," she said. "Well, since that's all I'm going to hear about from you until you find them, you might as well come down to the cafeteria and tell me all about it."

"I can't," I said. "I've got an official measuring at the Museum of Natural History."

"Oh?" she said, her face brightening. "Will Prudence Ashe be there?"

"Yes."

"I never see her since she left Braxton's. Do you mind if I come along?"

"Suit yourself," I said.

"Always the gentleman," she said sardonically. "I'll meet you in the lobby in fifteen minutes."

She was prompt, as always.

When I arrived at the lobby level, she was there waiting for me, makeup freshly applied, an outer garment of undulating colors covering her dull security uniform.

"We've got to stop meeting like this," she said with a smile. "Harold is getting suspicious."

"Is he?" I asked.

She snorted contemptuously. "Of course not. He knows the only thing you've ever really loved is an incomplete equation."

"I'm not a mathematician."

"All right, then—an unsolved problem."

The building's main doorway expanded to accommodate us, and we stepped out onto a northbound slidewalk.

"Why don't you tell me about this one?" she suggested.

"This what?"

"This problem, Duncan," she said patiently, as if speaking to a small, dull-witted child. "What is it about these elephant tusks that has so fired your imagination?"

"A number of things," I replied. "First, no one has ever asked me to track down a missing trophy before. It's something new."

"And you find that thrilling."

"Well, interesting, anyway," I responded. "And these would be among the oldest game trophies in the galaxy— maybe *the* oldest."

"I see," she said noncommittally.

"But there's more to it than that," I continued, as we reached the corner and the slidewalk began rising to avoid the cross-street traffic.

"Somehow I thought there was."

"I've been trying to track them down—and they vanish for hundreds of years, then suddenly appear thousands of light-years away."

"Isn't that usually the case with valuable trophies?"

"No," I said. "The more valuable they are, the sooner they show up in museums."

"And these obviously aren't in a museum."

"Not as far as I can tell," I said with a sigh. "They have been stakes in a card game, booty owned by a cyborg outlaw, and pawns in a power play by an unethical scientist —everything *but* museum pieces." I paused. "Well, not quite. They started out in a museum, but then they somehow passed into private hands. Just the opposite of the usual progression."

"Interesting," she said. "But insufficient."

"What do you mean?"

"There has to be more to it. What you've told me isn't

enough to make you stare blankly into space and forget to go home," said Hilda. "What else is so fascinating about these particular tusks?"

"All right," I said, turning to her. "Why is a private collector willing to pay two million credits for them?"

"How much?" she repeated, startled.

"Two million credits," I replied.

"Can they possibly be worth that much?"

"Not to any museum," I said. "And why this *particular* set of tusks? He was quite explicit about that: it can't be any other tusks. It must be these."

"Have you found a reason?" she asked, interested in spite of herself.

I shook my head. "Only a vague connection: the tusks were once owned by members of his social clan."

"A family heirloom?" she suggested.

"Highly unlikely," I replied. "No one knows the circumstances of the elephant's death, but the tusks were immediately sold at auction. They weren't owned by the Maasai in the beginning, and it's been almost two millennia since they were last possessed by a Maasai."

"What is a Maasai?"

"Mandaka's social group."

"Two million credits, you say?"

"Plus whatever he's already spent trying to find them," I answered. "Furthermore, I got the distinct impression that if the party who owns them isn't willing to part with them, Mandaka would be quite willing to break as many laws as necessary to obtain them."

"Including murder?" she asked curiously.

I remembered the glow of fanaticism on Mandaka's face when he told me that he would not be thwarted in his goal. "It wouldn't surprise me."

"Interesting," was Hilda's only comment.

The slidewalk came to a halt at a four-level intersection, and we stepped into the downflow and floated back down to street level, then stepped onto the expresswalk, stood behind the transparent windbreak, and secured our feet, then waited while the inevitable indecisive passenger delayed us for almost a full minute while deciding which windbreak to stand behind. Finally we began accelerating, and buildings and pedestrians both became a blur as we sped through the center of the city, maneuvered around the Big Swerve that bypassed the local commercial districts, and reached our maximum speed when we hit the Straight out to the suburbs. After we had gone about seven miles we began slowing down, and a moment later the expresswalk stopped at the Public Complex. We stepped off onto a slidewalk, went past the Observatory, the Science Complex, the Institute of Alien Art, the aquarium, the oxygen and chlorine zoos, and finally came to the Museum of Natural History.

"Nine minutes total," said Hilda, checking her timepiece. "Not bad for this time of day. I do wish they'd reroute it, though. Every time I go through the Swerve, I am painfully reminded that I'm not as young as I used to be."

"Oh."

She stared at me. "Duncan, I really hate it when you get like this. Ordinarily you're a reasonably polite man."

"What did I say?"

"It's what you didn't say," she explained. "You might tell me that I'm a fine figure of a woman, and I don't look a day over thirty."

"You're a fine figure of a woman and you don't look a day over thirty," I said mechanically.

"Thanks," she said caustically. "I wonder why I bother."

I looked ahead and saw a large group of children headed

for the museum. Since I was anxious to avoid them, I opted for the gravity lift rather than the enormous escalator that was designed to look like a stone stairway, and a moment later we had reached the huge main door.

We passed into the entry chamber, an enormous room dominated by a truly impressive revolving hologram of the galaxy, with each of the Monarchy's million worlds glowing vividly against the somewhat duller background of those worlds the race of Man had not yet assimilated. An overhead hologram, suspended just above the nearer spiral arm, announced times for the replays of some of the more famous military actions in our history: the Siege of Beta Santori, the Battle of Spica, the Sett War, the Battle of the Outer Rim, and three of the battles we had fought against Canphor VI and VII, the Canphor Twins.

We began walking around the exhibit until we came to an Information Area.

"How may I help you?" asked the computer.

"My name is Duncan Rojas. I am the head of the research department for Wilford Braxton's."

It registered my retinagram and bone structure in less than a second.

"Continue."

"Please confirm my appointment to see Prudence Ashe at the new Arrowhorn exhibit."

The computer fell silent for a moment, then glittered back to life.

"Confirmed. The Arrowhorn exhibit is in Centivarus Wing of the Albion Cluster Hall."

"How do I find it?"

"I have activated the red guideline. It will lead you to the exhibit. The Centivarus is closed to the public while the new exhibit is being set up, so you will have to pass a security check upon arriving there."

"I know," I said. "My companion is Hilda Dorian, who also works for Braxton's. Please certify her for entrance into the Centivarus Wing."

"Certified."

"Thank you," I said, watching the plethora of colored lines on the floor until one began blinking a bright red. We followed it, and it led us through the Hall of Sentient Beings, which had representations of some two hundred of the galaxy's sentient species, then took a left turn that skirted the multimedia holographic displays from Serengeti, the zoo world that had been established at the edge of the Inner Frontier. As we moved from one hall to another, we came upon a series of three-dimensional images that flashed constant updates not only of the museums's exhibits but of the status of more than a dozen exploratory expeditions as well. Still more images announced upcoming lectures, member donations, forthcoming museum-financed publications, and even new items in the lavish entry-level gift shops.

Finally we came to the Albion Cluster Hall, skirted a huge room devoted to the prehistory of the planet Darbeena, and arrived at the shuttered door to the Centivarus Wing. We waited until the computer confirmed our retinagrams, and then the doorway opened just enough to allow us to pass through.

It was an impressive exhibit, a series of enormous dioramas showing the incredible variety of life forms to be found on Centivarus III. The entire north end of the hall held a blindingly white polar scene, with the snow and ice so real that one could almost feel the cold.

There were two tropical displays—one a dense jungle, the other a waterhole at midday—plus a mountaintop, a sparse forest of sparkling bluegreen trees twisted into strange, angular shapes, and a flat highland savannah.

There were about a dozen laborers gathered in the savannah, positioning animals and foliage, and finally I saw Prudence Ashe, her thin, wiry figure sitting astride an enormous carnivore, doing some last-minute work on the fur behind its ear.

"Hello, Duncan," she called, clambering down off the beast with an agility that belied her years. Then her gaze fell on Hilda. "And you brought Hilda, too! What a pleasant surprise! How is Harold?"

"Just fine," replied Hilda. "And your children?"

"Geoffrey is back in school again, and the girls are still in the Navy. Diedre is out near the Binder system, and I'm not supposed to know where Carolyn is, though I have a feeling she's somewhere near Lodin." Prudence smiled. "She sent me a hologram of a local flower, and I took it to our Botany section."

"It looks like they're keeping you busy," said Hilda, looking around the hall.

"I can't complain," said Prudence with an air of satisfaction. "They put me in charge of the whole Centivarus exhibit." She turned to me. "I want to thank you again for your recommendation."

"Don't thank me just yet," I said. "You've got some ecological blunders here."

"You're referring to the Anderssen blue gazelle?" she asked.

"It's a night feeder," I replied. "You've got it out in the sunlight."

"I know," she said. "But we didn't have enough nocturnal animals to justify another diorama. There's a note about it on the computer display. Anything else?"

"Yes," I said. "You'd better replace that yellow-and-purple avian in the forest display, the one with the hooked beak." I pointed to a small birdlike creature that was perched on a limb just above a large reddish herbivore.

"What's wrong with it?" asked Prudence.

"It's not native to Centivarus III," I replied.

"Where *is* it from?" asked Hilda.

"I have no idea," I answered.

"If you don't know where it's from, what makes you so certain that it's not from Centivarus?" persisted Hilda.

"It has four toes. All Centivaran avians have three."

Prudence walked over to the diorama and stood there, hands on hips. "I'll have to find out who worked on it, and why it was scheduled for the Centivarus exhibit." She stared at the avian for another moment, then shook her head and sighed deeply. "Thank you, Duncan. Now that I know it's wrong, I'd better get one of my assistants to move it." She turned back to me. "I almost hesitate to ask, but is there anything else wrong?"

"Nothing that I can see," I replied. "But I'm totally ignorant of the flora; if I were you, I'd have one of the museum's experts check it out."

"I'll do that," she promised. "Would you like to examine the Arrowhorn now?"

"If it wouldn't be inconvenient," I said.

"Certainly not. That's why you're here." She led me over to the savannah display, and called for a floating staircase. "He's a wonderful specimen, isn't he?"

I looked at the Arrowhorn, a grotesque creature whose primary form of defense against large predators was its ability to lower its head, detach its sharp, poisonous antlers and shoot them with incredible force and accuracy up to a distance of forty feet. I had read up on the species earlier in the week, and learned that it took almost six weeks for the antlers to grow back. Once the horns had been used, a pair of fleshy pseudo-antlers appeared within a day, a very efficient bluff against predators that would attack if they sensed that the animal was hornless. The pseudo-antlers dried up and dropped off once the animal had regrown its true antlers.

"Very impressive," I said. "Who killed it?"

"A hunter named Demosthenes."

I shook my head. "I've never heard of him."

"He's just starting out."

"Has he supplied a referee?" I asked.

"No. He shot it on commission for the Museum."

"Then does the Museum have a referee?"

"No."

"You understand that you can't challenge my decision if you have no referee to represent you?"

"We just wanted an Arrowhorn. If it's a record—and I think it is—so much the better."

"Well," I said as the staircase arrived, "I suppose I'd better get on with it."

While Prudence showed Hilda the rest of the exhibits and directed the removal of the avian from the diorama, I spent the next twenty minutes measuring the Arrowhorn, thoroughly examining it to make sure that Prudence hadn't inadvertently enhanced the creature's dimensions. Finally I re-checked my figures and brought up the current Braxton's edition on my pocket computer.

"Nine feet four inches at the shoulder," I said. "That will place him 118th."

"Good!" said Prudence, her face lighting up. "We made the book!" She paused. "What about the horns?"

"155th on length, 183rd on spread," I replied. "Your hunter should have waited another week or two to shoot him."

"183rd on the spread?" repeated Prudence, surprised. "I thought he was a little better than that. What was your measurement?"

"67.2 inches," I said.

"I had 68.1."

"You probably measured them from the farthest point," I explained. "Arrowhorn spreads are measured from tip to tip, and you'll notice that his right horn angles in very slightly at the top."

She stared where I pointed, then nodded her head.

I paused, then continued. "Length from tip of nose to tip of tail, thirteen feet, three inches. That's not quite enough." I turned to Prudence. "Your Arrowhorn makes three of the four lists."

"Well," said Prudence, "I suppose that's not so bad, considering that they've been pretty much shot out for the past forty years."

"I might add that you did a beautiful job on it."

"Thank you."

I paused for a moment. "I wonder if I might ask you a question?"

"About Arrowhorns?"

"No."

She smiled. "About elephants, perhaps?"

"Why should you think so?"

"Hilda told me about your latest obsession."

"My latest *commission*," I corrected her. "I assume Mandaka has been to see you?"

"Yes," replied Prudence. "I wasn't able to help him."

"What was your opinion of him?"

She frowned. "I don't know. He's very courteous, but there's something almost sinister about him."

"I agree," I said.

Prudence was silent for a moment, as if recalling her meeting with Mandaka. Finally she looked up at me.

"Now, about your question . . ."

"It's simple enough," I said. "You know what I'm after. Do they still look like tusks?"

"I don't understand," interjected Hilda. "I thought we were all agreed that you're looking for a pair of elephant tusks."

"But tusks are ivory, and ivory has had many uses over the millennia," I replied. "They were still intact in 4400 G.E., but they could have been cannibalized since then."

"I doubt it," said Prudence thoughtfully. "They've certainly had a preservative applied, probably a number of them over the centuries. Uncarved ivory tends to lose moisture content, and as it does so, it starts cracking." She paused for a moment. "Did the owner—the one who had them in 4400 G.E.—know their value?"

"Their exact value?" I replied. "I have no way of determining that. But he did know enough about them to insure them."

She smiled. "There's your answer, then. No insurance company would have touched them unless they had been treated, and we've been treating ivory by molecular stabilization since 3100 G.E."

"So they still look like tusks?" asked Hilda.

"If they've been stabilized, there's not a carving tool around that could make a dent in them," replied Prudence.

"Well, that makes my life a little easier," I said.

"Can I help you with anything else?" asked Prudence.

"Not unless you can tell me why an obviously well-to-do modern man should be obsessed with an animal that died more than seven thousand years ago."

"It's a good question," she agreed.

"I've got more," I said.

"Such as?"

"Why *only* the Kilimanjaro Elephant? And how does Mandaka know that its ivory still exists? That's more than *I* know, and I've had the computer working on it all night."

"I thought you just said that it couldn't be carved," said Hilda, looking confused.

"The fact that it can't be carved doesn't mean that it can't be destroyed," I replied. "What makes him so sure it hasn't been?" I paused. "Which leads me right back to the main question: What does a man living in the 64th century of the Galactic Era want with an animal that died more than a thousand years before there *was* a Galactic Era?"

"I thought the main question was: Where is the ivory?" observed Hilda.

"That's no problem," I said. "I'll pinpoint it in a few more days. It's just detail work."

"He's tracing an item that's been missing for more than three thousand years and could be anywhere in the galaxy, and he says it's just detail work," said Prudence with an expression of disbelief.

"*You* talked to him," I retorted. "You came away with the same impression I did: that he's willing to do literally anything to get his hands on that ivory. Doesn't that make you curious?"

"It makes me want to stay as far away from him as possible," said Prudence fervently.

"Not the problem-solver, here," said Hilda. "Mandaka is the X in his equation."

"Speaking of Mandaka," I said, turning to Hilda, "I want you to do me a favor."

"I have a feeling that I'm not supposed to hear this," said Prudence, beginning to walk away. "I'll see you later."

"You can stay," said Hilda. "He's not going to talk me into anything."

"I really have to get back to work anyway," said Prudence, walking over to the savannah display, summoning the floating staircase, and going back to work on the carnivore's ear.

"Well?" said Hilda.

"Well?" I replied. "You know what I want."

"We both use the same computer system," she said. "Find out for yourself."

I shook my head impatiently. "I can't," I said. "I'm in Research. Before the computer will give me that information I'll need all kinds of permissions from the Executive Board, and that could take days. They might even cancel the assignment if they think there's something odd about him."

"Good!" said Hilda emphatically. "From what you and Prudence tell me, there's *plenty* that's odd about him."

"We both know that I'm going to get the information sooner or later," I explained patiently. "But you're in Security, Hilda—you could find out everything I need to know about Mandaka this afternoon."

"Not *this* afternoon, I couldn't," she retorted. "I told you: I've got a busy day ahead of me."

"As a personal favor to me?"

"Why is it that every time you fall in love with a problem we come down to personal favors? Have I ever asked you to do a personal favor for *me*?"

"I'll treat you and Harold to any entertainment in the city as soon as this is over," I said.

"I'm not asking for a bribe, damn it!" she said heatedly.

"It's a thank-you, not a bribe," I explained.

"A subtle distinction—especially coming from you."

"I really need this, Hilda," I persisted. "Just stay five minutes late and pull out his biography for me. Just five minutes, that's all it will take."

"Harold and I are going out to dinner tonight."

"So you'll spend five minutes less reading your menu."

She looked thoughtful for a moment, then shook her head. "If I do it after hours, someone is going to want to know why," she said. "I'll do it first thing tomorrow morning, and it will look like a routine security check."

"First thing?" I repeated. "You promise?"

"I promise, I promise," she said wearily.

"Good! There's got to be something in his dossier, some-where, that will tell me why he's got to have these particular tusks."

"Maybe he's just impulsive."

"Nobody's *that* impulsive," I said firmly.

"Oh, I don't know," she replied meaningfully, staring directly at me.

We rode the expresswalk back to the office in silence, as I kept trying to put together the pieces of the puzzle. As night fell, my computer glowed to life and informed me that it had uncovered yet another piece for me.

3

The Warlord
(5521 G.E.)

Lions ran from my path, and the few Samburu tribesmen I passed stared at me in awe.

I moved to the south, never hurrying, always staying within reach of water, secure in my strength and in my knowledge of the land. I never hungered, for I could pick up the smallest berry or bring down the stoutest tree. Many times I blew dust on my back to coat my skin against parasites and the burning rays of the sun, and so powerful was I that clouds of dust would remain in the air long after I had continued on my journey.

From time to time I would encounter others of my kind, but they could tell that I was somehow different from them, and they always retreated, trumpeting in fear.

It was lonely to be the king of all the world, but I had lived all my life with loneliness and I wore the mantle of my royalty with dignity as the ground trembled beneath my feet.

His official name was Alexander Korindus Kragan Gamma Sigma Philobus Nelson Nimbus Radillex Procyon Alioth Baaskarda Brakke Asterion New Holland Delta Hydra Galaheen Zeta Piscium, and it continued to grow with every system he conquered.

For the history books, and his numerous biographers, he chose the less formal name of Ghengis Marcus Alexander Augustus Rex.

His armies and navies knew him more simply as the Warlord.

He had a wife he hadn't seen in nine years, two concubines whose company he could no longer bear, a major-domo he distrusted, a political advisor that he had banished to the worlds of the Oligarchy, and a high priest who kept demanding his death.

He had a treasury with more money than he could count, let alone spend, in a lifetime. He ruled entire planetary populations that paid him tribute, and lived or died at his command. He possessed a luxurious palace on Asterion V that had been built exactly to his specifications, and deep within that palace he had his own grisly trophy room, which displayed the heads of seven rival warlords.

He sat now in the enormous throne room of his palace, surrounded by his elite, hand-picked bodyguards. The throne itself was a large chair constructed from the white bones of the huge polar beasts that stalked the northern frontiers of Asterion. Tossed with studied carelessness over the back of it was the pelt of a Dustdemon from New Holland that he himself had slain on a hunting trip. Framing the throne were two enormous pillars of ivory, the tusks of a legendary elephant (or so it was said) that he had appropriated during a raid on the Inner Frontier. Directly in front of the chair was an evil-looking stuffed lizard, some twelve inches in

height, that functioned as a hassock. The walls displayed
artwork and artifacts from all of the galaxy's many ages,
each piece pillaged during wars of conquest.

The Warlord himself disdained the sleek blue uniforms
of his troops. Instead he wrapped himself in the furs of
animals he had killed in mortal combat, leaving only his
powerful arms bare to the shoulder. His face bore two huge
scars which he wore with pride, and his curly black hair
was just starting to show signs of gray. His blue eyes glared
out at the world, rarely blinking, missing no detail, displaying no compassion.

Beside him, to his left, stood a slender young man, clad
in a formal one-piece suit of dark gray. A lifetime of slouch-
ing had taken its toll, and he appeared smaller than he was.

To the Warlord's right stood a smartly-uniformed man
whose insignia proclaimed him to be the captain of the elite
guard. He stood at attention, as he had been standing for
almost half an hour, muttered "He's here, sir!", and stared
at the doorway.

Standing in the entrance to the throne room, showing no
sign of uneasiness or apprehension, was a tall, clean-shaven
man dressed in the colorful silks and satins of a pirate of
old. His long, lean fingers sparkled with jewelry, his tunic
changed colors continuously as if it possessed a life of its
own, and even his boots glistened in the artificial light of
the throne room.

He made a production of displaying his empty holsters,
then opened his tunic, smiled as he held it out for the
Warlord's inspection, and finally extended his arms and
turned around very slowly.

"That's not necessary," said the Warlord in bored tones.
"You couldn't have gotten this far if you were armed."

"A matter of form, nothing more," said the man smoothly.
"I want you to know that I come in peace."

"As a matter of fact, you come in poverty," said the Warlord.

"If it pleases you to say so," replied the man, unperturbed. "Have any of the others arrived yet?"

"Only the alien."

The man frowned. "Not even the Blue Princess?"

"Not even the Blue Princess."

"When are they expected?"

"They're not," responded with Warlord.

"But I told them to be here!"

"Evidently they aren't as trusting as you are, Bellano."

"It's not a matter of trust," replied Bellano. "I have things to say that I don't want overheard, and any transmission signal that can be scrambled can also be unscrambled."

"Then perhaps they're not as desperate for my help as you seem to be."

"They are fools, and you and I will be better off without them," said Bellano, eliminating them from all further consideration with an eloquent shrug. "When all is said and done, the only one we truly need is the alien."

"Shall I send for him now, or would you prefer to relax for a while?" asked the Warlord.

"Perhaps a drink between two old friends, before we get down to business," suggested Bellano.

The Warlord nodded to his son, who walked to a hidden bar and poured two drinks. "Before you get too carried away, I think I should point out that we are not old friends, or even new ones."

"Friendly rivals, then."

"Not even that," said the Warlord. "You destroyed two of my ships last year. I haven't forgotten that."

"A simple misunderstanding," said Bellano smoothly.

"Surely you must agree, or else you would not have offered me safe passage here."

"That was business; so is this. But let's have no illusions of friendship. I'm sure there will be enough lying later on; there's no sense starting this early."

The young man returned with two drinks on a tray. Bellano took one, and then turned to the Warlord.

"To your very good health," he said.

"Thank you."

"And to a successful, if temporary, alliance," continued Bellano.

"To our alliance," echoed the Warlord, staring at him in amusement.

"Is something wrong?"

"I notice that you're not drinking," observed the Warlord. "I thought you were thirsty."

"It is impolite to imbibe before one's host," said Bellano smoothly.

"To say nothing of dangerous," agreed the Warlord. He lifted his glass to his lips and drained it in a single swallow. "Satisfied?"

Bellano offered a courtly bow and then emptied his own glass.

"Your son?" he asked, gesturing to the young man.

"Yes."

"I noticed a resemblance."

"Really?" said the Warlord dryly. "*I* haven't noticed any. Justin, pay your respects to Bellano, the King of the Wintergreen System."

"I'm very pleased to meet you," said Justin, extending his hand formally.

"I have a feeling that I've seen you before," said Bellano, staring curiously at him.

"It's possible," replied Justin. "I was on Margate IV just after you planted your flag on it."

"You should have introduced yourself."

"Your forces had just indiscriminately murdered a quarter of the planetary population. The timing seemed somehow inappropriate."

Bellano laughed heartily. "I admire your choice of words, young man!"

Justin inclined his head slightly. "Thank you, sir."

"Let him sit in on the meeting," said Bellano to the Warlord.

"Is there any particular reason why?" asked the Warlord.

"I like him. Besides, someday I may have to deal with him instead of you."

"Not for a long, long time," promised the Warlord. "But I have no secrets from him, and therefore I have no objection to his attending the meeting." He stared sharply at his son. "As long as he remembers that he is a spectator and not a participant."

Justin nodded his acquiescence.

"Fine!" said Bellano. "You might as well send for our alien friend, now."

"Would you rather eat first?"

"Why don't we eat and talk at the same time?"

"You won't keep your appetite for long if you eat at the same table as the alien," said the Warlord.

"Oh? What does he eat?"

"You don't want to know," the Warlord assured him.

"Doubtless I don't," agreed Bellano. He paused. "Is it alive?"

"Not by the time he finishes with it."

Bellano grimaced. "Let's speak first, by all means. If I have to watch him eat, I may not feel like speaking at all."

The Warlord nodded to his captain of the guard, who walked over to two of the bodyguards and spoke to them in low tones. They immediately left the throne room.

"Since you know that I am unarmed, I assume that you

won't find it necessary to retain the rest of your guards during our discussion," remarked Bellano.

The Warlord nodded his head. "No problem. They'll leave before we begin."

"I assure you I won't attack you," added Bellano with a smile.

"You're welcome to try," offered the Warlord with some sincerity.

"Another day," answered Bellano, equally sincere. He walked around the throne room, hands on hips, admiring the artifacts and paintings. "You've done yourself proud," he said at last.

"Pillage is a profitable profession," said the Warlord with a smile.

"How very true," replied Bellano, picking up a small Denebian crystal, fashioned in the likeness of a bird of prey. "I don't suppose you'd care to sell anything?"

"Not particularly," answered the Warlord. "I'm a conquerer, not a merchant." He paused. "But if you'd like that little bauble, it's yours."

"Really?"

"In honor of our truce," said the Warlord. "And it will save you the trouble of stealing it," he added wryly.

"What a terrible thing to say about a future ally," remarked Bellano in amused tones. "I'm a warlord, not a thief."

The Warlord shrugged. "Then put it back."

Bellano shook his head and placed the crystal in a leather pouch that hung down from a sash about his waist. "I'd rather keep it as a remembrance of you."

"Somehow I thought you might."

"Have you any objections to my examining your collection further?" inquired Bellano.

"There will be no more gifts."

"I'll look anyway."

"As you wish," said the Warlord.

"By the way, what are those things behind your throne?"

"Elephant tusks."

"Real ones?" asked Bellano, walking over to examine them.

The Warlord nodded.

"I'm impressed," said Bellano. "When did the last elephant die, anyway?"

"Five or six thousand years ago."

"Where did you get these?" he asked, gesturing toward the tusks.

"On one of my excursions to the Inner Frontier."

Bellano patted one of the tusks fondly, nodded his approval, and went back to examining the artwork.

"By the way," he remarked as he cocked his head to one side, trying to make sense of a non-representational blue-and-green hologram, "I assume that if you reject my proposal, you will not try to hinder me."

"I won't have to," said the Warlord calmly. "If you thought you could accomplish your goal without my help, you wouldn't be here."

"Or compete with me."

"Let's wait until I hear your proposal before we worry about what I will or won't do," said the Warlord.

"Sir . . ." said a guard at the doorway to the throne room.

The Warlord turned just in time to see a lithe, dark figure, vaguely humanoid in shape and with skin the color and texture of charred meat, leap nimbly to a window ledge some twelve feet above the ground, where it perched at a 45-degree angle.

"Don't you find it awkward up there?" asked the Warlord.

"Here I find comfort," replied the alien. "Here I will stay."

"You're Mylarrr?" asked Bellano, looking up at him.

"Mylarrr is me."

"Thank you for coming."

"I expect more than thank-you-for-coming," said the alien, flashing his yellow fangs in a toothy grin.

"And you shall have more, never fear," promised Bellano. "Shall we begin?"

"Begin and start and commence," agreed Mylarrr, purring like some gigantic cat.

Bellano turned to the Warlord. "I'm sure we're being recorded and monitored, but I would personally feel much more comfortable if you were to close the doors."

The Warlord turned to Justin and nodded, and the young man walked to the main doorway, directed the guards to leave and shut the massive doors, and then began closing various other doors to the throne room.

"You're *sure* you wouldn't rather come down from there?" suggested Bellano.

"Content, safe, secure, happy," replied the alien, shifting his position slightly so that his bullet-shaped head pointed downward, and Bellano could see now that he possessed a pair of vestigial wings, flimsy things that were never meant for flight but which seemed to aid his balance.

"May we offer you something to drink before we begin?" asked Bellano.

"Fly-by-Nights do not never ever drink human intoxicants, no," replied Mylarrr.

"As you wish," said Bellano.

"I wish to start and begin."

"And so we shall," said Bellano. He paused. "I have it on impeccable authority that the Oligarchy will be shipping a cargo of gold bullion to Denivarus II ten days from now."

The Fly-by-Night uttered a high-pitched shriek that sounded like a steam whistle.

"Gold is good," he said. "Gold is honorable. Gold is valuable. Gold is pretty. Gold is malleable. Gold is—"

"Gold is well-protected," interrupted the Warlord.

"Not this time," said Bellano confidently.

"Then why do you need my help?"

"There will be a Navy convoy of three hundred ships."

"And you don't think that constitutes protection?" asked the Warlord with a smile.

"Together, we have far more firepower, and that's all the protection there will be."

"Until they spot us while we're still two days away and send for reinforcements from the 12th and 14th Fleets," said the Warlord.

Bellano smiled triumphantly. "There will be no reinforcements no matter what happens."

The Warlord stared at him intently. "What makes you think that?"

"It's not generally known, but the 12th Fleet is committed to the Anderson Cluster for the forseeable future. There is a consortium of thirty-nine mining worlds that are trying to secede from the Oligarchy, and the 12th is there to make sure they don't."

"What makes you think they can't send reinforcements anyway?" asked the Warlord.

"Because those thirty-nine worlds are much more valuable to the Oligarchy than a shipful of bullion," said Bellano. He lowered his voice confidentially. "And they're better-armed than the Navy expected. In point of fact, the 12th Fleet is itself waiting for reinforcements. The mining worlds have actually fought them to a standoff."

"And the 14th Fleet?" asked the Warlord.

"It's only up to half-strength after the Volarian War. It won't be in a position to help anyone for another four months."

There was another shrill whistle from the Fly-by-Night. "You think you know. You don't know. Three months is all. Maybe two-point-nine. Maybe two-point-eight-five. Maybe two-point-eight-eight. You don't know."

Bellano looked up at the alien. "How did you find out?"

Mylarrr grinned at him. "Am I not the most beautiful and intelligent of all sentient beings? Do I not know the dying of the light and the onset of night?"

"What has that got to do with the 14th Fleet?" asked Bellano.

"It is just another thing I know," answered the Fly-by-Night firmly. "Three months. Maybe two-point-nine."

Bellano turned back to the Warlord. "Three months, four months, what's the difference? At least he confirms what I've said. The Fleet won't be ready for at least three months, and we plan to strike in eight days."

"I thought you said ten."

"I said it was due to land on Denivarus II in ten days. I plan to attack in eight. Why let them have the advantage of Denivarus' weaponry and police ships?" He paused. "Well?"

The Warlord shook his head. "Too simple."

"Sometimes good things are simple."

"Gold is a good thing," chimed in Mylarrr.

"How can I confirm that the 12th Fleet is pinned down in the Anderson Cluster?" asked the Warlord.

"You must have sources," said Bellano. "Use them."

"I'd prefer to know yours."

Bellano smiled. "I'm sure you would."

"If I can't confirm it, I won't be a party to this," warned the Warlord. "Are you sure you won't tell me who to contact?"

Bellano shook his head. "I've been sworn to secrecy."

"When did that ever stop you?"

"Touché," said Bellano. "Let us simply say, then, that your analysis of their data would be tainted by the fact that I supplied you with their names. I know you have sources within the Oligarchy; you will have to use them, or you would never truly believe my information."

"And the 14th Fleet?"

"That's easy," said Bellano, gesturing toward the Fly-by-Night. "*His* sources have to be different from mine, and he's got the same information."

"Why is the Oligarchy shipping gold bullion out to Denivarus II?" asked the Warlord. "Usually shipments go in the opposite direction, from the Rim to the Core. What's different this time?"

"I believe I can answer that, Father," said Justin.

"I believe *I* can, too," said the Warlord, annoyed at the interruption. "But I want to hear *his* answer."

"The Navy is spread too thin," said Bellano. "Humanity may have achieved primacy in the galaxy, but the Oligarchy has to constantly patrol a million worlds plus all the travel and cargo routes. It's my guess that the 12th Fleet is going to be hiring independent mercenary armies for the next few years, and will be paying them off in gold."

The Warlord nodded. "If that's true—and I believe it is—then that's where you'll find the Blue Princess."

"You think she's sold out to them?" asked Bellano.

"Rented, anyway. She knows there's going to be a lot of gold on hand; this is her way of getting closer to it."

"Then she's making a big mistake," replied Bellano promptly. "It's obvious that Denivarus II is going to be their bank. Even if she can figure out some way to steal the gold in transit from Denivarus to the paymaster, she'll only get as much as the Navy has committed to spend on a given action. We've got a shot at the whole bank, so to speak."

The Warlord stared at him thoughtfully. "Who, in your opinion, should command our forces?" he asked at last.

"You are the paramount warlord of the Rim," said Bellano with a courtly bow. "I will defer to you."

"Your fleet would bear the brunt of the attack," said the Warlord.

"They are just men and ships," said Bellano with a shrug. "Both are easily replaceable—especially the men." He paused. "The spoils will be split among the three of us. How we each choose to distribute it to our forces is no one's concern."

"Agreed," said the Warlord. "I must also tell you that under no circumstances will my ships fly my own colors in battle."

"I rather thought we would all go in without colors."

The Warlord shook his head. "If I decide to proceed with this, we will fly the colors of the Blue Princess." He paused. "The Navy is going to want an enemy to pursue, if not immediately then when they are up to strength. We might as well give them one."

"Excellent!" said Bellano with a smile.

"Next question: the Fly-by-Nights have no fleet. Why do we need them?"

"We'll have twenty-seven tons of bullion to get rid of in a hurry," said Bellano. "They understand its value. What better place to dump the gold than an empire of eleven alien planets that have no political ties to the Oligarchy? Nine-tenths of it will sit in their vaults, and the rest will come on the market as jewelry and art objects over the next ten years or so."

"Maybe only one-twelfth, possibly, perhaps," confirmed Mylarrr, swaying back and forth overhead.

"And what will they buy it with?"

"Credits."

"Traceable?"

Bellano shook his head. "Paper. And we are not to ask where they came by it."

"Rate?" asked the Warlord pointedly.

"Twenty percent of market."

The Warlord looked up at the alien. "The meeting's over. You can swing there for all eternity for all I give a damn."

"Twenty-six-point-two-two-three-one," said Mylarrr.

The Warlord smiled in spite of himself. "How did you come up with that figure so quickly?"

"Not quick or fast or prompt," Mylarrr assured him. "It is our absolute last, final, ultimate offer, for certain."

"Thirty percent or we stop right now," said the Warlord.

"Okay, thirty," agreed Mylarrr pleasantly, leaping to an adjoining window ledge and landing in a perfect handstand.

The Warlord turned back to Bellano. "How many ships can you bring to this little enterprise?"

"One hundred and thirty-five, perhaps one hundred and forty."

The Warlord smiled. "One hundred and seventy-five."

"I don't have that many."

"You see? I told you there would be ample time for lying later on."

"I can't leave my territory totally undefended," protested Bellano.

"You won't," said the Warlord. "If you commit one hundred and seventy-five ships, you'll still have twenty-seven in reserve."

"Twenty-nine," corrected Bellano with no show of embarrassment.

"I'll have to speak to my spies," said the Warlord, a look of amusement flashing across his face.

There was a momentary silence.

"Well, I suppose we'd better start working out the details of the attack," said Bellano at last.

"Let's not be premature," said the Warlord. "I haven't agreed to go through with this yet."

"Oh?"

"That's right," continued the Warlord. "For example, we haven't decided how you and I are splitting the gold yet."

"I assumed fifty-fifty," said Bellano.

"Are you supplying half the firepower?"

"I am supplying the necessary information."

"Which I will then confirm through my own sources."

"Well, I suppose we can split it up based on number of ships," offered Bellano.

"We can, but we won't," said the Warlord.

"Why not?"

"Because I'm not supplying three-quarters of the ships."

"You want to take seventy-five percent of the gold?" demanded Bellano. "Absolutely not!"

The Warlord shrugged. "As you will."

"Sixty-forty," countered Bellano.

"The percentage isn't open to negotiation."

"But you negotiated with the alien!"

"If I commit to this operation, I need him to take the gold off my hands. But I won't commit for sixty percent."

"Sixty percent of twenty-seven tons of gold is better than seventy-five percent of nothing," said Bellano.

"*I* didn't seek *you* out," replied the Warlord. "You need me for this operation—but if we can't reach an equitable agreement, I don't necessarily need you." He smiled. "There are no end of minority partners who would be only too happy to join me in this enterprise."

"Cut me out and I'll warn the Navy!"

"If your information checks out—and I won't proceed

until it does—warning the Navy won't do all that much good," said the Warlord. "But it *will* accomplish one thing: it will put the two of us at hazard, which I don't believe either of us particularly desires, but which I can weather far more easily than you. Now, let me have your answer: will you accept twenty-five percent, or is this meeting over?"

Bellano glared at him for a long moment. "I'll have to consider it. I'll let you know before we are finished."

"Let me know right now, or we *are* finished," replied the Warlord.

Bellano sighed and nodded his head. "All right."

"Good. I knew you were a reasonable man."

"What else remains to be done, before we plan our attack?"

"Now I will check out your information, and the Fly-by-Nights' ability to absorb that much gold without leaving an obvious trail, and then I will decide whether or not to proceed with the operation." He nodded to his son, who walked across the huge room and opened the main doors. "You will each be escorted to your quarters, where you can eat and rest. We will meet here again in three hours."

"Where the hell have you been?" demanded the Warlord as Justin entered his private chambers.

"Speaking to the Fly-by-Night," replied Justin, walking across the glistening floor and sitting down on a hand-carved chair of Doradusian hardwood.

"You must be a glutton for punishment," said the Warlord, swiveling in his chair to better face his son and ordering the door to slide shut.

"He can make himself understood, when he finds something he wants."

"Oh? And what does he want?"

"The elephant tusks."

"They're just a trophy," said the Warlord. "They have no market value. What can he possibly want them for?"

Justin shrugged. "I gather that the Fly-by-Nights practice some form of animist religion. They worship size and power, and these are the biggest teeth he's ever seen. He thinks they'll make him all-powerful."

The Warlord chuckled. "It'll take a lot more than a set of ivory to do that."

"I know," continued Justin. "But he offered to pay forty percent of market value for the gold if we'll agree to give him the ivory."

"Interesting," said the Warlord noncommittally.

"What shall I tell him?"

"Tell him no, of course. That's just a first offer. Let's see how high he'll go." The Warlord paused. "Besides, we've got more important matters to discuss. While you were spending your time with the Fly-by-Night, I've been confirming Bellano's data." He gestured to his private computer, which bore his personal seal. "It checks out."

"Does that surprise you?" asked Justin. "After all, he is practically our hostage. He had to know you would try to verify his story before committing yourself."

"What's your opinion?"

"About what, Father?"

"About Bellano. What do you think I should do?"

"You've never asked my opinion before," said Justin.

"And I won't be guided by it now," said the Warlord. "But you were there for the whole meeting. I want to see how much you've learned. What would *you* do?"

"I'd send him home and forget about the whole thing," said Justin.

"Why?"

"We don't need it."

"I thought everyone needed twenty-seven tons of gold bullion," said the Warlord sardonically.

"We don't need the exposure," continued Justin.

"Explain," said the Warlord, removing a large cigar from a jewel-encrusted thermidor and lighting it.

"I think the reason the Navy has left us alone is because we're so far out on the Rim. There are so few Oligarchic worlds out here that we're more trouble to destroy than we're worth." He paused. "Attack a Navy convoy and suddenly you've made it worth their while."

"It's a possibility," said the Warlord noncommittally.

"But you don't believe it."

The Warlord shook his head. "Bellano's information confirms what I've believed for a number of years. The Navy is spread too thin to care about what happens out here. The Oligarchy has more than a million of its own worlds to worry about." He paused. "In fact, they're probably delighted to have us operating out here. We've managed to pacify more than a hundred systems and put them on a credit economy; someday, in two or three centuries, they'll move in and reap the benefits of what we've done."

"Then why have they put a reward on your head?" challenged Justin.

"Oh, if some bounty hunter manages to bring me down, they won't weep bitter tears," said the Warlord. "But they'll be just as happy if the warlords continue to function out here against the day that they can move out and assimilate them into the Oligarchy."

"Are you willing to bet your life on it?" demanded Justin.

The Warlord seemed amused. "Of course not. But I'm willing to bet *Bellano's* life on it."

"I'm not sure that I follow you," said Justin.

"Then *learn* to," said the Warlord harshly. "Someday this will all be yours, and you'd better learn to use your brain by then."

"There is no need to insult me, Father."

"That's open to some debate," said the Warlord, still

annoyed. Finally he shrugged. "All right," he said. "I agree that the Navy isn't going to be thrilled about losing three hundred ships. If we go through with this, we're going to have to give them a villain, or they may decide upon one themselves."

"And the villain is to be Bellano?"

"It's got to be," said the Warlord. "They'll never believe in the Fly-by-Nights." He looked sharply at his son. "Would you?"

"I don't know," replied Justin. "Perhaps if I understood them better . . ."

"The Oligarchy isn't in the business of understanding aliens, just ruling them—or exterminating them," added the Warlord. "They're going to look for a human enemy, and flying the colors of the Blue Princess isn't going to fool them for more than ten seconds."

"How do you plan to convince them that Bellano is the one they want?"

"Before the convoy is totally decimated, I'll allow them to intercept a coded message to Bellano from one of his subordinates. They'll tightbeam it to the cypher section of the 12th Fleet, and within a few hours they'll know who they're looking for."

"When they find him, how can you guarantee that he won't implicate you?"

"Because all they'll find is what's left of him," said the Warlord. "His ship will regrettably be destroyed in the battle. In fact, the poor fellow will lose almost his entire fleet." The Warlord smiled. "He is a threat to my security; I see no reason why the Navy shouldn't be encouraged to eliminate him."

"Why shouldn't he suspect that you'll betray him and take steps to protect himself?" asked Justin.

"Oh, he will," the Warlord assured him. "He will take every precaution imaginable, for all the good it will do him." He leaned back on his chair, huge fingers interlinked behind his massive head, his gaze fixed on the oversized hologram of his most recent concubine that dominated the far wall of the chamber, just above a security console that allowed him to monitor all the rooms of his palace. "Bellano's fleet will bear the brunt of the Navy's firepower. Once the convoy has been destroyed, it shouldn't be too difficult to mop up what remains with our own fleet plus those ships that we've told him are committed elsewhere." He paused. "We'll also put five or six tons of bullion onto the remains of his flagship. After all, why should the Navy waste its time searching the Rim for the gold? We'll give them enough so they can assume that the rest of it was destroyed."

"You're sure they'll believe that?" asked Justin dubiously.

"I think there's every likelihood that they will—although I plan to take certain precautions, just in case they don't." He paused. "Anyway, when the operation is concluded, he'll have about fifty ships left defending eighteen systems; I think we can probably take all eighteen of them within a year." He paused thoughtfully. "And if I'm right about the Blue Princess, she can't have left too many ships defending her territory either." The Warlord smiled. "This situation may work out to our advantage all the way around."

"Then you're not doing this for the gold at all."

"The gold is certainly an added incentive," replied the Warlord, puffing on his cigar. "But eliminating the competition is my primary motive."

"I can't believe it will be as easy as you make it sound," said Justin.

"There's nothing easy about it," answered the Warlord. "A lot of good men and women are going to lose their lives in this action."

"You know what I mean."

"I didn't become Ghengis Marcus Alexander Augustus Rex by being tentative," said the Warlord. "Fleets and planets are just like people; they respond best to decisive actions by their leaders." He stared at his son. "That's what you must learn before you can hope to hold what I've put together. Once you've made a decision, there can't be any halfway measures. You can't rob the Navy of part of its gold, you can't cheat Bellano just a little bit, you can't take half of the Blue Princess' territory. You've got to go for the jugular, and once you find it, you must not let it go." He shook his head. "There's too much of your mother in you." The Warlord paused, trying to sum up his thoughts in a single sentence. "You've got to want more, and you've got to develop the cunning to get it."

"More what, Father?" asked Justin.

"Just *more*."

"I will try to remember that, Father," said Justin.

"You must also remember that a warlord has no friends and no allies. He has nothing but subordinates and enemies, and each of the former is potentially one of the latter."

"So you have told me."

"And I'll *keep* telling you until you know it as well as you know your own name." He leaned forward now, staring intently at his son. "Now, as for the Fly-by-Nights . . ." He paused. "Thirty percent of market value is ridiculous."

"Then shall we give him the ivory and take forty percent?"

"No."

"Why not?"

"Because I don't understand why he wants the ivory, and I don't trust what I don't understand." The Warlord paused. "We'll sell them five tons, no more."

"If you don't like their price, why sell them anything at all?" asked Justin. "That will leave us only sixteen or seventeen tons."

"Because the gold is simply a means to an end. There's always a chance that the Navy will see through our little ruse—and if they ever decide that Bellano didn't have all of the gold and start searching the Rim for the rest it, I want to make sure they know where to look for it—and if it's worth five tons to eliminate Bellano, it's certainly worth another five tons to insure that the Navy never finds out what happened."

"But the Fly-by-Nights will tell the Navy that *we* have the rest of it."

"It'll be my word against Mylarrr's—and the Oligarchy is predisposed to believe humans and distrust aliens," said the Warlord. "Besides, we'll have disposed of our share of the gold long before they start asking questions about it." The Warlord paused. "You look dubious."

"Personally, I'd be very careful about betraying a race that I didn't understand."

"But I do understand them," snorted his father. "That's why *I'm* the Warlord."

"Yes, Father," said Justin wearily.

Eleven days had passed, and the raid on the convoy had gone exactly as planned. Bellano was dead; the Navy believed—at least officially—that they had recovered that portion of the gold which had not been destroyed; the Warlord had lost only sixty-three ships of his own; and the Oligarchy was convinced that Bellano had been responsible for the raid.

The Warlord sat upon his throne now, a crystal glass in his hand, one foot propped up on his stuffed lizard, enjoying the pleasant aftermath of his victory. Justin stood near him, also sipping some wine, while Mylarrr perched precariously on a window ledge some dozen feet above the floor.

"It went more smoothly than I anticipated," the Warlord

was saying. "I wasn't sure that leaving some of the gold on Bellano's flagship would fool them."

"You are to be congratulated, Father," said Justin. "May I pour you some more wine?"

The Warlord nodded and held out his glass. "Thank you. Ask your friend if he wants some."

"No no no no!" said Mylarrr promptly. "Never do I ever drink intoxicants."

"Can we give you anything?" asked the Warlord.

"Oh yes, oh yes!" exclaimed the Fly-by-Night, leaping lightly to the floor and walking over to the ivory. "*This* is true intoxication!" he said as he reached out and placed his clawed hand against the larger of the two tusks.

"You enjoy touching it?" asked the Warlord, amused.

"It glistens with power, it glows, it sparkles," explained Mylarrr.

"And you think it transmits it power to you?"

The alien smiled. "When we touch, I am immortal."

"Whatever makes you happy," said the Warlord with a shrug.

"Ivory makes me happy and satisfied and immortal."

"Good for you."

"Fifty percent," said Mylarrr.

"No."

"Maybe fifty-one, perhaps, possibly."

"I'll think about it."

"Good! You think, ponder, meditate, consider, cogitate, then we shall talk and bargain and deal and trade."

The Warlord drained his goblet. "In the meantime, let's change the subject." He turned to his son. "Have you confirmed the disposition of Bellano's remaining ships?"

Justin nodded. "Yes, Father. His forces have fifty-three

ships remaining; all of their coordinates are in our computers."

"We'll regroup for a few days, then hit them before a new leader has a chance to emerge and consolidate his power." The Warlord held out his goblet. "This is excellent wine. I'll have some more."

Justin shook his head thoughtfully. "I don't think you need anymore, Father."

"Since when do *you* decide how much I can drink?" demanded the Warlord, trying to rise to his feet and finding to his surprise that they wouldn't support his weight.

"You've drunk quite enough to kill you already," said Justin calmly.

"Are you mad?" shouted the Warlord. "Do you know what you're saying?"

"It's quite painless, I assure you," said Justin. "A loss of feeling in the extremities, a sensation of cold, and then nothing."

"Guards!" bellowed the Warlord.

"They won't come, Father," said Justin gently. "They work for *me* now."

"But why?" asked the Warlord, struggling to comprehend.

Your time is done, Father. The day of the warlord has passed." Justin paused. "The mere fact that you believed all the false information I managed to plant with Bellano and your other sources meant that your days were numbered. Do you *really* believe that the most powerful military force in the galaxy is content to let a warlord rule entire solar systems and extract tribute from them? Is it rational to think that the Navy wouldn't protect its gold shipment with enough firepower to ward off any attack?"

"But we won!" protested the Warlord. "We destroyed them!"

Justin shook his head. "You destroyed an undermanned fleet that served its only purpose: it destroyed Bellano's forces before capitulating. I toyed with allowing the Navy to bring in a thousand support ships, but that would have decimated our own fleet, and I still have some use for it before it is disbanded."

"Disbanded? What are you—"

"Save your strength, Father," said Justin. "You haven't all that much left." He smiled. "While you were busy becoming the paramount warlord of the Rim, I ascertained through my own channels that the Navy would be much happier dealing with a single governor than a dozen warlords."

"You?" rasped the Warlord.

"Certainly," said Justin. "Haven't you always told me to use my initiative? As a gesture of goodwill, I have delivered Bellano and his fleet to them, and within a day or two they will take the Blue Princess into custody. And of course there's you, Father; I think that was what convinced them to do business with me. You are the one they wanted most of all."

"You've destroyed it all," whispered the Warlord.

"Nonsense," said Justin easily. "Eventually you would have lost your empire to a greater warlord . . . or, if you hadn't, *I* would have. Being a general has never been one of my ambitions anyway; I'm not very good at it, and I find it far too limiting. You never owned as many as thirty systems; tomorrow I will be the governor of one hundred and sixty-seven of them. Of course, we'll have to dispose of some of the lesser warlords, but the Navy is more than happy to do so, so that should prove no problem."

"And the gold?"

"Well, I'll get a ton of it for my troubles, but the rest will be returned to the Treasury planetoid in the Deluros system. They never needed it out here, of course; they use almost no mercenaries, and those that they do use are paid in credits. We arranged the shipment simply to lure Bellano into joining forces with you."

"Very clever," said the Warlord, almost inaudibly.

"*I* thought so," agreed Justin. "Anyway, in one stroke I've more than quintupled the size of your empire and acquired Oligarchic legitimacy as well." He paused for a moment. "Have I done well, Father? Do you finally approve of me?"

The Warlord spoke again, and Justin could barely hear him.

"You've made a mistake."

"Oh?" replied Justin. "What do you mean?"

"You should have killed the alien. You have no gold for him."

"Mylarrr?" replied Justin. "He is no problem. He will be content with the ivory."

"You are a fool," whispered the Warlord, and died.

Justin stood up and turned to the Fly-by-Night.

"He is dead."

"Sad and tragic and heartbreaking and inevitable," said the alien, still stroking the larger of the two tusks. "Now we discuss gold, which is good and bright and profitable."

"There won't be any gold," said Justin.

"No gold? No gold? But I saw gold!"

"Only a single ton, and I have use for it."

"But here is me!"

"I know you are here for the gold, but I'm sure we can come to a reasonable settlement."

"Reasonable and sage and just," said Mylarrr emphatically. "You propose, I dispose."

"As a gesture of goodwill, I would like to give you the ivory."

"The ivory!" exclaimed Mylarrr, jumping up and perching atop the larger of the tusks. "Immortal and invincible is me!"

"That is correct."

Mylarrr suddenly stared at Justin. "Now the gold."

"There is no gold for you."

"I know where it is and its location," said the Fly-by-Night.

"Then I will move it as soon as you leave."

"I will take it with me."

"You'll do no such thing," said Justin angrily. He turned to the doorway. "Guards!"

"Alas and sorrow, they will not come."

"Why not?" demanded Justin.

"Because I have killed them."

"You? How?"

"Me, as easily as this."

Mylarrr struck out swiftly with his clawed hand, and suddenly Justin fell to his knees, his fingers clutching at his neck.

"I have the ivory," repeated Mylarrr tranquilly. "I am immortal. I cannot be defeated. I will rule for eternity and infinity. Even the Oligarchy cannot touch me now."

"You're crazy! They will find my corpse and hunt you down!" promised Justin, his vision starting to blur.

"They cannot hunt me down," Mylarrr assured him. "I am the greatest of warlords. I have the ivory."

"My father had it, and it did not make *him* immortal!" rasped Justin.

"There is a difference," said Mylarrr confidently as he leaped nimbly to the floor.

"What is the difference?" asked Justin with his last breath.

"I have no son."

Third Interlude (6303 G.E.)

"Duncan?"

I muttered something unintelligible and rolled over onto my side.

"Duncan!"

This time the voice was louder, and a moment later a hand reached out and began vigorously shaking my shoulder.

"What happened?" I asked, sitting erect abruptly and almost banging my head against Hilda Dorian's. "Did I oversleep?"

"No."

"Oh." I was still disoriented, and my heart was pounding so rapidly that I was surprised she couldn't hear it. "What time is it?"

"Seven o'clock." She looked grim.

"Night? Morning?"

"In the morning." She paused. "I see you spent the night in your office *again*."

My brain finally began functioning. "I located the tusks again, almost twelve centuries after their last appearance."

"Really? When and where?"

"I found them in 5521 G.E., out on the Rim."

"That's less than eight centuries ago," she noted, impressed.

"But there's a problem."

"There are more problems than you think," she replied.

"Oh?"

"Let me hear yours first."

"An alien gained possession of the tusks, so I had to order the computer to redirect its search. There's no sense checking human records when the tusks are most likely to show up next in an alien society." I ran a hand through my hair, trying to smooth it down. "I must have fallen asleep while I was collecting data."

"Would you like some coffee?" asked Hilda, just a bit too solicitously.

"Not just now."

"You're sure?" she persisted.

"Yes, I'm sure," I replied. "Why have you suddenly become so nurturing?"

"Because you've got a bigger problem than some alien race that may or may not possess the ivory, and I want you to be fully awake when I discuss it with you."

"I'm awake," I said, getting to my feet and feigning some stretching exercise. "What have you got to tell me?"

"I came in early this morning and called up Bukoba Mandaka's dossier."

"And?"

She stared at me for a long moment, as if making sure that I was finally in possession of all my faculties before answering.

"He doesn't exist."

I frowned. "What do you mean, he doesn't exist? He was right here in my office. He deposited money in my account. I'm working for the man."

"I know," she said grimly. "But there is no official record of him."

"Computer." I ordered, "Bring up a hologram of Bukoba Mandaka."

The image of Mandaka shimmered to life and hung, suspended, above the computer.

"That is a *private* record," said Hilda. "The Commonwealth has no record of him."

"Have you checked his voiceprint and retinagram?" I asked. "Maybe Mandaka is an alias."

"I've got the computer working on it. So far it hasn't had any success."

"It's a big galaxy," I said. "It'll find him sooner or later." I paused, thinking of other avenues of pursuit. "What else did you learn?"

"His identification number is phony, his passport is forged, and the geneology program can't produce his parents."

"This is crazy!" I said. "Did we, or didn't we, check out his credit before I was permitted to accept his commission?"

"We did," she replied, frowning. "He has access to more than five million credits in two different banks, and he can stand a Level III credit check, which is as high as I'm empowered to go—but I can't determine the source of his money."

"What about his address?"

"A message-taking computer terminal in City Center."

"Does he pay taxes?"

"I haven't got clearance to tie into the Treasury computer."

"Can you get it?" I asked.

"Not without alerting a lot of people to the fact that I'm checking up on Mandaka. That's why I decided to speak to you first."

"Good thinking," I agreed. "If you told anyone higher up what you told me, they'd make me drop the assignment."

"Don't you think you should—at least until you learn something more about him?"

"What's wrong with you?" I demanded. "You yourself said his money's good!"

"But you don't know anything about him. He could be a criminal."

"He could also be exactly what he purports to be," I shot

back. "If I don't find the ivory, we'll never know *what* he is. He'll just vanish and hire someone else to find it."

"I should have known you'd react like this," she said, throwing her hands up in disgust. "All you care about is finding that damned ivory!"

"As soon as I locate it, I'll insist that he tell me who he is and why he wants it," I said soothingly. "But I don't have any leverage without it."

"You may not have much of a life expectancy *with* it," she pointed out.

I snorted contemptuously. "No one's going to kill me when my own computer is monitoring everything that happens."

"A man who has no past, no present, no future, and no identity might very well feel free to kill you."

"He's got a face and a bone structure and fingerprints and retinas," I replied. "Even if the police don't know his name, they'll know who they're looking for." I smiled at her. "I thank you for your concern, Hilda, but it really isn't necessary. I'll find the ivory in another two or three days —I've already run through two and a half millennia of its history in just two evenings, and I'm within eight hundred years of locating it right now—and as soon as I discover its location, we'll find out exactly who this Mr. Mandaka is and why he's so desperate to get his hands on a trophy that nobody else knows or cares about."

"And if he refuses to tell you?"

"He'll tell me," I said confidently.

"What makes you so sure?"

"You didn't see his face when he mentioned the ivory; I did. He'll do whatever he has to do to obtain it."

"Including murder?"

"I said so once before," I answered. "But in this particular case, murder won't get him the ivory. The truth will."

Hilda stared at me thoughtfully for a long moment. "Obviously you don't want my findings to go beyond this office."

"Absolutely not!"

"If I agree to keep quiet about this," she said, still staring intently at me, "I intend to impose two conditions on you."

"What conditions?" I demanded.

"First, I will personally monitor all future meetings or communications that you have with Mandaka."

"I agree—as long as you don't interrupt or let him know you're monitoring him."

"Second, if this isn't resolved within three days, I'm going to the executive board and the police with what I've got."

"You haven't *got* anything," I pointed out, exasperated.

"I've got a man who theoretically doesn't exist, but who has instant access to five million credits. I've got a man with no identity in a society where his identity should be imprinted in fifty million memory banks. I've got a man whom you consider capable of murder. Don't you think I can interest *someone* in my data?"

"But what if it takes me five days to track down the ivory? Or seven days? What if the aliens don't keep written records? They never joined the Oligarchy or the Commonwealth; for all I know they're extinct. You *can't* limit me to just three days!"

She paused to consider what I had said.

"All right," she replied carefully. "I'll go this far. If you haven't found the ivory three days from now, I'll give you a chance to restate your case—but I make no promises."

"That's unacceptable!" I snapped.

"The alternative is that I make my information public right now."

I glared at her and she glared right back at me.

"All right," I muttered. "It's a deal."

She seemed about to say something else, then changed her mind and walked out of the office.

I got up, ordered the door to admit no visitors, removed my rumpled clothing, and entered the small dryshower just next to the closet.

"Activate," I commanded.

"Done."

"Computer?"

"Yes?"

"Have you managed to trace the tusks any further?"

"No, I have not. There is very little recorded data concerning the alien race known as Fly-by-Nights."

"How long do I have before Braxton's is officially open for business?"

"One hour, fifty-one minutes, and nineteen seconds."

"How much of your capacity is currently at my disposal?"

"63.278%"

"That's all?"

"I am readying the building for its human occupants, and working for a number of early arrivals."

"Very well," I said. "Of that percentage, I want you to utilize half of it on the Fly-by-Nights to see if you can find out what happened to the ivory after Mylarrr gained possession of it."

"Understood. Working . . ."

"Now make my window opaque until I get dressed."

"Done."

I stepped out of the dryshower and faced the glowing crystal. "I want you to use the remaining half of your capacity to learn everything you can about Bukoba Mandaka."

"There is no official record of Bukoba Mandaka."

"I know you just checked his credentials against the Monarchy's records," I said. "But there are other places yet to look."

"Waiting . . ."

"To begin with, you might access any records relating to the Maasai, if they exist."

"Understood. Working . . ."

"Next," I said, "see if the words Bukoba or Mandaka have any special meaning in the Maasai dialect."

"Understood. Working . . ."

"Next, let me have some music."

"Have you a preference?" asked the computer.

"Barjeenan's Concerto in B-flat Minor."

"Done," said the computer, and the atonal alien music flooded the office.

"That's better," I said, sitting down, still naked, on my contour chair. "Let me have a mild vibration, please."

"Done," replied the chair.

"And heat the small of my back. I'm a little stiff."

"Heated," said the chair.

"Thank you." I turned back to the glowing crystal. "Whether or not he exists officially, Mandaka must have done something that we can trace. We know he paid a visit to Prudence Ashe at the Natural History Museum before approaching me, so I want you to check all museums and private collectors that have large collections of Earth animals. Start with this star system, then check all nearby systems, and finally check this entire star cluster. I want to know if he's been to visit any of them."

"Understood. Working . . ."

I paused, letting Barjeenan's music flow over me, trying to blend my thoughts with the exotic interior rhythms.

"Next," I added, "I want you to access the Realty Board and all the various rental agencies and hotels, and find out if a Bukoba Mandaka—or anyone answering to his description—has recently rented or purchased living quarters anywhere on the planet."

"Understood. Working . . . I have checked all Maasai

dictionaries in my language banks, and in those on Deluros VIII. Bukoba is a traditional Maasai name. Mandaka is a traditional East African name, and has been used by the Maasai, the Kikuyu, the Luo, the Wakamba, and the Samburu. Neither name has any analog meaning."

"Well, it was a thought," I said with a sigh.

"Have you any further instructions?"

"Yes," I said. "Let's see how well organized he is. I want you to take out a classified advertisement to the effect that the advertiser has inherited a trophy collection that he doesn't want, and is dispersing it to the highest bidder. I want it stated that the collection includes a Bafflediver, a Demoncat, a number of small mounted carnivores, and a pair of elephant tusks."

"Where would you like the advertisement placed?"

"At least thirty thousand light-years from here."

A cross section of the galaxy appeared above the crystal. Seven of the planets were blinking a bright blue.

"Those planets that are blinking are all members of the Oligarchy, at a distance of from 30,346 to 31,112 light-years."

"Which is the closest?"

"Nelson Twenty-Three."

"People live on the twenty-third planet out from the sun?" I asked, surprised.

"No. This planet is the only one in the system."

"Then how did it get such a name?"

"It was the twenty-third planet to be terraformed by a member of the Pioneer Corps named Nelson, who lived and died in the second century G.E. Its inhabitants call it Meadowgreen."

"Population?"

"72,349."

"All right," I said. "Place the ad in any media that accepts it. Route all replies to our office on Genovaith II, and then back to me."

"Working . . ."

I began getting dressed. I had briefly considered going home for a fresh outfit, but I didn't want to take the time, so I ordered my garment to display a different orange-and-brown pattern, each color snaking around my limbs until it gently flowed into the other.

"Give me a 360-degree viewpoint of myself," I ordered.

Suddenly, standing almost within arm's reach, was a holographic replica of myself, which spun very slowly in a circle. I examined it carefully and decided that there was every chance that Hilda wouldn't recognize it as the same outfit I had worn the day before. Besides, she had so many other things on her mind that there was an excellent possibility that I wouldn't receive her standard lecture on the importance of personal appearance and hygiene for department heads, even if she saw through my little ruse.

"Thank you," I said, and the image vanished.

"Will there be anything else?" asked the computer.

"Yes," I said. "There is one last thing."

"Waiting . . ."

"I want you to access the police computer and see if anyone answering to Mandaka's description has been arrested for any offense within the past twenty years."

"The result will be negative," responded the computer. "If he had been arrested, the Commonwealth would possess a record of his voiceprint and retinagram."

"All right," I said with a sigh. "No further orders."

"Working . . ."

I returned to my chair and ordered it to adjust its contours to conform to my position. I found myself vaguely uncomfortable, finally remembered that I had ordered the chair to apply heat to the small of my back, and instructed it to bring its temperature back to normal.

I considered ordering breakfast, but decided instead to get another hour's sleep before the workday commenced. It seemed that I had just closed my eyes when the computer summoned me back to consciousness.

"Duncan Rojas?"

"Yes?" I said, instantly alert.

"I have ascertained what happened to the tusks after they fell into Mylarrr's possession."

"Excellent!"

The computer made no response.

"Well?" I demanded.

"I must point out that Wilford Braxton's opens for business in two minutes and seven seconds," replied the computer, "and I cannot relate the next phase of their history to you in such a brief period of time."

"Then I'll start work a bit late."

"I am programmed to help you search for the ivory only during that time when you are not actively employed by Wilford Braxton's."

"I always take a break halfway through the morning," I said. "Today I will take it the moment the office opens. Will that satisfy you?"

"I must make a value judgement," announced the computer. It glowed an eerie red for a moment, then returned to normal. "Yes, that will satisfy me."

I leaned forward intently as the computer revealed yet another step of the ivory's remarkable odyssey.

4

The Thief
(5730 G.E.)

It was early morning as I descended the escarpment into the Rift Valley, and Lake Bogoria was hidden beneath layers of steam and fog. I drank deep, paying no attention to a pair of bull buffalo who stood staring sullenly at me.

From time to time I wished that I might obtain some askaris—young bulls who had recently been cast out from their herds—that I might teach them what I knew, for this is the way we pass on a lifetime's accumulation of wisdom from one generation to the next, but though many saw me, none dared to approach, so huge and awesome was I.

Though my belly was full and the lake was at hand, still I felt compelled to move on, to follow the circuit I had established so many decades ago. As I flapped my ears to help cool my blood, a thousand birds burst shrieking from the nearby bushes. I watched them for a moment, and then turned my gaze once more to the south.

Tahiti Benoit poured herself an Alphard brandy, then sat back in her chair and examined the hologram of the two enormous tusks that hung, suspended in space and time, above her computer.

"Three hundred and sixty degrees, please," she ordered, and the image slowly rotated.

"Give me the weight again," she said.

"237 and 225 pounds when first auctioned in 1898 A.D., 226 and 214 pounds when officially weighed in 1932 A.D., 487.22 and 459.48 Galactic Standard Kilos when weighed just prior to molecular stabilization in 3218 G.E."

She stared at the tusks, then took another sip of her brandy. "Show me their owner."

The tusks vanished, to be replaced by the image of a thin, wiry Fly-by-Night.

"This is Meglannn," announced the computer. "He claims to be the duly-elected Prime Minister of Winox IV, but in fact he was a minor military officer who usurped power eleven Standard years ago."

"Eleven years," she mused. "Have there been any attempts to overthrow him?"

"Three. All were unsuccessful."

"What happened to the perpetrators?"

"They were all executed."

"How well-guarded is he?"

"He possesses a personal bodyguard of fifty-seven Fly-by-Nights, who work in round-the-clock shifts. He is never in the company of less than nine bodyguards, even when he is within his own dwelling."

"Where does he keep the tusks?"

"They are on display in the Governmental Resource Building."

"What is that—some kind of museum?"

"It is the center of the Winox IV bureaucracy."

"I assume they're also under constant guard?"

"The building is under constant guard. I have no information about the tusks."

"Does the Governmental Resource Building ever hire human help?"

"Checking . . . never."

"Do they have any exchange program with the Oligarchy?"

"No."

She paused for a moment. "All right. Now show me the restoration team they've called in to repair the crack in the larger tusk."

A group of aliens, all very tall, very blue, and very bald, appeared above the computer.

"They never use Men on the team?" she asked.

"Never," replied the computer.

"Who's in charge of it?"

The team vanished, to be replaced by a hologram of a tall, attenuated blue female.

"This is Tsavos Tvisir, age one hundred and six Galactic Standard years. She possesses degrees in Artifact Restoration from Lodin XI and Canphor VI, and has been an independent businesswoman for more than sixty years."

"She owns her own ship?"

"Yes," answered the computer.

"All right," said Tahiti. "No soft spots so far. Let's keep going. Who is the Oligarchy's Ambassador to Winox IV?"

The alien disappeared, to be replaced by a middle-aged, somewhat overweight human male.

"This is Ambrose Seaton, age forty-seven, former Ambassador to Golden, former aide-de-camp to Admiral Isaac Kindlemeier."

"Golden?" she repeated. "Isn't that a major trading world on the Inner Frontier?"

"That is correct."

"And the Winox system isn't even a member of the Oligarchy," she mused. "This posting hardly constitutes a promotion." She stared at the image thoughtfully. "Why did he leave Kindlemeier's service?"

"That information is classified. I am unable to access it."

"Would moving here be considered a demotion?"

"In terms of pay, no."

"But in terms of power and authority?"

"Yes."

She allowed herself the luxury of a small smile. "I think we've found our weak link. Computer, go to subjective mode."

"Done."

"Give me a subjective analysis of Ambrose Seaton's character."

"He is a well-educated but unimaginative public servant, totally loyal to the Oligarchy. From his constant messages asking Deluros VIII for instructions on protocol, I must conclude that he is very insecure, and probably lacks those human character traits of self-reliance, intuition and imagination that are so vital to an ambassador this far out on the Galactic Rim, where decisions must frequently be made without Oligarchic approval."

"What exactly did he do that cost him his last two postings?"

"That information is classified."

"Is he happy in his current position?"

"He has twice applied for transfers to Oligarchic worlds, so I must conclude that he is not happy in his current position."

"Better and better," said Tahiti. "Cancel subjective mode."

"Cancelled."

"You know, of course, why I am asking these questions?"

"You have been hired by a collector named Leeyo Nelion to steal the tusks from the Fly-by-Nights of Winox IV."

"I have been offered the job," she corrected it. "I haven't accepted it yet." She paused. "Let me see the tusks again."

The ivory instantly appeared.

"How much are they worth on the open market?"

"Ivory is no longer used in any commercial or artistic process," replied the computer. "Thus, it is of value only to collectors and museums, and that value depends entirely upon how much a given collector or museum is willing to pay for it. The last commercial transaction was for four hundred and twenty-five credits per Standard kilo, in 5409 G.E.; since then, two sets of tusks have been donated, without compensation, to museums."

"All right," she said. "Let's go over the details once more."

"Waiting . . ."

"Nelion had been hunting for the ivory for years, without success. Then he managed to learn, through private sources, that the Fly-by-Nights have called in a restoration team to fix a tusk that has a new crack in it. He performed whatever research was necessary and determined that the tusk was one of the pair he'd been searching for." She paused. "It sounds reasonable enough."

"Have you some reason to doubt his account?" asked the computer.

"The best reason: self-preservation. Before I commit to the operation, I want to be sure that his proposition is exactly what it seems to be. After all, he's not the one who stands to go to jail if things go wrong." She paused again. "If he's lying, I can't see what purpose it would serve; he won't be able to take possession of the ivory until I'm safely off the planet." She stared long and hard at the ivory. "He must want it pretty badly; he's offering an enormous amount of money for it."

She sipped her brandy again, creating and discarding various scenarios until she finally came to one she liked. She analyzed it, decided that it would work, and went to work on the details. Finally, an hour later, she re-activated the computer.

"Send a message to Mr. Nelion," she commanded. "Tell him that I've agreed to his terms. As soon as my bank on Binder X confirms that the first half of the money has been deposited in my numbered account, I'll carry out my end of the contract."

Tahiti, dressed in a severely-cut gray business garment, entered Ambassador Seaton's small, rather spare office and immediately took a seat opposite the ambassador's desk. The wood-panelled walls were covered with holograms of Seaton in the company of important Men and aliens, all smiling at the camera.

Seaton, dressed in full military regalia, complete with an impressive display of shining medals, rose to greet her. He seemed taller than the computer's description of him, and she concluded that he was wearing some kind of lift in his highly-polished shoes. His hair glowed an attractive but unnatural silver, and his thick moustache had been waxed to within an inch of its life.

"I trust you will forgive the surroundings, my dear," he said, waving a hand at his office.

"They seem quite elegant," she replied.

"They are," he answered. "But what one really wants in an embassy is not elegance, but ostentation." He wrinkled his nose in a show of distaste. "One *must* impress the natives, or one simply cannot function—yet the government simply will not spend what is needed on Winox IV until it joins the Oligarchy, thereby almost certainly assuring that it will never join."

"We've brought recalcitrant worlds into the fold before," said Tahiti. "I'm sure we will again."

"True," he agreed, interlacing his pink, pudgy fingers on the desktop, "but those were worlds that had something the Oligarchy wanted—minerals, farmland, fissionable materials, whatever. Winox IV is too poor and too far out on the Rim for anyone in authority on Deluros VIII to pay attention to it."

"They've sent *you* here, haven't they?" she said admiringly.

"I'm a career diplomat," he replied with false humility. "I go where I'm posted."

"You're being much too modest," she protested. "One of your aides told me that you've served with Admiral Kindlemeier."

"That's true," he admitted. "An excellent commander. I truly miss our afternoons together, sipping port and playing chess." He smiled. "He used to get so annoyed when he lost . . ."

"You've also been our Ambassador to Golden," continued Tahiti. "Surely the Oligarchy wouldn't send a man with your credentials out here if they weren't interested in Winox IV."

"You're a very perceptive woman," he said in self-satisfied tones. "And of course they *are* interested in Winox. Sometimes I simply get annoyed—not without justification—at the bureaucracy's sluggishness."

"Well, I, for one, am impressed that a man of your stature still remains accessible. I can't tell you how much I appreciate this audience, Ambassador Seaton."

"Part of my job is to help human visitors in any way that

I can, my dear," he replied smoothly. "And just how may I help you, Miss Benoit?"

"Please call me Tahiti."

"All right—Tahiti," he amended. "How long do you plan to be on Winox?"

"I'm not sure. Possibly a week, possibly two."

"According to my assistant, you're here to build a jail?"

She smiled. "If that were the case, I'd be here for a year. No, my job is merely to produce a feasability study for a detainment center."

"I'm at a loss to understand whom we would be detaining," said Seaton, puzzled, "since we have no real authority here beyond the embassy grounds."

"We've launched an interesting experiment out here on the Rim," said Tahiti. "We have found that we can achieve maximum security by building chlorine jails on oxygen worlds, and vice versa. It virtually eliminates the possibility of a detainee escaping, since he or she would be unable to breathe the atmosphere beyond the prison walls." She paused. "It also tends to dispel any fears the local populace might have that they have been placed in any danger by the erection of a nearby penal structure."

"I hadn't heard of this before!" exclaimed Seaton. "It's an excellent idea!"

"Thank you," she said modestly. "I was partially responsible for it."

"You are a very interesting young woman."

"And you," she replied with a smile, "are a professional diplomat."

He chuckled. "True. But even diplomats don't lie all the time, my dear."

"Then, since you've convinced me that you're being sincere, I wonder if I might ask one more favor of you?"

"Certainly."

"I'd like to take a tour of the city. Can you possibly arrange for a member of your staff to escort me?"

"I'll be happy to escort you myself."

"Oh, that's really not necessary," she protested. "I'm sure you're much too busy."

"I can always make time for a fellow human," he assured her. "Especially one as lovely and charming as yourself."

"Then, thank you."

He paused. "You must understand, however, that there's really not much to see. This is not the Fly-by-Nights' home planet. It's primarily a mining world, which supplies their empire with certain metals and fissionable materials that have been exhausted on their other worlds. There's just the one city, and it's hardly as grand as the cities of the Oligarchy."

"Nevertheless, I'm always interested in seeing new worlds."

"Then you shall be my guest this afternoon," he insisted.

"Thank you, Ambassador. I truly appreciate it."

"If so, you can do me a favor in return."

"Certainly. What is it?"

"Please call me Ambrose."

"I'd be delighted to, Ambrose."

"What truly good fortune it is that you came here!" said Seaton. "You have no idea how boring it is to speak only to other diplomats and military officials."

"To tell the truth, I was a little hesitant about forcing myself upon you during my very first day on the planet."

"Nonsense!" scoffed Seaton. "You had letters of introduction from Admiral Nakashima and Ambassador Craig. What better credentials could one need?"

Suddenly she frowned.

"What is it, my dear?" asked Seaton.

"My letter from Ambassador Craig," she replied. "I wonder if I might have it back? I wanted to send him a little personalized note of thanks, and I'll need the address of his embassy."

"Certainly," said Seaton, getting to his feet. "It's doubtless with your dossier in the outer office. I'll get it for you right now."

"You needn't bother," she said, half-rising. "I can get it myself."

"It's no trouble," he replied. "Besides, you wouldn't know which staff member to ask."

"Thank you very much," she said, watching him strut out of the office.

The moment the door slid shut behind him, Tahiti arose and walked quickly to his computer. She studied it briefly but expertly, made a minute, almost indetectable adjustment, and was back in her chair a good twenty seconds before Seaton returned and handed the letter to her.

"Now," he said, "I insist that you join me for lunch, and then we'll take that tour."

"I don't want to impose further on your time," she said hestitantly. "I can eat at my hotel and then come back."

"Nonsense," he replied with mock sternness. "Consider it an official order."

She smiled at him. "In that case . . ."

Ninety minutes later, locked away from the planet's thin, dry air inside the embassy's chauffeur-driven landcar, they carefully traversed the crazily-twisting streets of the city, avoiding the perching posts to which the Fly-by-Nights clung by the thousands while driving past the needle-like domiciles that seemed to house more residents on the exteriors than the interiors.

"Fascinating!" exclaimed Tahiti. "Are all the buildings set into the ground at such odd angles?"

"Most of them," replied Seaton. "The Fly-by-Nights

seem positively uncomfortable standing erect. They love to hang or swing from things—the more precarious the perch, the better."

"And I notice they don't have any street lights. Are they nocturnal?"

"I have no idea. To the best of my knowledge, no one has ever seen them sleeping. We had an exobiologist out here to study the Fly-by-Nights a few months ago; he decided that they recharge their energies when they hang upside down, that their muscular reactions are such that they're at total rest then." He paused. "I tend to doubt it."

"Oh? Why?"

"Because I was present at the signing of a trade agreement between Winox IV and Roosevelt III, and Meglannn—he's their Prime Minister—hung upside down during the entire ceremony, and still managed to demand five or six changes in the wording."

"I've heard of Meglannn," said Tahiti. "What's he like?"

"Cold and ruthless as only an alien can be," said Seaton. "I feel uncomfortable when I'm in the same room with him—though of course I never give any indication of it. It would never do to let one of *them* think he's got the upper hand." He paused. "I have no idea why he has chosen to live on Winox instead of one of the Fly-by-Nights' more populated worlds."

"Perhaps he fears assassination," suggested Tahiti.

"Perhaps," said Seaton. "More likely, he simply prefers the climate, or the amenities—such as they are. You must remember that aliens are not the most logical of creatures —and occasionally they can be quite warlike. I would guess that Meglannn killed off a tenth of the Fly-by-Nights' population in his rise to power—and since he's taken possession of the tusks, he's even more willing to risk confrontations."

"Tusks?" she asked innocently. "What tusks?"

"The tusks of an elephant."

"From Earth?"

"It's ridiculous, I know, but the Fly-by-Nights have owned them for centuries, and tradition has it that the possessor is immortal and unconquerable."

"Wouldn't the fact that Meglannn took them from a previous owner tend to disprove that?"

He smiled. "It would to *me*. I refuse to speculate on the vagaries of the alien mind."

"Isn't that your job?"

"The job of any planetary ambassador out here on the Rim is to hold the fort until the Oligarchy finally moves in."

They continued driving through the city, passing an occasional alien walking among the Fly-by-Nights, taking a brief detour to see the newly-erected Canphor and Lodin embassies, and finally stopping before a structure which was much larger than the others.

"Where are we now?" asked Tahiti as the doors slid open and the strange, almost-stale alien odors of the city once again assailed her nostrils.

"The Governmental Resource Building," replied Seaton, getting out of the landcar and then helping her descend to the pavement. "Smells awful, doesn't it? This is where the Fly-by-Nights do the little work that gets done around here." He ordered his chauffeur to remain with the car, then took her arm and led her through the front door.

She found herself in a seven-sided entry foyer, the height varying from one end to the other by as much as six feet. There were numerous plaques on the walls, each written in an alien script, and a few non-representational pieces of art, mostly in blues and violets, which made her wonder if the Fly-by-Nights could see as far into the infrared as humans could. Dominating the room was a gold statue of a female Fly-by-Night.

"Myvesss," explained Seaton. "She was one of their greatest warlords, or so I'm told."

"Is that solid gold, or merely gold-plated?" asked Tahiti with professional curiosity.

"I have no idea," replied Seaton. "I can find out for you, if you wish."

She shook her head. "No. I was just wondering."

He led her through a maze of irregularly-shaped rooms, each with Fly-by-Nights perched all over the walls and ceilings, and finally they came to a large, well-lighted chamber.

"Ah, here we are!" said Seaton, turning immediately to his left. "On this wall here we have what passes for the crown jewels, though as you can see, they're all quartz. Some of them are quite unique, though."

"Unique is the word, all right," said Tahiti, studying the display. "I see a couple of things that might pass for necklaces, and maybe a crown over there on the right, but I can't begin to guess what functions the rest serve."

"I'm afraid I can't help you."

"How does Meglannn dress for ceremonial occasions?"

"He's just as likely to show up naked as clothed," said Seaton distastefully. "The only time I've seen him in full regalia, he spent the better part of ten minutes juggling five or six of these stones"—he indicated a number of rounded pieces of quartz—"and then gave them to an underling as if they were so much rubbish."

"Did the juggling have some special racial or religious significance?" she asked.

"I really have no idea," said Seaton in bored tones. "I suppose it's possible." He led her to another display case.

"Now, these are considered to be the culmination of the Fly-by-Nights' religious art."

There were some forty wood and stone carvings, each resembling a spikey undersea creature, though she could find no detailing on them except for the protrusions.

"Is this supposed to represent some kind of life form?" she asked at last.

"In a manner of speaking," he answered. "It's their deity."

"Their god looks like a sphere with spikes?"

"*They* think so," he replied in condescending tones.

"The carvings seem quite primitive," she noted.

He shrugged. "These are considered to be the best that the race has produced over the millennia—which is not saying all that much for the Fly-by-Nights' taste in art."

"And *these*," she said, turning and indicating two enormous pillars of ivory, "must be the tusks." She studied them for a moment. "I wonder how the Fly-by-Nights ever came into possession of an elephant's tusks?"

"I really don't know their history," responded Seaton. "I gather they've been here for some two hundred years."

She examined the smaller tusk closely, then moved on to the larger one.

"What are you looking for?" he asked.

"I've never seen an elephant's tusks before," she replied. "I'm curious." Suddenly she pointed to the base of the tusks. "There's a crack starting here."

"Yes, there is," he replied. "It's so small that I'm surprised you spotted it."

"How soon is the restoration team due?"

"What restoration team?" he asked sharply.

"I assume that if the tusks have such significance to the Fly-by-Nights, they'll want the crack repaired—and if it hasn't been repaired yet, then obviously there are no Fly-by-Nights qualified to repair it, so they've probably sent for a restoration team."

"Why a team?" he persisted. "Why not just one being?"

"No reason," she replied with a shrug. "I suppose it could be one man or alien."

He bent over and stared at the larger tusk, still unable to see the minute crack, then straightened up. He stared at her for a long moment, then quickly led her through the remainder of the building and drove her back to her hotel.

"Dinner tonight?" he asked.

"I'd be delighted," she replied.

Tahiti sighed as yet another coded message from Seaton's office was unknowingly routed through her computer; this one dealt with staple foods for the human contingent of Winox IV.

"Forward it to its destination," she instructed the computer through her miniaturized communicator.

"Done."

"What's the matter with him?" she muttered as she leaned back on the oversized chair which the hotel had supplied for humanoid (but not necessarily human) guests and stared at the none-too-clean wall of her small room. "How big a hint does he need?"

"Another message coming through," announced her computer.

This one concerned two malfunctioning hand weapons.

"Damn! If he isn't even suspicious, he might be *too* stupid to deal with."

"What shall I do with the message?" asked the computer.

"Forward it to its destination."

She sat silently in her room, glaring at her communicator, for another ten minutes, and began mentally running through a number of alternate plans, none of which she especially liked.

"There another message coming through," announced the computer. "This one bears Ambassador Seaton's personal code."

"That's the one we're waiting for!" she said. "Intercept!"

"Done."

"What does it say?"

"It is a personal request from Ambassador Seaton to Pietre Kobernykov, the Oligarchy's Chief of Intelligence for this sector."

"Ambrose, I could kiss you!" she said happily. "I *knew* you couldn't be that stupid!" She paused. "What does he want to know?"

"He requests your dossier, and also wants Pietre Kobernykov to run a standard security check on you. He further requests that he be given the information within the next three hours, if possible."

"So he can arrest me at dinner," she said, nodding her head. "I want you to reply, in standard military code, that I am working directly for Kobernykov, that my mission and dossier are classified, but that Ambassador Seaton is to render me any assistance I might request."

"How shall I sign it?" asked the computer.

She paused thoughtfully for a moment. "Don't use any name at all; just use Kobernykov's service number."

"I must point out that it is highly irregular not to sign a coded message," noted the computer.

"I know, but until I know if they're friends, I don't know whether Kobernykov would sign it formally or informally. Send it under a For Your Eyes Only imprimatur, and label it Top Secret. At least this way it will smack of intrigue, and a bored little bureaucrat on a dull little planet might just feel like he's part of the game for the first time."

"What shall I do with the Ambassador's message?"

"Destroy it."

"This is an excellent wine," commented Tahiti. She took another sip, then placed her glass down on the table and smiled at Seaton, who was seated across from her in the embassy's private dining room.

"It was imported from Kalimar II."

"Kalimar II?" she repeated. "I've never heard of it."

"It's an agricultural world on the Outer Frontier."

"I must go there sometime," said Tahiti. "Imagine the fun I could have," she added with a smile, "visiting their vineyards while evaluating locations for chlorine detention units."

"You've never seen one in your life," said Seaton with a smug smile.

"A vineyard?"

"A chlorine jail," he replied. "Oh, they're an excellent idea, and for all I know the Oligarchy is starting to build them—but you don't have anything to do with them, do you, my dear?"

"I've already told you: that's the reason I'm on Winox IV."

"I know what you've told me."

"What seems to be the problem, Ambrose?" she asked.

"You're not at all what you pretend to be, are you?" said Seaton.

"You've seen my credentials and my letters of introduction."

"I know—but I've also had a communiqué from Pietre Kobernykov this afternoon."

"Damn him!" she snapped furiously. "I told him I could handle this job alone!"

"Then you *are* working for Intelligence," he said triumphantly.

"I haven't said that."

"You don't have to."

She studied his face carefully for a long moment. "All right," she said at last. "I'm on a very sensitive and potentially dangerous assignment here. Now that you know, you *must* help me maintain my cover. My life may depend on it."

"Your life?" he repeated, surprised.

"It's possible," she said grimly. "Now, do I have your promise?"

"Of course," he replied. "But I do have a question: if there is a dangerous situation developing here, why wasn't I informed of it? After all, I *am* the ambassador."

"Because I'm on a mission that is not directly concerned with either the human or Fly-by-Night populations of Winox IV."

"Then what are you here for?"

"I'll tell you if and when I think it's necessary," she replied, gesturing to a robot waiter to refill her wine glass.

"I think I know already."

"I very much doubt that," replied Tahiti.

"It has something to do with the tusks, doesn't it?"

"What makes you think so?"

"You have *your* secrets," he replied smugly. "I have *mine*."

"You're mistaken," she said uneasily.

"No, I'm not," he replied with growing confidence. "But you may rest assured that my lips are sealed. All I want is to help you." He paused. "You mission *does* concern the tusks, doesn't it?"

She stared at him but made no reply.

"Come, come, my dear. If you can't trust your own ambassador, who *can* you trust?"

Finally she sighed and nodded. "You were right."

"I thought so."

There was a long silence.

"Have you nothing further to say to me?" asked Seaton.

"I'm trying to decide if I can trust you," replied Tahiti.

"We're both on the same side," he said. "I'll help you in any way I can."

"That's what bothers me," she said. "You already know that my mission may be dangerous, and that it doesn't deal directly with the human contingent on Winox IV. Why are you so anxious for me to accept your help?"

He smiled wryly. "If we succeed, maybe I can finally get off this boring little world." He paused. "I've had some bad luck in my career," he continued, "but I deserve better than Winox IV. I'm capable of far better things. I need a posting commensurate with my abilities." He suddenly looked uncomfortable. "I realize how I must sound to you, but I am meant for something better than this! You can help me, simply by letting me help you."

She studied him for another moment.

"All right," she said at last.

"Good!"

The robot waiter brought her a new glass of wine, setting it down carefully upon the table. It wobbled slightly, and the robot steadied it before Tahiti could reach for it.

"Intelligence received word last week that there is going to be an attempt made to steal the tusks by members of an alien race representing themselves as an artifact restoration team."

"Why bother?" asked Seaton. "It's not as if they're worth anything. They're just an old hunting trophy from Earth."

"Perhaps, but Meglannn believes in them, and so do his followers. If the aliens steal them, they'll be able to demand an enormous ransom."

"Meglannn's a barbarian," said Seaton. "Why should the Oligarchy care what happens to the tusks?"

"Barbarian or not, he's the leader of the Fly-by-Nights,

and we've been trying, without success, to get them to join the Oligarchy for more than five centuries. If we can use our good offices to prevent the theft, it might provide us with just the leverage we need."

"Then I'll arrange for an audience with him tomorrow," said Seaton. "The restoration team isn't due to land for another week. We can warn him in plenty of time."

"No," said Tahiti firmly.

"Why not?"

"We want to set this up so that *we* can catch them in the act. If Meglannn's troops save the tusks, he might be less willing to respond to the Oligarchy's overtures— and besides, if we simply scare them off, they'll strike elsewhere and all our planning will have been for nothing."

"But how do you propose to stop them?" asked Seaton. "I have a grand total of thirty-six military and fifty-three civilian personnel working for me. We're hardly geared for a pitched battle."

"We have Winox IV under surveillance. As soon as I inform our people that the tusks have been stolen, we'll move against the thieves."

"What if the aliens manage to escape anyway? If they reach light speed before you stop them, they're gone. Or what if their ship is destroyed with the tusks in it?"

Tahiti smiled. "In my ship is a duplicate pair of tusks, identical in almost every respect, right down to the tiny crack in the base. My job is to replace the real tusks with the fakes, and then alert our ships the moment the duplicates are stolen."

"I see," said Seaton thoughtfully. "What will you do with the real tusks in the meantime?"

"I'll have to find a secure place to keep them," she responded. "That's where I might be able to use your help."

"I have no place to hide them," said Seaton. "The Fly-by-Nights have always been allowed full access to the embassy. They would get suspicious if we were suddenly to deny it to them." He paused. "Can't one of our ships take them for a week?"

"No," she said, shaking her head.

"But why not?"

"First, because we don't want anyone to know that our ships are in the vicinity. And, more importantly, because the Fly-by-Nights would never allow it. They think *we're* the enemy."

"Then what do you propose to do?" he asked.

She shrugged. "I'm not sure—but I've got five days to figure something out." She paused, then added wryly: "It may very well be that I'll have to steal the real tusks in order to let the aliens steal the fake ones."

"An intriguing concept," he said.

"A dangerous one," she replied grimly. "If I'm caught, I'll be summarily executed by the Fly-by-Nights, and you'll be absolutely powerless to help me."

"Yes, I see," he said, frowning. "What would you do with them if you managed to steal them?"

"I had planned on keeping them in the embassy for that week."

"I already told you—the embassy isn't secure."

"Then I'll have to think of something else."

"What about your ship?"

"I haven't got the authority to take them off the planet."

"That shouldn't be a problem," said Seaton. "Just get Kobernykov's permission."

She shook her head. "I'm not allowed to make tightbeam contact with him until the mission is completed. We don't know how sophisticated the aliens' decoding devices are." She sighed. "It's a shame. I feel certain he'd give me the authorization if I could just contact him."

"Possibly the embassy's computer . . ." suggested Seaton.

She shook her head. "We can't take the chance."

Seaton lowered his head in thought for a moment, then looked across the table at her. "That still won't be a problem. *You* may not have the authority to remove them, but *I* do."

"Are you quite sure?" she asked dubiously.

"In my capacity as governor, I have the authority to act autonomously in the best interest of the planetary population—and in my opinion, protecting the tusks is in the best interest of both the humans and the Fly-by-Nights. I can give you written authority to remove them."

"Then that's what we'll do!" she said decisively. "I'm so glad that I took you into my confidence! Now it's just a matter of figuring out how to get the tusks from the Government Resource Building to my ship."

"And to replace them with the fake set," added Seaton.

"Have you any suggestions?" she asked.

"Give me tonight to think about it and let me see what I can come up with."

"All right," said Seaton, instructing his computer to cast an image above his desk. "This is a blueprint of the main floor of the Government Resource Building."

"However did you manage to obtain it?" asked Tahiti, who had an identical floorplan in her ship's computer.

"I am not without my resources, my dear," he replied smugly. "Now, *here* is where they keep the tusks"—he pointed to one of the chambers—"and *here* is the nearest exit."

"How many guards?"

"At the exit, two. In the room itself, none—at least, not

on a regular basis. In and around the corridors, anywhere from fifteen to thirty-five."

"And no humans work in the building?"

"That's correct."

She studied the plans, as if for the first time. "It's going to be difficult," she said at last. "I'm certain that I can't lift them, and even if I use an aircraft to take them to the nearest door, I'm certain to be heard or seen."

"The trick, I suppose, is to get the guards out of the building," suggested Seaton.

Tahiti breathed a sigh of relief, grateful that she wouldn't have to hand-feed him *every* detail. The more it seemed like his own plan, the more willing he'd be to carry it through to completion.

"That would certainly make it easier," she agreed. "But how can we get them to desert their posts?"

"An air raid?" mused Seaton. "No, that's no good. They're not at war with anyone." He paused for a moment. "I wonder if there's some way to convince them that the building is structurally unsound?"

She shook her head. "It hasn't collapsed yet, so they'd probably remove its contents before leaving, even if they believed you."

"True," he agreed.

"Besides," she added, "we not only have to convince them to leave, but we also have to make them understand that *I* have a right to be there."

"You'll need help."

"Not for this part of the job. I just need your permission to take the real tusks off the planet."

"My dear, you've already admitted that you can't lift the tusks," said Seaton patiently. "I think I'll have to send some of my men along, just to make sure everything goes smoothly."

"How can we possibly justify bringing along human soldiers?" she asked, hoping that he could come up with the answer before she had to provide him with it.

Suddenly Seaton smiled triumphantly. "I've got it!"

"What is it?" she asked excitedly.

"As far as the Fly-by-Nights are concerned, your specialty is chlorine environments, right?"

"That's the way I registered when I passed through customs," she confirmed.

"Then that's the answer!" he continued enthusiastically. "We'll explain to them that there's a chlorine leak, and that they'll have to leave the building while we find the source of it and fix it."

"That's very good, Ambrose!" she said, and he practically glowed with satisfaction. "Very good indeed. I *like* the idea of getting them to abandon the building!"

"It *is* a good plan, isn't it?" he said proudly.

"It's excellent," she replied. "If you ever decide to give up diplomacy, you've got a career waiting for you in Intelligence. Now we just have to sort out the details." She paused. "I'm not here to work on the Government Resource Building itself, so we can't claim that there's a chlorine leak there and nowhere else." She paused as if in thought. "Probably the best thing to do is release some chlorine into the sewer system; that way it will seep into all the buildings in the area. We can show up in multi-environmental outfits and explain that it was a test that got out of control. That way they won't be concentrating on any particular building. We can tell them that it is potentially dangerous, but that we've pretty much got it under control and are just checking for any major sewer leaks."

"I like it!" exclaimed Seaton. "We can even justify our presence at the Governmental Resource Building by saying that we want to secure the most important building first, and then go on to the smaller ones. We can cordon it off, substitute the tusks, and be out of there within five minutes!"

"Do you have access to any chlorine?" she asked.

"More than enough for our purposes," he replied. "The embassy has two multi-environmental meeting rooms. I can appropriate the chlorine we need from the system and replace it after the crisis is over."

"You're *sure* I'm not putting you in an awkward position?" she asked solicitously. "I mean, the men who steal the tusks will be under your direct orders, not mine."

"Not at all," he answered happily. "In fact, you're doing me a favor. Once the Oligarchy finds out that I've helped you, I have every expectation of being transferred to another planet."

"I can almost guarantee it," said Tahiti sweetly.

Fourth Interlude (6303 G.E.)

"So she actually got the Ambassador to steal the tusks for her!" murmured Hilda, and I was suddenly aware of her hologram hovering just above the glowing crystal. She was sitting at her desk, sipping from a cup of tea and nibbling on a biscuit.

"That is correct," replied the computer.

"Computer," I said, "freshen the air and let the sunlight in."

"Working . . . done." The east wall of my office became translucent, letting in the morning sun, and the stale odors vanished from the room.

"All right," I said. "At least we know that the tusks

belonged to Leeyo Nelion five hundred and seventy-three years ago."

"Incorrect."

"I don't understand," I said.

"Nelion died of *eplasia*, a rare disease caused by a mutated virus, while Tahiti Benoit was on Winox IV."

"Then what happened to the ivory?"

"I possess insufficient data to answer that question at this time," responded the computer.

"Then we'll use another approach," I said calmly. "What happened to Tahiti Benoit once she left the Winox system with the tusks?"

"She committed three major robberies in the next two years, after which I can find no record of her actions or whereabouts."

"The tusks were worth nothing to her," I continued. "She must have tried to sell them at one time or another."

"It seems likely, but I am unable to ascertain that at this time."

"Well, at least we're back to tracking them down through human records," I said. "It has to be easier than trying to trace them through the Fly-by-Nights' archives."

"Do you mind if *I* ask a question?" interjected Hilda.

"Not at all," I replied.

"Computer, why did Leeyo Nelion want the tusks?"

"I possess insufficient data to answer that question at this time," replied the computer.

"Has Leeyo Nelion anything in common with any of the other humans who either owned or sought possession of the tusks?" she continued.

"Working . . . done. Leeyo and Nelion are both Maasai names."

Hilda looked inordinately pleased with herself.

"So Nelion was a Maasai?" I said, curiously unsurprised by the revelation.

"I am unable to confirm that at this time," said the computer. "I can only confirm that his given name and his surname are both common Maasai names."

"Check the census databank of five hundred and fifty years ago and see if you can confirm it," I ordered.

"Working . . . done. I can now confirm that Leeyo Nelion was a Maasai."

"Why do we keep running across the Maasai whenever we find the ivory?" I wondered aloud.

The sun rose above a nearby building, and I directed the computer to make the wall opaque again.

"I have another question," said Hilda. "Just to satisfy my own curiosity, what became of Ambrose Seaton?"

"He was relieved of all responsibilities, tried for theft and espionage, found guilty, given a suspended sentence, and spent the remainder of his life in obscurity."

"Poor man," muttered Hilda.

"He was a fool," I said.

"What difference does *that* make?" she retorted. "Do you reserve your sympathy only for geniuses?"

"He let a total stranger talk him into committing a criminal act," I said.

"Well, *I* know a man who has let a total stranger talk him into lying to his company and asking his Security Chief to act in collusion with him. Is *he* a fool, too?"

"Mandaka didn't talk me into anything," I explained patiently. "He hired me to do a job. How I do it is *my* business."

"How you do it is *our* business," she corrected me. "Or have you forgotten our little agreement?"

Suddenly I remembered that we weren't alone.

"Why are you saying this in front of the computer?" I demanded. "It's making a record of it!"

"It won't draw any value judgments unless we order it to go to subjective mode," she replied calmly. "And only the Chief of Security knows where that record will reside. I can delete it if I choose."

"Good," I said. "When do you plan to delete it?"

"Oh, I think I'll leave it alone for a few days, until I'm sure I don't need it to bring you to your senses."

"I haven't done anything wrong," I said stubbornly. "I'm just doing what I'm being paid to do."

"By a man who doesn't exist."

"His money exists, and the ivory exists," I replied. "That's all that concerns me."

"Well, it's not all that concerns *me*," said Hilda. "You've got three days, less about two hours, to come up with your solution."

"I've got three days, and if I haven't got the tusks by then, you promised to renegotiate," I reminded her.

"I said I would *consider* extending your time," she corrected me. "Don't go putting promises in my mouth, Duncan."

She terminated the connection, and I spent the next hour certifying a Sillyworm from the Inner Frontier. I had my lunch sent up to my office, ate quickly and silently, and then began studying a challenge to one of my rulings by a disgruntled guide whose client's Devilowl had not qualified for a listing.

"Duncan Rojas, you have an incoming call," announced the computer.

"Give it to someone else," I said. "I'm busy."

"I cannot."

"Oh? Why?"

"Because it is from Bukoba Mandaka, whose business is with you, rather than the firm of Wilford Braxton's. My programming compels me to—"

"Never mind!" I said quickly. "Put it through!"

"Verbal or visual?"

"Visual."

An instant later Bukoba Mandaka's face appeared above the glowing crystal.

"Mr. Rojas? I have called to find out what progress you are making."

"I've managed to trace the tusks to within six centuries of the present," I replied. "They have quite an engrossing history."

"When can I expect to know where they are now?" he demanded, displaying no interest in my last remark.

"That's difficult to say," I answered. "Possibly two or three days, certainly no more than a Standard week."

He nodded his approval. "That is satisfactory."

"In the meantime, Mr. Mandaka, I would appreciate it if I could speak with you."

"We are speaking right now," he said.

"But my time is not my own right now," I pointed out. "I wonder if I could meet you somewhere for dinner?"

"Is it necessary?"

"It could prove most helpful to me."

He considered the proposition for a moment, then nodded in agreement.

Hilda's image suddenly appeared directly above Mandaka's, signaling silently that she wanted to accompany me.

"Are you acquainted with Ancient Days?" asked Mandaka.

"I've heard of it," I said as Hilda's gestures became more urgent, "but I've never been there."

"It's in the directory," said Mandaka. "I'll be there at eight o'clock this evening."

"May I bring a friend?"

"I would prefer that you didn't."

"She works for Braxton's and is acquainted with my investigation."

"I am paying only you; I will speak only to you."

"You're quite certain?" I asked.

"Those are my conditions."

"Very well, Mr. Mandaka," I said, shrugging and shoot-ing an almost-apologetic smile in the direction of Hilda's hologram. "I will come alone."

"Eight o'clock, Mr. Rojas," he repeated, and the con-nection was broken.

"Duncan," said Hilda harshly, "I thought we had an understanding!"

"What could I do?" I said. "You heard him."

"You didn't argue very forcefully."

"I was afraid he'd call the whole thing off."

"I'll remember this if you haven't found the tusks in three days," she promised.

"I'm sure you will," I said grimly.

"I'll also expect a full report on what he said when I return from the theater tonight."

"Tonight?" I complained. "How about tomorrow morn-ing?"

"I said *tonight*," she repeated grimly as her image faded from view.

I arrived ten minutes early, fearful that Mandaka might not be there if I were so much as a minute late. The address given in the directory was in a wealthy section of the city, but when the slidewalk finally dropped me off I found nothing but a large office building, its glass walls blindingly reflecting the setting sun.

I walked up to an elegantly-clad doorman and told him that I was looking for Ancient Days. He smiled and ushered me to a small door just to the left of the main entrance, waited until I had tipped him, and then fiddled with a small device on his wrist. The door dilated, I stepped onto an air cushion, and a moment later I had floated gently down some fifty feet, where an impeccably-dressed headwaiter greeted me, took my name, informed me that a table had been reserved for me, and began leading me to it.

I had the distinct impression that I had wandered into a segment of human history, for instead of the the confining walls of a restaurant I saw endless cultivated fields on the banks of a huge river. An enormous stone sphinx towered over me, and in the distance I could see a number of slaves pulling blocks up the slope of a half-completed pyramid.

"Is this your first time here, sir?" asked the headwaiter, waiting politely until I had finished staring at my surroundings and was ready to continue walking to my table.

"Yes."

"This week we are displaying panoramas from the Egyptian dynasties," he explained. "We work in concert with various archaeological and historical societies, and we pride ourselves on the accuracy of our depictions."

"You said *this* week?" I replied.

He nodded. "Our subject matter changes every ten days. In our last exhibit, for example, we displayed the prehistoric life of the Late Cretaceous period, and eight days from now we will be presenting scenes from the opening of the American West."

"Fascinating," I said sincerely, staring at the pageant being played out before me. "How many holographic projectors does it take to create an effect like this?"

"More than three hundred," he replied.

"And how many different eras do you present over the course of a year?"

"We have thirty-seven in our library at present, but the number is growing. We hope to have a presentation covering the entirety of Earth's continental drift ready by the end of the year."

"If the food's half a good as the presentation, I'll be back for it," I promised him.

"We're quite proud of our cuisine, Mr. Rojas," replied the headwaiter. "The finest ambience in the galaxy will not keep a restaurant in business if the food does not measure up. Despite the fact that our reputation extends throughout the entire cluster and brings us many tourists and curiosity-seekers, the bulk of our patrons are repeat customers."

"Is Mr. Mandaka one of them?" I asked.

"Oh, yes. He has a passion for our African panoramas."

We finally reached the table, which boasted not only a leather-bound menu written in glowing blue calligraphy, but also a small booklet explaining the scene that was transpiring all around me. Printed menus were rare and booklets of any type were even rarer, and I opened the menu to find out just how much a patron was expected to pay to finance this combination of visual and gustatory experience. There were no prices listed, which meant that it was *very* expensive.

Now that I was seated, I re-examined my surroundings more thoroughly. The room itself was quite large, easily capable of accomodating three hundred diners, while a polished bar along one wall seated another forty. A gaudier establishment might have costumed their personnel as ancient Egyptians, but the servers of Ancient Days were dressed in immaculate formal attire. It was almost impossible to see where the room actually ended and the holographic images began, for the displays were much more sophisticated than those of my own computer. As I sat there, I could almost feel the harsh Egyptian sun beating down upon my head and catch the scent of the sandlewood and incense that the wooden dhows were bringing up the Nile.

As the scene shifted to the creation of the Temple at

Karnack, a large man, dressed in conservative gray, suddenly sat down opposite me, and I found myself staring at Bukoba Mandaka.

"Good evening, Mr. Rojas."

"Good evening," I responded.

"Have you made any further progress since we last spoke?"

I shook my head. "I can only use the computer after business hours, Mr. Mandaka."

"Well, Mr. Rojas," he said, staring at me, and I realized that he was even larger and more muscular than I had remembered, "what prompted you to request this meeting?"

"I have a number of questions," I replied.

"Then ask them. I *must* have the ivory of the Kilimanjaro Elephant. I will give you any information that will help you with your quest."

"*That* is my first question," I said. "*Why* must you have the ivory? You have mentioned your willingness to pay a price far in excess of its worth."

"It is worth it to me."

"Why?"

He paused for a moment, as if considering his reply, and then said: "I cannot see how answering that question will help you find the ivory."

"You refuse to answer it?"

"For the moment, Mr. Rojas," replied Mandaka.

Just then a waiter stopped by for our drink orders and Mandaka asked for a glass of milk.

"Milk?" I repeated, surprised.

"It is the traditional beverage of my people," he replied. "In the old days we mixed it with the blood of our cattle."

I ordered an Alphard brandy, and the waiter walked off, casting sidelong glances at Mandaka as if he expected him to rip off his clothes and dance on the table in another moment.

"Proceed," said Mandaka when the waiter had finally retreated to the bar.

"I beg your pardon?"

"Your next question, Mr. Rojas."

"Why do the Maasai feel that they have a proprietary interest in the tusks?"

"What makes you think we do?" asked Mandaka, without denying it.

"As I trace the tusks through the galaxy, I keep running into members of the Maasai—Maasai Laibon, Tembo Laibon, Leeyo Nelion, yourself."

"Leeyo Nelion never possessed the tusks," he replied with an air of absolute conviction.

"He came very close, though," I said.

"Oh?" said Mandaka, leaning forward intently.

I nodded. "He hired a thief named Tahiti Benoit to steal them from a race known as the Fly-by-Nights. She succeeded in her mission, but Nelion died before she could deliver them to him. That was five hundred and seventy-three years ago."

"What became of them?"

"The computer is working on it right now," I said. I paused and stared at him. "How did you know that Nelion never received the ivory?"

"I am not without my own sources."

"You could make my job a lot easier by sharing them with me," I suggested.

He shook his head. "My information is entirely negative, Mr. Rojas. I know only which Maasai possessed the ivory, and at what point we lost possession of it.

"You mean Tembo Laibon, of course."

"That is correct."

"You don't deny that the Maasai spent three thousand years trying to get the ivory back?"

His face remained impassive. "Next question."

"You're making this very difficult for me, Mr. Mandaka," I said.

"I'm making it very lucrative for you, Mr. Rojas," he responded, "and it is my considered opinion that you do not need to know the answer to that question."

"I will find the answer with or without your help," I said earnestly.

He stared at me for a long moment without saying anything, and suddenly I felt very uneasy.

"It will do you no good, Mr. Rojas," he said, and his voice was less menacing than I had anticipated, "for even if you should discover the answer, you will not believe it."

"Once the facts are before me, I will accept them," I assured him.

He smiled wryly. "Facts are frequently the enemy of truth."

The waiter returned just then with Mandaka's milk and my brandy, and we each ordered dinner. I chose a mutated shellfish in a wine sauce; Mandaka requested an unadorned cut of meat, extremely rare.

"You have more questions, Mr. Rojas?"

"Yes," I said, "but if you didn't answer the ones I asked, you're not very likely to answer the others."

"Perhaps not," he agreed, "but as long as we're here you might as well ask them anyway."

"All right," I said. "Who are you?"

He stared directly into my eyes. "You know who I am."

"*I* do, but the Oligarchy doesn't."

"I am Bukoba Mandaka, and I am the last member of the Maasai."

"Then why can't I find any record of you?"

He paused before answering.

"Perhaps I have a passion for privacy."

"Many men have a passion for privacy," I noted. "You are the only one I know whose very existence cannot be proven."

"It can be proven," he replied, "if you know where to look."

"And where is that?"

"We are getting rather far afield, Mr. Rojas," he said, draining his glass of milk. "None of this has anything to do with the ivory." He paused. "You seem suddenly nervous, Mr. Rojas."

"I am," I admitted. "It occurs to me that I may have asked a very dangerous question."

"Then why did you ask it?"

"Because I want to know."

"Just as you want to know why the Maasai have such a long-standing obsession for the tusks of the Kilimanjaro Elephant?" he said.

I nodded.

Suddenly he smiled with satisfaction. "I chose the right man for the job, Mr. Rojas," he declared. "The whereabouts of the ivory will eat away at you until you have located it."

"And the other questions?"

"When you have found the ivory, perhaps I will tell you some of the things you want to know."

"Perhaps I will not tell you where it is *until* you have told me what I want to know," I said.

His eyes narrowed and he leaned forward, speaking softly. "*Now* you have said something dangerous, Mr. Rojas," he said, articulating each word carefully. "Murder is the least of the crimes I will commit to obtain the ivory."

"But *why*?" I asked, my curiosity outweighing my apprehension.

"I need it."

"For *what*?" I persisted. "What can you possibly do with it? There are other tusks on display in various museums and collections. Why will only the Kilimanjaro Elephant's tusks suffice?" I paused. "If you're willing to kill for it, why aren't you willing to kill for a Morita sculpture or the Blasingame Diamond?"

"They are meaningless baubles," he said contemptuously. "It is the ivory I must have."

"I repeat: why?"

He stared long and hard at me.

"Because it was ordained millennia ago."

"Ordained?" I repeated. "Where? By whom?"

"I believe you have asked enough questions, Mr. Rojas."

"Then give me some answers," I persisted. "If the ivory is so valuable to the Maasai, why did Tembo Laibon gamble it away?"

"Because he was a fool!" snapped Mandaka, his eyes shining with passion. "He knew what had to be done, and he could not bring himself to do it!"

"What had to be done?"

Mandaka was staring at his clenched fists so intently that he didn't even hear my question. I waited for him to relax so that I could ask it again, but then, from somewhere, I heard an amplified drum roll, and suddenly an elderly man with a long white beard and a multi-colored robe began walking through the room, a bent wooden staff in his hand.

"Moses," said Mandaka, directing my attention to the old man as he changed his staff into a snake and back again.

"He's very good," I commented as he began duplicating the magical feats of his Biblical counterpart. "I've always been fond of magicians."

"You have always been fond of *illusionists*," Mandaka corrected me.

"What's the difference?"

He stared at me again. "You would not like magicians, Mr. Rojas."

"Have you ever met one?"

"No, I never have," he replied as Moses muttered an incantation and the water in some nearby glasses changed to blood and back again.

"Then what makes you so sure that I wouldn't like them?" I asked over the applause of the patrons.

"My people had magicians—witch doctors—while we were still Earthbound."

"You mean sorcerers?" I asked dubiously.

He shook his head. "No. These magicians gave us strength in battle, brought rain for our crops, and kept our cattle fertile."

"It sounds very primitive."

"That is true," he agreed. "But I will tell you this, Mr. Rojas: a *mundumugu*—a witch doctor—could put a curse on a man or a beast hundreds of miles away, and as surely as you are sitting here, that man or beast would die."

"I very much doubt that, Mr. Mandaka."

"I am not surprised, Mr. Rojas," said Mandaka, staring intently at Moses, who had created a tiny plague of locusts, bejewelled, glittering creatures that flew above his head in almost hypnotic patterns.

The performance continued for another five or six minutes, each illusion an episode from the Bible. Finally the old man raised his hands and parted the hologram of the Red Sea. He walked a few feet onto the dry river bed, turned, bowed, and was instantly covered by millions of tons of water. This seemed to signal the onset of a new era, and the holograms now displayed a youthful Cleopatra touring her kingdom while riding in a golden chariot.

"Fabulous!" I exclaimed, joining the rest of the audience in enthusiastic applause.

"For an illusion," qualified Mandaka. He turned back to me. "Are we finished, Mr. Rojas?"

"I believe you were about to tell me what Tembo Laibon was unable to bring himself to do when you were interrupted by the magician."

"No, I was not, Mr. Rojas."

"Then I agree that we are finished, at least at this time," I said. "I would like to know where I can reach you, though."

"That won't be necessary," he replied. "I will contact you daily until you have located the ivory."

I took a sip of my brandy, then looked across the table at him.

"I don't know how to put this next question tactfully . . ." I began.

"You have been without artifice all evening, Mr. Rojas," said Mandaka, and I could not tell if he was annoyed or amused. "Why change now?"

"I would like your assurance that what I am doing is not illegal."

"It is totally legal."

"And that you are not a fugitive?"

"No, I am not a fugitive." Mandaka paused, staring directly across the table at me. "Now *I* have a question."

"Yes?"

"If my answers had been different, would you have stopped hunting for the ivory?"

"No," I answered truthfully. "I would not."

He looked satisfied. "I thought not."

"*Were* you telling me the truth?"

"Yes, Mr. Rojas, I was."

"Then I will find your tusks for you."

"I know you will."

"I suppose I should point out to you," I added, "that as

far as I have been able to determine, they haven't brought any lasting happiness to their various owners."

"I am not surprised."

"Then I hope that you'll be the exception to the rule, and that they will bring you fame and fortune."

He smiled ruefully.

"They will bring me only death, Mr. Rojas," he said with absolute certainty. "And now, if you will excuse me . . ."

He got to his feet and walked out before I could utter another word, leaving me to ponder his final fatalistic statement.

"Computer," I said, entering the office an hour later and collapsing into my chair, "have you located the tusks after they left Tahiti Benoit's possession?"

"No."

"Divert two percent of your capacity for this conversation and keep the remainder working on the problem."

"Done," announced the computer. "What do you wish to discuss, Duncan Rojas?"

"Tell me about the Maasai."

The computer glowed brightly as it summoned up the information.

"They were an extremely aggressive tribe of nomadic pastoralists located in southern Kenya and northern Tanzania."

"How can they have been aggressive and pastoral at the same time?" I asked.

"They were not militarists, such as the Zulus," explained the computer, "but they raided neighboring tribes to obtain cattle and women, and they were highly successful over the centuries. Although they never numbered more than 300,000, at one time they controlled almost a third of the grazing land of Kenya and Tanzania."

"Against which tribes did they make these raids?"

"Primarily the Kikuyu and the Wakamba, although they also fought numerous minor battles against the Luo, the Nandi, and the Kisi."

"Did the Maasai ever rule Kenya or Tanzania?"

"No. Prior to colonization there were no national borders in sub-Saharan Africa. When Kenya was first colonized, it was administered by the British. After obtaining its independence, it was ruled primarily by the Kikuyu, and, to some lesser extent, by the Luo and the Wakamba."

"But not the Maasai?"

"No."

"That's curious," I said. "If they dominated the other tribes, why didn't they take over the leadership of the government?"

"The most charismatic leader of the independence movement was Jomo Kenyatta, a Kikuyu, and his tribe held most of the major governmental positions."

"And the Maasai didn't object?"

"The Maasai continued their pastoral existence for another century, oblivious to all social and political change, and were totally without political power until an overpopulation crisis forced the government to purchase their tribal lands."

"What about the Tanzanian Maasai? Did *they* exercise any power?"

"Tanzania was first a German colony, then a British protectorate. The Maasai were always a distinct minority, and took no interest in the independence process or the formation of a government."

"That's very strange," I said. "It's almost as if, having achieved primacy among their neighboring tribes, the Maasai then willingly relinquished it without a fight."

"The relinquishing of their primacy may not have been

willing," replied the computer. "The British forbade them to use their weapons or to make war on neighboring tribes."

"When was that?"

"Approximately 1900 A.D."

"Could it have been 1898 A.D.?" I asked.

"It is possible," answered the computer. "Communications were very primitive, especially in Africa, and orders were often slow to be implemented."

"1898 is also the year that the Kilimanjaro Elephant was killed," I noted.

"We do not know that," contradicted the computer. "We only know that the Kilimanjaro Elephant's ivory was first auctioned in 1898 A.D."

"Still, I wonder if there is a connection?"

"What kind of connection?"

I frowned. "I don't know yet." I paused. "Was it the Maasai who originally put the tusks up for auction?"

"The records are incomplete and contradictory, but no mention has ever been made of any Maasai in connection with the auction of the tusks."

I lowered my head in thought, certain that I was close to some link, some revelation that would explain the connection between the Maasai and the ivory, but not knowing what it might be or how to search for it.

"The British Museum of Natural History came into possession of the ivory in 1932 A.D. Is that correct?"

"Yes."

"How long did the Museum keep the ivory?"

"One hundred and twenty-five years."

"And then what happened to it?"

"Working . . ."

5

The Politician
(2057 A.D.)

    A million flamingoes flew by me as I walked slowly along the shores of Lake Nakuru. I did not slake my thirst there, for the water was foul and bitter, but instead I dug a hole in a nearby glade and waited patiently for it to fill with fresh water.

  I ate the bark of the baobab tree, and the tall grasses, and the acacia pods, and sprayed my body with dust to rid it of parasites and protect it from the sun. Then I read the wind and found, almost hidden among its messages, the pungent scent of citrus. I followed it to its source, a small village, and began raiding the orchards, for my appetite, like my body, was huge. The natives ran out to drive me away with spears and arrows, but as soon as they saw me they lowered their heads and clapped their hands, as if I were some long-lost god returning to claim his homeland.

  I remained there, unmolested, for three days, and I could

have stayed longer, for I was old and stiff from the battles of my youth, the gouge of a rhino horn above my knee and the three musket balls I still carried inside my flesh. But instead I moved once again to the south, and as the honey badger follows the honey bird to the bees' nest, so I followed the enormous rift in the earth's crust to confront my destiny.

Matthew Kibo, a harsh Kenyan cigarette dangling from his mouth, his sleeves rolled up past his elbows, his skull shining beneath his thinning gray hair, got up from his computer, walked across the small, cluttered office, pulled a soft drink out of the portable refrigerator, and hit a switch that increased the speed of the overhead paddle fan.

It was February in Nairobi—hot, lazy weather. Kibo sighed and tried not to think of the beach at Malindi or his cool, spacious country home in the mountains of Uganda. He returned to his chair, took a long swallow, and looked out through the dirty window to the City Square, where a handful of people walked across the hot pavement in front of Jomo Kenyatta's statue, moving as if in slow motion.

He finished the drink, tossed the bottle atop an overflowing wastebasket, and was about to turn back to the computer when the door opened and a young man, clad in a colorful *kikoi*, entered the office.

"You seem to be settling in here comfortably," noted Tom Njomo.

"One office is very much like the next," replied Kibo wryly. "How are things in the Nakuru District?"

"Hot and dry, just like everywhere else." Njomo grinned. "I think we have more dust devils than voters out there."

"Did Baroti give us his endorsement?"

"He says that he's still making up his mind," replied Njomo.

"He's lying," said Kibo firmly.

"Perhaps," agreed Njomo. "He promised that he'll make his decision in the next three or four weeks."

"That will be too late to do us any good, even if he was telling the truth."

"It looks that bad?"

"It doesn't look good," acknowledged Kibo, gesturing to the figures on his computer screen. "Jacob Thiku, seventy-two percent; John Edward Kimathi, twenty-one percent; undecided, six percent; and the three other candidates share one point between them."

"Well, what did you expect?" said Njomo with a shrug. "Thiku is the most popular president we've had since Jomo Kenyatta. Look at what he's done: employment is up, inflation is down, the literacy rate is over ninety percent, the debt is down, he built the Lake Turkana Pipeline, the West loves him, the East courts him, and the conservationists have practically deified him—to say nothing of his working out a settlement to the war between Zambia and Zaire." He paused. "How can you win an election when you have to run against God?"

"No one said it was going to be easy," replied Kibo with a wry smile. "Still, I'm being paid to manage Kimathi's campaign."

"Such as it is," said Njomo caustically.

"Kimathi requires special handling," answered Kibo. "He scares the hell out of people—including me. He'd have had a difficult time beating a *normal* candidate, let alone Jacob Thiku."

"Then why are you working for him?"

"Because he fired his campaign manager and got rid of his staff, and because the other side didn't see fit to hire me at the outset," said Kibo sardonically. "My job is to make them wish they had—and then get the hell out of

Kenya before Kimathi brings the whole damned country tumbling down around him."

"With eleven weeks to go before the election, that hardly seems a likely prospect," commented Njomo, walking to the refrigerator and opening up a cold bottle of beer.

"Oh, I don't know," said Kibo. "A lot can happen in eleven weeks."

"Like what?"

Kibo shrugged. "I don't know yet; I've only been on the job for three days. But our first order of business is clear: we've got to find an issue."

"Thiku has a monopoly on them, and he's on the right side of each one."

"Then we'll find one that he's overlooked."

"I wish you luck."

"You wish *us* luck," corrected Kibo.

"I mean what I said," replied Njomo seriously. "I'm just a graduate student in Political Science, getting experience for my Master's thesis. I don't know about you, but I happen to love this country, and I don't want to see a demagogue like Kimathi running it. I just want to get him close enough to lose respectably, so I can hire on with a better candidate next time around."

"I trust you'll forgive me if I do my best?"

"Go ahead, for all the good it will do you," said Njomo. "You know, Kimathi was even against the Turkana Pipeline. If he'd had his way, the Northern Frontier would still be a desert." He paused. "Have you ever thought about what would happen if you actually win?"

"It's sacrilegious for campaign managers to think one minute beyond the election," answered Kibo. "And the instant the election's over, they start looking toward the next one. Or didn't they teach you that in college?"

"I'm beginning to think they taught me all the wrong

things," said Njomo wryly. "Here I've been wasting my time studying the intricacies of our political system, and all the time I should have been reading Machiavelli."

"It wouldn't hurt," replied Kibo seriously.

"So I gather."

"And it would take some of the mystique away from being a political organizer," continued Kibo. "You do your homework, you study your opposition, you analyze your market, and you set your goals. It's just a job, like any other—and in all immodesty, I do it damned well."

"I know," said Njomo. "That's why Malawi's economy is in a shambles."

"I got my man elected," said Kibo. "It's *his* job to govern the damned country." He lit up another cigarette and stared at the younger man. "Let me give you a little advice, if I may."

"Go ahead."

"It's a political leader's job to stake out moral and ethical positions. If that's what you want to do, you're in the wrong end of the business. Campaign managers work backstage and make deals with the devil so that their bosses can get up there in front of an audience and invoke God."

"And when the political leader is John Edward Kimathi?"

"No matter what you may think, people tend to get the leaders they deserve. If they're crazy enough to vote Jacob Thiku out of office, then they deserve Kimathi."

"And it's your job to give them the opportunity to do just that."

"That's right," said Kibo. "Or do you think that only candidates you personally approve of should be allowed to run for office?"

"I never said that," replied Njomo defensively.

"Good. Then I'll expect your wholehearted support. Besides," added Kibo seriously, "if you want to have a future in this field, you'd better make an earnest effort on Kimathi's behalf. The *people* may be watching Thiku and Kimathi, but the *politicos* are watching you and me and our counterparts."

Njomo made no comment.

"All right," said Kibo, getting to his feet. "After you've finished your beer, I want you to start contacting our fundraisers, especially in the Tsavo District, and gently but firmly urge them to be a little more productive. I'm going over to the library."

"What for?" asked Njomo.

"Because we can't run a campaign without funds, and the treasury's almost empty."

"No. I meant, what are you going to the library for?"

"I told you—I'm looking for an issue."

"And you think you'll find one there?" asked Njomo dubiously.

"Who knows?" replied Kibo. "I certainly haven't found one anywhere else."

He put on his jacket and hat, went out into the hot equatorial sun, and tried to ignore the sounds and smells of the central city as he walked down Moi Avenue. When he came to Biashara Street, he turned left, continued on past a score of gift shops, and finally came to the newly-renovated and expanded MacMillan Library. He wasn't sure exactly what he was looking for, but he requested a stack of books and disks, carried them to the reading room, appropriated a small desk and computer by a window that overlooked the golden dome of the exquisite Jamia Mosque, and went to work.

It couldn't be a contemporary issue, he knew; Thiku was on top of every one of them. Economics was out, too; the average Kenyan had never been better off. Ditto for foreign policy; Thiku was the Peacemaker of Africa.

It would have to be, he decided, an emotional issue, one that could arouse passions, since the intellect was so firmly committed to Jacob Thiku. That meant that Kimathi needed an enemy—not Thiku, who was close to being a God-figure—but a tangible, visible enemy, one Thiku had over-looked, against whom he could rage and rail and inflame the populace.

Kibo leaned back, clasping his hands behind his head, and stared out at the mosque. It couldn't be a nearby coun-try; the press was already afraid of Kimathi, and they'd be convinced that he wanted war.

So it had to be a large country, one so powerful that no matter what passions Kimathi aroused, the thought of war was inconceivable. The United States? No, they'd been pouring money into Kenya for a century; it would be too hard to paint them as an enemy. Russia? No, they had nothing to do with East Africa; never did, never would. China or India? No, their African client states were all on the West Coast, thousands of miles away.

So it came down, as he had known it would, to Britain. They had colonized Kenya, had overlaid it with their own culture and laws, had bent over backward to keep it in the Commonwealth. Somewhere in the past, thirty or seventy or ninety or one hundred and fifty years ago, there had to be *something* he could use, something so trivial that Thiku had overlooked it, something so meaningless that no prior president had cared about it, something so potent that, given the proper approach, Kimathi could rally a nation to his banner.

And, seven hours later, he found it.

"You're joking, right?" said Njomo uncomfortably.

"I never joke about business," replied Kibo.

"You honestly think you can win the election for Kimathi

because of some elephant that's been dead for more than a century?"

They were seated at an outdoor restaurant in Muthaiga, a suburb some eight miles out of town, their table near a large circular barbecue pit. White-jacketed waiters scurried from table to table, offering a choice of freshly-cooked meats, and a huge crowd of informally-dressed men and women had gather at the horseshoe-shaped bar at the far end of the restaurant. The sun had set, and there the usual chill in the night air.

"That's correct," said Kibo calmly as he shook a spicy seasoning over his impala cutlet.

"Then you're as crazy as he is!"

"They didn't teach you very much in college, did they?" asked Kibo, making no attempt to hide his amusement.

"They taught me enough to know when a politician is grasping at straws," shot back Njomo.

"Nonsense," said Kibo confidently. "What I've done is find an issue that Kimathi can make his own."

"A non-issue, you mean," said the younger man.

"It'll be an issue by tomorrow night," replied Kibo, "which is all that matters." He paused. "You know, most elections aren't won or lost because one candidate has a better fiscal policy than the other, or manages his parliament better. Usually it comes down to who tells the best jokes or kisses the most babies."

"Or who can make an issue out of a dead elephant?" said Njomo caustically.

"Precisely," agreed Kibo. "Kimathi needs a cause; this gives him one. He needs an enemy; this pinpoints one. Since he's going to be a one-issue candidate, he needs an issue so simple that everyone can immediately understand it; this gives him such an issue. He needs to appeal to national pride; this is an issue that surpasses tribalism and appeals to all Kenyans. Even his name will help: Deedan Kimathi was the most effective general in the Mau Mau emergency a century ago. I'll make sure the press is aware of that." Kibo took a sip of his wine and leaned back with a contented smile. "It's perfect."

"You *really* believe what you're saying, don't you?" said Njomo.

"Of course I do. And a week from today, so will everyone else in this country."

"It will never work."

"Yes it will. There are precedents."

"Someone else became President because of a dead elephant?" scoffed Njomo.

"No," replied Kibo patiently. "But Hassin became President of Egypt in 2023 with the same kind of issue."

"Hassin? He won because he made peace with Jordan."

"That was *after* he was elected. His entire campaign was based solely on the accusation that Great Britain had appropriated a number of Egypt's national treasures; he promised to get them back if he was elected President."

"And did he?"

"No. All the treasures are still in the British Museum— but he *did* manage to get himself elected. He wasn't all that bad a President, either."

"Even if he did demand the return of his national treasures, he was talking about mummies and gold and jewelry," protested Njomo. "*You're* talking about the tusks of an elephant."

"I'm talking about national honor," replied Kibo. "It's not Kenya's fault that we didn't have any temples and pyramids for the British to loot. They took what they could find, and we want it back."

"But *tusks*, for God's sakes!"

"The tusks are a symbol, nothing more," said Kibo. "It

doesn't matter whether they have a market value or not. They constitute the greatest trophy ever taken. They belong on display right here in the Nairobi Museum, not the British Museum of Natural History." He paused. "As far as anyone can tell, the elephant wasn't even killed by a European but by an African."

"Who cares?"

"*Everyone* will care after Kimathi makes his next speech. This is the last remaining stain of colonialism, and it has to be eradicated. Those tusks are part of Kenya's heritage, not Britain's." He paused, and then leaned forward. "You want to know something else? They're not even on display. They're locked away in a vault in the museum's basement, gathering dust, when they should be here for every Kenyan to see."

"They're not on display?"

Kibo shook his head. "Sounds contemptuous, doesn't it?"

"You know, it could be construed that way," admitted Njomo.

"Especially coming from the mouth of our fire-breathing political dragon."

"Let me think about this for a few minutes," said Njomo.

"Be my guest," said Kibo, finishing his wine. As the waiter passed by, Kibo signaled to him.

"Yes, Mr. Kibo?"

"Bring me the richest dessert you've got," he said.

"I thought you were watching your weight," noted Njomo as the waiter scurried off.

"I deserve it," said Kibo expansively. "A good politician gets maybe three or four brilliant notions in a lifetime. This one should keep me in business for the next five years."

Kimathi took to the airwaves the next night. His voice strained, his eyes wild with passion, the veins on his forehead standing out as if they would burst, he ranted and railed against the British. He raised the twin spectres of racism and colonialism, he threatened certain vaguely-defined actions if the tusks of the Kilimanjaro Elephant were not returned immediately, and he demanded that Kenyans boycott all British products.

It was the British, he screamed, who had decimated Kenya's wildlife, who had profligately slaughtered species after species, and who now refused to relinquish the symbol of Kenya's vanished wilderness, the ivory of the most fabulous animal of all.

It was the British who had accumulated vast treasures from all of their former colonies, and not only refused to return them but kept them hidden from public view in a blatant display of contempt for their former subjects.

And it was Jacob Thiku, he added pointedly, who refused to demand the return of the ivory, who had once been a brilliant leader but had lost his courage and would not stand up to the British.

What did the British want with the tusks anyway, demanded Kimathi. They refused to display them, they refused to sell them, and they refused to return them. When would this condescension cease?

Only, he concluded, when Kenya elected a President who did not fear the British and would eradicate this final affront to black African dignity.

"Not bad," said Kibo, going over the preliminary figures the next afternoon. "Not bad at all."

"You mean it actually worked?" asked Njomo contemptuously. "I thought they were going to have to put a straitjacket on him halfway through the speech, the way he kept leaping and screaming and shaking his fist."

"He picked up four points," replied Kibo with a smug smile. "Not too shoddy for a madman."

"Let me see that!" said Njomo in disbelief, stalking over to the computer. He studied the screen for a moment, then straightened up with a surprised expression on his face. "It's unbelievable!"

"Wait until tomorrow afternoon, when he gives his speech at the University," promised Kibo. "I guarantee he'll pick up two more points."

"I wonder what the reaction is like in Britain?" mused Njomo.

"They probably wonder why we're making all this fuss about a pair of tusks."

"Will they return them?"

"Not while he's making threats," replied Kibo. "It's too much like giving in to blackmail. And he won't be through making threats until after the election."

"What about Thiku?"

"What about him?"

"What will he do?" persisted Njomo.

"The reasonable thing."

"And what is that?"

Kibo shrugged. "Who knows? But it will be ineffective. This is an emotional issue; reason has nothing to do with it."

Kimathi made four more speeches—and picked up nine more points in the polls—before Jacob Thiku finally agreed to address the issue of the tusks.

The elephant, he pointed out, had not been killed by the British, nor by any European.

The elephant, he noted, had been killed on the slopes of Mount Kilimanjaro, which was entirely within the borders of Tanzania, and hence Kenya actually had no claim to it at all.

The tusks of the elephant, he reminded, had been legally

auctioned in Zanzibar, which was then an independent country, not Mombasa.

It was some thirty-four years *after* the initial auction, he explained, that the British Museum of Natural History finally obtained the ivory.

While he would certainly welcome the tusks of the Kilimanjaro Elephant if the British were to make a gift of them, it was obvious that Kenya had no legal or moral claim to them. Indeed, if *anyone* had a right to demand the return of the ivory, it was Tanzania.

Kimathi, he concluded reasonably, was trying to arouse passions and make political capital out of a meaningless issue while severely straining Kenya's ties to its oldest ally, Great Britian. Once the people understood what Kimathi was doing, they would surely reject his fiery calls to arms.

It was a splendid, reasoned response, and was printed in all the British newspapers and carried on most of the international video networks.

And the next morning Kimathi had narrowed the gap between them by three more points.

"You look morose for a man whose candidate is only trailing God by six points," said Njomo a month later, as he walked into Kibo's office.

"Five, if you read the *Nation*," Kibo corrected him.

"Then why the long face?" persisted Njomo. "You've got money coming in faster than you can count it, Kimathi made the covers of *Stern* and *Time*, and poor old Jacob Thiku is probably seeing elephants in his sleep."

"The British ambassador wants to talk to him."

"To Kimathi?"

Kibo nodded grimly. "I've been putting him off for two weeks, but I can't keep them apart much longer."

"What's wrong with letting him speak to Kimathi?"

"Everything."

"I don't see why. Kimathi will wait until all the cameras are trained on them and then threaten the ambassador with death or worse if he doesn't take the next plane to Britain and bring back the tusks."

"That's what I'm afraid of," said Kibo.

Njomo blinked his eyes rapidly. "I don't think I understand you," he said.

"That's because you're very young and very naive," said Kibo. "Just believe me—the last thing we want is for Kimathi to meet face-to-face with any representatives of the British government."

"You've spent more than a month creating this myth that Kimathi is the sole defender of Kenya's honor," said Njomo. "Now he finally has the chance to meet one-on-one with the enemy and you're trying to prevent it. Why?"

Kibo sighed deeply. "What do you think the British or the Americans or the Russians see when they look at Kimathi?" he asked.

"I don't know. Probably they see a colorful politician making headlines with an unlikely issue."

"They see a clown," replied Kibo. "A big, bumbling clown whose country gave away his toys, and who wants them back." He paused. "Half of them probably think he wears a loincloth and lives in a mud hut."

"I don't see your point," said Njomo.

"He amuses them, the way Idi Amin amused them a century ago. If they ever actually listened to what he said, if they saw the way he can manipulate an audience, if they realized that he graduated at the top of his class at the Sorbonne, they wouldn't be amused any longer. They'd be frightened."

"What's wrong with frightening the British ambassador?" asked Njomo. "It will be one more nail in Jacob Thiku's political coffin."

"Maybe," said Kibo. "But I doubt it." He paused long enough to light another cigarette. "At the rate Kimathi is gaining support, he'll catch Thiku two weeks before the election and beat him by a good two million votes. Only one thing can stop him."

"What?"

"If he loses his issue, I haven't got time to come up with another one—and if the ambassador meets with him personally and sees for himself that Kimathi really is crazy enough to go to war over the tusks, he may very well recommend to his government that they return them." He looked across the desk at Njomo. "That's the bottom line: no issue, no victory."

"I see," said Njomo, a look of dawning comprehension on his face.

"One more thing they didn't teach you at school," remarked Kibo wryly.

Njomo pulled a beer out of the refrigerator. "So what do you do now?"

"I'll do my damnedest to convince Kimathi that it's beneath his dignity to meet with the opposition."

"I thought Jacob Thiku was the opposition."

"Nobody could have gotten this far running again Thiku; Kimathi's running against the British. I just hope he'll listen to me."

"If reason won't work, appeal to his vanity," suggested Njomo. "It's never failed yet."

"You're learning," commented Kibo.

"Oh?"

Kibo nodded. "When all is said and done, it's more important for a campaign manager to understand people than politics."

"I suppose it is, at that," admitted Njomo.

"As long as you remember that, you've got a future in politics," said Kibo. Suddenly he smiled. "And if you forget it, you can always make a living teaching politics at the University."

Kimathi's next major address was delivered in Malindi, but was broadcast throughout the country. Five minutes after it was over, Kibo's phone rang.

"Yes?"

"Mr. Kibo?"

"Speaking."

"This is Sir Robert Peake."

"What can I do for you, Ambassador?" said Kibo, lighting a cigarette.

"Did you hear John Edward Kimathi's speech this evening?"

"Yes."

"This vilification of my government really cannot be permitted to continue, Mr. Kibo," said Peake.

"The candidate writes his own speeches, Ambassador," replied Kibo. "What do you expect *me* to do about it?"

"I expect you to compel him to exercise some restraint in his attacks, Mr. Kibo," said Peake. "His Majesty's Government will look upon a repetition of this evening's harangue with extreme disfavor."

"Then you'd better speak directly to Mr. Kimathi," responded Kibo.

"I have repeatedly tried, and you have repeatedly prevented me, Mr. Kibo."

"That's simply not true, Ambassador," lied Kibo. "Mr. Kimathi has a very full schedule, but I am still trying to arrange a meeting between the two of you."

"Don't bother, Mr. Kibo."

Kibo frowned. "You no longer wish to speak to him?"

"No."

Kibo quickly analyzed his options and alternatives. "I

can arrange for you to have dinner with him tomorrow night," he said after a brief pause.

"I'm afraid I will be quite busy tomorrow night," said Peake. "Just remember what I told you, Mr. Kibo. We will not tolerate another such attack."

Kibo heard the disconnecting click, and immediately tried to raise Kimathi on the phone. The candidate was unavailable, and finally he managed to reach Njomo.

"What is it?" asked the young man after he had identified Kibo's voice.

"Trouble," said Kibo. "I want you to cancel all of Kimathi's speaking engagements for the next two days, until I can get to him."

"What happened?"

"I had a call from the British ambassador. He insists that Kimathi stop attacking his country."

"So what?"

"Just do what I said!" snapped Kibo, breaking the connection and trying once again to reach Kimathi. Finally, an hour after midnight, the candidate picked up the phone in his suite.

"John, this is Matthew Kibo."

"How did you like my speech tonight?"

"It was excellent." Kibo paused. "John, we've got a problem. I've canceled your schedule for the next two days. Can you fake an illness?"

"Why?"

"It's very complicated," answered Kibo. "But the election is only twenty days away. It's time to start mending fences."

"With Thiku?" said the candidate contemptuously. "He's a powerless old man."

"With the British."

"Not without the ivory!"

"John, this is *me* you're talking to. I *gave* you the damned issue."

"I will never relent until the tusks have been returned."

"John, I've never given you bad advice yet, have I?" demanded Kibo. "You've got to believe me. The people know what you stand for. If you stop attacking the British right now, you can still win this election. If you don't, then I promise you you're going to lose."

"Nobody gives orders to John Edward Kimathi!" bellowed the candidate. "I fear no man and no nation, and I will not be silenced! Let them bring their guns; I stand ready."

"It won't be guns that they bring," said Kibo. "Can you just stay where you are until I fly up and speak to you?"

"I'm scheduled to speak in Lamu Town tomorrow morning," replied the candidate. "If you want to speak to me, you can meet me there."

"It's been canceled."

"Then I will stand on a street corner and shout my message. I will not be silenced until the ivory has been returned!"

Kibo slammed down the receiver, then tried to call Kimathi again but received nothing but a busy signal.

He spent another hour trying to raise Kimathi on the telephone, then went home to enjoy what he knew would be his last night as the campaign manager of a potential president.

Njomo walked across the office and turned off the television set.

"I'd call it one of his better speeches," he said.

"I'd call it one of his last ones," replied Kibo. "And turn the television back on."

"Why?"

"Because I know the difference between a threat and a bluff."

"You mean the British ambassador?" asked Njomo. "What can he do? The more he protests, the better Kimathi looks."

"You've still got a lot to learn," said Kibo, leaning back on his chair and staring at the historical drama on the set.

Njomo sat in his chair for another twenty minutes, then walked over to the computer on Kibo's desk.

"Do you mind?" he asked. "I just want to check the network ratings for the speech."

"Be my guest," said Kibo, staring through his window at the statue of Jomo Kenyatta that dominated the City Square. An ambulance raced by, sirens screaming, and two hundred birds took off in frightened flight, only to alight on the pavement once the vehicle had passed from sight.

"Not bad," commented Njomo, as the figures began appearing on the screen. "We did especially well on the Coast."

"It's one hundred and fifteen degrees on the Coast," replied Kibo. "They've got nothing better to do than sit around watching television."

Suddenly he sat erect, his attention centered on the television.

"Here it comes," he announced.

Njomo deactivated the computer and turned to face the video screen.

"And now," said a smooth, polished voice, "we interrupt our regular programming for a special announcement."

The scene shifted to Jacob Thiku's private residence in Muthaiga. Thiku and Sir Robert Peake stood on the stone steps leading to the house, surrounded by reporters.

"I have a brief announcement to make," said Thiku.

The press crowded closer.

"At 11:30 this morning, less than fifteen minutes ago, the government of Kenya concluded its friendly and peaceful negotiations with the government of Great Britain, as represented by Ambassador Sir Robert Peake. As a result of these negotiations, the ivory of the Kilimanjaro Elephant will be placed on public display in the National Museum of Nairobi at noon tomorrow."

The old president shook Peake's hand, then shot a triumphant smile at the cameras. Kibo felt that he was smiling directly at *him*.

"Well," said Kibo wearily, "that's your final lesson: never manage a single-issue candidate unless you can be sure the issue will last until election day."

"What do we do now?" asked Njomo, still stunned by Thiku's announcement.

"Now?" repeated Kibo. "Now we go home and relax. And the day after tomorrow we try to figure out what Kimathi can say during the final three weeks of the campaign so that he loses respectably instead of by a landslide."

"And what about tomorrow?"

"I don't know about you," said Kibo, getting to his feet, walking to his closet, and donning his jacket, "but I'm going to go over to the museum and see what all the commotion was about."

Fifth Interlude (6303 G.E.)

I returned to my apartment a little after midnight, more for a change of clothes than from any desire to spend the night there. I nodded pleasantly to the tripedal doorman from distant Hesporite III, waited for the airlift to scan my retina and bone structure, and gently ascended to the seventh floor. When the corridor came to a stop in front of my door I stepped off, placed my palm to the scanner, uttered the unlock code, and entered.

And found myself facing Bukoba Mandaka.

"What are you doing here?" I demanded.

"Waiting for you," he said calmly, rising from the chair in which he had been seated.

"How did you get in?"

"I have my methods."

I stared at him, huge and muscular and towering above me, and decided not to press the issue.

"All right," I said. "Why are you here?"

"I have come to talk."

"I thought that's what we did at dinner."

He shook his head. "We *sparred* at dinner, Mr. Rojas. Now we will *talk*."

"I would welcome that," I said. "Do you mind if I fix myself a drink first?"

"Not at all," he said. "Your liquor is in the kitchen."

"I know," I replied dryly.

"You have an interesting home, Mr. Rojas," commented Mandaka, following me as I walked through the dining area.

"It's rather ordinary, actually," I replied with a shrug.

"I didn't say it was extraordinary," he corrected me. "I said it was interesting."

I looked around at the sterile white walls and pristine furniture. "Oh? What's so interesting about it? I find it rather dull, myself."

"It is interesting because it tells me absolutely nothing about you," he answered. "And that, in turn, tells me everything about you."

"You're not making yourself clear," I said, approaching the liquor cabinet and ordering the door to dilate.

"How long have you lived here, Mr. Rojas?" asked Mandaka.

"About seven years."

"In seven years you have not made this place your own. I find that interesting."

"I still don't understand you," I said, reaching in and pulling out a container.

"The furniture is functional but without character," he noted. "The artwork is bland and reflects nothing of the owner's taste. The carpet is old but shows no wear, nor do the kitchen appliances show any sign of use. There is no wife, no family, no sign of a lover's presence. You pay for an apartment, Mr. Rojas, but you use it like a hotel: There is nothing of *you* here. Even the books and tapes are nothing but light entertainments, chosen by a man who occasionally seeks a few minutes of diversion, nothing more." He paused. "And the puzzles, Mr. Rojas,"—he shook his head sadly—"the puzzles."

"What about them?"

"What kind of man keeps hundreds of puzzles in his bedroom and study? Only a man who wishes to fill the empty hours between the things that are important to him."

I stared at him, but made no answer.

"I contrast this to your office, Mr. Rojas," he continued. "Books everywhere, the walls covered with photographs and holograms of the rarest animals in the galaxy, food and coffee always in evidence, furniture chosen for comfort rather than anonymity, a certain amount of clutter that seems on the verge of getting out of control—*that* is where you live, Mr. Rojas, and what you live *for*."

"You came here just to tell me that?" I asked, annoyed that he had so accurately analyzed my life on the basis of a few rooms of old furniture.

"No," he responded. "I came here to tell you that I am seriously displeased with you, Mr. Rojas."

"Oh? Why?"

"Does the world Nelson Twenty-Three mean anything to you?"

"You traced the ad here that quickly?" I said.

"Of course."

"I'm impressed."

"*I'm* annoyed," he replied. "Why did you run it?"

"I was curious to know just how far-reaching your sources are."

"Neither my sources nor myself appreciate being an experiment designed solely for the edification of your curiosity, Mr. Rojas," he said sternly. "You cost me a considerable amount of money tracing that advertisement to Genovaith II and then to your office."

"Perhaps I shouldn't have done it," I admitted. "You can deduct it from my fee."

"It could very well come to a third of what I'm paying you."

"It makes no difference," I said with a shrug. "I was at fault."

"Was it worth it, Mr. Rojas?" he asked, studying my expression.

"Not really," I answered. "In fact, I would have been surprised if you or your sources hadn't noticed it."

"That is a lot of money to spend merely to test your theory, Mr. Rojas," he noted. "Or have you no desire for money?"

"Everyone wants money," I replied.

"But not everyone *needs* it," concluded Mandaka. He stared thoughtfully at me for a moment, and then nodded. "All money can buy you is sterile apartments and trivial little puzzles such as you keep here. Only people like myself can set you tasks such as finding the tusks of the Kilimanjaro Elephant." He smiled ironically. "I think, Mr. Rojas, that you may need me as much as I need the ivory."

"Just how long have the Maasai needed the ivory?" I asked.

"A long time," he replied.

"Since 1898 A.D.?"

"Not quite."

"But surely before 1914 A.D.?" I suggested.

"Yes, Mr. Rojas," he acknowledged.

I smiled with satisfaction. "I thought so."

"Perhaps I should not denigrate your little games and

puzzles," said Mandaka wryly. "They have made your mind very agile."

"Thank you."

He stared at me again. "I assume that you have learned something more from your computer since we had dinner earlier this evening."

"A bit," I replied, finally withdrawing a glass and pouring my drink. "Mostly it confirmed what I had already suspected." I turned to him. "May I fix you a drink as well?"

"As I believe I told you once before, I drink only milk," he answered.

"I'm afraid I don't have any. Shall we sit down, Mr. Mandaka?"

"There is only one chair in your kitchen," he pointed out.

"We'll go to the living room," I said, leading the way.

He walked to a corner and sat down on a large chair which had more resiliency to it than he seemed to expect; at any rate, he seemed to sink into it, then awkwardly shifted his position until he was sitting erect. I ordered my couch to approach me, suddenly remembered that the furniture in my apartment did not respond to verbal commands, and walked over to it. I adjusted the controls so that it floated some six inches above the ground, swaying gently, and then seated myself.

"What did your computer tell you this evening?" he asked when I had taken a sip from my drink and placed it on an end table.

"How and why the British returned the ivory to Kenya."

"That happened in the 21st century A.D.," he noted sternly. "I thought you were tracing the tusks *forward* in history."

"I am," I replied. "This took a very small portion of the computer's capacity, and I was curious to learn more about their history."

I half-expected him to react with a show of anger, but instead he merely nodded his head. "John Edward Kimathi," he mused softly. "He put them right within our grasp, and still we did nothing!"

"What *should* you have done, Mr. Mandaka?"

"We should have taken them from the Museum and done what had to be done," he replied. He paused, then added grimly: "What *still* has to be done."

"And what is that?"

He looked at me thoughtfully. "If there was any chance at all that you might believe me, I think I would tell you, Mr. Rojas."

"Why not tell me anyway, and let me make up my own mind?" I suggested.

He shook his head. "I can't expect you to do your best if you believe you are working for a madman."

"I already think I am working for a criminal, and it hasn't slowed me down," I noted.

He seemed amused. "A criminal? Why? Because I know how to bypass your apartment's security system?"

"And because you obviously are not Bukoba Mandaka."

"I've told you that I am."

"But the government has no record of you," I pointed out.

"You accepted my answer at dinnertime."

"It was in my best interest to accept it: I'm every bit as anxious to find the tusks as you are." I paused. "You are a physically imposing figure, Mr. Mandaka. Therefore, I will accept it again, if you insist upon it—but I would rather know the truth."

He smiled. "An intelligent decision, Mr. Rojas. However, at the risk of disappointing you, I must repeat that I truly am Bukoba Mandaka."

"When and where were you born?"

"On Earth, fifty-three years ago."

"On Earth?" I repeated, surprised, for I had never met anyone who had been born on our mother planet.

"That is correct."

"Why is there no record of you?" I asked.

"Earth is practically deserted, Mr. Rojas; no more than fifty million people remain there, and the census bureau was half a world away. It was not very difficult for my parents to hide the record of my birth."

"Why should they wish to?"

"Because they knew that the day would come when I would require absolute freedom of movement, and they surmised, correctly, that I would desire freedom from governmental scrutiny as well."

"Why would you desire freedom from governmental scrutiny if you were acting within the law?"

He paused, as if considering how much to tell me. "There are things required of me that the government will not condone," he answered at last. "And while I have committed no felonies to date, I will, without hestitation, break any law that comes between myself and possession of the ivory."

"Traveling under a false passport is a felony," I noted.

"Not as far as I'm concerned," he replied firmly, closing the subject.

The computer flashed to life just then.

"There is a message coming in for Duncan Rojas," it announced.

"Put it through," I ordered.

"Do you desire video contact or only verbal?"

"Video."

Suddenly Hilda Dorian's image appeared above the coffee table.

"Do you know what time it is?" she demanded.

"A little after midnight," I replied.

"You were supposed to contact me the minute you got back from dinner!" she snapped. "I checked your office after Harold and I returned from the theater, and the computer told me you had gone home. Why haven't you reported in to me?"

"I have company," I replied, gesturing to Mandaka. She made an adjustment at her end which allowed her image to swivel so she could see him.

"Are you in trouble?" she asked promptly.

"Not at all."

"You're sure?" she insisted.

"I'm sure, Hilda," I said. "Stop treating me like a child."

"I'll stop treating you like one the day you stop acting like one," she said harshly. "The only thing you know about this man is that the Commonwealth doesn't have any record of him, and yet you've invited him to your apartment."

"I didn't exactly invite him," I said wryly.

"What does that mean?" she demanded.

"Nothing, Hilda," I said quickly. "I assure you that I'm in no danger, and I'm happy to have him here."

She looked from one of us to the other, then paused and cleared her throat. "Mandaka, I'm warning you: he'd better show up for work healthy tomorrow morning."

Before the Maasai could reply, she had terminated the connection.

Mandaka stared at the spot where her image had been for a long moment.

"Who was *that*?" he asked at last.

"Hilda Dorian," I replied. Then I realized that the name meant nothing to him, and added: "She's Braxton's Chief of Security."

"The woman you wanted to join us for dinner?"

"Yes," I said uncomfortably, shifting my position on the couch.

"It would have been an interesting meal," he said with an ironic smile.

"I'm sorry—sometimes she can be overly protective. I hope she didn't offend you."

"She didn't," he replied. "In fact, I wish I had someone to feel that way about me."

"I wish I didn't," I said with a grimace.

"You say that only because you are annoyed with her. If you were ever to find yourself alone, *truly* alone, you would cherish her."

"Are you truly alone?"

He nodded somberly. "As alone as any human being has ever been."

"You have no wife?"

"None."

"Or children?"

He shook his head. "They are not permitted me."

"Friends?"

"None."

I paused awkwardly, unaware of what to say next. "Well, there are worse things," I finally ventured. "Many people choose solitary lives."

"I did not choose this life, Mr. Rojas," he said earnestly. "All that I have I would gladly give for the comforts of family, or even for a person who worried about me the way your Chief of Security worries about you."

"Then what is preventing you from acquiring a family?" I asked.

"It is my *destiny* to live alone and die alone." He paused. "In point of fact, our lives are very similar, Mr. Rojas— cold and sterile and solitary."

"I don't find them similar at all," I said defensively.

"If there is a difference, it is that you live this way by choice."

"You make me sound like a recluse," I objected. "I see people all the time."

"So do I."

"And I have my work," I added.

"And I have my mission."

I felt uncomfortable with the path the conversation had taken, and decided to change it.

"Obtaining the ivory is only the first step of that mission, isn't it?" I asked.

He nodded.

"Surely you haven't been searching for it for fifty-three years, or you'd have found it by now."

"You are a very perceptive man, Mr. Rojas," he said. "In fact, I have been seeking the ivory for only seven years."

"What happened seven years ago?" I asked bluntly.

He stared thoughtfully at me, then shrugged.

"I finally determined, beyond any possible doubt, that I was the last existing Maasai."

"If this is something the last Maasai must do, why did Leeyo Nelion seek the tusks?" I asked.

"It is something *any* Maasai could have done," he replied, a trace of anger in his deep voice. "It is something that the last Maasai *must* do."

"And you won't tell me what it is?"

"You would think me quite mad."

"All of this has something to do with the Maasai's fall from power, doesn't it?"

"Power is a very elastic term," responded Mandaka. "When we were the most feared tribe in East Africa, do you know how many of us there were?"

"No."

"Twenty-five thousand, Mr. Rojas—as compared to perhaps two million Kikuyu."

"Twenty-five thousand?" I repeated incredulously. "And you still managed to control more than a third of the country?"

"There *was* no country until the European heads of state

artificially created one," he replied. "There was the land upon which the Maasai had always lived, and we made no attempts to appropriate any other tribal lands." He paused and forced a smile to his lips. "And then, in 1880 A.D., the greatest of our witch doctors, the *mundumugu* Mbatian, foresaw the imminent arrival of three plagues from the North which would come close to destroying the Maasai race. In 1881 we were striken with smallpox, and almost ninety percent of us died, and in 1882 rinderpest struck our herds of cattle and killed all but a handful of them."

"And the third plague?" I asked.

"In 1883, a 29-year-old Scotsman named Joseph Thomson walked west from Mombasa into Maasailand."

"Thomson was the third plague?" I asked, frowning.

"Not Thomson himself, but the white man, who appropriated our lands and tried to take away our culture," answered Mandaka. He paused. "Everything Mbatian predicted came to pass, and yet we weathered all three plagues and remained the greatest warriors in East Africa. No young man could become an *elmoran*, an adult, until he had killed a lion with his spear." He paused, frowning. "And then the British took away our spears, and made it illegal for us even to carry a shield. We could no longer kill the lion, even when he attacked our herds. We had been warriors, and they turned us into defenseless shepherds." He suddenly chuckled, as if at a memory. "We never got along very well with the British. Did you know that the Maasai were the only tribe that did not fight in Man's first great world war? The British demanded that all able-bodied African men report for duty, and we said: Oh, no, we are no longer warriors, we have no weapons with which to fight. You have turned us into cattle-breeders and goat-herders; we will stay here with our cattle and our goats."

"Excuse me for asking," I said, trying to comprehend, "but what has this to do with the tusks?"

"More than you can imagine," he said in a voice suddenly tinged with bitterness. "What enrages me the most is that they were there, in Nairobi, for centuries, and yet we never took them away from the Kikuyu. For all I know, we never even tried." He paused thoughtfully. "It was *then*, before the ivory was turned over to private interests, that we should have taken it."

"I'm surprised the government relinquished it," I said. "Given the emotions it aroused during the Thiku-Kimathi campaign, I would have thought it was a national treasure."

"It was."

"Then why would the government have given up possession of it?"

"Some Kikuyu or Luo bureaucrat doubtless was bribed," offered Mandaka contemptuously.

"Don't you know the details?" I asked, surprised.

"No. Only that at some point in the first millennium of the Galactic Era the tusks passed into private ownership." He paused. "I have always been less concerned with their history than their whereabouts."

"Then you don't care to know how it happened?" I asked, disappointed, for I was suddenly anxious to know the answer.

"It is obvious that *you* care," he replied. "How long will it take you to unearth the facts?"

"I'm sure that it's a matter of public record," I said. "And if it is, my computer at Braxton's should take no more than three or four minutes to come up with what we want to know." I looked at him hopefully. "I can tie into it right now, if you'd like."

He nodded his consent, and a few minutes later the computer began glowing and revealing its information to us.

6

The Curator (16 G.E.)

My years weighed heavily upon my massive body as I climbed the escarpment of the Rift Valley, still drawn to the South. Once, as I slept, ants crept up the inside of my trunk; the pain almost maddened me before I could reach water and drown them. I had seen others of my kind die from such physical invasions, or from starvation when they ground away their final set of teeth, or from predation when they lay down, too weak and tired to defend themselves—but I knew that such fates were not meant for me.

Time pressed heavily upon me, burning at my insides as the sun burnt upon my back, urging me onward. A lioness, feeding upon a waterbuck, growled at me, prepared to hold her ground; I raised my trunk and bellowed at her, and she retreated, not even daring to snarl as I passed by. A crocodile attacked my leg as I crossed a shallow stream; I picked him up and broke him in half. A herd of impalas blocked my path; I rushed down upon them, asserting my right to be there, and they fled in terror.

*I became foul of temper and sore of spirit as I urged my
ancient body along its journey. I did not suffer silently, but
broke the stillness of the African air with shrill, high-pitched
blasts of anger, as I warned both men and beasts not to stand
in my path as I hurried onward to confront my destiny.*

The Museum of African Antiquities was a mag-
nificent if misnamed structure. For one thing, it covered a
period of only three hundred years, from 1780 to 2080 A.D.;
for another, it dealt not with all of Africa, nor even East
Africa, but solely with the relics of Kenya's past, as befitted
an institution that had been moved in its entirety from
Nairobi to its new marble-and-glass edifice on the colony
planet of New Kenya.

New Kenya itself was an abundant world, teeming with
life, crisscrossed by hundreds of clear rivers, blessed with
fertile soil, which had been ceded to the overpopulated
nation of Kenya by the Republic just after the dawn of the
Galactic Era in the 30th century A.D. There had been
considerable sentiment for calling the capital New Nairobi,
but eventually it bore the name of Kenyatta City in honor
of the *Mzee*, the Wise Old Man, who had delivered Kenya
from the British and guided it through its first tentative
years of independence. Kenyatta City now numbered half
a million citizens, with another million residing in the prin-
cipalities of New Mombasa, Little Naivasha, Nyerere City,
and Kericho Town, and the remaining two hundred thousand living and working on the farms that were making a
vigorous attempt to encircle the colony world at the equator.

Like all successful colony planets, New Kenya had survived some minimal terraforming, some major population
influxes, and some serious political adjustments as it became
a functioning member of Mankind's infant-but-burgeoning
Republic. New bacterial infestations were met with new
medications, new soil conditions were met with new crop

hybrids, new responsibilities as a member of a galactic community were met with new governmental departments, and new debts were met with new sources of taxation.

And when the taxation reached limits beyond which the government dared not go, then belts were tightened and expenditures were cut. One such expenditure was the operating budget for the Museum of African Antiquities.

"The situation is as follows," announced Joshua Kijano, the museum's Chief Curator, to his department heads. "We will now be open to the public only three hours a day, four days a week. Our maintenance and security staffs have been cut in half. All museum personnel have been asked to take a fifteen percent cut in salary. Your new salaries will be frozen, and there will be no cost-of-living increases for the foreseeable future. If any of you feel you cannot work under these conditions, I will certainly understand, and will be happy to write a glowing letter of recommendation for your resumé." He paused and looked at his six senior employees, then sighed. "Well, we all knew it was coming. I'm sure you'll all want time to consider your options. I'll be in my office for the rest of the day, as well as tomorrow morning." He looked directly at a plump, white-haired woman. "Esther, I'd appreciate it if you'd stay behind for a few minutes."

The others all left, speaking in low, worried whispers, and Esther Kamau remained in Kijano's curiously uncluttered office. It bore the usual diplomas and commendations, but was lacking in the artifacts and oddities that usually filled a curator's office to overflowing.

"Please sit down, Esther," he said, walking behind his sleek, polished desk to his own chair.

"Just how bad is it, Joshua?" she asked, seating herself opposite him.

"Terrible," he answered. "How many years have the

two of us put into the museum between us—seventy-five? Eighty?"

"Eighty-three," she responded. "And now they want to kill it, don't they?"

"Not all of it."

"Just the important parts," she said.

"They're *all* important parts."

"The parts you and I have spent our lives working on, then," she amended.

He nodded. "You are no doubt aware that we have had an offer for the butterfly collection."

"It took more than five centuries to put that collection together back on Earth," she said. "Doesn't that mean anything to them?"

"Evidently not," he replied. "At any rate, the Natural History Museum on Far London had made a very substantial bid."

"There is no possible way that we can put a price on the butterfly collection. It's the most extensive such collection ever assembled."

"We *didn't* put a price on it," he replied unhappily. "*They* did. And, unfortunately, they made their bid directly to the government."

"They're no fools," she said. "They knew we'd turn them down."

"They also knew that some pretty bureaucrat would suddenly see the museum as a new source of income," replied Kijano. He stared across the desk at her. "That's what I've been fighting about during the past two weeks."

"I thought you were fighting for our budget."

He shook his head grimly. "That's what I told the others. In point of fact, I lost *that* battle in the first twenty minutes." He paused. "I've been fighting to save the museum."

"And?"

"We've reached a compromise."

"The butterflies?"

"The butterflies are just the beginning," he said bitterly.

"What, then?" she demanded apprehensively.

"They agreed that all departments pertaining directly to New Kenya's cultural heritage should remain intact." He paused. "I thought I should warn you, before you make any serious plans to remain here as Curator of Animal Exhibits, that I was unable to protect *your* department."

"I knew it," she said in a dull monotone.

"I've tendered my resignation in protest, effective two weeks from now," he said. "Why don't you consider doing the same, Esther? The Republic has plenty of museums that would be happy to have two curators with our experience."

"And let some bureaucrat who doesn't know a mammal from a reptile dismantle what it took you and me a lifetime to build?" she demanded. "Our wildlife is every bit as much a part of our heritage as our artwork and tribal costumes, Joshua. Our relationship to it helped make us what we are!"

Kijano sighed deeply. "You know it and I know it, but I couldn't make the government see it that way." He fidgeted nervously with his hands and finally clasped them together with fingers interlaced. "Their position is that the other departments are displaying the history and cultural heritage of the people who live here on New Kenya, while the Department of Animal Exhibits is merely offering displays that are more appropriate to a natural history museum located on Earth itself."

"That's utterly ridiculous!"

"I know," he said wearily. "But they were bound and determined to sell *something* off, and this was the best I could do."

"Don't they know that these exhibits are irreplaceable?" demanded Esther Kamau heatedly. "Once you sell the butterflies or the seashells, you can never put a collection of them together again!"

"Of course they know it," replied Kijano. "But there is a difference between knowing and caring. These are politicians: right now all they care about is a twenty-nine percent inflation rate and the poor showing that the shilling makes against the Republic credit."

"The economy will improve with or without selling off a collection of priceless exhibits that took more than a millennium to put together."

"They don't *care* what condition the economy's in five or ten years from now," he explained patiently. "They're all up for election in the next year or two."

"One butterfly collection isn't going to solve their problems," she said adamantly.

"We're talking about more than the butterfly collection," he said.

"Will there be *anything* left when they're done with their auctions, Joshua?"

"I hope so. They've agreed to let us keep a few of the major exhibits: the bongo and okapi, Ahmed of Marsabit, the record Nile perch, the last impala, the last cheetah . . ."

"We have more than six thousand items on display, and you're telling me that keeping *six* of them is a compromise?"

"No," he replied. "Keeping the other five departments intact is the compromise."

"Well, I think it stinks!"

"So do I, but the alternative was worse."

She paused, considering her options. "Can't we get the press on our side?" she asked at last.

"I've already tried," said Kijano. "The networks don't care, and the kind of publications that do care reach perhaps two percent of the populace, all of whom were on our side to begin with."

"You didn't try hard enough," she said accusingly.

"That's not fair, Esther," said Kijano reproachfully. "You're concerned with your department; I was fighting for the whole museum."

"I'm sorry," she said more gently. "I know you did your best." She paused. "But it wasn't good enough. We've got to think of something more. We can't let a bunch of self-centered, short-sighted, ignorant, immoral politicians dismember a collection that took fifteen centuries to build!"

"There's nothing left to do," he said helplessly.

"There's always something."

"I can't permit you to do anything that will jeopardize the rest of the museum," he warned her.

She stared at him for a long minute. "You're a sweet man, Joshua, but you're very naive," she said at last. "Don't you realize that if you let them get away with this, the other departments will go next? You're sitting on millions of shillings' worth of gemstones. How long do you think you can keep them, once they've run out of seashells and stuffed lions?"

"I have their assurances . . ." he began.

She snorted contemptuously. "How much do you suppose their assurances are worth, once they've decimated the Department of Animal Exhibits?"

"Not much," he admitted. "That's why I've tendered my resignation. I've devoted too much of my life to the museum to watch them sell it off piece by piece." He paused. "Are you sure you won't consider resigning too?"

She shook her head. "We can't all run away, or there will be no one left to fight them. They've got to be stopped, Joshua."

"They're the government," he said. "You *can't* stop them."

"I can try," she responded.

* * *

The museum's Board of Directors, many of them political office holders, refused to accept Joshua Kijano's resignation, but insisted that he remain to serve out his contract and oversee the dispersal of the Department of Animal Exhibits. He tested their decision in court, lost, and reluctantly agreed to stay on for the remaining fourteen months of his contract.

The butterfly collection was the first to go. The agreement had been made, and Esther Kamau was powerless to stop it.

After that, it became a holding action, a war of attrition with the hope that the economy would improve before the final climactic battle.

The museum on Binder X wanted the plains animal collection. She got in touch with her counterpart through an intermediary, explained the situation, and managed to save the buffalo and the carnivores while giving up the gazelles and the antelope.

The university on Sirius V wanted the Lake Turkana fossils. She forged the inventory and kept the nineteen finest specimens, shipping off the remaining 236 after dragging out the process as long as she could.

The seashell collection, some 18,000 pieces strong, went on the block next, bid for by both Greenveldt and Pollux IV. She had an understanding friend on the board of the Greenveldt Museum, accepted their bid, and with her friend's collusion managed to keep two hundred of the rarest shells.

And then Gregory Rousseau, Governor of Daedalus II, a millionaire who had made his fortune building spaceships for the military and spent most of his spare time hunting on the Inner Frontier, announced that he wanted the tusks of the fabled Kilimanjaro Elephant for his private collection.

She waited two weeks, then sent him a message explaining that the tusks were not among the items that the museum had placed on the market.

When she did not hear from him again, she assumed that the matter was over—but a month later she was summoned to Joshua Kijano's office.

He waited until she had seated herself before producing a personal letter from Rousseau, which he pushed across the desk to her. She glanced at it briefly, sighed, and placed it back on the desk.

"Did you tell Governor Rousseau that the tusks of the Kilimanjaro Elephant are not for sale?" he asked.

"Yes, I did."

"You have the list of exempt exhibits that I negotiated with the government, Esther—and the tusks aren't on it."

"This is a special case," she replied. "The tusks of the Kilimanjaro Elephant are not only the greatest single trophy ever taken, but they have historical significance as well."

"What significance?"

"They were the major issue in a presidential campaign in Kenya in the year 2057 A.D."

"Really?" he said, surprised. "I knew nothing about that."

"Then allow me to recommend some history books and tapes to you," she replied. "They are the most important exhibit the museum owns."

"I'd like to see those books," he said earnestly. "If what you say is true, I can go to the government and present the case for keeping the tusks." Suddenly the enthusiasm vanished from his face.

"What's the matter, Joshua?"

"They'll never accept it," he said with a sigh. "Governor Rousseau has offered us three hundred thousand credits. That's more than two million New Kenya shillings!"

"But I thought we were talking about selling our collections off to museums, so the people could always have access to it. This man isn't even a Kenyan, Joshua, and he wants it for his own private collection!"

"The government won't look at that," said Kijano. "They'll look at his three hundred thousand credits, and they'll jump at his offer."

"We can sell him one of our last two rhinos for that amount."

"He doesn't want a rhino," said Kajano. "He wants the tusks. He was quite explicit about that."

"If it's tusks he wants, tell him to triple his offer and he can have Ahmed," she said. "But the Kilimanjaro Elephant's tusks must stay here."

"Ahmed of Marsabit is the most famous elephant in our history," replied Kijano, "the only animal that was ever protected by presidential decree—and not just any president, but the *Mzee* himself. The government has already agreed to let us keep him."

"The ivory of the Kilimanjaro Elephant is more important," she insisted.

"But it's not on the list."

"I don't care about the list!" she snapped. "I'm the curator of the Department of Animal Exhibits, and I say that the tusks are the most important item we possess!"

He stared at her for a moment, then sighed wearily.

"Esther, if I turn him down, he's just going to contact the government, and they'll accept his offer. All a refusal will do is postpone the inevitable."

"Then let's postpone it," she said. "What can they do to you—fire you? You've already tried to quit and they wouldn't allow it."

He smiled. "You have a point." The smile vanished. "But he *will* go to the government after I turn him down. After all, he's a planetary governor; he has highly-placed friends."

"I'm sure he will," she replied. "But you and I aren't exactly an army. We can only fight this battle one day at a time."

Three weeks later Rousseau's representative went directly to the government of New Kenya, money was exchanged, and Esther Kamau, after considerable thought, overcame her grief and her rage long enough to choose her last battlefield.

Seventeen days later, almost to the minute, the computer beeped, and Esther Kamau looked up from her cluttered desk.

"Yes?"

"This is Joshua," said Kijano. "He's here."

"Who's here?"

"Governor Rousseau." Kijano paused awkwardly. "If this will be too painful for you, I can take him to the tusks."

"No," she replied, rising. "I'll meet you there."

She walked through the pristine corridors, past the empty display cases and barren pedestals, and finally entered the small room that housed the two pillars of ivory in a huge glass case.

Kijano entered the chamber a few minutes later, accompanied by a tall, tanned, muscular, middle-aged man who sported a shock of bushy gray hair. A quartet of younger men followed them at a respectful distance.

"Esther," said Kijano, "this is Governor Gregory Rousseau of Daedalus II."

"I know," she said, ignoring the governor's extended hand while staring intently at him.

"Is something wrong?" asked Rousseau curiously.

"I just want to see what kind of man buys the trophies of some other hunter," she said bluntly.

"I am not merely a hunter," answered Rousseau smoothly. "I'm also a collector." He paused. "I realize that you were unhappy to sell the tusks. Let me assure you that they will be protected with the finest security system that money can buy."

"I'm sure they will," she said. "And I'm also sure that no one but you and your friends will ever see them again."

"From time to time I open my country estate to the public," he replied easily.

"Our museum is open to the public every day," she said.

"But your public is more concerned with the national debt than with the national treasures," he noted with a smile. "Believe me, this will work out best for all parties concerned."

"I do *not* believe you, Governor Rousseau," she said.

He seemed about to answer her, then shrugged and turned questioningly to Kijano.

"The governor has brought a crew along to take the ivory to his private ship," Kijano informed her.

"I've given the matter considerable thought," said Esther, "and I can't allow it."

"What?" demanded Rousseau.

"The economic crisis is a momentary thing," she said slowly. "The tusks of the Kilimanjaro Elephant belong to the ages. I am sorry that you have been cast as the villain in the piece, but I have devoted my entire life to preserving antiquities for the public. I have done it because once lost, they can never be replaced or recreated, and I cannot let some crass political agreement rob us of our most precious artifacts."

"I don't think you understand the situation," said Rousseau. "I sympathize with your point of view, but the tusks are mine. They have already been paid for."

"Then I implore you, a man who has spent most of his life in public service, to serve the public one more time and donate them back to the museum," said Esther.

"It's out of the question," he said bluntly. "I paid for

them, they're mine, and I'm here to take them back to the Daedalus system with me."

"They're not going anywhere," she replied calmly.

"What are you talking about?" demanded Rousseau.

"Esther, what's going on here?" added Kijano, looking very worried.

"Joshua," she said, turning to him, "we have to draw the line somewhere. We can't let them destroy what took almost fifteen hundred years to build."

"That sounds remarkably like a threat," said Rousseau, no longer either amused or solicitous.

"That is precisely what it is, Governor," she replied.

"And how is one unarmed woman going to stop my crew from taking the tusks with them?" he asked.

"One unarmed woman couldn't possibly stop you," she said. "That is why I have placed an explosive device in the base of one of the tusks. The moment anyone touches it, it will destroy this wing of the museum and everything in it."

"Which tusk?" asked Rousseau, frowning.

"I don't believe I'm going to tell you."

"This is ridiculous!" he snapped. "I will simply have an anti-demolition team come here and disable the device, and the only thing that will have changed is that you will spend the next few years in jail."

"It is a very sensitive device," she said calmly. "The slightest vibration will trigger the explosive mechanism."

Rousseau turned once again to Kijano. "Is she telling the truth?"

"I have no idea," admitted Kijano.

"What do you think?"

"I think," said Kijano, considering his answer carefully, "that I would not like to be inside the museum if you decide to move the tusks."

Rousseau ordered his men to wait outside, then turned his attention back to Esther Kamau.

"All right," he said. "What is it you want? More money?"

"If I wanted money, your offer would have been more than sufficient," she replied.

"Then what *do* you want?"

"Perhaps I should tell you what I *don't* want."

"Please do," said Rousseau.

"This museum—not the building, which is new, but the exhibits, which are ancient—has been my whole life. More to the point, almost two thousand dedicated scientists have made it their life's work over the past fifteen centuries. They did it for personal glory and out of driving curiosity, to be sure—but they also did it for the people of Kenya, and now we are perpetuating their work for the people of New Kenya. This is our history, our past; it is everything we have been and everything we are now, and as such it belongs to the people. What I don't want, and cannot allow, is the museum's slow, day-by-day emasculation." She paused. "I would sooner destroy it all at once."

"But surely the sale of its treasures is preferable to their destruction," said Rousseau. "I, for one, am willing to sign an agreement allowing you the option of repurchasing the tusks if I or my heirs should ever resell them, and I am certain that all other purchasers would be willing to make the same concession."

"What good is such an agreement when the items in question will be spread across two hundred thousand light-years, when some of them may not come on the market again for millennia?" she responded.

"The agreement offers you at least the possibility of eventually correcting what you think is a cataclysmic mistake on the part of your government," said Rousseau. "The destruction of the tusks and the other exhibits would eliminate even that possibility."

"There is a third alternative," she said.

"Oh?"

"Let the tusks remain here, where they belong."

He shook his head, not without compassion. "I can't let you blackmail me."

"Then hear what I say about the museum rather than the device, and let me reason with you."

"First disable the device, and then I'll listen."

"I don't trust you, Governor."

"To listen?"

"To make the right decision *after* you've listened."

He fell silent for a moment, staring at the two pillars of ivory, then turned to her again.

"Why the tusks?" he asked at last.

"I don't understand."

"I know for a fact that you've sold off most of your stuffed animals, as well as your shell and butterfly collections. What it is about the tusks that made you decide to take this stand?"

"They represent everything that made Kenya great," she said.

"What do you mean?" he asked. "I know I'm not that well-acquainted with their history, but I assumed that they were the trophies of a hunting expedition."

She shook her head and gazed at the ivory.

"They *are* Kenya," she said passionately. "Kenya was wild animals, and they belonged to the greatest animal of all. Kenya was an ivory market, and they were sold at auction. Kenya was a colony that gained its independence from Great Britain, and they were the last vestige of British colonialism. Kenya has produced great men, and they were instrumental in allowing one of the greatest, Jacob Thiku, to finish the work he had begun. Kenya has expanded to the stars, and they have made the trip with us. Kenya is the microcosm of human evolution, from primitive man to city dweller to star traveler, and they have survived every era. They are the exemplar of Kenyan history." She paused and stared at him. "Everything we are resides in them."

"I see," said Rousseau, scrutinizing her carefully. "They must have enormous meaning to you."

"To all Kenyans," she corrected him.

"But especially to their curator."

"It is my job to preserve them for the ages," she said. "That is why I cannot allow you to take them with you. Do you understand now?"

He smiled at her.

"Oh, yes," he replied. "Now I fully understand." He turned to Kijano. "You have the keys to the case?"

"It has no keys," said Kijano. "It responds to the thumb-prints of senior staff members."

"Please open it," ordered Rousseau.

"But the device . . ."

"There is no device," said Rousseau confidently.

Kijano approached the case gingerly and placed his thumb over the scanner, and the glass door swung open.

Rousseau walked over and touched each of the tusks, then turned to Esther Kamau.

"I will not press charges against you," he said. "It would be like jailing a priest for protecting the Holy Grail."

He left the chamber to get his men, and Esther, after a moment's silence, turned to her old friend.

"I'm sorry, Joshua," she said. "But I had to try."

"I know," said Kijano.

"I couldn't bring myself to do it."

"I never thought you could," he said gently.

The Museum of African Antiquities sold off its last item—a hand-crafted Nandi spear—less than a year later.

Esther Kamau was not around to observe that event. She had died, for no reason the doctors could determine except an absence of the will to live, seven months earlier. Joshua Kijano put in a request to the government that they purchase a small, tasteful monument for her grave. The request did not come up for consideration for six years, by which time Kijano, too, was dead, and nobody quite knew what Esther Kamau had done to deserve such a governmental expenditure, so the request was tabled and soon forgotten in the wake of the news that the government's austerity program had been so successful that the economy was now stagnating and experts were desperately looking for new methods of stimulating it.

The museum, which had been standing empty for half a decade, was gutted and redesigned, emerging from its facelift a few months later as the massive new Bureau of Economic Development. Everybody in the New Kenyan government took pride in the fact that they had finally found a meaningful function for a run-down old building that had seemingly outlived its usefulness.

Sixth Interlude (6303 G.E.)

The computer stopped glowing, and Mandaka looked across the room at me.

"Has your curiosity been assuaged?" he asked.

"For the moment," I replied.

"The ironic thing is that the one Kenyan who actually tried to save the tusks wasn't even a Maasai," he said.

"Oh? How do you know?"

"Kamau is a Kikuyu name," explained Mandaka. "But

the mere fact that she held a position of prestige and authority was enough to tell me that she did not belong to the Maasai," he added bitterly.

"Why?" I asked.

"It is late, and I am thirsty, Mr. Rojas," he replied, getting to his feet and stretching his massive body. "I think I should be going home."

"I'm not at all sleepy," I said. "I'll be happy to walk you home if you live nearby."

"I do not live nearby," he responded. "Are you still willing to accompany me?"

"Yes."

"And to see how the last Maasai lives?" he asked, amused.

"Like anyone else, I would suppose," I offered.

"You do not believe that for a moment, Mr. Rojas," said Mandaka.

"No, I don't," I admitted.

"That gnawing curiosity again," he said, unperturbed. "All right, Mr. Rojas—I will show you what no one else has seen since I took up residence on this planet."

"Thank you."

He walked to the door, waited until I ordered the lights to dim, and went out into the hall, waiting patiently while I reprogrammed the security system and the lock.

"I don't suppose this will keep you out," I commented, "but there is always a chance that someone was watching you. At least this will make them go to some extra effort."

"I would not worry about it, Mr. Rojas," said Mandaka. "You don't have anything that anyone would want."

I was about to make an angry retort when it occurred to me that he was quite correct, so I remained silent and led him to the airlift, and we gently descended to the main floor. The Hesporite doorman had been replaced by a female Mendorian, a lovely catlike creature with supple muscles and flowing yellow fur. I told her that I probably would not be back until the following night, as I planned to go to the office after leaving Mandaka's apartment.

We walked out the front door, took a slow-moving slide-walk to the next intersection, and then crossed over to a westbound expresswalk that took us through the city and deposited us on the west side in less than five minutes. We transferred to three more local slidewalks, and eventually found ourselves standing before a tall glass-and-chrome building that glistened in the moonlight.

"My humble thatched hut," announced Mandaka with a sardonic smile.

We passed through a rigid security system at the main entrance, then walked to the left side of the lobby and boarded a private airlift that took us directly to the top floor, emerging some seventy-eight levels above the ground. We stepped out into a long, carpeted corridor that was brightly illuminated by some hidden source, turned to our right, and rode it halfway down the hallway, stopping when we came to the first door.

Mandaka murmured something in a language I had never heard before, waited for the security system to identify his retina and bone structure, and then placed his palm to a sensing device, after which the door dilated long enough for us to enter his apartment and then closed quietly but securely behind us.

"Lights," ordered Mandaka, and suddenly the entire apartment was bathed in light.

I found myself standing in a small dirt yard surrounded by an almost-impenetrable fence of thorn bushes. To my right was was a thatch-roofed hut, the walls of which seemed to be made of dried mud. Where there should have been white, polished walls, there was a panoramic view of a barren, parched savannah.

I followed him through the compound into the interior of the hut. Where there should have been furniture, there was only a trio of primitive mats. A fire blazed in the middle of it, yet cast no heat—which gave me the clue I needed.

"A holographic projection?" I asked.

Mandaka nodded. "Yes. You are actually standing on a carpet, and I am reasonably certain that the management would look upon huts made of cow dung with some disfavor. I chose this particular apartment because the ceiling is some twenty feet high, which allows more scope to the projections." He smiled. "I must change my clothing. I'll be with you in a moment."

With that, he lowered his head and walked through the small doorway of the imaginary hut, though of course he could have remained erect and walked right through the projection. As I waited for him, I examined my surroundings more carefully. Leaning against the wall were two long spears, the metal points at least as long as the wooden shafts; I touched one of them gingerly and discovered that it was quite real. I thought I could hear a small animal bleating, but I could see no trace of it, and decided that it was another projection. A pot containing some kind of crushed vegetable was on the fire, but it, too, proved to be merely an illusion.

"Welcome to my home, Mr. Rojas," said Mandaka, reentering the hut.

He had completely removed his outfit and now wore a single red garment that was slung loosely over one shoulder and hung down to just below his knees. In one hand was an ancient gourd containing milk, which he lifted to his lips; after he took a long swallow he placed it carefully on the floor.

"It's . . . unusual," I said.

"I am the last Maasai," he said, sitting down cross-legged

on a mat by the fire. "There is no one else to honor or observe the ancient ways."

"This isn't here just to impress me," I noted, puzzled. "You actually *live* like this."

"I follow such of the old rituals that will not bring me into conflict with the authorities," he replied. "Which means that I do not slaughter goats and read their entrails, nor have I proven my manhood by killing a lion with a spear."

"It would be a good trick," I said. "The last lion died in 2088 A.D."

"Ah, yes—the Wilford Braxton's expert!" he said with a chuckle.

"The Maasai also measured their wealth by the number of cattle they owned," I said. "But I see no holographic cattle outside your doorway."

"That is because my cattle are real, Mr. Rojas," he replied. "I own meat herds on eleven different worlds. That is how I have made my fortune."

"I assume all the other rooms of your apartment are equally . . . evocative of earlier times?"

"Except for my office, from which I control the purchase and sale of my herds."

I paused, trying to think of a polite way to word my next question. None came to me, so I simply blurted it out:

"Don't you find it uncomfortable?"

"I find it *necessary*, Mr. Rojas," he replied seriously. "When I am gone, there will be no one to remember our traditions or to carry them on. We were a noble people, Mr. Rojas; we disdained all the trappings of Western civilization long after every other tribe had been assimilated into your culture. We lived in harmony with our environment, we asked no favors of anyone and we offered none. We asked only to be allowed to live as we had always lived . . ." His voice trailed off for a moment, and he seemed lost in thought.

"Did you know, Mr. Rojas, that we even practiced conservation with our own cattle? We mixed their blood with their milk, but we never killed them."

"Your whole race lived on milk and blood?" I asked, surprised.

"For the most part." He paused, looking off at some point in space and time that only he could see, and the flickering fire cast strange shadows on his dark face. "We were a great people once. Our *elmorani*, our young warriors, were feared by all who saw them, our women were coveted by all other warriors, our lands were the richest in East Africa. We spoke only our own language, and disdained Swahili and all European tongues." He looked over to me and smiled bitterly. "And then the changes came, so slowly that they were imperceptible. We lost a battle against the Lumbwa. The Nandi fought us to a standstill. Our young men began wearing shirts and shorts. We went to the hospital rather than the *mundumugu* when we were ill. Before long more of us spoke Swahili than Maasai and we were reduced to begging shillings from tourists in exchange for having our photographs taken—and yet we were numerically far stronger than in the years of our greatness."

He sighed and continued, barely aware of my presence. "And when independence came, they handed the countries to men like Kenyatta and Nyerere, who were not too proud to take them. When Man achieved spaceflight, he colonized New Kenya and Uganda II and Nyerere, but the Maasai were left behind with no lands, no cattle, not even the memory of their own language." He paused and seemed to come back to the present. "And now there is only me, Mr. Rojas," he concluded. "I alone can redeem my race."

"How?"

"There is something that I must do, that only I *can* do."

"And that is why you need the ivory?"

He nodded. "That is why I need the ivory."

"How can the ivory redeem your people?" I persisted.

"I will tell you that, Mr. Rojas, when you have found the ivory and I have taken possession of it."

"I'll hold you to that promise."

"I hope that I have the opportunity to keep it."

"You will," I assured him. "Even as we speak, the computer is searching for the ivory."

"I know," he said with a deep sigh. "But even now, you have no idea how important it is. I will never marry, nor have a child. If I do not redeem my people, no one ever will."

"Why will you never marry?" I asked. "I know that the Maasai used to steal women from other tribes, so it obviously can't be that you must find a pure-blooded Maasai woman."

"Since the 24th century A.D., no Maasai has married outside the tribe," he replied. "Or at least none was supposed to; I imagine a few broke the law and took non-Maasai mates."

"But surely they never found themselves in the situation of having no Maasai women to choose from," I said. "Certainly that rule cannot apply to the last Maasai."

"It doesn't, Mr. Rojas," he acknowledged.

"Then I repeat my question: why can you never marry?"

"Because I am not a man."

I stared at him uncomprehendingly. "I don't understand."

"No Maasai boy can become an *elmoran*, a man, until he has been circumcised. He cannot take his place among his peers, he cannot offer counsel to his elders, and he cannot wed." He paused to make sure I was following him. "I have never been circumcised, Mr. Rojas. By the law of my people, I am still a boy."

"Circumcision is a very minor operation," I said. "Surely any competent doctor can perform it upon you."

"Unquestionably."

"Then why not have it done so that you can marry and live a normal life?"

"I will tell you that when you find the ivory," he said. "But as I told you earlier this evening, I am not destined to marry or to father children. I wish this were not the case, for a family would bring me great joy—but I must tread a different path."

"What kind of path?"

He stared at me, and for the first time his face briefly reflected his emotions.

"A more terrible path, Mr. Rojas, than I hope you can imagine."

Then the mask of the arrogant Maasai fell back in place and he offered me a sip of his milk. I had a feeling that this was a singular gesture that he had made rarely, if at all, during his life, and I accepted the gourd.

Just before lifting it to my lips, I peered into its dark interior.

"It's all right, Mr. Rojas," he said with an amused smile. "There is no blood in it."

I took a long swallow—the first milk I had had since I was a boy—and handed it back to him.

"Thank you for sharing it with me," I said sincerely.

"I have a great deal of milk and no one to drink it with," he said with a noncommittal shrug. Suddenly he got to his feet. "Come, Mr. Rojas—I will show you the rest of my apartment. There will never be another Maasai domicile, so you might as well satisfy your curiosity."

I stood up and followed him, instinctively ducking my head to avoid bumping into the top of the imaginary doorway, and a moment later I found myself in yet another room that resembled the inside of a Maasai dwelling, albeit a much larger one.

There were a number of lion's hair headdresses, each carefully displayed and labeled, and next to each was a distinctive spear bearing the design of its owner.

"They look like museum pieces," I said admiringly.

"No museum has such a collection," he replied with a note of pride. "This headdress," he said, pointing to a particularly impressive one, "belonged to Nelion, after whom they named the highest peak of Mount Kenya."

He spent the next few minutes giving me the history of each headdress and weapon, his face alive with such interest as I had heretofore seen only when he discussed the ivory. Finally we came to a last headdress, quite insignificant in comparison with the others, and constructed entirely of dried grasses.

"And what is this one?" I asked, gesturing toward it.

"That is my own headdress," he replied. "There are no lions left on Earth, so I was forced to use the materials at hand."

"Are you telling me that you grew up in surroundings like these?" I asked unbelievingly. "That you lived in a hut?"

"A *manyatta*," he replied. "The hut is merely a part of the whole, which also encompasses all neighboring huts and the thorn barrier surrounding them."

"But how was that possible?" I asked. "Surely the authorities would not permit you to live like—pardon me—but like a savage."

"I told you: Earth is almost deserted, and the few authorities who remain have no interest in telling a family living miles from anyone else in Kenya how they must house and feed themselves." He paused. "I was thirteen years old before I saw any human being other than my parents and my grandparents."

"You never saw or played with any other children?" I asked, astonished.

"Never."

"And you actually lived as your ancestors lived?"

"We observed the form, but not the letter," he replied. "It is true that I lived in a hut made of mud and wattle—but the hut contained three computers. And while I have never physically attended any school, I hold advanced degrees in economics, business, and African history."

"African history I can understand," I said. "But why the other two?"

"Because I knew that someday I would have to leave Earth to determine if I were truly the last Maasai; and if I were, that I would have to search for the ivory. Both quests were certain to prove very expensive."

"When did you finally leave?" I asked.

"Twenty-six years ago, when my parents had both died."

"And you've never been back?"

He shook his head. "Not yet."

"That sounds like you plan to return someday."

"Someday," he said noncommittally.

"I envy you," I said.

"Oh? Why?"

"Because I've always wanted to see the birthplace of our race," I said.

"You're a wealthy man," he said. "Why haven't you made the trip?"

"I've planned it a couple of times," I admitted. "But something always came up."

"Like the ivory?"

"Similar things," I acknowledged. "Problems that were so fascinating that I couldn't walk away from them." I sighed. "Perhaps someday I'll actually find the time to get there."

"I wouldn't be at all surprised," he said.

There was a momentary silence.

"Perhaps I had better be going," I said at last. "It's been a long day, and I'm tired."

Mandaka walked to another doorway.

"Come with me for just a moment before you go, Mr. Rojas," he said. "I have something that I think may interest you."

I followed him, and entered another holographic projection of a large hut. This one contained several primitive drawings and carvings, and he directed my attention to one drawing in particular, that of a huge elephant with such disproportionately large tusks that it seemed totally out of balance. It had been crudely executed on a large piece of bark, and had been meticulously framed and preserved.

"What do you think, Mr. Rojas?" he asked, studying my reaction.

I walked over to the drawing, studying it intently.

"Is that *him*?" I asked.

"I believe so," he replied. "The dates are right, and the artist drew several other elephants, none of them with ivory like this."

"How big was he?" I asked, feeling a strange sense of awe.

"We know that the tusks were each over ten feet in length," he answered, "so a normal man would have come up to *here*." He indicated a spot a little more than halfway up the elephant's leg.

"He must have been a monster!" I mused.

"He was the greatest animal that ever lived," said Mandaka with conviction.

Even in the drawing he had such presence, such vitality, that I found it hard to imagine that he did not still tread across the plains and scrubland of East Africa, his footsteps reverberating through Kenya's troubled history, his trumpet louder than the thunder.

"Have you any other representations of him?" I asked at last.

"Just the one," replied Mandaka.

"I thank you for allowing me to see it," I said.

"You are welcome."

"And now I really must leave," I announced. "I have work to do."

"I thought you were going to bed," he noted.

"I can sleep in my office," I said. "There is something I must do first."

"I know."

I stared at him curiously. "I thought you didn't approve of my delving into the ivory's history."

"I was wrong," he said. "I have concluded that the hunter can never know too much about the hunted."

He led me through the various projections until we reached the front door.

"I'll hear from you tomorrow?" I asked.

He nodded.

"Thank you for your hospitality," I said as the door dilated.

"Thank you for coming. You are the first guest I have had."

"Since you moved here," I said, stepping out into the corridor. "You told me that before."

"Since I left Earth," he replied, as the corridor began transporting me to the airlift. I looked back to see if he was jesting, but the door had already closed.

The office was dark when I entered it. I ordered the computer to set the illumination at low intensity and to make me a cup of coffee, then sat down on my chair, adjusted it to the angle at which I wished to recline, and clasped my hands behind my head.

"Computer?"

"Yes, Duncan Rojas?"

"What percentage of your capacity are you currently using to search for the ivory?"

"Seventy-two point three percent."

"Divert five percent to my next request and continue the search."

"Working . . . done."

"I just saw a drawing, supposedly from life, of the Kilimanjaro Elephant," I said.

"According to the data I possess, no such drawing exists. I will adjust my databank to coincide with your observation."

"Fine," I said. "But it occurs to me that if one such eyewitness account, so to speak, exists, then perhaps there may be others."

"That is logical."

"I want you to access the African history databank in the Main Library Computer at Deluros VIII and see if you can find such an account. Limit your search to accounts ranging from, oh, 1875 A.D. to 1898 A.D." I paused. "They may have been written later, but that is the era they should cover."

"Working . . ."

"And please play Kronize's Missing Concerto."

"Done."

The room was flooded by Kronize's atonal yet compulsively rhythmic music, and a moment later I was sipping my coffee, unconsciously tapping my fingers against the container in time with the concerto.

When I had finished the coffee I tossed the container into the atomizer, then took a dryshower and changed my clothing. As I lay back on the chair, I became unpleasantly aware of a bright series of lights shining in my eyes, realized that I had not ordered the windows to become opaque, issued the order, and lay back, sifting over what I had learned from Mandaka while drifting on the edge of sleep.

"I have found what is very likely a reference to the Kilimanjaro Elephant," announced the computer suddenly.

I sat erect, fully alert.

"Turn off the music," I ordered.

"Done."

"There is an atypical vagueness in your statement," I said. "Why?"

"Because there are no other eyewitness accounts to which this can be compared. However, I have cross-referenced it with all known secondary sources, and the time, the location, and the physical description indicate a 94.32% probability that this was indeed the animal that you know as the Kilimanjaro Elephant."

"Good!" I said eagerly. "Tell me what you have found."

"Working . . ."

7

The Hunter
(1885 A.D.)

I had spent two months walking the baking earth of the Rift Valley, and now, with the last of its major lakes behind me, it was time to ascend once more to the high plateau.

I tested the wind, not once but many times, for with my years had come caution. From the west the scent of green grasses came sweeping across the Loita Plains, and I knew there was cool water in the Mara River, but I turned to the southeast, for it was upon the Loita Plains that I had first met the one being in all the universe capable of instilling fear in me, a pale man who had the power to kill from afar, and I had never returned there.

I paused to rub the parasites from my skin against the base of an acacia tree, then smothered those that remained with dust I blew on them with my trunk. I took a last look at the great rent in the earth's surface, then followed an ancient path up the wall of the eastern escarpment. Birds and monkeys screeched *and fled before me, and when I met a lioness who was coming down the same path she snarled and slunk off into the bushes.*

Then, finally, I reached the high grassland, and began the final stage of my journey.

Old Van der Kamp looked around the barroom at the dusty shack he called the Mbogo Trading Post and totaled up the white faces: three—four, if he counted himself—which was more than he could ever remember being here at the same time.

Named for the buffalo that had given him a game leg before he'd finally managed to put a bullet through its eye, the trading post had been sitting there on the Sand River, gathering customers and termites in equal proportions, for the better part of two decades. In the back room the old Boer kept piles upon piles of skins and ivory, each carefully labeled as to supplier and amount paid, against the day that the rains would come again and the riverboat could come by and pick them up. In an adjacent cellar, buried deep in the earth to help keep them cool, were some twenty kegs of beer. Van der Kamp offered no menu and no food, but if a passing traveler brought enough for everyone, he had no objection to cooking it up.

Hanging on the wall behind the bar were the gleaming white skulls and horns—Van der Kamp could not afford a taxidermist—of kudu, sable, roan, eland, a clutch of gazelles, and the buffalo who had given the outpost its name.

The old man drew himself another beer and observed his clientele. Sitting at one end of the bar in neatly-pressed clothes was the Englishman, Rice, his carefully-trimmed goatee almost pure white, his hands strong and calloused, most of the color washed out of his face from too much exposure to the tropical sun. It was odd, reflected Van der Kamp, but instead of getting darker, the English seemed to lose such color as they had acquired after a few years and wind up paler than when they had come out.

At the opposite end of the bar was Guntermann, the German: bald, moustached, with blue eyes and a suit that had once been white but was now the color of the scorched African earth. Even here inside the shack he wore his pith helmet, more to hide his bald head from view than to protect it from the sun. Still, as strange as he looked, he knew his business; forty-two tusks bearing his name now resided in the storage room.

Sitting quietly at the lone table at the back of the room was Sloane, the first American Van der Kamp had ever seen. Americans were rare in Africa, since their government had no colonial ambitions anywhere on the continent. This one certainly looked out of place, with his cowboy stetson and his Confederate Army uniform, but he had already made a name for himself as an ivory hunter, leading the old Boer to conclude that if there was one thing that the men who stopped at the Mbogo Trading Post had in common, it was that they had nothing in common.

Outside the building, sitting in a sheltered area near the bore hole, were some twenty blacks, bearers and trackers for the three white men. They weren't allowed inside, but Van der Kamp saw to it that they got all the beer they wanted, a foul-smelling Kisi brew that packed quite a punch and for which he charged their employers what he thought was a nominal fee. He had checked them out carefully: a Lumbwa, a Kikuyu, nine Wakamba, half a dozen Nandi, a Wanderobo, and a pair of Bugandas. No Maasai, praise be, which meant that there probably wouldn't be any bloodletting. He stuck his head out the window every few minutes, keeping a watchful eye on the big, well-muscled Lumbwa, just to be on the safe side, but the Lumbwa, sitting off by himself, seemed oblivious to the presence of the other Africans.

"I'll have another," announced Rice as he drained his glass. He looked around the room for a moment. "My treat, if anyone should care to join me."

Sloane, the American, looked up, nodded his agreement, and went back to rolling a cigarette.

"I would be delighted," said the German, taking out a handkerchief and wiping the sweat from his face. "Allow me to introduce myself: I am Erhard Guntermann, late of Munich."

"Guntermann, Guntermann," mused Rice. Suddenly he looked across at the German. "Didn't I hear your name in connection with a slave-running operation some years back?"

"I hope not," said the German with a hearty laugh. "I have done my best to disassociate myself with that particular part of my past." He shrugged. "There wasn't much money in it anyway," he added with a sly smile. "Too much competition from the English." He paused. "Besides, ivory pays much better."

"Gentlemen, the Queen," said Rice, holding his glass up. Nobody followed suit, which didn't seem to bother him at all. "So you're an ivory hunter now?"

Guntermann shook his head. "I'm an ivory *trader*."

"Oh?"

The German nodded. "I go to the Congo, into the rain forest, and when I find tribes that are starved for meat, I supply antelope for them in exchange for ivory." He paused and wiped his face again. "Very profitable," he added with satisfaction.

"But if they can kill elephants, why can't they kill their own meat?" asked Rice, slapping at a tsetse fly that had landed on his neck.

"They don't kill many elephants themselves," explained the German. "But they know where to find the carcasses, and when they find them, they collect the ivory." He paused long enough for a series of hippo grunts from the nearby river to subside. "One pygmy village had so much ivory they used it for fenceposts around their bomas!" The German shook his head in mock sorrow. "Poor people. They have no idea what it's worth."

"Where was this village with ivory fenceposts?" asked Rice curiously.

Guntermann smiled. "Ah, my friend, you do not really expect me to tell you that, do you?"

Rice returned his smile. "No, not really." He continued staring at the German as the bellowing of the hippos began again. "So you're Guntermann."

"That's me," said Guntermann. "And you?"

"Blaney Rice, formerly of Johannesburg."

"Johannesburg," repeated the German. "You were born in Africa?"

"I was born in Manchester, England. I emigrated to South Africa and started a farm there, and when it went broke, I began trading my way north." He paused. "I ended up here twelve years later. That was, oh, about ten years ago."

"You trade ivory?" asked Guntermann with professional interest.

"Not any longer," replied Rice, picking up a nut from a bowl on the bar and tossing it to a vervet monkey that appeared in the window. The monkey screeched and ducked, then picked it up off the ground and reappeared in the window a moment later, looking for another tidbit.

"What *do* you trade?"

Rice smiled. "Photographs."

"Photographs?" repeated the German disbelievingly.

Rice nodded. "I use architect's blueprint paper," he explained. "I trade the photos to the village headmen for salt, trade the salt for copper, the copper for goats, the goats for more salt, and the salt for cattle. It takes half a year to make my circuit and get to the Sudan, where I sell the cattle to the army—but when I'm finished, I've usually made about three thousand pounds on an initial investment of six shillings."

"Before you sold photographs, what?" asked the German, plucking a small insect from his handkerchief, studying it idly, and flicking it to the floor.

"I started out to make my fortune as an ivory hunter," replied Rice, "but I must confess I wasn't very good at it. When I quit, I hadn't so much as a halfpenny to my name, and I discovered that the only thing I had that was worth anything at all to the locals were my cartridges. I traded them for salt, sold the salt for more cartridges, traded them for goats, and kept on going until I reached Ethiopia and sold out for almost two thousand Maria Theresa dollars. It was too hot up there, so I came down here where the weather was more pleasant and there were more tribes to trade with, bought a couple of cameras, and went into business."

"You call *this* pleasant weather?" asked Sloane sardonically.

Rice turned to him. "Have you ever been up in Ethiopia?"

"A couple of times."

"Then you know how hot it gets there."

"Not a hell of a lot hotter than right here," said Sloane.

"You're quite wrong," said Rice adamantly. "No man was meant to live in that heat."

Sloane shrugged and turned his attention back to his beer.

"I have a question for you, my good sir, if you don't mind?" continued Rice.

Sloane stared at him for a moment. "Go ahead," he said at last.

"The native you arrived with," said Rice. "I don't seem to recognize his tribal markings."

"He's a Kikuyu."

"I've never seen one before," said Rice. "I had heard that Kikuyuland was closed to whites."

"It is."

"Then how did you acquire him?"

"He broke a law, and escaped before they could kill him," said Sloane.

"What did he do?"

Sloane shrugged. "I never asked him."

"Are the Kikuyus good trackers?" asked Rice.

"This one's all right," said Sloane noncommittally.

"Not like the Wanderobo, though," said Guntermann with a touch of pride as a change of breeze brought the unmistakable odors of hippopotamus and crocodile to them on the hot, moist air.

"I noticed that you had one with you," commented Rice, fanning himself with his hat, more to chase the smells of the river away than from any serious belief that the effort might make him feel cooler. "Are they as good as people say?"

"My Wanderobo could track a billiard ball down the smoothest street in Berlin," responded Guntermann.

Rice chuckled and finished his beer, then held up his empty glass. "I believe it's someone else's turn?"

"Acknowledged," said Guntermann, slapping down a few coins. "Now that you have brought up the subject of Wanderobo, I saw a Wanderobo woman behind the building when I arrived."

"She is Kisi," answered Van der Kamp. He paused, then added defensively: "And she belongs to me."

"You're a Boer, aren't you?" asked Guntermann.

"Yes."

"I thought Boers hated the blacks."

Van der Kamp shook his head. "We do not hate blacks. We hate only the Zulus, not because they are black but because they are the enemies of our blood."

"And it gets very lonely out here during the long rains, eh?" chuckled Guntermann with a knowing wink.

"Sometimes," said Van der Kamp, still defensive.

"When the British make this land a protectorate," continued Guntermann, "they're going to tell you to get rid of her."

"I've had dealings with the English before," said Van der Kamp grimly. "They do not frighten me."

"May I respectfully suggest that we keep politics out of our discussion, gentlemen?" said Rice. "There's no reason for nationalism out here in the bush."

"Agreed," said Guntermann. He gestured toward Sloane with a smile. "In the interests of international unity, perhaps we should ask our American colleague to remove his military uniform."

"You can ask," said Sloane.

Rice studied the outfit for a moment.

"I see you were a captain, sir," noted the Englishman.

Sloane shook his head. "Nope."

"But your insignia—"

"I bought this outfit after the war."

"Then you didn't see any action?"

Sloane paused before answering. "I saw my share of it."

"Which side were you on?" asked Rice.

"I thought we were supposed to avoid politics," noted Sloane.

Rice loosened a couple of buttons on his shirt and began fanning himself again. "This isn't politics, it's just curiosity," persisted the Englishman. "Why did you choose to buy a Confederate uniform? After all, they lost."

"Reflects the sun more, shows the dust less," answered Sloane.

"And is this hat that which your American cowboys wear?" asked Guntermann, pointing to Sloane's stetson.

"You'd have to ask an American cowboy."

Guntermann threw back his head and laughed. "Well said, sir! By the way, we haven't been introduced. I'm Erhard Guntermann, and this gentleman is Blaney Rice."

"Hannibal Sloane."

"*The* Hannibal Sloane?" asked Rice, raising his voice as the chorus of hippos started up once again.

"Unless there are two of us."

"Your reputation precedes you, sir," said Rice. You're said to be one of the most successful ivory hunters in East Africa."

"One of 'em," agreed Sloane.

"They mention you in the same breath with Selous and Karamojo Bell," said the Englishman, obviously impressed.

"Never met them," said Sloane.

"How many elephants have you killed?" asked Rice.

Sloane finished rolling his cigarette and lit it up.

"A few," he said at last.

"You're being modest."

"Possibly he's the strong, silent type," said Guntermann with an amused smile.

"Possibly," said Sloane.

"Actually," continued the German, "while I don't doubt your accomplishments, the very best elephant hunter of all is less than fifty feet away from this bar at this very minute."

"The big Lumbwa with the hand-axe?" asked Sloane.

The German smiled. "The very one! Have you ever seen a native hunt elephant with an axe?"

"Once," said Sloane.

"This one—Tumo is his name—is the best," said the German proudly.

"Are you suggesting that he can actually kill an elephant with a hand-axe?" asked Rice skeptically.

"With ease."

"I hate to call you on it," said the Englishman, "but I've

hunted a few elephant in my day, and I simply don't believe you."

"I have seen him kill eleven elephants with no weapon but his axe," said Guntermann.

Rice stared thoughtfully at his glass. "Perhaps in the rain forest, where they don't have any maneuvering room," he mused. "Perhaps there—but surely not out here on the savannah!"

"Anywhere," said the German adamantly.

"You're not talking about females or totos?" said Rice, turning to Guntermann. "You're stating that he can bring down a full-grown bull elephant?"

"That is correct."

Rice shook his head. "It can't be done."

"I have seen it done many times," replied Guntermann.

"A six-ton elephant, with nothing but a hand-axe?"

The German nodded emphatically.

"I don't want to call you a liar," said Rice, "but I'm willing to wager that it can't be done."

"Name your price," said the German confidently.

The Englishman pulled a wad of notes out of his wallet, counted them off, and laid them on the bar. "How about fifty pounds?"

"Certainly," agreed Guntermann. He smiled confidently at Rice. "How about one hundred pounds?"

"That's an awful lot of money."

"Either he can kill the elephant or he can't," said the German. "The amount of the bet will not effect the outcome." He paused. "Of course, if you'd rather not . . ."

Rice counted out another fifty pounds. "Done!"

"I accept!" said the German happily. He rummaged through his pockets and pulled out an equivalent amount in marks and Maria Theresa dollars. He pushed both piles of money toward Van der Kamp. "You can hold the stakes."

The Boer nodded his agreement, picked up the money, and tucked it into a pocket.

"There's one condition," said Rice.

"Oh?"

"He's got to make his kill tomorrow. I'm due in Kampala five days from now, and I'll never make it if I don't start tomorrow afternoon."

"That was never mentioned as part of the wager," said the German. "What if we cannot find a bull elephant tomorrow?"

Rice lowered his head in thought, then turned to Sloane. "Mr. Sloane, would you be willing to be my representative on the hunt, to make sure the conditions are fulfilled?

"It could take days," said Sloane. "And I don't work for free."

"That was never my intention," said Rice. "I'll pay you half my winnings."

Sloane shook his head. "I'll take the ivory."

"But if he doesn't make a kill, there won't be any ivory," noted Rice.

"He'll make the kill."

"What make you so certain?" demanded Rice.

"I told you: I've seen a Lumbwa work with an axe before," answered Sloane.

"How the devil can a man kill an elephant with nothing but a hand-axe?" persisted Rice.

"He'll hamstring him," said the American.

"What do you mean?" insisted Rice.

Sloane turned to Guntermann. "It's your Lumbwa; *you* tell him."

The German smiled coyly. "If I start telling people how he does it, who would bet with me?"

"Well, since I've already put up my money and I won't

be here to see it, I'd like *someone* to tell me," said Rice irritably.

"All right," said Sloane. "The Lumbwa will track down the elephant, and approach to within maybe forty yards. Then he'll wait until the wind is right, sneak up behind him, and sever the tendons of a back leg about a foot above the ground." He turned to the German. "Right?"

Gunterman merely smiled.

"Most animals can get along just fine on three legs," added Sloane, "but an elephant's got to have all four. Hamstringing him nails him to the spot."

"All right," said Rice grudgingly. "That demobilizes him. How does he kill him?"

"All elephants are right-handed or left-handed," said Sloane. "The Lumbwa won't strike until he figures out which side the elephant favors."

"What has *that* got to do with anything?" demanded Rice.

"Once he's hamstrung, the elephant will spin around to the side he favors with his trunk outstretched, trying to locate his attacker. Then the Lumbwa will either hack off the trunk with a single stroke, or put a deep gash in it."

"And then?"

"If he's in the middle of a herd, he'll run for cover; otherwise, he'll just stand twenty feet away and wait for it to bleed to death."

"It sounds gruesome!" said Rice.

"It's not a pretty sight," agreed Sloane. "Once I determine that the elephant's done for, I'll stick a bullet in his ear and put him out of his misery."

"And you're sure the Lumbwa can do this?" said Rice.

"Unless he's clumsy," said Sloane. "Everyone makes a mistake sooner or later."

"If it's as easy as you make it sound, why are there still any elephants left at all?" said Rice bitterly.

"I didn't say it was easy," replied Sloane. "I said it was possible.

"I suppose I might as well concede the bet right now," said Rice.

"No," said Guntermann. "We go hunting tomorrow morning."

"Why bother?" said the Englishman.

"You are not the first man to bet against Tumo," answered the German. "I always give him a brand-new Maria Theresa dollar when he wins my money for me. Why cheat him out of it?"

"Why not just pay him?" suggested Sloane.

"He does not work, he does not get paid," replied Guntermann firmly.

"Besides," said Sloane, "there's always a chance he'll mess it up. If he does, you can pick up your winnings from Van der Kamp next time you come through."

"Say, that's right!" said Rice suddenly. "How many chances does he get? I mean, if he's such a clumsy tracker that he scares the elephant off, does that count?"

"He will require only one chance," said Guntermann. "Once he begins his final close stalk, that is the elephant that we bet on."

"You're willing to make that a condition of the wager?" asked Rice.

"I am."

Rice ordered another round of beers as the light began to fail and millions of frogs began croaking in the nearby river.

"For all the ivory and half the winnings, I'll take the Lumbwa out alone," offered Sloane. "We can probably travel much faster that way."

"No," objected Guntermann. "I am going too. I love to watch my Lumbwa in action."

"All right," said Sloane. "But just you and him—no entourage. If we start shooting meat for your boys we may scare all the elephants out of the area—and I don't plan to spend a month of my life waiting for one set of ivory."

"Agreed," said the German. "Will you be taking your Kikuyu?"

"He goes where I go."

Guntermann nodded his approval. "Good! We will need two boys to carry back the ivory."

They set out the next morning, the four of them, walking inland from the river. Tumo, the Lumbwa, and Karenja, Sloane's Kikuyu tracker, studiously ignored each other, and Guntermann was nursing a hangover, so they proceeded in total silence for the first two hours. They saw huge herds of wildebeest and gazelle, but nothing larger except for an occasional giraffe, and after another hour they unloaded their packs and rested in the shade of a ten-foot-tall termite mound.

"How soon before we come to elephant spoor?" asked Guntermann, taking a long swallow from his canteen.

"It'll be a while yet," replied Sloane, removing his left shoe and cutting a jigger out from beneath the nail of his big toe. "This area's been pretty well shot out. The elephant have moved east and probably a bit north, and they're getting pretty timid."

"Will it be today, do you think?" persisted Guntermann.

"Probably not for two or three days," replied Sloane. "If we're lucky."

"You're sure?"

Sloane shrugged. "You never know. There are always a few lone bulls around, if you're lucky enough to find them, but the rule of thumb for an ivory hunter is that you walk twenty-five miles for every shot you take, unless you're the type who blows away cows and calves." He paused and swatted a tsetse fly away. "Why? Thinking of going back to the trading post?"

"Rice virtually conceded the wager," noted Guntermann.

"Whether he conceded or not is between you and him," said Sloane. "But if I don't get the ivory, I want half the money."

"Then we proceed!" snapped Guntermann, getting to his feet.

"Whatever you say," said Sloane, putting on his shoe.

"What are you doing in this area if there is so little ivory here?" asked Guntermann irritably.

"I came back from Uganda for porters," said Sloane. "I got the chief of an Acholi village mad at me and had to leave in a hurry. My men all deserted, except for Karenja here."

"I do not understand," said Guntermann. "A tribe of Acholi wants to kill you, and you say you are going back there? Why?"

"I buried three tons of ivory before I left," said Sloane. "Once I hire myself some porters, and maybe a few *askaris* who know how to use their rifles, I'm going back there to dig it up."

"I see," said Guntermann, wiping his face with his ever-present handkerchief. "But why have you come so far for your porters?"

"They're less likely to desert if they don't speak the local language and don't know how to get home," replied Sloane.

They proceeded in silence across the vast plains, spotting some distant herds of impala, zebra and eland, but approaching within five hundred yards of nothing except a lone ostrich, which scurried away when it spotted them. When they stopped to eat beneath an acacia tree, a pair of lionesses suddenly appeared and strode past them, no more than thirty yards away, ignoring them with regal disdain. Shortly thereafter a rhino approached them, snorted ferociously, faked a charge, and then trotted off with its tail held high.

By nightfall they had seen thousands of antelope and tens of thousands of birds, but no sign of elephant, and they camped out in a grove of thorn trees while Tumo and Karenja took turns standing guard, surrounded by the night sounds of the veldt: the high-pitched giggling of hyenas, the coughing of a lion on the prowl, the frightened bark of a zebra.

The next morning began as uneventfully as the previous one, but before the sun had risen very high in the sky they came to a pile of elephant dung. Karenja walked up to it, squatted down, and stuck his hand into it.

"*Baridi*, Bwana," he announced as the Lumbwa walked over to examine it.

"What does he say?" asked Guntermann.

"He says it's cold, by which he means that it's old and dry," replied Sloane. "No sense following this one."

"This is ridiculous!" said Guntermann in exasperation as Tumo confirmed Karenja's finding. "Just last year there were thousands of elephants here!"

"They're not houses, Guntermann," said Sloane.

"What does that mean?" snapped the German.

"It means they don't stay put where you find them."

They covered another seven miles, passing several more herds of wildebeest and a large troop of baboons, then settled down for a meal while Tumo, the Lumbwa, went off by himself. He returned excitedly half an hour later, announcing that he had found fresh elephant spoor.

"How many?" asked Sloane.

"Just one," replied Tumo.

"Full-grown?"

The Lumbwa nodded. "Big bull," he said.

"Okay," said Sloane. "It looks like we're in business. Where did you find it?"

The Lumbwa pointed off to the east, and explained that it was less than a mile away.

"No sense sitting around here," said Sloane, loading his pack and picking up his rifle. "You ready, Guntermann?"

The German got to his feet. "Yes."

"Then let's go."

They walked due east for almost a mile, then turned slightly north. Finally the Lumbwa pointed out a fresh pile of elephant dung.

Karenja walked over, examined at it, then looked at the nearby ground and walked back to Sloane, a frown on his handsome face.

"It is *Malima Temboz*, Bwana—The Mountain That Walks," he announced so softly that only Sloane could hear him.

"You're sure?" asked Sloane.

Karenja led him over to the spoor. "You see?" he said, pointing out the twin furrows where the elephant's tusks had plowed up the dry earth as he walked. "The Makonde call him *Bwana Mutaro* because of the marks he leaves, and my own people know him as *Mrefu Kulika Twiga*, for he is taller than giraffes, but he is truly *Malima Temboz*."

Sloane called Guntermann over.

"Yes, what is it?" asked the German, still excited over finding the fresh spoor.

"Tell your boy that we don't want any part of this elephant," said Sloane. "We'll find another one, and you'll still win your bet."

"Why?" demanded Guntermann. "What is wrong with this one?"

"I know this elephant," explained Sloane. "He's killed

more than a dozen natives, including a Wanderobo who was probably every bit as good with an axe as your Lumbwa is."

"You have actually seen him?"

Sloane shook his head. "No. But I've heard about him."

"How can you possibly know this is the same elephant?" scoffed Guntermann.

Sloane led him over to the spoor. "That's the biggest footprint I've ever seen," he said. "Just on size alone, this has to be the same one. And see the way his tusks plow up the ground whenever he walks? That's why they call him *Bwana Mutaro*. He must be carrying two hundred pounds a side." He paused. "That's a lot of elephant to kill with a hand-axe. He's an old boy, and he's been around. Your boy isn't going to sneak up on him or catch him napping."

"If he carries so much ivory, why don't you want him?" asked Guntermann.

"I do," replied Sloane. "And now that I know he's in the area, I'll be back for him when this wager is over. But you didn't bargain on sending your boy against *Malima Temboz*. We'll find another one."

"The Mountain That Walks?" repeated Guntermann excitedly. "I want to see this elephant!"

"Maybe someday you will."

"I mean now!"

"I've already explained to you . . ."

"But if Tumo *does* kill him, think of the publicity!" said Guntermann.

"What publicity?" snorted Sloane. "You're five hundred miles from the coast, and five thousand miles from anyone who cares."

"I will have him stuffed and mounted, and bring them both back to Europe: the world's greatest elephant and the savage who killed him armed only with a hand-axe."

"You're crazy."

"We are wasting time," said Guntermann, ignoring him. "Tumo!"

The Lumbwa looked questioningly at him.

"*Kwenda*—let's go!"

The Lumbwa nodded and began trotting alongside the twin furrows in the earth.

Karenja turned to Sloane.

"It's his show," said the American. "Let *him* do the work." He fell into step behind the Lumbwa, followed by Karenja and Guntermann.

They spent the next nine hours traveling in a relatively straight line, occasionally losing the distinctive spoor but always finding it again, then diverted to the east where the elephant had found a small, muddy water hole. Since the full moon was out, the Lumbwa elected to keep following the furrows rather than let the elephant start distancing them, and at daybreak they came to a pile of dung that was less than twenty minutes old.

"We're getting awfully close," said Sloane after calling Guntermann over. "He's probably only a mile or two ahead of us, and since he's been traveling all night there's every chance that he'll sleep as soon as the sun's a little higher. Are you still sure you want to go through with this?"

"Absolutely!" responded the German.

Sloane paused and stared at Guntermann for a long moment, then nodded. "All right," he said. "From here on, we don't talk, cough, hum or whistle. Watch my hand signals, and when I motion you to stop, you obey me instantly. Understand?"

Guntermann nodded.

"I'm going to send Karenja out ahead of us, just in case there are any other elephants in the vicinity who might cause a problem."

"And if he finds some?"

"If he does, he'll come back and let us know how many and where."

Sloane gave his instructions to the Kikuyu, who set off at a right angle to them at a fast trot, then nodded to the Lumbwa, who once again began following the spoor, though much more slowly and silently this time.

And then, as they came to a small glade of flowering trees, the Lumbwa stopped, standing stock-still, and Sloane motioned Guntermann to do the same.

The Lumbwa carefully removed his hand-axe. Then, reaching down to a pile of dung, he smeared it all over his body to mask his own odor. He picked up a handful of grass and tested the wind, then silently entered the glade, crouching low, setting each foot down carefully.

Sloane and Guntermann remained where they had stopped for five minutes, then ten more.

"What's taking him so long?" Guntermann whispered, but Sloane merely gestured him to silence and continued staring at the glade.

Then a loud trumpeting came to their ears, following by the shrieking of birds and monkeys breaking cover, and then all was silent again.

"Let's go!" muttered Sloane, entering the glade. He entered the glade carefully, checking every tree, every movement of grass, every fluttering leaf. Guntermann was about to pass him when he reached out an arm and stopped the German.

Finally, after another five minutes, they came to what was left of the Lumbwa—a blood-stained *kikoi* and a pulpy mass that bore no resemblance to a human being. They found his hand-axe fifty yards away. Though Sloane spent another few minutes checking his surroundings, there was no sign of the elephant.

"He's gone," he announced when he was sure they were

alone. "I'm sorry about your boy, but I warned you: this isn't just another elephant."

Guntermann shook his head sadly.

"What a tragedy!" he muttered. "I could have toured Europe!"

"I'm glad to see you're so deeply moved," said Sloane sardonically.

Guntermann glared at him. "I have lost one hundred pounds. Isn't that enough?"

Sloane shrugged noncommittally. "If you say so," he replied.

There was a crackling of bushes and Sloane leveled his rifle in the direction of the sound, but it was only Karenja, racing up to see what had happened. The Kikuyu read the scene instantly.

"*Malima Temboz* knew he was coming," said Karenja, pointing to the ground. "You see, he led him deeper and deeper into the trees, then turned *here*"—he indicated the place—"and silently came back *here*"—he gestured again —"by his trail to lie in wait. Truly he is the wisest and most terrible of elephants!"

Sloane studied Karenja's reconstruction of the scene, then nodded. "He probably never knew the elephant was behind him until it grabbed him." He sighed. "Well, there's nothing left to bury. We might as well be going."

"Where?" asked Guntermann, as they began walking out of the glade. "Back to the trading post?"

"*You're* going back to the trading post," said Sloane. "I've got an elephant to hunt."

"I'm coming with you," said Guntermann firmly.

Sloane shook his head. "Your bet's over and done with. This is business now; you'd only slow me down."

"But I want to see him!"

"Tumo probably saw him—for a couple of seconds, anyway," said Sloane. "Do you think it was worth it?"

* * *

The pale man did not see me, but I had seen him as he approached the trees, and some inner instinct told me that it was he, and not the black man, who was my true enemy. After I killed the black man I raced out the far side of the clearing and turned to the east, across the sun-scorched Loita Plains, nor did I stop to sleep for two days and two nights. I did not slow down until I could see mighty Kirinyaga, which men called Mount Kenya, in the distance. Then I stopped by the place of cool waters and drank deeply.

Sloane knelt down and examined the pile of dung.

"Dry," he muttered. "You'd think he'd have slowed down by now."

"He is *Malima Temboz*," said Karenja, as if that explained everything.

Sloane leaned up against a dying baobab tree and set to work rolling a cigarette as he scanned the horizon.

"Where's the nearest water?" he asked.

The Kikuyu pointed to the east.

"How far?"

"Half a day," said Karenja. "Maybe more. Maybe less."

"Well, we might as well get going," said Sloane with a grimace. "No reason why he should be the only one to drink today."

They set off beneath the high tropical sun, the Rift Valley behind them, the coast and Mombasa an unimaginable march to the east through hundreds of miles of thorn trees. The ground became so hard that the elephant's tusks no longer plowed it up as he walked, and their rate of pursuit diminished as they twice lost touch with his spoor and had to backtrack to pick it up again.

They came to a Wakamba village three hours later, asked if anyone had seen *Malima Temboz*, and received the kind of looks usually reserved for madmen and fools. Sloane pulled three cartridges out of his belt and offered them to anyone who could tell him how recently the elephant had passed by and what direction it had been headed, but there were no takers.

Finally, as night fell, they came to a narrow, dirty river and slaked their thirst, then made camp beneath an acacia tree.

"Terrible place!" muttered Sloane, alternately shivering and slapping at mosquitos.

"The Maasai call it *Nairobi*," Karenja informed him.

"*Nairobi*? What does it mean?"

"The place of cool water."

"The place of a million mosquitos is more like it," grated Sloane.

"We call it the place of cold swamps," added Karenja.

"Well, that's closer, anyway," said Sloane, pulling his blanket over his head, more for protection from the insects than from the chilling breeze that swept across the plain.

Sloane spent an uncomfortable night, getting up twice to add to the fire and wishing that he could strangle the one particular hyena whose high-pitched giggling seemed to rouse him every time that he was on the brink of sleep. He was actually relieved to see the morning come, and, though sleepy and ill-tempered, lost no time breaking camp and taking up his quest once again.

They had been on the trail for no more than half an hour when they came to a flat, dusty plain where a herd of buffalo had obliterated all sign of the elephant.

"Wonderful," growled Sloane. He stood erect, placed his hands on his hips, and surveyed the area. "Which way, do you suppose? South to Tsavo, north to Kikuyuland, or straight ahead?"

"Not to Tsavo, Bwana," said Karenja. "Too dry."

"Lot of elephants down there, though," noted Sloane.

"*Malima Temboz* does not like his own kind. Always he walks alone."

"All right," said Sloane. "Let's turn north and see if we can pick up his trail."

They began walking to the north, examining the ground every few minutes, but after two hours Sloane concluded that the elephant must have headed east or south.

"I do not think so, Bwana," said Karenja. "He is next to a god, so it is logical that he would go to *Kirinyaga*, where *Ngai* dwells."

"He's just an elephant, Karenja."

"He is *Malima Temboz*."

"Even *Malima Temboz* leaves a spoor," said Sloane. "You've been following it for three days."

Karenja had no answer to that, so he remained silent.

"Let's go back and see where we lost him," continued Sloane.

"*Ndio*, Bwana," agreed Karenja reluctantly.

They backtracked toward the place where the buffalo herd had obliterated the elephant's tracks. At one point a pride of lions blocked their path, huddled about the carcass of a dead eland, and Sloane made a large semicircle around them through a heavy stand of thorn bush.

"*Bwana!*" whispered Karenja excitedly as they came opposite the pride.

"What is it?"

The Kikuyu pointed toward the ground, where two furrows, about six feet apart, were plainly visible.

Sloane frowned. "Why the hell would he go through bush when there was a plain track to follow?"

"He is *Malima Temboz*," explained Karenja patiently. "Thorns are no more to him that the petals of a flower."

They began following the trail, and came to a pile of dung half a mile later.

"Warm," announced Karenja, sticking two fingers into it.

"How old?"

"Maybe ten minutes. Maybe fifteen. Maybe twelve."

"I'll be damned!" muttered Sloane. "The son of a bitch is stalking *us*!"

"He knows we are here, Bwana," said Karenja. "We came back with heavy feet."

"I know *he's* here, too," said Sloane, "so we're even."

Karenja picked up a handful of dirt and ground it to powder between his fingertips, watching it drift to the north.

"The wind favors *Malima Temboz*, Bwana."

"Then we'll even the odds," said Sloane. He headed off to his left, followed by the Kikuyu. When he had gone half a mile, he turned right and continued walking rapidly. After walking through the oppressive heat for an hour he felt reasonably secure that he was once again ahead of the elephant. He then turned back into the thorn bush, looking for a likely place of concealment. Once there, he sent Karenja up a nearby tree as a lookout, placed two shell in his rifle, and waited.

An hour passed, then another, then a third.

"Any sign of him yet?" asked Sloane without much hope.

"*Hapana*, Bwana."

"You're sure?"

"He is not here."

"All right," said Sloane with a sigh. "Come on down."

Karenja clambered down the tree while Sloane slung his rifle over his sweat-soaked shoulder.

"Let's get out of this bush and back onto the grass," said Sloane.

They walked half a mile to the east, emerging from the scrub thorn onto the broad plain—and almost immediately came upon the elephant's spoor.

"Christ!" snapped Sloane. "He walked right past us while we were sitting in there being eaten by insects!" He knelt down and examined the furrows. "This is one goddamned smart elephant."

"He is *Malima Temboz*," said Karenja, nodding sagely as if the Bwana had finally realized what Karenja had been saying all along.

Sloane didn't bother to respond, but simply began following the spoor again.

They soon reached a drier, hotter area, free of trees and scrubland, brimful of gazelles and zebra and impala and wildebeest. Sloane sought out a nearby termite mound, climbed to the top of it, reached into his pack, and pulled out his spyglass.

"I've got him!" he announced a moment later.

"Where?" asked Karenja.

Sloane pointed off to the northeast.

"Are you certain it is *Malima Temboz*?"

"He's too far away to see his ivory," answered Sloane. "But he's a big one, and he's traveling alone."

He jumped down from the mound.

"All right," he said. "We know he likes to play games, so let's see if we can't outsmart him this time. See that grove of trees about six miles ahead?"

"*Ndio*, Bwana," said Karenja, nodding.

"If he thinks we're still after him, he's going to lie up and wait for us there."

"He is not a lion, to lie in wait," said Karenja.

"He's not your run-of-the-mill elephant, either," said Sloane. "He knows he's being followed, and he knows he's more vulnerable out on the grass. He'll head for the trees, believe me." He paused, wiping some dust from his eyes. "You go off to the right and circle around that grove. If he breaks out, I want to know which way he's going."

"And you, Bwana?"

"I'm going straight into the trees. There's a waterhole about four miles ahead and maybe a mile to the left; if he stops to drink and take a mud bath, I think I can beat him to the grove."

"And if he does not stop to drink?"

"Then I'll go in after him. You give a holler if you see him break cover."

Karenja held out his hand. "*Kwaheri*, Bwana."

"What do you mean, Good-bye?" said Sloane. "I'll see you in two hours."

"*Ndio*, Bwana," said the Kikuyu without much conviction. Then he set off at a trot.

Sloane looked across the plain, tried without success to spot the huge bulk of the elephant, took a sip of water from his canteen, and began walking toward the distant grove of trees.

Herds of gazelle and impala scattered out of his way and he slowed his pace, not wanting to alert the elephant to his presence. Soon he found the right rate of speed, and was able to walk past the grazing animals without distressing them. He was just congratulating himself on the ease with which he had crossed the plain when he found a lone rhino blocking his path.

It peered at him, snorting, then began trotting in a large circle until it was able to get his wind. Sloane slowly unslung his rifle and laid it across his chest, hoping that he wouldn't have to use it and reveal his presence to the elephant.

The rhino came to a stop about sixty yards away, then began pawing the earth and snorting vigorously. A moment later it trotted within twenty yards of him, then cut away at a right angle.

Sloane remained motionless, and the rhino circled him again, obviously troubled by his scent. Once again the animal lowered its head and charged, and once again it veered off when twenty yards away. Finally, shaking its head furiously, it turned its back on him and galloped away, burping violently from both ends.

Sloane waited another minute to make sure that it wouldn't be returning, then continued his trek toward the glade of trees. As he approached them, the animals became more skittish, possibly because the trees offered cover for carnivores, and began racing off as he approached them. He checked the ground for signs of the elephant's spoor, saw none, and slowly began circling to his left, hoping that he might be able to spot the elephant on the open plain.

He had gone almost a third of the way around the glade when he heard Karenja's voice call out.

"Bwana, he has gone back into the trees!"

"Back *into* them?" muttered Sloane to himself. "How the hell did he get here without my seeing him?"

He checked his cartridges, placed two extras between the fingers of his left hand, and entered the glade, which he estimated to be about two hundred yards in diameter.

Twenty feet into the trees he stopped, and listened for telltale signs: the rumbling of the elephant's stomach, the breaking of a twig, anything to help pinpoint the animal's location. He heard nothing, and after another moment he walked in another twenty feet. Again he stood still, and again he heard nothing but the trilling of birds and the chirping of crickets.

He wanted to yell to Karenja, to see if the elephant had emerged again, but he didn't dare give away his own location, and so, foot by foot, he continued walking through the glade. Visibility was rarely more than ten feet, frequently five, and he suddenly became aware of the idiocy of tracking *Malima Tembo* through such dense cover. He quickly retraced his steps, and emerged into the open with an enormous sense of relief.

Now he stood back some fifty yards and called out to Karenja:

"Is he still in the glade?"

"*Ndio*, Bwana!"

"Wait about ten minutes for him to forget I'm here, and then start making noise on your side. Maybe we can frighten him out in this direction."

"He is not afraid of noise, Bwana!" yelled Karenja.

"Do it anyway!"

Karenja made no reply, but about fifteen minutes later he began beating the branches of the trees and screaming at the top of his lungs, while Sloane, kneeling, rifle in hands, scanned the length of the glade, waiting for the elephant to burst out.

Nothing happened.

The noise stopped ten minutes later, and half an hour after that Karenja timidly circled the glade and approached Sloane.

"What are you doing here?" demanded the hunter.

"I thought you must be dead, Bwana, for I heard no shots," explained Karenja, "so I came to take your body to the missionaries."

"Thanks," said Sloane sardonically.

"Shall I go back to beating the branches, Bwana?"

Sloane shook his head. "No, that doesn't seem to do any good."

"Then what shall we do?"

"Wait," said Sloane. He tapped his canteen meaningfully. "We've got more water than he does. That water hole is a mile away; sooner or later he has to come out."

"Sooner or later men must sleep."

"Always the optimist," said Sloane.

"Shall I go back to the other side, Bwana?"

"Yes, I think so. And take this with you"—he handed Karenja the spyglass—"just in case he sneaked out while you were over here talking to me."

Karenja took the glass and headed off at a trot, while Sloane pulled his pack off and took out a piece of biltong and began chewing laboriously on it. Day turned to twilight, and twilight to evening, and still the elephant remained hidden within the glade.

Finally Sloane decided that it was too dark to see, so he built a large fire, more to aim by than to keep the carnivores away, and sat down beside it, his back propped up against his pack, his rifle laid gently across his legs.

A lion coughed in the distance and a herd of wildebeest stirred uneasily about half a mile to the west. Somewhere a leopard roared and an antelope screamed, and then all was silent again.

And then, instinctively, Sloane looked up—and there, charging as silently as the night, with no scream, no warning trumpet, was *Malima Temboz*.

The hunter raised his rifle to his shoulder and stared at the great beast. Its huge ears blotted out the moon and stars, its enormous bulk made the earth shake with each step it took, its twin pillars of ivory seemed to extend to Eternity.

"You're everything they said you were!" murmured Sloane, staring awestruck as the elephant bore down upon him.

At the last possible instant he got off a shot. The bullet raised a swirl of dust on the elephant's skull, but didn't stop him, or even slow him down, as Sloane had somehow known it wouldn't.

He continued staring in wonder as the thick trunk and

shining ivory reached out for him. It was, he decided, a sight that could last a man a lifetime.

And a lifetime was all he had left.

Karenja found what was left of his Bwana a few minutes later. He waited until morning and buried the tattered gray outfit, and then, because he had seen the way white men treated their dead, he placed a cross upon the grave and carefully hung Sloane's weatherworn stetson atop it.

Then he went back to his village, paid a large reparation to his chief, bought a wife, and spent the rest of his years tending his goats, for once a man has hunted *Malima Tembo* there are no challenges left to him.

Seventh Interlude (6303 G.E.)

"Duncan—don't you *ever* sleep at home? Wake up!"

I murmured something and reached out to pull the blanket over my head, only to realize that I didn't have any blanket and that I had fallen asleep in my office.

"Duncan!"

I sat up, rubbing my eyes and yawning.

"What time is it?" I asked.

"Seven-thirty," said Hilda, who was standing before my contour chair, her arms folded resolutely across her chest.

"I don't suppose you'd like to come back in an hour?"

"I would not. Now get up and on your feet; you'll feel much better."

I stood up gingerly, my back stiff, my right leg aching, a stale taste in my mouth.

"You're wrong," I rasped.

"About what?"

"I feel worse."

"Then try sleeping in your own bed, just for a change," she said sarcastically. She paused and stared at me. "Duncan, I spent half the night wondering if you would even be alive this morning. I'll give you two minutes to collect yourself, and then you're going to tell me exactly what happened last night."

"The elephant killed him."

"What are you talking about?" she demanded.

"Hannibal Sloane," I said. "He was the first white man to see it."

"I don't care what you learned from the computer!" she snapped. "I want to know what went on between you and Mandaka!"

"Oh," I said dully, trying to concentrate. "The computer found three more pieces of the puzzle last night."

"You're getting closer to the tusks?"

I shook my head. "Not to the tusks."

"Then to what?" she asked, confused.

"To the *reason*."

"Come on," she said. "Let's get some breakfast into you while we talk. You look dreadful and sound worse."

"Thanks," I said, sitting back down on the contour chair. "Why don't you just come back at nine?"

"Computer," she ordered, "let's have some light in here."

Instantly the wall became transparent and the morning sunlight flooded my office.

"All right!" I said, wincing. "I'll come to breakfast! Just make it stop!"

"Fifty percent opacity," ordered Hilda, and suddenly the room became bearable again.

"That was a terrible thing to do," I said sullenly as I got to my feet. "I only had about three hours' sleep."

"I'll apologize later," she said, walking to the door and ordering it to open.

"Where are we going—second floor or nineteenth?" I asked, running my fingers through my hair and trying to remember where I had left my hairbrush.

"The nineteenth," she said. "Why let the rank-and-file see you like this?"

We walked to the airlift and ascended to the Executive Dining Room, which was nothing but an exclusive cafeteria, then chose a table that hovered by a large window in the farthest corner of the room and seated ourselves. I watched the holographic representations of the menu pass by, ordering the pastry and a cup of coffee, while Hilda chose, in bits and pieces, her usual sturdy breakfast.

"All right," she said, after the display vanished and the food slid up through the base of the table. "Are you awake now?"

I nodded, trying to ignore the view of the waking city that the window afforded me.

"Then I want a full report."

"Hilda," I began, "you won't believe his apartment! I've never seen anything like it in my life."

"*His* apartment?" she said. "The last I knew, the two of you were in *your* apartment."

"He doesn't like it," I said. "Too sterile."

"He's got a point," she admitted. "Start at the beginning."

"The beginning?"

"Tell me what happened at Ancient Days, and why he was in your apartment later."

I told her everything that had happened, including my

visit to Mandaka's unlikely quarters. She finished her breakfast just as I finished my recounting.

"You know," she said after considering my report, "I have the strangest feeling that you *like* him."

I shook my head. "I don't know him well enough to like him. I *empathize* with him."

"How can you empathize with a man who grew up in a grass hut half a galaxy away, and is convinced that he will die when you finally find the tusks?"

"All right, then," I amended. "I *sympathize* with him."

"Why?"

I shrugged. "Because he'd rather be someone else."

"You?"

"Never me," I said. "I willingly chose to live the life he hates." I looked across the table at her and smiled. "He'd much prefer to be *you*."

"I don't understand."

"All he ever seems to have wanted was a job and a family and a normal, orderly life," I explained. "Instead, he grew up without ever seeing another child, he's burdened with the knowledge that he's the last of his race, and he seems compelled to spend his fortune and even his life acquiring the tusks of an elephant that died seven millennia ago." I thought about it as I gazed down at the bustling traffic and nodded. "Yes, I think he'd much rather be you."

"Then why doesn't he make some attempt to live a normal life?" she asked.

"I told you: he can't get married."

"Billions of people never get married and still manage to lead normal lives," she said. "Most of them," she added meaningfully, "are even on record with the Commonwealth."

"I explained that to you."

"Oh, he's got a slick explanation for everything," she

said. "He must be quite a talker for you to have believed it all."

"You weren't at his apartment," I said. "You didn't see how he lives."

"But *you* did," she said. "And you still think that you both live the same kind of life."

"Yes."

"But he lives in an expensive penthouse that he's made over to look like a primitive hut, and you live in a middle-class apartment whose colors you couldn't describe to me if your life depended on it. He travels the galaxy, and you spend all your time in your office. He wants relationships, and you go out of your way to avoid them. He wishes someone else had found the ivory so he wouldn't have to search for it, and you can think of nothing else except finding it. And somehow he's convinced you that your lives are identical. I repeat: he must be some talker."

"Our lives are alike in the things that matter," I said defensively.

"They're as different as night and day."

"The only substantial difference is that he is unhappy with his life and I enjoy mine."

She seemed about to comment on that, then decided not to. Instead she ordered up a pastry for herself, stared at her fingernails for a few moments, and then looked across the table at me.

"All right, Duncan," she said. "You've spent a few hours with him, you seem—for reasons I cannot fathom—to have taken a liking to him, you've seen how and where he lives. Have you any idea why he is willing to pay millions of credits, and even to kill, for possession of the ivory?"

"I have an *idea*," I responded carefully. "I don't have an *answer*."

"What's the difference?" she asked as the pastry arrived.

"I don't know the exact reason he needs them, but it's

connected to the fact that he's a Maasai," I said. "More to the point, I think he's desperate for the tusks not just because he's a Maasai, but because he's the *last* Maasai."

"What has that got to do with it?"

"I don't know," I said. "But from various comments he made, I gather that there is something that must be done with or to the tusks, or at least some reason for possessing them, that *could* have been done by any Maasai, but which absolutely *must* be done by Mandaka precisely because he is the last Maasai."

"It sounds like a lot of gibberish to me," she said. "Something that could have been done, might have been done, must be done." She paused and stared impatiently at me.

"When you say it that way, it sounds like gibberish to me too," I admitted uncomfortably. "But there's an answer buried in there somewhere. I know there is!"

"*What* must be done, for goodness sake—and *why* must it be done?"

I shrugged helplessly. "I don't know."

"Didn't you ask him?"

"Of course I did," I answered irritably.

"And?"

"He wouldn't tell me," I replied. "He said I'd think he was crazy."

A caustic smile crossed her face. "Not you, Duncan—not if it added to the mystery. *I* might think he was crazy, everyone else might think he was crazy—but you, you'd just add it to the interminable list of puzzles you're working on."

I said nothing, but simply toyed with my empty coffee cup.

"All right, Duncan," she said with a sigh. "*Do* you think he's crazy?"

"No, I don't."

"Would you care to hazard a guess as to why he wants the tusks?"

"Only that it's tied in with his being a Maasai."

She stared intently at me. "Why do I have the feeling that you know more than you're telling me?"

"I *suspect* more than I'm telling you," I replied. "I don't *know* anything."

"Why should the Maasai be more interested in this elephant than the Kikuyus or the Zulus?"

"The Zulus were thousands of miles to the south," I said.

"I'm just using names," she said, obviously annoyed. "I don't know one tribe from another. Let's try again: why should the Maasai be more interested than any other tribe?"

"I don't know."

"Did a Maasai kill the elephant?"

"Probably not. No one knows for sure."

"Then why do you say probably not?"

"The Maasai didn't hunt for meat and they didn't collect ivory; they'd have no reason to kill him." I paused. "Also, based on what I learned about him this morning, it would take more than a naked warrior with a spear to bring him down."

"Well, if a Maasai *didn't* kill him, what claim do they have to his tusks? Did a Maasai buy them at auction?"

"As far as I can tell, no Maasai ever possessed them while they were on Earth," I replied. "They were initially put up for auction by an Arab, they were bought by Caucasians, the British Museum turned them over to the Kenya government, and they remained in the Nairobi Museum until the dawn of the Galactic Era—and even then, I haven't been able to find any Maasai who owned them until the time of Maasai Laibon in the eighteenth century G.E."

"Then what possible claim can the Maasai have on them?"

"I get the feeling that it's not so much a claim as a *need*," I replied.

"We're right back where we started," she said. "I'm going to ask why they need them, and you're going to say you don't know, that you have some vague notion but you're not prepared to share it with me. Am I right?"

I nodded. "You're right. More coffee?"

"You can be the most frustrating man!" she snapped.

"I don't mean to be."

"Two days, Duncan!" she said, shaking a pudgy forefinger at me. "That's all the time you have left."

"Then we renegotiate," I reminded her.

"Not if you haven't got some better answers by then."

"Once I have the answers, I won't need the extension," I promised.

"Well, you'd better get them, because you don't seem to be making much progress with the ivory."

I returned to my office, walked over to my private bathroom, threw some cold water on my face, and decided that I needed a shave.

"Computer?"

"Yes, Duncan Rojas?"

"How is your search for the ivory proceeding?"

"I have found no sign of it since it was stolen from Winox IV by Tahiti Benoit," answered the computer.

"I want you to do me a favor."

"Yes?"

"While I'm shaving, I want you to assemble a brief history of the Maasai race for me, starting in 1898 A.D."

"You will have to be more precise."

I frowned. "You want an actual date in 1898 A.D.?" I asked.

"I need a definition of the word 'brief'," responded the computer.

"Less than five hundred words," I said.

"Working . . . done."

"I'm not through shaving."

"Waiting . . ."

I walked over to my desk a moment later and sat down behind it. "All right, computer."

"The Maasai race, in 1898 A.D., numbered twenty-five thousand, and owned most of the land in the Kenya's Rift Valley, as well as the southern area of Kenya that encompassed Tsavo, Amboseli and the Maasai Mara, and the northern sections of Tanganyika encompassing the Serengeti Plains, Mount Kilimanjaro, and the Ngorongoro Crater. They were the most feared warriors in East or Central Africa, with a reputation—though not the military accomplishments—rivaling the Zulus of South Africa.

"By 1910 the British had created numerous laws that deprived the Maasai of much of their power, as well as their way of life. They were no longer allowed to carry spears, or even shields, and raids against other tribes were not permitted. By 1940 they were no longer allowed their traditional rite of passage to manhood, the slaying of lions with spears.

"At independence, they numbered two hundred and fifty thousand, far less than the Kikuyu, the Luo and the Wakamba. They clung to their traditional pastoral way of life, and hence fell behind the other tribes in terms of literacy, health, and economic power.

"By 2010 A.D. their lands had been appropriated by the governments of Kenya and Tanzania. By 2050 A.D. their numbers had decreased to thirty thousand. By 2093 A.D. they no longer spoke their own language, known as *Maa*, but wrote and conversed exclusively in Swahili. At the dawn of the Galactic Era and the colonizing of New Kenya, no Maasai had ever held a position of major responsibility within the Kenyan or Tanzanian government. The race has no accomplishments of note since Man achieved space travel."

"A very unhappy story," I said.

"I am not programmed to make judgments in that area," replied the computer.

"I know," I said, lost in thought. How long I sat motionless I do not know, but finally I looked over to the computer again.

"Computer?"

"Yes?" it responded, glowing brightly.

"Is it possible for you to analyze the situation in East Africa prior to 1898?"

"Analyze it in what regard?"

"I want you to assess the tribal situation in all its aspects circa 1897 A.D. and tell me the likelihood that the history of the Maasai would proceed as it did, totally devoid of power or accomplishments."

"Working . . ."

I ordered a cup of coffee, decided that I had already had too much coffee in the past twenty-four hours and canceled it, and instead ordered a glass of fruit juice. Before it arrived the computer had the answer for me.

"The probability that Maasai history would follow the course it did, which I have calculated using all data up to and including 1897, was 1.43%."

"Now calculate it again, circa 1910 A.D."

"Working . . . 51.23%."

"Again, circa 1950 A.D."

"Working . . . 93.78%."

"Thank you, computer," I said, sipping my fruit juice.

Suddenly Hilda's image appeared, hovering above me.

"I've been monitoring the computer, Duncan," she announced.

"Who gave you permission?" I asked.

"I don't need permission; I'm the Chief of Security." She stared at me. "As angry as I am at you, I can't help being fascinated by what you've been asking the computer. May I guess the next question?"

"Be my guest," I said.

"Computer," she said, "let me offer a hypothesis: the Maasai race's loss of power and primacy was a direct result of the death of the Kilimanjaro Elephant in 1898 A.D." She paused. "Analyze, please."

"Working . . . Your hypothesis has a .00034% chance of probability."

"Very interesting," I said.

"What's interesting about that?" she said. "You were wrong." She looked disappointed. "You know, you even had *me* half-believing there was a connection."

"There is," I said.

"But the computer only gave you a .00034% chance of being right," she said. "I'd hardly call that encouraging."

"You're wrong," I said. "Based on the information it has, there should have been no chance at all."

"Oh?" she said, interested in spite of herself.

I nodded. "There is no known connection between the elephant and the Maasai. It shouldn't have affected the history of the race at all."

"The likelihood is that it didn't."

"The computer shouldn't be dealing in likelihoods in this case, but in absolutes," I said.

"Then ask it why it didn't simply say zero," she insisted.

"I will. I'm trying to think how best to word it." She fell silent and allowed me to think for a moment. "Computer," I said at last, "what factors changed the likelihood of the

Kilimanjaro Elephant's death influencing the history of the Maasai from zero to .00034%?"

"Secondary sources referring to certain pronouncements of Sendeyo."

"Who was Sendeyo?"

"A Maasai *laibon*, and brother to Lenana, who was paramount chief of the Maasai in 1898 A.D."

"What pronouncements did Sendeyo make?" I demanded.

"Insufficient data," replied the computer.

"If you don't know what he said, why does it influence your computation?" I persisted.

"The mere fact that he was a major *laibon* in 1898 A.D. and that he mentioned the Kilimanjaro Elephant is sufficient to change the likelihood from zero to .00034%."

"Thank you," I said. Then I turned back to Hilda's image. "I was wrong," I said with a sigh. "I had no idea that a simple reference to the elephant could affect the computation."

"Probably you were wrong," agreed Hilda. "But it nevertheless raises another question. Computer?"

"Yes?"

"It is my understanding that there is no known connection between the Maasai and the death of the Kilimanjaro Elephant. Is that correct?"

"That is correct."

"Then how did Sendeyo know the elephant was dead—or that it had even existed?"

"Insufficient data," responded the computer.

Hilda's image turned to face me. "I don't know if it's a meaningful line of pursuit—but it *is* interesting, don't you think?"

"*Very* interesting," I replied.

It got less interesting during the next thirty minutes,

for no matter how I approached the subject, I could not make the computer draw any connection between Sendeyo and/or the Maasai and the Kilimanjaro Elephant. The *laibon* may possibly have mentioned it once—the source, after all, was not a primary one, and hence could not be taken as absolute truth—and that one possible mention was enough to affect the computer's calculations. It possessed no further data, and could not be drawn into offering any hypotheses of its own.

Finally Hilda interrupted my questioning.

"We open for business in twenty minutes," she announced. "I've got to start making my rounds."

"All right," I said.

"Let me know if you come up with anything."

"I will."

Her image vanished, and I turned back to the computer, not knowing how to attack the subject next. I stalled for a moment by asking if it had managed to locate the tusks, and it replied again that it had been able to find no trace of them since Tahiti Benoit had stolen them from the Fly-by-Nights.

I was completely out of ideas, and yet I hated to stop questioning the computer, since once we had opened it would be another nine hours before I could bring up the subject again.

"Please create a holographic representation of the tusks," I said, hoping that the sight of them just a few feet away from my desk might inspire another line of pursuit.

"Done," announced the computer as the image of the tusks took shape directly in front of me.

I stared at them, impressed as always, but unable to think of a way to get the computer to positively tie them to either Sendeyo or the Maasai. I leaned back, propped a foot up against my desk, and sighed.

"They look so clean for all the blood they're carrying with them," I said.

"They are merely extended molars," the computer corrected me. "They never carried any blood, Duncan Rojas."

"I was speaking metaphorically," I replied. "Many people have died because of them."

"Six thousand nine hundred and eighty-two, based on my data," said the computer.

"That must be wrong," I said. "There was the Warlord, and Hannibal Sloane, and Tumo the Lumbwa, and Esther Kamau. We don't know for a fact that they caused the deaths of the Iron Duchess or Tahati Benoit."

"I do not consider the Iron Duchess or Tahiti Benoit in my total."

"How did you arrive at that total?"

"A minor war was fought for possession of the tusks in 882 G.E."

"A war?" I repeated, surprised.

"A military action between two worlds," explained the computer. "My databanks define such action as a war."

"And it was fought over the ivory?"

"That is correct."

"Tell me about it," I said eagerly.

"Working . . ."

8

The Potentate
(882 G.E.)

I reached the dust-filled plains of Amboseli, and now, for the first time, I could see mighty Kilimanjaro in the distance, its slopes a dull blue-gray, its snow-capped peak lost in the clouds. I continued walking south toward Kilimanjaro, the greatest of elephants making his pilgrimage to the greatest of mountains, for if the God of Men dwelt on Mount Kenya, then perhaps the God of Elephants dwelt here.

Not much time remained to me. I felt no fear or sorrow, for death comes to all things, and it seemed better that I should seek out my God now than that He should find me, weak and starving and unable to stand in His presence, or mad with pain as ants ate away at the inside of my trunk. I wanted to ask Him why He had made me different from all others of my kind, why He had ordained a life of loneliness for me, why I had survived bullets and spears and arrows that would have killed any other living thing. I wanted to know for what purpose

He had created me, and if I had served that purpose well and honorably.

And so, pausing only long enough to drink and to spray dust on my cracked, irritated skin, I turned once again toward Kilimanjaro and continued my journey.

General Arab Chagalla, feeling slightly uncomfortable in his dress uniform, looked up from his morning tea as Major Juma entered his office.

"Sir?" said Juma.

"Stand at ease, Major," said Chagalla. He issued a brief order to his computer, and the various battle maps that lined the walls of the room went blank.

"Thank you, sir," said Juma. He paused, trying unsuccessfully to calm himself. He held up a slip of blue paper. "Sir, what is this all about?"

Arab Chagalla barely glanced at the paper. "I should think it is perfectly clear. We have been ordered to attack Plantagenet II."

"Have they threatened our security?" asked Juma, leaning forward and pressing his fingertips on Chagalla's desk.

"No."

"Have they attacked any of our nationals?"

"No."

"Then why, in Allah's name, are we going to war against a planet that is located seventy-three thousand light-years away?"

"Why does our King do anything he does?" said Chagalla sardonically. "Allah has whispered in his ear that we must attack Plantagenet II."

"And that is his *only* reason?"

"Of course not," said Chagalla. "But it *is* his official reason."

"And what is the true purpose of our attack?"

Arab Chagalla sighed. "I don't think you'd believe me if I told you."

"Is that the only answer I am to be given?" demanded Juma.

"No," said Chagalla. "But at least *I* won't be the one to tell you, Allah be praised. The King has ordered a meeting of all senior military personnel after the mid-morning prayer; some junior officer will be stupid enough to ask him." Chagalla paused and looked thoughtfully at Juma. "Let me give you a warning: try not to smile when he explains his reasoning."

"I beg your pardon?"

"You heard me," replied Chagalla seriously. "Appear attentive and serious, and we may actually make it to Plantagenet II before suffering any casualties, *Inshallah*."

They gathered in the throne room in their finest dress uniforms, the seventy-eight senior officers whom Amin Rashid XIV, absolute monarch of Alpha Bednari IV, had chosen to carry his colors into holy battle against the infidels of the Plantagenet system. No chairs had been provided, and they all stood at attention, awaiting the arrival of the king.

Finally he entered the room. He was not an imposing figure—small, fat, slightly bowlegged, with an uncontrollable swirl on the left side of his beard—but he held, by heredity, murder, and the grace of Allah, an imposing title. He was forty-seven years old, and he had sat on the throne ever since murdering his brother and his uncle three years ago. During that time he had taken forty-seven wives, one for each of his years. He was a devout believer in a form of Islam that did not quite conform to the Koran, a profligate spender, a compulsive gambler, a breeder of mutated lizards and an avid student of their bloodlines, and a man who achieved publicity totally out of proportion to his minimal power within mankind's vast and sprawling Republic.

He was xenophobic in the extreme, confiding in no man who had not been born upon Alpha Bednari IV (which he had renamed Mohammed in honor of the Prophet, but which still appeared as the fourth planet of the Alpha Bednari system in all official books and maps), trusting no woman at all, declaring (though never actually waging) a Holy War against all alien races. He had disenfranchised all citizens who did not practice his particular form of Islam until the Republic stepped in and slapped him smartly where it hurt the most—in his treasury—and his attempt to deny women the right to own property was still making its way slowly through the planetary court system.

He held a blue-green lizard lovingly in his left hand, stroking its head absently as he surveyed his audience.

"Gentlemen," he said at last in his high-pitched voice, "it is good to see such brave men standing before me." He paused to clear his throat. "Tomorrow we shall begin on a Holy Jihad against the infidels of Plantagenet II, and I shall take my place aboard our flagship, sharing all the dangers with you, as all worthy kings must do."

He paused to raise the lizard to his lips and kiss its head.

"I am Amin Rashid XIV, King of Mohammed, Beloved of Allah. I cannot be defeated, and therefore, if I am with you, *you* cannot be defeated. No laser shall touch our ships, no sonic disrupter shall reach us, no molecular imploder will function if it is aimed against us. We are immortal, for we are on a mission proclaimed by Allah."

"A question, Lord?" said a young colonel.

"Yes?" answered Rashid, turning to him.

"May I inquire as to the strategic value of capturing Plantagenet II?"

"You may not!" snapped Rashid. "Is it not enough that I have declared *jihad?*"

"Yes, sir," said the colonel quickly.

Rashid, still annoyed, continued stroking the little lizard. "We make war upon Plantagenet II because Allah has appeared to me and told me that they possess something that I must have. All who stand in our way will be destroyed. All who raise their swords against us will know the wrath of the One True Lord."

"*Swords?*" whispered Major Juma, frowning. "He thinks they're going to fight with swords?"

"The rivers will flow red with blood, birds of prey will feast on the charred flesh of the infidels, and the carnage will continue until the last voice raised against us has been silenced. So Allah has decreed; so it must be."

No one cared to be the one who asked what Allah's purpose might be, and so they all remained silent and at attention until Rashid finally addressed himself to it.

"On display in a museum in the city of New Avon are the tusks of an animal known as the Kilimanjaro Elephant, the largest mammal ever to walk the Earth which gave birth to our race. Allah has told me that I must possess those tusks." He paused and looked across the stunned faces. "This is what I want, and this is what Allah wants. Any man who does not pledge his life to the accomplishment of this goal denies not only my sovereignty but Allah's." A cold smile gave an ample hint of what both Rashid's and Allah's reaction to such an action might be.

Shortly thereafter Rashid dismissed them to prepare for the invasion.

"We're actually going to war over a pair of tusks!" repeated Major Juma, in the privacy of Arab Chagalla's office. "I can't believe it."

"You'll believe it when they start shooting at you," replied Chagalla grimly.

"But why?"

The general sighed deeply, lit a cigar, took a puff, and looked directly at his junior officer. "Because our beloved monarch has sired thirteen daughters and no sons since ascending to the throne, and he wants some heirs."

"What has one to do with the other?" asked Juma, taken aback by the answer.

"In ancient days, when the race was still Earthbound, there was an animal, a relative of the elephant, known as the rhinoceros. It was hunted to extinction because of a horn that grew at the end of its nose."

Juma stared at him, but said nothing.

Chagalla took another puff of his cigar, and continued. "The reason that this animal was hunted for its horn was because the horn took the shape of a phallus, and it was thought by various potentates that consuming the horn— in powdered form, to be sure—would give them unlimited virility." The general paused, reflecting upon the sheer idiocy of what he was trying to explain. "There are no more rhinos, and no more rhino horns—but there *are* these two enormous tusks. If you look at their shape, which is not dissimilar to that of a rhinoceros horn, and recall that thirty-four of our beloved monarch's forty-seven wives are barren and that he himself is getting neither younger nor more sexually vigorous, you can draw your own conclusion."

"We're going to attack Plantagenet II so that he can enjoy his wives more frequently?" said Juma disbelievingly.

"Of course not."

"But—"

"We're going to attack Plantagenet II because he *thinks* he will be able to enjoy his wives more frequently."

"But this is ridiculous!" exclaimed Juma. "Why don't we merely *buy* the tusks?"

"We offered to, and we were turned down," replied Chagalla. He smiled sardonically. "I believe *that* was when Allah suggested that we should go to war."

"*Was* rhinoceros horn an aphrodisiac?" asked Juma.

"Certainly not."

"Then the ivory won't be either," he concluded. "Why doesn't someone tell him that?"

Chagalla stared at him. "Are you volunteering?"

"No, but . . ."

"Well, when you find someone who is willing to tell our beloved monarch that there is no hope for his lackluster abilities in the bedroom, please let me know. Until then, I suggest that you prepare for battle."

Juma shook his head in dismay. "So we're going to war because no one is willing to tell a madman that an oversized tooth is not an aphrodisiac."

"That is the gist of it," agreed Chagalla grimly. "Try to remember that we serve our planet, which is eternal, and not our ruler, who is ephemeral."

Juma shook his head. "This is an evil war," he said with conviction. "Allah will not permit us to win."

"It is my reading of history that Allah usually favors the side with the best firepower," replied Chagalla.

The invasion began poorly. (In fact, it almost didn't begin at all, for when Rashid's personal mullah, Shereef Hassim, learned the purpose of the military action, he refused dispensation for the troops to eat condensed rations. Rashid had him executed, but his successor also refused, and by the time the monarch had found a mullah who declared that for the duration of the battle the army and navy could eat meat that had not been ritually slaughtered, eight mullahs had been killed or tortured and the fleet had been forced to remain in port an extra thirty-six hours.)

Finally, though, the fleet took off for the distant Plantagenet system, and Major Juma, after spending the first two days in his tiny compartment, once again requested an audience with his general.

"Come in," said Arab Chagalla, as the young major appeared in the doorway to his relatively spacious private quarters.

"Thank you, sir."

"Will you share some unsweetened coffee with me?" asked Chagalla, gesturing to the pot that sat on the table next to him.

"No, thank you, sir."

"Then please be seated." He inclined his head. "My house is your house. Such as it is," he added wryly.

Juma entered the cubicle, and the door slid shut behind him.

"Is this room secure, sir?" asked Juma, walking over to a bench that was suspended from a bulkhead.

Chagalla frowned. "Secure?"

"Can we be overheard?"

"No."

"Good," said Juma, sitting down and leaning forward. "I tell you this because I trust you, and because I cannot accomplish it alone." He paused uneasily. "I've worked out a plan."

"To conquer Plantagenet II?" asked Chagalla, giving the younger man a chance to veer away from the subject that he obviously wished to discuss.

"To kill Amin Rashid."

"I will pretend I did not hear that," said Chagalla, unsurprised. "And you, for your part, will never refer to it again."

"But the man is crazy!"

"He is also our king, to whom we have sworn our loyalty."

"He is not responsible for his actions."

"Is not Allah said to look with compassion upon the madman?" asked Chagalla, sipping his coffee.

"Allah may, but that will be small comfort to tens of thousands of the dead and dying on Plantagenet."

"Enough!" said Chagalla sharply. "He is your monarch; you are his vassal. He is an imperfect man, to be sure, but perfection dwells only within Allah. You must serve him, and allow Allah to judge him."

Juma pursed his lips impatiently.

"You don't think the Republic is going to let us get away with this, do you?" he persisted. "Up to now, Rashid has merely been an irritant. This act of aggression will make him a criminal—or do you happily anticipate defending him against the military might of twenty thousand worlds?"

"I will listen no further," said Chagalla firmly. "You must be quiet, or it will be my duty to report you."

"Then report me!" snapped Juma. "But the blood of Plantagenet II will be on your hands if you do not listen! And for what? For a pair of tusks that a madman thinks will give him the fertility of one of the lizards that he breeds!"

"I suggest that you pray to Allah for guidance and forgiveness," said Chagalla.

"Allah must be preoccupied with other problems, or Amin Rashid would never have ascended to the throne."

The older man stared at him thoughtfully for a long moment, as if trying to make up his mind about something. Finally he sighed and leaned back on his cushioned chair.

"Allah sees and knows more than you might think," said Arab Chagalla.

"What does *that* mean?" demanded Juma, pouncing upon the statement like a cat.

Chagalla stared at him, seemed about to say something, then changed his mind. "Pray for guidance, both for yourself and your king," he said at last.

"Something's going on!" said Juma excitedly. "Something I'm not aware of!"

"There are many things going on in the galaxy and the universe of which you are not aware," replied Chagalla.

"It must happen soon," continued Juma. "We reach the Plantagenet system in three more days."

"You have *your* timetable and Allah has *his*," said the general.

"May I help?" asked Juma eagerly.

"Certainly," answered Chagalla, his face an emotionless mask. "Pray for a swift and bloodless victory over the infidels."

There was no reason why it shouldn't have worked. They planted the bomb inside a ripe citrus fruit, and placed it at the bottom of a huge bowl of similar fruit.

Nine senior staff officers were involved in the plot, and all nine were present, fully prepared to sacrifice their own lives to insure the death of their monarch. Chagalla, who wasn't aboard the flagship, was nonetheless involved, and was ready to take over command of the fleet and order it to return to Alpha Bednari IV the instant he received confirmation of Amid Rashid's unfortunate demise.

A staff briefing had been scheduled for 1600 hours, ship's time, aboard the flagship, and when Rashid insisted on attending it, the plan went into effect. By the time he arrived and seated himself at the end of the briefing table, the bomb had been activated and the officers had cleared the room of all those who were not directly involved in the assassination attempt.

But Allah, as Chagalla had noted, had a soft spot in His

heart for madmen, and the bomb exploded just as Rashid
had bent over to pick up a piece of fruit that he had dropped
on the floor. Thus protected by the table, he suffered minor
bruises and some slight damage to his lungs from the in-
halation of smoke. Seven of the nine officers died from the
explosion, and the other two died later that night before
they could be tortured into divulging the names of their
co-conspirators.

And the fleet continued on course to Plantagenet II.

When they were three hours from their destination, Rashid
announced that the invasion had to be fought on the ground;
he would not risk destroying the tusks accidentally by firing
upon the enemy from orbit.

Chagalla, now his ranking officer, explained that the
Plantagenet military had doubtless spotted them already,
and was unquestionably tracking them with their weaponry.
If he, Chagalla, were not allowed to soften up the enemy's
defenses, there was considerable doubt that he could land
a single ship safely.

Rashid listened politely and then explained that Allah
had whispered to him that very morning that the invasion
would be a success and that he would shortly possess the
mystic power embedded in the tusks of the Kilimanjaro
Elephant.

Chagalla then requested that he at least be allowed to
put the fleet into orbit around Plantagenet V or VI until he
could calculate the enemy's firepower.

Rashid refused, for Allah had told him that all enemies
would fade away before his holy onslaught.

Chagalla's final suggestion was that they make one last
attempt to parley, since the presence of the fleet might have
some effect on the government's previous decision not to
part with the ivory.

A very reasonable suggestion, agreed Rashid—under other circumstances. But the time for reason and reconciliation was past. Allah had told him that he must attack the infidels and wrest the ivory from their grasp.

Chagalla, who didn't think much of Rashid's *or* Allah's grasp of military tactics, merely nodded and saluted.

The first eight ships that attempted to land were instantly blown apart. A ninth entered the atmosphere, weapons blazing, and managed to destroy two farmhouses and a three-mile section of dirt road before it was destroyed.

Finally Chagalla activated his communicator.

"My Lord," he said furiously, "you have *got* to let me hit their military installations! We've lost nine ships and have yet to disable a single one of their weapons!"

"Are you giving orders to *me*?" demanded Rashid. "I am the Chosen One, the conduit of Allah! We will not attack them from space! I will not take the chance of destroying the tusks!"

"But we've lost more than six thousand men!"

"They were only men," said Rashid with a shrug. "They died for the greater glory of Allah."

"They died for your tusks," explained Chagalla, forcing himself to retain an outward appearance of calm, "and we're no closer to getting them than when we started."

"We cannot be defeated," replied Rashid serenely. "Allah has so decreed it."

"Sir, I hate to contradict you, but if you don't allow me to defend our men, we can and we will lose. You *must* let me bomb the planet or we will suffer a defeat of catastrophic proportions!"

"I will not destroy the tusks!" said Rashid. There was a momentary pause. "However, I will allow you to inject chemical or toxic substances into the atmosphere if that will assuage your doubts, General Chagalla. *But*," he added meaningfully, "no radioactive materials may be used. The tusks are no use to me if I cannot . . . cannot *use* them," he concluded lamely.

You mean if you cannot grind them to powder to eat with your breakfast, corrected Chagalla silently. Aloud he merely said "Yes, My Lord," and quickly severed the connection.

"So now he wants to poison the atmosphere and kill off the entire civilian population?" demanded Major Juma furiously.

"What he wants and what he's going to get are two different things," replied Arab Chagalla to his subordinate. "I want you to check the various nerve gases and chemical agents we have aboard, run them through the computer, and have it come up with a mixture that will be disabling without being fatal." He paused. "Then we'll dump it on New Avon and their military bases, land a commando force, grab the tusks, and beat a very hasty retreat, *Inshallah*."

"And what about Rashid?"

"I am sure that Allah, in His infinite wisdom, will solve that problem. Right now, however, I'm trying to keep my forces from being decimated."

"You are now the most powerful man in the military," continued Juma. "If you were to lead a coup, you would have the backing of ninety percent of your officers."

"The military was created to fight, not to rule," replied Arab Chagalla. "I have neither the desire nor the capacity to govern a planet." He activated his holographic screens and studied the position of his fleet. "Now access the computer, check our chemical stores, and order it to create the compound we discussed. And Juma?"

The major, who had started to leave, turned and faced the general.

"Yes?"

"I want no more talk of a coup. I will not lead it, and should any of my subordinates attempt it, I will oppose them. This is the army of Alpha Bednari IV, and I expect it to behave with discipline and honor."

A few minutes later Arab Chagalla raised the flagship on his communicator, and asked to speak to Amin Rashid.

"Yes, General?" said the monarch.

"The chemical compound has been created, and is being dispersed in the atmosphere even as we speak."

"Excellent!" said Rashid. "How soon will its effects be evident?"

"In less than five minutes, My Lord," responded Chagalla. "I am about to order two of my ships to land at New Avon and appropriate the tusks." He paused. "Would you like to accompany them, My Lord?"

"Absolutely! I will march into the city at their head!"

"I must warn My Lord that the effects of the compound are not fatal, and will dissipate within three hours. I cannot guarantee your safety if our enemies recover while you are in their midst."

"Three hours is far more than I will need," Rashid assured him.

"Very good, My Lord. A protective outfit will be supplied for your convenience."

"The gas is not fatal," said Rashid. "I will wear no suit."

"But, My Lord—"

"I am immortal!" declared Rashid. "Ordinary men must wear protective suits, but the Blessed of Allah will not! I shall walk into New Avon clad only in my white robes."

"As you will, My Lord," said Chagalla with a shrug.

"Good. Now let the invasion begin!"

Amid Rashid XIV wound his way through a sleeping populace at the head of his army. When he reached the museum he mounted the great stone steps in solitary splendor while his official biographer captured the moment with a holographic camera. The monarch then entered the building, followed closely by his armed men, and personally broke open the glass case that held the tusks of the Kilimanjaro Elephant. Once the ivory was secured, he led an orderly march back to the ships.

Upon returning to the flagship, he passed briefly through the decontamination chamber, supervised the careful packing of the ivory, and announced his triumph over the intercom.

Then, just before the evening prayer, he collapsed.

"Will he live?" asked Major Juma.

"He will live," answered Arab Chagalla.

"And he will retain all his senses? Those that he hadn't already lost?" qualified Juma.

Chagalla lit a cigar and leaned back comfortably on his chair.

"He will retain all his senses."

"Then Allah has truly deserted us!" muttered the young major bitterly.

"Allah has done no such thing," replied Chagalla.

Juma stared at him curiously.

"Allah not only has a sense of justice," continued the general, "but I think He has a sense of the ironic as well."

"I do not understand," said Juma.

"I've just received the medical reports on our monarch's condition," said Chagalla.

"But you just said that he will live and retain his senses."

"That is true," said Chagalla, enjoying himself enormously. "But there is one thing that he will not retain." He took another puff of his cigar and smiled. "What was the purpose of this invasion, Major Juma?"

"To obtain the ivory, which he thinks in his madness will endow him with the potency of a stallion."

"That is correct," said Chagalla. "And according to the medical reports, the only lasting ill effect he will suffer from exposing himself to the poisons in the atmosphere will be permanent sexual impotence."

Juma grinned. "Truly?"

Chagalla nodded. "I told you that Allah would redress all grievances." He paused, taking a long puff on his cigar. "Such exquisite justice! Our God is a sly one, is He not?"

"I would trade Him for no other," agreed Major Juma happily.

Eighth Interlude (6303 G.E.)

I went to work verifying a Bafflediver measurement after learning the story of Amin Rashid XIV. Mandaka contacted me just before lunchtime.

"Have you any further information?" he asked.

"I learned that a war was fought over the tusks in 882 G.E.," I replied.

He frowned. "You know what I mean."

I shook my head. "The computer has been unable to locate them since Tahiti Benoit stole them from the Fly-by-Nights."

"You knew that two days ago."

"They'll turn up," I assured him. "It's just a matter of the computer being thorough and us being patient."

"Will you be spending the night at your office?" he asked.

"Yes."

"I'll contact you again toward midnight."

"You needn't bother," I replied. "I'll get in touch with you the instant I've located them."

"I'll contact you tonight," he repeated, breaking the connection.

"I'm sure you will," I said to the empty space where his image had been.

The remainder of the day passed slowly, as I brought some of my routine bookkeeping up to date, and parceled out the coming week's authentication assignments to my staff. I had a short meeting with the artist who would be illustrating the Quinellus Cluster edition, explained to her once again how our color process worked and what guidelines our technicians would need, and then, at four o'clock, I ordered a glass of fruit juice and sat back on my chair, trying to think of any further suggestions I could give the computer that would help it to locate the ivory.

"I hope you're going to dress somewhat better than *that*," said a familiar voice, and I looked up to see Hilda Dorian standing in my doorway. She had done something with her hair since breakfast, and was wearing a very elegant pink and green outfit that I hadn't seen before. She was even wearing the old diamond-and-starstone engagement ring that Harold had given her some twenty-odd years ago.

"What's the occasion?" I asked, staring at her.

"The company party."

"Didn't we just have one?"

"That was a year ago."

"Really?"

"And you missed it," she continued.

"I must have been sick," I said.

"Hah!"

There was a long silence.

"Well, enjoy yourself," I said at last.

"You're coming too, Duncan."

I shook my head. "I have work to do."

"Duncan, it's been four years since you attended the company party."

"Everybody gets drunk and plays stupid games," I replied. "It's not the kind of thing I enjoy."

"Believe it or not, it's not the kind of thing *I* enjoy either," she said. "But I go because it's expected of me—and *this* year you're going too."

"Not a chance," I said. "Mandaka's checking in with me at midnight."

"Mandaka doesn't pay your salary, and he doesn't own your computer," she said patiently. "Wilford Braxton's does, and they suggested very strongly to me that your presence is desired."

"Oh, come on, Hilda—they won't even know if I'm there or not," I said. "I've got more important things to do."

"You have *nothing* more important to do," she said firmly. "Your employers feel that your constant absence from the parties harms staff morale."

"My staff came here to research and authenticate records of big game, not go off to play party games and listen to boring speeches," I shot back. "If they really want to increase staff morale, tell them to hand out a general raise."

She glared at me. "Duncan, I promised them that you would come, and I'm not going to let you make a liar out of me."

"You had no business telling them that," I said. "I happen to have a deadline, remember?"

"I'll extend it six hours."

I shook my head. "No deal. The last time I went, old Hammond's wife latched onto me and talked my ear off for four hours."

"Mr. Hammond's wife has been dead for more than three years," she said. "You can't use her as an excuse."

"That long?" I said, surprised.

"You went to the funeral."

"I thought it was just a few months ago."

"Three years, Duncan."

"You're sure?"

"Duncan, I don't know why I waste my time with you! You're so wrapped up in your work you don't have any conception of time or propriety or anything else!"

"I don't know why you bother, either," I said honestly. "Maybe you should just give it up as a lost cause and let me get back to tracking down the ivory."

"Duncan, you've got to stop thinking about yourself and what makes *you* happy!" she snapped, and this time she was truly furious. "It won't hurt you to go to the party, and you'll make life much easier for me! Your employer wants you to go, your staff expects you to go, and I insist that you go. That's all there is to it."

"I don't have any formal clothing," I said.

She walked over to my closet and studied the outfits hanging there, then pulled one out. "This will do just fine."

"Everyone will be dressed better than me," I said. "I'll feel awkward."

"Then it will be your own fault," she replied. "You've known about this night for months."

"I just heard about it now."

"Nonsense. The company mailed out invitations to all of its employees."

"I never got one."

"Computer?" she said.

"An invitation was received one hundred and eight days ago," said the computer. "There have been four subsequent messages requesting confirmation of attendance, all of which have been ignored."

"Thanks a lot, friend," I muttered, glaring at the glowing crystal.

"You are welcome, Duncan Rojas," responded the computer.

"Now, if you're all through pouting and protesting, I want you to change into this outfit and be ready to leave at five o'clock sharp."

"Why torture *me*?" I demanded. "You've got a husband. Why not make *him* take you?"

"Harold will be meeting us there."

"Then go in peace, have a good time with him, give him my regards, and leave me alone."

"Harold is coming because he is an adult, and he accepts the responsibilities of adulthood," replied Hilda. "It's about time you learned to do the same."

"It's about time I found the ivory."

"The ivory can wait," she said. "Besides, the computer will be working while you're at the party."

"The computer isn't making any progress," I said. "It's going to need more direction."

"Then you'll direct it when the party's over."

"That's eight hours from now!"

"You're breaking my heart, Duncan," she said sarcastically. Then she paused. "Why not try going with an open mind?" she suggested at last. "You might enjoy it."

I stared at her but made no reply.

"You might even find a nice young woman," she continued. "Although what a nice young woman would see in you is utterly beyond me."

"What do *you* see in me?" I asked.

She looked at me thoughtfully and sighed. "I'll be damned if I know anymore," she said. "Once upon a time I saw a brilliant young man with a good sense of humor. You were a little eccentric, and I've always liked eccentric people." She paused. "But as the years go by, the eccentricity has evolved into a monomaniacal work ethic and the sense of humor is usually absent."

"And the brilliance?"

"You're still brilliant, but brilliance isn't enough, Duncan. You have no social graces, and you care about nothing but your work. You have a tendency to hurt people through carelessness rather than malevolence, and I'm not at all sure that that's preferable; it implies that they aren't worth the effort to avoid hurting, or even to hurt on purpose."

"Then why do you still bother with me?"

"Because I've known you for almost half my life, and you don't walk away from half a lifetime, even if it didn't work out the way you had hoped." She paused. "Besides, if Harold and I didn't care about you, who would?"

I shrugged, unable to come up with an answer.

"I realize that you'd probably be happier if no one took an interest in you," continued Hilda, "but you can't have everything you want in this life. Now, are you going to change into this outfit, or I am going to have to deny you access to the computer?"

"You'd actually do that?" I demanded.

"I would."

"I don't suppose you'd consider just yelling at me for another ten minutes and leaving alone?"

She shook her head adamantly. "You're only thirty years or so past adolescence," she said. "I still hold out some slight hope that you'll grow up someday."

"Five o'clock?" I said, defeated.

"Right." She pointed a pudgy forefinger at me. "And you'd better be ready, Duncan."

I nodded my acquiescence, she left the room, and I immediately began scribbling down possible channels of inquiry to give to the computer before I left for the evening.

I got back to the office at eleven o'clock, having decided half an hour earlier that Hilda was having such a good time that she'd never notice my absence.

The party had been as tedious and boring as I had feared. Everyone, even the Braxton heirs, threw themselves into a group songfest and seemed to feel a sense of camaraderie and goodwill that somehow eluded me, and then a live band arrived and Hilda actually made me dance once around the floor with her, despite my protestations that I hadn't danced in years. Everyone else seemed to be having such a good time that I began wondering if she was right, if there was something missing within me—but then I thought of Mandaka sitting on his floor, wrapped in an ancient tribal blanket and seeking the ivory for God knew what purpose, and I decided that it must be the rest of them who were out of step with reality, that no amount of party games and social chatter measured up to the thrill of tracking the ivory through the eons. I knew then that I had more in common with this strange black man who had been raised in a hut and had never seen another child than I did with any of my co-workers, even with Hilda. They sought the warmth of others, while we sought the solitary path of the hunt.

Well, I amended, *we* didn't seek it. Even Mandaka would rather have lived the life of a Braxton's employee if he had had a choice. *I* sought it. I could observe Hilda with Harold, could see the fondness and tenderness they still felt for each other after all these years written clearly upon their faces, but it seemed somehow empty. They would be returning to their house, to waste more time with idle chatter and perhaps watch a holo or two, and another evening would have slipped away from them forever, an evening without challenge, without accomplishment, without the excitement of the hunt. They'd awake happy and tranquil and fulfilled eight hours from now—but *I'd* awake another step closer to the tusks, and I realized that I wouldn't trade places with them for anything.

"Computer!" I said.

"Yes, Duncan Rojas?"

"Have you found the tusks yet?"

"No."

"Have you amassed any data whatever concerning them since they were stolen by Tahiti Benoit?"

"No."

I sat down and frowned. "Give me some warmth in the small of my back," I ordered the chair.

"Done."

"Computer, I need to think. Please play Ghanetski's *Altairian Rhapsody in B-flat Minor*, and make the west wall opaque."

"Working . . . done," said the computer as the room was flooded with Ghanetski's passionate rhythms.

I sat motionless for perhaps ten minutes, letting wave after wave of the music sweep over me, emptying my mind of all thought and then starting to construct the comprehensive whole of the puzzle anew.

"Computer?"

"Yes, Duncan Rojas?"

"What percentage of your capacity are you devoting to searching for the tusks?"

"Seventy-three point two-three-one percent."

"And how far have you progressed since the year the year 5730 G.E.?"

"I have made no progress."

"I must not have made myself clear," I said. "Surely you are progressing in a logical pattern. You must have eliminated the years 5731, 5732, and so on. Where are you at now?"

"I am searching for the tusks chronologically, alphabetically, pictorially, by subject, by location, by museum, by auction, by description, and by accounts in biographical memoirs. I have completed none of the searches as yet."

"I see," I said. "All right. I want you to take half of the

capacity that you are expending on this problem and find out when and where Tahiti Benoit died. There's always a chance that if the tusks don't surface again, she never got rid of them." I paused. "She died two years after stealing them; there probably wasn't much of a legitimate market for them. It's possible that because Leeyo Nelion was willing to offer so much for them, she was holding out for a comparable offer, which of course would not be forthcoming from museums or collectors, or from anywhere else unless one of Nelion's offspring knew not only that she had the ivory but how to find her. And since we know that the Maasai never got their hands on it . . ." I let my voice trail off.

"Working . . ."

"Good," I said, leaning back and ordering my chair to adapt itself to the contours of my body and to vibrate very gently. "Computer?"

"Yes?"

"Why do *you* think he wants them?"

"I do not understand your question."

"The tusks—why do you think Mandaka wants them?"

"Insufficient data."

"What do you think he plans to do with them?"

"Insufficient data."

I paused. "How many men my age spend more nights at the office than at home?"

"You must be more explicit," replied the computer. "Do you refer to men with your identical birthdate or those who currently share your chronological age—and do you refer to men on this planet, in this system, within the Commonwealth, or in the galaxy?"

I sighed. "Never mind, Computer." I closed my eyes and listened to a particularly moving strain of the *Rhapsody*. "Computer?"

"Yes?"

"Is there more than this?"

"I do not understand your question."

"Should I want the things that other people want?"

"You must be more explicit," replied the computer.

"Friends, family, children, a wife."

"I am not programmed to make value judgments in that area."

"Create a sub-program and answer my question."

"Working . . . No, Duncan Rojas, there is nothing more than the quest for knowledge."

"You're certain?"

"No, Duncan Rojas, I am not certain. I have created a sub-program based on my own imperatives. If you were a machine, I would be certain."

"Thank you anyway, computer," I said.

I must have dozed off then, because the next thing I knew it was two o'clock in the morning, and I had a stale taste in my mouth.

"Computer?"

"Yes, Duncan Rojas?"

"Have you located the ivory yet?"

"No."

"Have you pinpointed the time and place of Tahiti Benoit's death?"

"No."

I got up, used the bathroom, and took a quick dryshower. Then the computer summoned me.

"Bukoba Mandaka is attempting to communicate with you."

"Put him through, on visual."

Mandaka's face appeared above the computer.

"I tried to contact you at eleven o'clock," he said accusingly, "but you weren't there."

"I had an unavoidable engagement," I explained.

"Did it have to do with the ivory?"

"No."

"Then you had no right to go," he said sternly. "I am paying for your time."

"It was a company function," I replied, "and I was told in no uncertain terms that if I failed to attend, my use of the computer would be curtailed."

He stared at me for a moment, then nodded his head.

"Have you located the ivory?"

"No," I said. "I've instructed the computer to go back and try to find out when and where Tahiti Benoit died. This line of inquiry is based on the assumption that Leeyo Nelion's descendants never got their hands on it. Can you confirm that?"

"Tembo Laibon was the last Maasai to possess the tusks," he responded. His expression darkened, as it always did when he mentioned Tembo Laibon. "We had them for thirteen centuries and that fool gave them away in a card game!"

"Perhaps he didn't know their value," I suggested.

"He knew," said Mandaka with conviction. "Every Maasai knew. It should never have come down to him, or to me. The first Maasai who owned them should have done what had to be done."

"The first?" I said. "You mean Maasai Laibon?"

He nodded silently, his gaze fixed on some distant place and time that only he could see. There was such pain on his face, such infinite bitterness, that I wanted to comfort him somehow.

"I'll find them," I said lamely. "You have my word, Bukoba Mandaka."

"I know you will," he said, his expression unchanging.

"I'll contact you the moment I know where they are," I continued awkwardly.

"Yes," he said softly.

I watched him for another minute, wondering what to say next, and finally he took the burden from me by breaking the connection.

"Computer?" I said after another moment's silence.

"Yes, Duncan Rojas?"

"*Was* Maasai Laibon the first Maasai to own the tusks?"

"Yes."

"And he passed them on to his descendants, and so on all the way down to the time of Tembo Laibon?"

"That is correct."

"I wonder how Maasai Laibon came into possession of the ivory in the first place?"

"Is that a direct question?" asked the computer.

"Yes," I said. "Do you know the answer?"

"Working . . . Yes, now I know."

9

The Artist
(1701 G.E.)

As I approached the base of Kilimanjaro, I stopped more and more frequently to fill my belly with water, for though I possessed an enormous hunger, my teeth were worn down and I could no longer chew my food. My head ached, my joints were stiff, and I had to stop to rest more and more often.

I tested the wind many times, for men lived at the base of the mountain, and I had no desire to encounter them. I had barely enough strength to climb to the top of Kilimanjaro and confront my God, and I knew that I would never come back down. Even the white egrets which had been my constant companions seemed to sense that I was preparing to die, for all but one of them deserted me as I neared the mountain. I lingered at one last waterhole, dusted my skin one last time, and then approached a narrow pathway leading to the lower slopes.

He stood six feet four inches tall, and his skin was black. She measured eleven feet two inches from tip of nose to tip of tail, and her skin was an intricate pattern of blue and green.

He saw his world through cold brown eyes; she saw what no one else could see through her glowing red orbs.

He was a Man; she was a Nightcrawler.

His name was Maasai Laibon; her name was Eyes-of-Fire.

They had never met . . . but eventually they would, for she possessed something he wanted. It was her greatest treasure and his greatest need.

She lived in a cave on Belamone XI, where the temperature never rose above zero degrees centigrade, and swirling gases diffused the light from the distant red sun.

From birth she had been something rare, a blind creature born into a sighted race and yet somehow not *of* that race, a Nightcrawler who could not see normal sights but could read far into the infrared spectrum, who observed life as a series of electrical patterns rather than solid forms. With the tendrils that extended from her neck she carefully and delicately etched what she saw, and though at first her execution lacked sophistication, the exquisite figures that she created were beautiful beyond belief.

Some races would have killed a blind infant at birth. Others would have used every scientific innovation at their command to restore her normal vision. A few would have treated her as a helpless invalid, to be cared for and cosseted for the rest of her life. But the Nightcrawlers did none of these things. Instead, they encouraged her to master her art, to produce more accurate renditions of the things their instruments could sense but that they themselves could never see.

By the time she was forty-five years old, she was considered one of the finest artists of her generation. When she reached her true maturity, at age eighty, she decided that

it was time to embark upon the project for which she had
been training all her life. It was to be a scrimshaw of the
Nightcrawlers' racial history as seen from her unique per-
spective, an intricate series of images that would chronicle
the evolution of her race from mindless grub to starfaring
intellect, and would bring a new depth of understanding
to the race's experience.

When it came time to begin her project, one of the planet's major trading houses presented her with two columns
of ivory, which had been obtained from the humans whose
Republic, though currently under economic siege from a
number of races, remained the dominant force in the galaxy.
The ivory had come from the largest mammal to walk across
Man's home planet, and had survived for almost 3,000 years.
Eyes-of-Fire agreed that any organic material that could
maintain its structural integrity for so long was an ideal
substance upon which to produce her history; furthermore,
the Nightcrawlers had signed treaties with Man, and had
joined the list of Man's allies, so it was only just and fitting
that a treasure from Man's home world should be an integral
part of her exhaustive depiction of her race's history.

She began her creation on the day that Maasai Laibon
was born.

She worked slowly, carefully, with incredibly delicacy
and precision, while Maasai Laibon grew to manhood, finished his schooling, served four years in the Republic's
navy, took a wife, and sired two sons and a daughter. He
was a serious young man, more concerned with the past
and the future than with the present, and when he turned
thirty he moved his wife and children into his parents' house
while he set off to find the tusks of the Kilimanjaro Elephant.

His search spanned the entire galaxy, beginning with
Alpha Bednari IV and leading him to the Spiral Arm, the

Rim, the Outer Frontier, and the Inner Frontier, as well as to twenty-six worlds of the Republic itself. It took him through museums and millionaires' retreats, through grubby barrooms and alien cities, and twice it landed him in hospitals when people didn't like the questions he was asking or the way he asked them.

But finally, after twelve years, he pinpointed the location of the ivory: it was on Belamone XI, a frigid little oxygen world inhabited by the Nightcrawlers, snakelike beings that had recently pledged their allegiance to the Republic.

He flew to the Belamone system, landed on Belamone XI, and had the Republic's ambassador begin making inquiries about the location of the ivory. Finally he learned that it was in the possession of a female named Eyes-of-Fire, and he submitted a formal request to meet with her.

It was ignored.

He waited patiently while another, more urgent request was sent.

It was rejected.

Finally, he found out where her cave was, and, telling no one of his intentions, he unpacked a coldsuit, stocked it with provisions for six weeks, and quietly set off to meet Eyes-of-Fire.

It took him four days to find her, the four coldest days of his life, but at last he entered her cave. It was totally dark, for she had no need of light, and he activated the power-pack attached to the lamp on his helmet.

The cave seemed empty, but it showed signs of habitation and so, step by cautious step, he proceeded into the winding, twisting interior until, after more than a quarter of a mile, he came to her.

To his eyes she looked like an enormous gray slug, with two glowing red coals for eyes, and half a dozen long, delicate tendrils emanating from her neck.

To her, he seemed like a geometric pattern, the heat of his body extending in all directions, the path of his bloodstream like tiny little rivulets of electricity racing in an endless but not unpleasing procession.

"You are the one they call Eyes-of-Fire?" he asked, his voice echoing through the cave.

"Yes," she replied in a sibilant, moaning whisper.

"My name is Maasai Laibon."

"I know who you are," she replied. "Twice I have refused to see you. You have broken protocol by entering my dwelling place without permission."

"I apologize," said Maasai Laibon, "but I come on a matter of the utmost importance to my race."

"I know why you are here, Maasai Laibon," she said, her glowing eyes focusing on him.

"You do?"

"Am I not Eyes-of-Fire, who sees things that others may only guess at?"

"You have something that does not belong to you," said Maasai Laibon. "It is something for which my people have searched over the centuries."

"You refer, of course, to the ivory," said Eyes-of-Fire, the shadows flickering off her huge, ungainly body as her side rose and fell in time with her breathing.

"I do."

"But it is no longer the ivory that was brought to me more than forty years ago," she said. "It is now the housing for what will become the Sacred Art of my race."

"It belonged to my race first," said Maasai Laibon, "and we must have it back."

She stared at him with her sightless but seeing red eyes. "It will do you no good, Maasai Laibon," she replied calmly.

He sat down on the hard floor, and propped his back up against a stone wall.

"You do not know why we need it," he said.

"Yes I do, Maasai Laibon, for my blind eyes can see into the past as well as the future, and I tell you again that the possession of the ivory will bring you no fulfillment." She paused. "I foresaw that you would come here, against all advice, seeking the ivory. You are even in the scrimshaw, Maasai Laibon."

"I am?" he asked, surprised.

"Yes."

"If you can see into the future, what will I say next?"

"I do not know."

"Then you can't see into the future."

"Poor human, who like my own race sees only the Here and the Now," said Eyes-of-Fire. "The past is fixed and immutable, but the future hinges upon an infinity of choices. I have seen the choices you are most likely to make, and I say that possession of the ivory will not restore your people to their former glory."

"Possession of it is just the first step," said Maasai Laibon.

"Will you do what must be done, Maasai Laibon?" she asked. "Will you take your uncircumcised son to the mountain on Earth and redeem your people?"

"No," he said, trying to hide his surprise at the extent of her knowledge. "It is enough that I will bring the ivory back to the Maasai. Others will carry on from there."

"No others will carry on, Maasai Laibon," whispered Eyes-of-Fire. "And eventually the ivory will pass from the possession of the Maasai."

"Never!" he exclaimed. "Once we have it, we will never relinquish it!"

"Yes you will, Maasai Laibon," she said serenely. "There are two equally probable futures for the ivory. In one, it will remain on Belamone XI for all eternity, someday to become the Holiest of Holies of my race. In the other, it shall travel to the farthest ends of the galaxy, bringing death to many and unhappiness to more."

"It will become the property of the Maasai, and there it will stay," he said firmly.

She shook her sightless, reptilian head. "No, Maasai Laibon—that is not the futures that I read."

"Then you are mistaken."

A shrug began at her head and slithered down the entire length of her body, sending harsh shadows racing throughout the cave.

"Perhaps," she said.

"I must have it."

"I cannot relinquish it to you," she replied. "I have worked on it for more than forty years. The larger tusk is complete, the smaller one more than half-done. They represent my life, and I will not part with them."

"I am not without resources," he said. "Name your price."

"There is no price high enough, Maasai Laibon," she answered.

"Perhaps we can reach a compromise," he suggested. "Can your artwork be transferred to another medium?"

"No," she said. "Nowhere have I cut deeper than a thousandth of a millimeter, nowhere is there a line so bold that it can be seen without instrumentation or special enhancement. What I have done cannot be copied or transferred." She paused. "So delicate is the work that the tusks cannot even be moved. The mere touch of your hand would wipe away centuries of my race's history. This mountain shall become a shrine, and all who wish to see the completed work will make their pilgrimage to this very cave, where they will use special instrumentation that will enable them to see my artistry."

"I am very sorry," said Maasai Laibon, "but that will not come to pass. When I leave Belamone XI, the ivory leaves with me."

"You still mean to take the ivory, even after what I have told you?"

"I do."

"I cannot permit it, Maasai Laibon."

"And I will not be denied it, Eyes-of-Fire."

"You have come here without weapons," she noted ominously.

"I came only to talk—this time."

"If you come back, I will kill you."

"When I come back, I will take that chance."

Maasai Laibon entered the ambassador's office and walked, aloof and arrogant, to a chair.

"I'll come right to the point," said the ambassador, looking up from his computer terminal. "Two hours ago I was ready to throw you off the planet."

"Oh?" said Maasai Laibon, his face an expressionless mask, his gaze fixed on the endless white landscape just beyond the ambassador's window.

"Did you or did you not visit the Nightcrawler known as Eyes-of-Fire?"

"I did."

"You had been expressly forbidden to do so."

"I obey a higher imperative than Nightcrawler law," replied Maasai Laibon.

"Well, you don't obey any higher imperative than human law, and I'm all the human law there is on this planet," said the ambassador severely. "I told you not to go and you went anyway. I could have had you arrested for that!" The ambassador glared at him for a long moment, then sighed. "But half an hour ago I received a direct communication from the Nightcrawlers."

"Oh?"

"It seems that Eyes-of-Fire doesn't want you harmed, detained, or forced to leave against your will." He paused. "I have no choice but to honor her request—but I'll be damned if I can understand it." He shook his head in frustration. "The longer I deal with aliens, the more convinced I become that *none* of them make any sense!"

"If you are not arresting me or ordering me to leave, why have I been summoned here?" asked Maasai Laibon.

"Because I want to know what's going on," said the ambassador. "For example, what is so damned important about Eyes-of-Fire, anyway? No one beyond this planet has ever even heard of her."

"She has something that doesn't belong to her."

"Something you think belongs to you?"

"To my people."

"Damn it, man, *I* am one of your people, and I assure you that she has nothing that belongs to me!"

"My people are the Maasai race, and she has something which must be returned to us."

"What the hell is the Maasai race? I've never heard of it."

"A race of men."

"There are no races of men, Maasai Laibon," said the ambassador firmly. "There is only Man, and then there is everything else. It's us against the galaxy."

"If that is true, then in the long run the galaxy will win," offered Maasai Laibon.

"Not before we give it a good run for its money," the ambassador assured him confidently. He paused for a moment. "But we're getting away from the subject. What does she have that you think belongs to you?"

"A set of ivory tusks."

"The ivory?" said the ambassador, surprised. "She's been working on it for almost half a century."

Maasai Laibon stared expressionlessly into the ambassador's eyes. "She had no right to," he said with conviction.

"It's a little late to come barging in to tell her that now. I gather her project will be complete in another decade."

Maasai Laibon shook his head. "Her project will never be complete. I am taking the ivory with me when I leave."

"Can you prove that it's yours?"

"Not to your satisfaction," replied Maasai Laibon.

"Then you have no legal claim to it."

Maasai Laibon paused. "I have a *racial* claim to it," he said at last.

"Not that any court of law would recognize."

"That is why I have not gone to a court of law."

"Why did you wait more than forty years before arriving to claim it?" asked the ambassador.

"It took me many years to track it down."

"Why do you think it belongs to you?"

"I don't think you would understand," said Maasai Laibon.

"Try me."

"No."

"Damn it, man, I'm your only representative on this snowball of a world! If you can't convince *me* of the justice of your claim, how to you expect to convince *them*?"

"Eyes-of-Fire knows why I must have the ivory."

"You told *her* and you won't tell *me*?" demanded the ambassador heatedly.

"I did not tell her; she knew."

"She's an oversized earthworm who's never been ten miles from her cave," said the ambassador. "How could she know?"

Maasai Laibon shrugged.

"Aren't you even curious?" persisted the ambassador.

"No."

"Let me put it another way: doesn't her knowledge imply that she has already been contacted by one of your Maasai? And if *he* was willing to let her keep the ivory, then perhaps you should be guided by his actions."

"She has never seen a Maasai."

"Then how—?

"She is a mystic," continued Maasai Laibon. "She sees things that others cannot see, and she knows things that others do not know. She knows the history of the tusks, and can see their future. She knew that I would come for them."

"But she refused to give them to you," said the ambassador. "So doubtless she knows that you will leave here without them."

"As she explained to me, there is one past, but there are many possible futures; she is trying to manipulate events so that they will favor the future she most desires." He paused. "She is doomed to fail."

The ambassador stared at him, half-convinced that the man before him was fully as mad as the alien race with which he had to deal—and considerably more dangerous. "I tell you here and now, Maasai Laibon, that should anything happen to Eyes-of-Fire or to the ivory, I will not rest until you have been apprehended and punished."

"You have your duty," said Maasai Laibon, rising to his feet and walking to the door. "And I have mine."

The next morning Maasai Laibon landed his ship about half a mile from Eyes-of-Fire's cave. He once again donned his awkward but essential protective suit, checked the power packs on his laser pistol and molecular imploder, inserted both weapons into their slots on his broad belt, waited for the shot he had administered himself to raise his adrenaline level, and finally set off for his destination, ignoring the winds that howled around him and limited his vision.

Twenty minutes later he entered the cave, and though his suit had kept its internal temperature constant, he *felt* warmer simply because of the lack of snow and wind. He began walking toward the spot where he had first encountered Eyes-of-Fire, the shadows jumping ominously before his headlamp.

She was where he expected to find her, her glowing red eyes visible long before he could make out the rest of her massive, boneless body.

"You have come again, Maasai Laibon," she said in her sibilant whisper.

"I have come again," he replied, startled once again by the echoes his voice created in the bleak interior of the cave. "Why did you tell the ambassador to allow me to stay on the planet?"

"Because it has been ordained that you would come again, and there was no need to involve your ambassador, or ask him to stand against the inevitable."

He withdrew the laser pistol and pointed it toward her. "I will have the ivory," he said. "Please do not make me kill you to get it."

"My life is of no consequence," she said calmly. "It is my art that matters."

"You shouldn't have used the ivory."

"It was ordained that I should use the ivory," replied Eyes-of-Fire, "just as it was ordained that you and I would meet under these circumstances at this exact time and place."

"Ordained by whom?" asked Maasai Laibon.

"By the Creator of All Things," she said.

"You believe in a God?"

"The same God that you believe in, Maasai Laibon," said Eyes-of-Fire. "The same God who has removed the seed of greatness from your race, and who will not return it simply because a thief has traveled to a distant world to rob an artist of her work."

"I *must* take it back with me," he said.

"I know. But it will bring the Maasai nothing but unhappiness, and eventually it will pass from their hands."

"Is that the curse of a doomed Nightcrawler?" he asked sardonically.

"No," replied Eyes-of-Fire calmly. "It is the insight of a gifted Nightcrawler. You will kill me and take the ivory, but it will not bring you what you hope for."

"I don't have to kill you," he said. "Move aside and let me take the ivory in peace."

She shook her head, casting fearsome shadows on the floor and walls. "You must kill me first."

"It's not necessary."

"It *is* necessary," she replied. "Yesterday I stopped working on the scrimshaw. The very last scene I depicted was my death, which I suffered at your hands."

"Art doesn't have to mirror life," he said. "I have no wish to kill you, Eyes-of-Fire. Let me have the ivory and leave in peace."

"You shall never know peace again, Maasai Laibon," she whispered. "Your number shall diminish, your power shall evaporate on the wind, your children's grandchildren will not even know the meaning of the ivory, and eventually all shall become dust."

"You are wrong!"

"I am right," she said, slithering her enormous bulk across the floor toward him. "And now you must kill me, Maasai Laibon, or I shall surely kill you."

He took a step backward, then another, but when she

kept approaching him he finally fired his weapon. She collapsed in a shuddering heap, but it was a full five minutes before the light of life left her glowing eyes, and another ten before he finally was able to force himself to walk around her body.

He found the ivory in a small chamber some thirty feet away, and dragged it back to the shuttlecraft, one tusk at a time. Long before he reached his destination, the last of the delicate etchings had been destroyed.

NINTH INTERLUDE (6303 G.E.)

I had come full circle. The next chronological appearance of the ivory was during Tembo Laibon's fatal poker game. I knew everything there was to know about the tusks of the Kilimanjaro Elephant except the two most important things: where they were and what Bukoba Mandaka intended to do with them.

"Computer?"

"Yes, Duncan Rojas?"

"Have you amassed any data on the whereabouts of the ivory since Tahiti Benoit stole it from Winox IV?" I asked wearily.

"No, I have not."

"Have you pinpointed the time and place of Tahiti Benoit's death?"

"No, I have not."

"Well, keep working on it."

"Yes, Duncan Rojas."

"I'm going to take a nap," I said, leaning back on my chair. "Wake me in two hours."

"That will be at five-fifty-three A.M.," announced the computer.

"Whatever."

"Would you like some music?"

"No," I replied. "I'm sleeping, not thinking."

But I was wrong. The harder I tried to sleep, the more active my mind became. Why had the ivory disappeared from view for the past six centuries? Why had Maasai Laibon killed for it? Why had Leeyo Nelion risked lifetime imprisonment to have it stolen? Why was Bukoba Mandaka prepared to commit any crime from murder to treason to possess it?

And in the back of my mind there was yet another Maasai name: the ancient Laibon Sendeyo. Why did the mere fact that he once mentioned the ivory imply a chance, slight but measurable, that the ivory was in some way responsible for the Maasai race's fall from power and primacy?

I was still pondering these questions when the computer informed me that it was 5:53 A.M.

"Did you locate the tusks yet?" I asked without much hope.

"No. But I have learned when and where Tahiti Benoit died."

"Please tell me."

"She died in 5732 G.E. on the planet Bartus III, also known as Skyblue."

"How did she die?"

"She died from a brain aneurysm. According to the coroner's report, death was instantaneous."

"Then Skyblue was her headquarters at the time of her death?"

"Yes."

"Excellent!" I exclaimed. "That means if she hadn't sold

or traded the ivory, it was on Skyblue at the time of her death."

"That seems logical."

"And if she *had* sold or traded it, you would have found some reference to it by now."

"The probability, at this point in my search, is 54.231%."

"Then there's a better than even chance that the ivory is on Skyblue."

"No, Duncan Rojas," corrected the computer. "There is a better than even chance that it *was* on Skyblue at the time of her death."

"All right," I said, getting to my feet. "I'm going out for breakfast. I want you to use all your available capacity to discover if the ivory left Skyblue after 5732 G.E."

"Working . . ."

I walked out of my office, caught the airlift down to the lobby level, nodded to a couple of the guards, and had one of them let me out the front door of the building. I took the slidewalk to a nearby restaurant that I frequented when I felt like eating outside the building, but as I approached its entrance I realized that I was too excited to eat. If the ivory hadn't been sold or traded, *if* the computer could find no record of it leaving Skyblue, *if* Tahiti Benoit had kept possession of it from the time of the theft until her death two years later . . .

Finally, too tense and keyed up to stand passively on the slidewalk as it took me from one location to the next, I stepped off it and began walking briskly down a major thoroughfare. My actions would have been impossible two hours later, and might even have gotten me an official reprimand, but the city was just now coming to life, the streets were relatively empty, and I continued working off my excess energy until it dawned on me that I had finally worked up an appetite after all.

I stopped at the first restaurant I came to, only to discover that it did not serve breakfast and would not open for another five hours. I walked a few yards further and came to a small, bustling little restaurant that had a mixed clientele of humans and aliens. I looked in through the window, saw that a few small tables were empty, and entered.

The tripodal manager from Hesporite III led me to a table in the back, activated his translator mechanism, and explained that unless I was a regular customer whose daily dietary needs were on file with the restaurant's computer, I would have to call up a menu and order while at the table.

I thanked him, ordered the tabletop to display the day's fare, studied it as each item was cast in a rather crude hologram above the table, and then announced my choices. My meal, somewhat undercooked, arrived less than a minute later, enclosed in a vacuum pack which opened upon voice command.

While I was sipping my coffee and wondering exactly what kind of mutated chicken my omelet had come from, the tabletop glowed to life again, flashing news, business and sports headlines and informing me that I could watch a hologram replay of the previous night's freehand middleweight championship bout for an extra ten credits. It seemed a reasonable price, especially since it would take my attention from the food (which was not of very high quality), but when the fight appeared I found out the reason for the price: it had lasted only two minutes and 43 seconds, and was such a one-sided contest that it killed that small portion of my appetite that remained after my first mouthful of the omelet.

I had the meal debited from my petty cash account, then left the restaurant and slid back to the office, my excitement mounting as I neared the Braxton Building.

"Back so soon, Mr. Rojas?" asked one of the guards pleasantly.

"I've got a long day's work ahead of me," I said, hoping that I was right.

I waited impatiently for an airshaft, ascended to my office level, and practically ran down the corridor.

"Computer!" I said as the door opened for me.

"Yes, Duncan Rojas?"

"Did the ivory ever leave Skyblue?"

"No, it did not."

"Then we've got it!"

"Skyblue is a world approximately eight thousand miles in diameter," noted the computer, "with a dry land mass covering approximately twenty-eight percent of the planetary surface. Knowing that the ivory is there does not mean that you have found it."

I checked the time: it was 6:51. "I'll find it before Braxton's opens for business this morning," I said confidently. "I want you to tie into every museum and art gallery, every public and private trophy collection, and every natural history society on the planet to see if you can locate the tusks."

"Working . . ."

"And patch through a call to Bukoba Mandaka."

"Done."

A moment later Mandaka's image appeared above the computer. Evidently I had awakened him, for he was blinking his eyes rapidly and frowning as he tried to focus them on me.

"Mr. Mandaka, this is Duncan Rojas."

"Mr. Rojas!" he said excitedly. "Have you found the tusks?"

"Almost," I said. "I've pinpointed the planet that they're on."

"How soon before you locate them precisely?"

I shrugged. "No more than an hour or two," I replied. "Probably less."

"I'll be right over!"

"That's not necessary. I can call you again when I've found their exact location—or you can simply remain tied into my computer."

"No," he said adamantly. "I want to be there, in person."

"But—"

"We may have some further business to discuss," he said. "In private."

"Whatever you wish."

"*That* is what I wish," he said, breaking the connection.

"Computer," I said, turning back to the glowing crystal, "have you found the ivory yet?"

"No, I have not."

"What is the population of Skyblue?"

"Three million."

"How many museums and galleries and collectors can there be?" I asked.

"There is only one museum," replied the computer. "There are eleven art galleries and twenty-four proclaimed collectors. There is no natural history society."

"How many have you checked?"

"All but one gallery and two private collections. Still working . . . done. None of them have the ivory."

"One of them's *got* to," I muttered.

"All responses have been negative, Duncan Rojas."

"Maybe it belongs to a gallery or collector who doesn't want to part with it," I said without much conviction.

I considered the possibilities for a moment, then turned back to the glowing crystal.

"Computer, what time is it at Skyblue's museum?"

"It is midafternoon."

"Connect me with the museum's Natural History Curator."

"Working . . ." It paused. "There is no Natural History Curator."

"Then connect me with whoever is in charge of the museum."

"Working . . . done."

The image of a middle-aged woman who wore mannish earrings and not enough makeup appeared in the air above the computer.

"Good afternoon," I said. "I am Duncan Rojas, Chief Researcher for Wilford Braxton's."

"I am Hazel Guthridge, the Curator of the Skyblue Planetary Museum. What can I do for you, Mr. Rojas?"

"I have reason to believe that the tusks of a certain elephant may be on Skyblue," I began. "I have a client who is prepared to pay quite handsomely for them."

"An elephant?" she said, frowning. "No, we have no elephants on display here."

"I'm not searching for an entire elephant," I explained patiently. "My client just wants the tusks."

"I understand that—but we only display flora and fauna that are native to Skyblue."

"I have virtually irrefutable data that the tusks were on Skyblue five hundred and seventy-five years ago, and that they have never been exported. Possibly they were mistaken for the tusks or horns of a local life-form."

She shook her head. "My understanding is that the elephant was an enormous beast. None of our native life-forms begin to approach it in size." She paused. "Why are these tusks so valuable?"

"They're a family heirloom," I answered. "In truth, they are valuable only to my client."

"And not to a museum that specializes in Earth animals?" she asked sharply.

"Let me rephrase that," I said hastily. "My client is the only private party who will pay above and beyond their standard value as established by museum auctions."

"I see," she said. "But I still don't know how I can help you, Mr. Rojas. As I said, we display only local fauna. Also, Natural History is one of our weaker divisions; our flora and fauna collection is far from extensive. I myself specialize in native gemstones and rare minerals."

"Have you ever seen the tusks of an African elephant?" I persisted.

"No," she replied, "but I would certainly know if they were on exhibit in my own museum."

"Let me transmit a holograph of them," I said. "This is very important to my client."

"I have a better suggestion," she replied. "I was on my way to a board meeting when you contacted me. Why don't I instruct our computer to transmit holograms of our Natural History wing, and if you see the tusks you can let me know. Although," she added, "even then I won't be able to be of much help to you. None of our exhibits are for sale."

"Thank you very much," I said. "I accept your generous offer."

"You're quite welcome," she replied with a businesslike smile. An instant later her face vanished, to be replaced by a hologram of the main hall of the Natural History wing. There was a diorama of a scene that seemed to be from the planet's tropical zones: a river, with numerous snakes and long, low, sturdy lizards. The museum's camera slowly turned 360 degrees, giving me a total view of the hall, but there was nothing there except a number of wood and bone carvings made by the humanoid native race.

There followed a chamber filled with exhibits of rather mediocre taxidermy, and it soon became apparent that the museum was in serious need of a Natural History curator: polar animals were mixed with grassland herbivores, and one particular diorama actually displayed a fish-eating amphibian grazing on some forest ferns.

Still, there was no sign of the ivory, and I waited impatiently while the camera took me through two more rooms of wingless avians and six-legged reptiles. Finally it came to the fossil display, and I leaned forward, since this was the most likely place for the ivory to be. The camera dwelt lovingly on numerous skeletons of small, rodent-like carnivores, a few sturdy herbivores, and even a giant, 25-foot-high dinosaur, but when it had completed its survey of the room I still hadn't seen the ivory.

The next room was filled with avian and reptile eggs, and then the hologram vanished.

"What happened?" I demanded.

"You have now seen the entire Natural History wing," announced my computer. "The transmission has concluded."

"But I didn't see the ivory!"

"There is no ivory listed in the museum's catalog," answered the computer. There was a brief pause. "What would you like me to do next, Duncan Rojas?"

I paused and considered my answer. "You've checked the more obvious places on Skyblue," I said at last. "Now start checking the less obvious ones."

"I will require guidance."

I sighed wearily. "Give me a minute to think."

I sat motionless, staring at the wall, trying to see if there was something I had missed. If there was, I couldn't think of it. If Tahiti Benoit hadn't sold the ivory, it was still on Skyblue—and if it was still on Skyblue, why hadn't it surfaced? The obvious answer was that she had hidden it somewhere—but if she had hidden it, it wouldn't have been inaccessible; it would have been with everything else she had hidden from the authorities.

"Computer?"

"Yes, Duncan Rojas?"

"When Tahiti Benoit died, what became of her possessions?"

"Checking . . . her house was purchased by a James Cawthorne. Her jewelry was sold at public auction for estate taxes. The money from the Torrance III robbery and the diamonds from the Sirius V robbery were returned to their rightful owners."

That was it. The ivory *couldn't* still be buried away somewhere, not if thorough searching had turned up everything else.

But if it had been found, where was it? It hadn't left the planet, that much was certain. But if it wasn't in the museum or the art galleries or any of the private collections . . .

And then a thought came to me.

"Computer?"

"Yes, Duncan Rojas?"

"I want a complete atmospheric, geological and climatic history of Skyblue."

"Working . . ."

"When you've got it, please make a hard copy for me."

"Understood."

I ordered a cup of coffee, then adjusted the opacity of the walls to allow more of the early morning light into the room. Then I lit a cigar, put my feet up on my desk, and waited for Bukoba Mandaka to arrive.

He showed up five minutes later, his face alive with anticipation.

"Have you found them yet?" he asked eagerly.

"No."

"But you definitely know what planet they're on?"

I nodded. "Bartus III, more commonly known as Sky-blue."

He looked blank. "I've never heard of it."

"Most people haven't. It's a colony planet about halfway to the Inner Frontier."

"And you say you'll have the location before Braxton's opens for business?"

"I may have been a little bit optimistic about that," I replied. "I've checked the museum, the art galleries, and all the private collections, and I haven't come up with the tusks yet."

He frowned. "What will you check next?"

"I'm working on an idea I had," I said. "Or rather, the computer is."

"It's *got* to find them!" he muttered, more to himself than to me. "I can't be thwarted this close to my goal!"

"While we're waiting for the computer," I said, "can you tell me anything about an ancient Maasai named Sendeyo?"

His jaw dropped. "What do you know about Sendeyo?"

"Not as much as I'd like to," I replied.

He stared at me but said nothing.

I was about to repeat my question, but just then the computer concluded its work and produced a printed read-out. I skimmed it quickly until I came to the pertinent items, then tossed it on my desk and leaned back on my chair once again.

"Mr. Mandaka, I think I know where the ivory is," I said.

"Thank God!" he whispered. He picked up the readouts and scanned them, looking more and more confused. "*This* is what told you?"

"Yes."

He shook his head in wonderment. "I chose the right man for the job. I wouldn't begin to know what to make of all this."

"Would you care for some milk?" I asked.

"No, thank you."

"Have a seat," I offered him.

"I'm too excited to sit," he said. "You don't know what this means to me, Mr. Rojas!"

"I'd *like* to know," I said.

He stared at me for a long moment. "And so you shall, before too many more days have passed."

"I don't understand," I said. "Our business is done as soon as you confirm that I've found the ivory."

He continued staring at me, and finally he spoke. "I would like to enter another covenant with you, Mr. Rojas."

"Oh?" I said, trying to hide my interest.

"What I have to do cannot be done alone," he said. "I will need the help of at least one man, and since I have found you to be trustworthy and efficient, you are the man I wish to have with me." He paused. "You will have to take a leave of absence, for which I will compensate you."

"How long a leave of absence?"

He rubbed his chin thoughtfully. "Perhaps four weeks."

"Where will I be going?" I asked.

"Initially, to Skyblue."

"And then?"

"To Earth."

"Why?"

"There is something I must do there that I cannot do alone."

"And what is that?"

He stared at me. "I will tell you, but only after we have

reached Earth and there is no chance of your changing your mind."

I shook my head. "I'm sorry, Mr. Mandaka, but if I'm to take a leave of absence from my job and accompany you to Earth, I have to know why."

"If I tell you why," he said earnestly, "you will not come."

"If you *don't* tell me why, I will not come," I replied.

He seemed to be fighting a battle within himself. Finally he sighed, summoned a chair, and sat down on it after it had floated over to him. "All right, Mr. Rojas—I suppose you deserve to know."

"Thank you."

"But I must put it in its proper context, or you will think you are dealing with a madman."

"Eccentric, yes," I said. "Mad, no."

"Thank you for your confidence," he replied wryly. "I will have that milk now."

I ordered it for him, and it arrived within a few seconds.

"In the absence of champagne," he said, raising his glass to me and then drinking it down in a single swallow.

"You're going to tell me about Sendeyo, aren't you?" I asked.

He nodded, summoned a small table, and set the empty glass down on it.

"You know," I said, noticing that my cigar had long since gone out and relighting it, "when I woke up this morning, I realized that I required only two more facts to know the full history of the ivory: I needed to know where it is now, and I needed to know what you planned to do with it." I paused. "Sendeyo was the only loose end; I couldn't figure out what he had to do with either of them."

"That is because you were mistaken in your initial

assumption, Mr. Rojas," said Mandaka. "There is a *third* thing you must know before you have the full history of the ivory, a history that has not yet seen its final chapter."

"Oh?" I asked, leaning forward intently. "And what is that?"

"You must know how the Kilimanjaro Elephant died."

"Nobody knows how he died," I said.

"*I* do," replied Mandaka—and then, his eyes focused on a spot trillions of miles and thousands of years away, he told me the story of Shundi, and Butamo, and Rakanja, and Sendeyo, and of the Kilimanjaro Elephant.

10

Himself (1898 A.D.)

I reached the base of Kilimanjaro and began climbing. The slopes were gentle at first, punctuated by glades and clearings, and there were frequent ice-cold streams of water flowing down from the frozen summit.

I ascended leisurely, for I knew that if my God was at the top of the mountain He would wait for me. The lower slopes of the mountain were teeming with life, but except for the new flock of egrets that rode on my back and head, everything fled from my presence. Lions snarled as they retreated, leopards hissed and disappeared into the bushes, rhinos grunted and raced away, even men stood aside and watched me in awe as I passed by their bomas.

His name was Butamo, and he had been running for two days and two nights.

He had been taken into slavery in Uganda by the notorious Shundi, the Kavirondo tribesman who ranked second only to the Arab, Tippu Tib, as a dealer in human flesh. Shundi himself had been a slave of Tippu Tib's when he was a small boy, but when he learned that the Koran forbade one believer to hold another in slavery, he had converted to Islam and been given his freedom. He thereupon entered the only trade he knew. He had no intention of freeing any Islamic slaves, so he set up shop farther inland than Islam had penetrated and began amassing his fortune.

Shundi had only two rules: one fed one's slaves well, for sickly, underweight bodies did not bring good prices on the auction blocks of Zanzibar and Mombasa; and one never permitted an escaped slave to survive, for it would simply encourage others to do the same.

So when Butamo escaped during the night, Shundi turned his expedition over to his second in command and set off, with three Wanderobo trackers, determined to bring Butamo back or kill him.

The trail was hard to follow, for Butamo was very skilled in his bushcraft, but there are none so skilled as the Wanderobo, and although they lost Butamo's trail many times, they always came back to it, and to the huge mountain looming ahead of them.

As the air became cooler, the pain in my stomach subsided somewhat, and I was able to lower myself gently into a shallow depression and rub mud over my parched, itching skin. Another of my kind approached, a young bull, ready for his afternoon wallow, but when he saw me he stood back until I had finished, nor did he approach the wallow until I had recommenced my journey and passed from his sight.

Butamo saw a village on the lower slopes of the mountain and made directly for it. It took him three hours, and when he entered it he was immediately surrounded by armed warriors, each menacing him with a spear or a *panga*.

"I need help!" panted Butamo. "I have escaped from the slavers, and I have not eaten for two days!"

"You are not a member of our tribe," said one of the elders. "Why should we help you?"

"If you do not give me food, I will die."

"If we give you food and the slavers find out, we will *all* die," replied the elder. "You must leave our village."

"I am unarmed," said Butamo. "At least give me a spear that I may kill an animal for its meat."

The elders conferred quickly. It was likely that the slavers would follow their escaped property, and if they did so, they would stop at the village and would find the ancient muzzle-loader that had been taken from the German hunter years ago. They might even start asking questions about the German and arrest the elders for murder.

But if the muzzle-loader were given to the escaped slave, no one would ever know where it came from, and if he were tried for murder, well, his suffering would be so much the shorter than were he to live many years as a slave.

"Do you know how to use the white man's gun?" asked one of the elders, when the conference was over.

"I have seen how the white men use them," replied Butamo.

"Because you run from the slavers, and because we hate slavery, we will help you," said the elder. "We will not give you a spear, because our spears bear our tribal symbol and we do not wish the enmity of the slavers. Instead we will give you a gun, if you will promise never to tell anyone where you obtained it."

"I will tell no one," said Butamo.

The elder sent one of his warriors to fetch the gun.

"Give him water to drink," commanded another elder, and Butamo was given water.

The warrior returned and handed the muzzle-loader and a bag to Butamo.

"The bag contains the power that makes the gun explode," explained the elder.

"I know," said Butamo. "I have seen Shundi use such a gun."

"Who is Shundi?"

"He is the slaver from whom I escaped."

"Shundi does not sound like a white man's name."

"He is black," said Butamo.

"Why does a black man sell other black men to the white men?" asked the elder.

"For money."

"And what does he do with this money?"

"He buys many cows and goats and wives," said Butamo.

"*How* many?" asked the elder, with what Butamo thought was a little too much interest.

"I thank you for your help," he said, backing away carefully. "Now I must go, lest I lead Shundi to your village."

Butamo saw a pair of warriors heading down a narrow path, and he decided that the safest means of retreat was to go higher up the mountain.

When I had climbed halfway up the mountain my legs and my stomach started hurting again. I trumpeted my rage at my body's weakness, but finally my energy departed, and for the first time in almost seventy years I lay down to sleep.

Butamo climbed rapidly for almost three hours, until he was absolutely certain that he had not been followed by the tribe that had given him the weapon. He saw a warthog staring at him, and for a moment he was tempted to use the gun, but finally he decided not to, for he didn't want the noise giving away his location. Instead he shook some fruit down from a tree and ate it, then turned over a large rock and found some edible grubs, and continued his ascent up the mountain, always being careful to cover his trail.

I awoke to a burning pain in my side, the worst agony I had ever felt, and climbed awkwardly to my feet. I had slept for no more than three hours, but my massive weight had partially crushed my right lung, and I stood, weak-legged and groggy, gasping for breath. The pain wouldn't go away and finally, in my agony, I began ripping down trees and hurling them down the side of the mountain. Birds screeched and flew away in terror, but it was many minutes before my rage and my pain subsided enough for me to begin climbing the mountain again.

Butamo spent a chilly night on the mountain. In the morning he found a stream, stood knee-deep in it, and tried unsuccessfully to catch a fish with his hands. When his legs became numb with cold, he climbed out of the water, found some edible berries, and perched atop a rock outcropping, looking for Shundi and his three Wanderobo trackers.

There was still no sign of pursuit, but Butamo knew that sooner or later the Wanderobo would strike his trail and come up the mountainside. The more he thought about it, the more certain he was that they wouldn't give him much warning, so he decided to unpack the powder bag and load his rifle.

Then Butamo—cold, hungry, and fearful of going back down the mountain—began walking forward, using all the skills at his command to hide his tracks from those he knew would be looking for them.

Cold and hungry, my belly filled with pain and emptiness, my right lung burning with every breath I took, I raised my eyes, trying to see how far I had to climb to reach the summit, but the top third of the mountain was shrouded in clouds. I raised my trunk and tested the air, hoping that I might find the scent of God drifting on the gentle wind.

What I found was the odor of a man.

Butamo walked up a steep rocky grade for perhaps one hundred yards, then found his path blocked by a grove of giant groundsels and circled to his left to avoid them.

He paused to wipe the dust and sweat from his eyes, then looked ahead—and found himself less than sixty yards from the largest elephant he had ever seen, an elephant so big that he towered above the trees, with tusks so large that they dragged through the earth as he walked.

I forced the pain back long enough to focus my eyes. He stood there, less than sixty yards away from me, carrying a rusty weapon and wearing nothing but a loincloth.

"Are you God?" I asked, extending my trunk to him. "Are you He whom I seek?"

Butamo looked around to see if the elephant had any companions in the nearby glade, but couldn't see any. He looked admiringly at the huge beast's ivory, but knew that he didn't dare to take it—not with Shundi and his three Wanderobo listening for telltale noises that would betray his location on the mountain.

Regretfully, for he had watched Shundi trade ivory and he knew what these tusks would be worth, he began slowly backing away.

He made no answer, no acknowledgment of any kind at all. He was not God; he was just a man.

The pain came rushing back then, and I knew that I would never live to reach the summit. Only if God lay directly ahead of me, only if this man stood between us, would I be able to confront Him before I died.

I began walking forward.

Butamo surveyed the clearing. There was no place to hide except the glade, and he did not know what might be waiting for him in there: a glade like that could easily hide a leopard and her cubs. And yet he couldn't simply stand still and watch as the elephant approached him, for it was now within forty yards and showed no sign of turning.

He yelled and waved an arm, hoping to scare the animal away.

The man yelled at me, and I raised my trunk and screamed back. This is my mountain, I thundered, and I will not be stopped before I confront my God.

At thirty yards, Butamo raised the old muzzle-loader and took aim.

At twenty yards he fired.

I felt a searing pain in my left shoulder, and blood began spurting from my wound. I knew that it would be just a matter of seconds before my heart stopped, but I did not let those seconds go to waste: I charged across the intervening space, wrapped my trunk around the man, and hurled him against a tree some twenty yards away.

Then, with a grunt, I fell over on my side. I took one last look toward the top of Kilimanjaro, hoping to see God and ask Him why He had done this to me, but the summit was still hidden in clouds, and I closed my eyes, suddenly at peace, as I realized that this had always been His plan and that I would be meeting Him momentarily.

* * *

It was five hours before Rakanja chanced upon the carnage. He had taken his cattle high up on the southeast side of the mountain the previous week, and two had not come back, so, leaving his two young sons in charge of the herd, he had ascended Kilimanjaro once again in search of them.

What he found was the carcass of the largest elephant he had ever seen, and the broken body of Butamo, which still retained a spark of life.

"Who are you?" demanded Rakanja.

"Water," rasped Butamo, barely able to move his parched, blood-covered lips.

Rakanja gave the dying man water.

"Who are you?" he demanded again.

"I do not understand you."

Rakanja repeated his question a third time, switching from Maasai to Swahili.

"I am Butamo."

"Why are you on our mountain?"

"*Your* mountain?" whispered Butamo uncomprehendingly.

"God has given the Maasai all the land between Kirinyaga and Kilimanjaro," stated Rakanja with absolute conviction.

"I escaped from slavers, but the elephant that I killed has killed me," murmured Butamo. "Please do not let them find my body."

"What is that to me?" asked Rakanja.

"They will string my body up and carry it back to my village so that my brothers will know that no one can escape from Shundi, and the birds will eat my eyes, and the ants will eat my flesh, and the hyenas will devour my bones. Do not let them do this to me. Bury me, or find a deep gorge and throw me there."

"It will make no difference once you are dead," replied

Rakanja, "and I must find my missing cows." He stood up to leave.

"Wait!" cried Butamo with his remaining strength.

"What now, slave?" asked Rakanja.

"If you will hide my body, I will tell you how to become rich."

"I am already rich," said Rakanja. "I have many cattle and goats, and already I have three wives."

"In one day you will double your wealth."

Rakanja squatted down beside Butamo. "How?" he demanded.

"The man who hunts for me trades not only slaves but ivory. If you will sell him the ivory of the elephant I killed, he will pay you many pieces of silver, with which you may buy more cows."

"The Maasai do not trade ivory, and we have no use for the white man's pieces of silver."

"You can buy fifty cows with what he pays you."

Rakanja considered the likelihood of finding his two missing cows, computed the bride price of the young woman he had recently taken a fancy to, and looked thoughtfully at the elephant's carcass.

"What is the name of the slaver?" he asked.

"You will hide my body?"

Rakanja nodded. "I will hide it."

"He is Shundi the Kavirondo. He will have three Wanderobo trackers with him."

"How do I remove the tusks?" asked Rakanja. "I have never taken ivory before."

"If you wait for three or four days, you can pull them right out of the sockets."

"I cannot waste that much time."

"Then you can . . ." Butamo's body was shaken by a paroxysm of coughing, and when it subsided he was dead.

Rakanja looked around the ground until he found a large pointed stone, the kind that he might have used for an axe had he found it near his boma. He approached the carcass, felt the side of the jaw until he came to the end of the tusk, and then began chopping through skin and muscle.

It was long, hard work, and it was dark before he had removed both tusks. He ignored the near-freezing temperature as he carried each of them in turn half a mile up the mountain and hid them under a number of bushes that he uprooted. Then he returned to Butamo's body, slung it over his shoulder, walked to the edge of a nearby precipice, and hurled it into space, waiting until he heard the thud it made on the mountainside almost a thousand yards below him before returning to the elephant's tuskless carcass.

Then he made a fire, and waited.

The Wanderobo found him at midmorning, but it was noon before Shundi himself arrived. The slaver walked over to the elephant's carcass, half-smiled when he saw that the tusks were missing, and finally turned to Rakanja.

"You're Maasai, aren't you?" asked Shundi.

Rakanja nodded.

"I have been chasing a slave up the mountain. His trail led to this spot."

"He was here," said Rakanja.

"Where is he now?"

"Dead."

"I want his body."

"You may not have it," said Rakanja, staring contemptuously at the three Wanderobo.

"I will have it," repeated Shundi.

"You will go away, unless you desire a blood-feud with the Maasai," said Rakanja.

Shundi stared at him. "You are the only Maasai I see."

"I am enough," replied Rakanja.

"I don't like the arrogance of the Maasai," said Shundi. "I think perhaps a lifetime of taking orders might be just what you need."

Before anyone could react, Rakanja had hurled his spear through the chest of one of the Wanderobo, and picked up a wooden spear that he had fashioned the night before.

"There is your lifetime," he said. "How many more do you wish to spend?"

"One will be enough," said Shundi, pulling a bolt-action pistol out of his robe and aiming it at Rakanja.

Rakanja stared at the gun with no show of fright. "If you kill me, you will never find the tusks of the elephant."

"Ah!" said Shundi, smiling. "So now we talk business!"

"We do not talk at all until you throw your gun away."

Shundi replaced the gun inside his robes.

"You must throw it away," said Rakanja. "Otherwise, you will kill me after I show you the ivory."

"I give you my word that I won't," said Shundi.

"What is the word of a slaver worth?" said Rakanja contemptuously.

Shundi withdrew the gun, looked at it lovingly, then sighed and hurled it into a small gorge.

"Come," said Rakanja, starting to climb up the mountain. "I will show you the tusks."

They climbed for perhaps fifteen minutes. Then Rakanja came to the place where he had hidden them, pulled away the bushes, and stood back while Shundi approached.

"By Allah!" exclaimed the slaver. "I have never seen such ivory!" He squatted down next to the tusks and examined them. "You did a sloppy job, Maasai," he noted. "You hacked away five or ten pounds from the base of each."

"They are still the greatest tusks you have ever seen," said Rakanja.

"Yes, they are."

"How many pieces of the white man's silver will you pay for them?" asked Rakanja.

"I will give you forty silver shillings," said Shundi.

"Each," said Rakanja.

"That is a lot of money," said the slaver.

"That is what I want."

Shundi shook his head. "Too much."

"They will stay here until they rot," replied Rakanja, "and you will never be allowed on Kilimanjaro again."

Shundi looked at the tusks again, then shrugged. "All right," he said at last. "Eighty shillings."

"You will count them out on the ground, and I will take them," said Rakanja.

Shundi nodded, pulled out a sack of coins, and began laying out eighty shillings.

"I want that, too," said Rakanja, pointing to a large gold coin.

"That is a Maria Theresa dollar," said Shundi. "It is worth many shillings."

"I want it," repeated Rakanja.

"All right," said Shundi, leaving it on the ground. "If you will lead us down the mountain so that we do not become lost, you may have it."

Rakanja gathered all the coins up and placed them in his water gourd. He waited until each Wanderobo had lifted a tusk, then began walking down to the clearing where the elephant had been killed.

A single gunshot rang out and Rakanja pitched forward, face first, dead before he hit the ground.

"Arrogant son of a pig!" said Shundi, a smoking pistol in his hand. "Did you really believe that the great Shundi travels with only one handgun, and that he would throw it away because some ignorant barbarian tells him to?"

He approached Rakanja's corpse and retrieved his money, then turned back to his trackers.

"Follow me!" he ordered them. "And woe betide the first one of you who damages the ivory."

I was no longer in pain. All feeling had vanished; even hunger and thirst were gone—yet I was restless and somehow incomplete, and I screamed my misery, louder and louder, the intensity increasing instant by instant, until at last it reached into the dreams of Sendeyo himself.

The fire blazed brightly, illuminating the fronts of the dung-and-straw huts that formed the *manyatta*, the thorn-fenced village. The elders sat in a small circle around the fire, and beyond them, in a much larger circle, stood fully five hundred *elmorani*, proud Maasai warriors, their faces painted, their spears gleaming in the firelight.

Suddenly the tall thin figure of Sendeyo, brother of the paramount chief of all the Maasai, appeared from out of the darkness, and stood inside the circle of elders.

"I have had a vision, my children," said Sendeyo, the shadows flickering off his black skin and his lion's-mane headdress.

He stared at the assemblage, and waited for the foremost of the elders to speak.

"Tell us your vision, Sendeyo."

"My sleep has been troubled for many nights," said Sendeyo. "Tonight all became clear."

He paused and looked at his audience.

"In this vision, I saw the *laibon* of all elephants lying dead on the slopes of mighty Kilimanjaro."

He paused again, as the elders and warriors waited for his next statement with rapt attention.

"The elephant was not killed by a Maasai," continued Sendeyo, "for the Maasai do not kill animals for meat or for ivory. We kill only the lion to affirm our manhood."

"Who killed the elephant, O Sendeyo?"

"The elephant was killed by an escaped slave."

The foremost elder spoke again: "What has this vision to do with the Maasai, O Sendeyo?"

"In my vision, a Maasai *moran* named Rakanja came to the body of the dead elephant." Sendeyo paused again, as the fire blazed higher behind him. "The *moran* chopped out its tusks and sold them."

"I know Rakanja," said another elder. "He has been missing for six days."

"You will find his body on Kilimanjaro," said Sendeyo with absolute conviction, and a little moan of terror escaped from the assemblage—not terror of death, for the Maasai did not fear death, but terror at the power of this man, who could see the death of another from such a great distance.

"I order you not to look for his body," continued Sendeyo. "He has broken custom and disgraced his people. He has desecrated the *laibon* of all animals, and has entered into commerce with the white man." Sendeyo frowned contemptuously. "He has dishonored the Maasai."

There were fearful looks and mutterings as the warriors waited for Sendeyo's pronouncement.

"From this day forth," continued Sendeyo, "all that the Maasai possess will turn to dust. It will not happen overnight, for the Maasai are a strong and numerous people, but it has already begun. Our lands will become less fertile, the Kikuyu and Luo and Wakamba will become more numerous, the white man will corrupt our *elmorani*, and in time even our language will be lost and the Maasai will speak only Swahili or the white man's tongue. Our numbers will decrease, our weapons will be taken from us, and our people will forget what it means to *be* Maasai. The spirits of all Maasai from this day onward will wander alone in the void between this life and the next."

There were moans of misery and fear.

"Tell us what we must do, O Sendeyo!" cried the elders. "Tell us how we may lift this *thahu*, this most terrible of curses!"

"There is a way," said Sendeyo, the shadows flickering off his painted face, and suddenly a hushed silence fell upon the assemblage.

"You must find the ivory, and bring it back to Kilimanjaro, to the very place where the elephant died. There you must make an altar of it, and wash it in the pure blood, the blood of an uncircumcised Maasai male. Only then can the honor of the Maasai be redeemed; only then can the spirits of those gathered here and those yet unborn be freed of this *thahu*; only then can the spirits of the Maasai dead finally come to rest."

Sendeyo stared at the elders and *elmorani*.

"I have spoken," he concluded. "What you do is up to you."

He turned on his heel and retired to his boma, his dreams finally free of the image of the Kilimanjaro Elephant. He never mentioned him again, and died seven years later.

And so my spirit wandered the void, waiting and watching, watching and waiting, as Sendeyo's thahu came true, and the Maasai fell from grace, and their numbers decreased, and their wealth vanished. I saw Maasai Laibon gain possession of my ivory, and I saw Tembo Laibon gamble it away, and I saw Leeyo Nelion die before he could claim it, and finally only one Maasai remained—a tall, driven man named Bukoba Mandaka, who was a trillion trillion miles away from the sacred mountain Kilimanjaro.

Tenth Interlude (6303 G.E.)

His story finished, Mandaka fell silent and stared at me, watching for my reaction.

"*That's* what you plan to do with the ivory when you get it?" I said at last.

He nodded. "I have no choice."

"Of course you have a choice," I said. "You can choose not to sacrifice yourself."

"It must be done."

"Why? Because some witch doctor pronounced a curse seven thousand years ago?"

"It has come true, has it not?" asked Mandaka ruefully.

"You don't know that the decline of the Maasai has anything to do with him."

"It is not a matter of knowledge, but of belief," said Mandaka.

"Well, *I* don't believe it."

"You don't have to."

We fell silent again. I noticed that my cigar had gone out, and relit it.

"When will you be leaving for Skyblue?" I asked.

"Tomorrow morning. I would like you to come along."

"That's very short notice," I said. "Braxton's probably won't permit me to leave."

"They will permit it," he said confidently.

"You sound very sure of yourself," I noted.

"They are in business to make money. I bought you from them once; I can buy you from them again."

"You mean you paid them a stipend in addition to my own commission?" I asked, surprised.

He nodded. "I am always prepared to pay for what I want, Mr. Rojas."

"And once you have the ivory, what then? Will you fly directly to Earth with it?"

"Yes." He paused awkwardly. "And again, I would like you to accompany me."

"Why?"

"I have my reasons."

"Then you'd better tell them to me," I said, "because I don't intend to be a participant in any ceremony that culminates in your death."

"You will not be, I assure you," said Mandaka.

"Then what do you want me for?" I persisted.

"When the ceremony is over, my body must be burnt and my bones scattered. There are very few people that I would trust to carry out such a task; you are one of them."

"It is really necessary?" I asked again. "After all, you are the last Maasai. Whatever you do, there will be no more of you—so why sacrifice your life for the honor of a people who no longer exist?"

"I am not doing it for the Maasai who are yet to come, for as you properly point out, I am the last." He paused. "I am doing it for all those Maasai since the time of Sendeyo whose souls are wandering in limbo, awaiting the sacrifice he ordained atop Kilimanjaro to send them home."

"Sendeyo gave them a bunch of primitive mumbo-jumbo, nothing more!"

"These are my most deeply-held beliefs," replied Mandaka with an almost-detached serenity. "They cannot be shaken by your arguments."

I looked at him for a long moment and finally nodded my agreement. "All right," I said. "The subject is closed —at least for the time being."

"Thank you," he replied. "Will you accompany me?"

"If you can arrange it with Braxton's, I'll come at least as far as Skyblue. I think I'd like to see the ivory in person."

Mandaka got to his feet. "I have preparations to make and affairs to put in order. Will you meet me at my ship tomorrow morning?"

"Where is it?"

He named his hangar and dock number at the local spaceport.

"When will we take off?" I asked.

"At daybreak, Mr. Rojas. Please do not be late; after all this time, I am very eager to finally get my hands on the ivory."

Then he rose and left my office, leaving me to consider the full consequences of his forthcoming odyssey.

"Have you gone crazy?"

Hilda was sitting opposite me in the executive cafeteria, her round face flushed with frustration.

"No," I said thoughtfully. "I don't think so."

"What do you know about this man?"

"Enough," I said, nibbling on a piece of pastry.

"Enough?" she repeated. "What's enough? He comes out of nowhere, he isn't listed with any agency in the Monarchy, he freely admits that he'll commit murder to get what he wants, he lives like some animal in that crazy apartment of his—and *you*," she added furiously, "you decide to take a four-week leave of absence to go off to Earth with him to perform some pagan ceremony that you won't even describe to me!"

"He needs my help," I said. "And I've only promised to go as far as Skyblue with him; I haven't made up my mind about Earth yet."

"What about all the times *I've* needed your help and you've always been too preoccupied with your work?" she demanded, pounding the table with a pudgy fist and practically spilling her tea.

"This *is* my work," I explained.

"Your work ended when you found the ivory!"

"I'm haven't found it yet," I pointed out. "That's why I have to go to Skyblue."

"Don't play games with me, Duncan. You've found it, all right. I can tell by that smug expression on your face."

I couldn't deny it but I didn't feel like confirming it, so I simply stared at her and said nothing.

"Tell me the truth," said Hilda after a long pause. "Do *you* think whatever he's going to do will somehow restore the honor or the prestige of the Maasai?"

"It doesn't matter what *I* think," I replied. "*He* thinks it will, and that's all that matters."

She shook her head wearily. "Why do I persist in wasting my time with you, Duncan?"

"Why do you?" I asked, suddenly interested.

She shrugged. "I wish I knew."

"*You* can't explain why you keep putting up with me; *I* can't tell you why I've decided to help Mandaka. Why don't you just accept that I'm finally doing what you wanted?"

"When did I ever say that I wanted you to go to Earth with Mandaka?" she demanded.

"You're always saying that you want me to make a commitment to someone. Here I've made a commitment to help Mandaka, and all of a sudden you're complaining."

"Oh, Duncan, Duncan," she murmured, "what am I going to do with you? How can you be so smart and so stupid at the same time?"

"Why don't you just wish me a happy voyage, and tell me what you'd like me to bring you from Skyblue?"

"Just come back safe and sound from Earth," she said. "That will be enough."

"I haven't decided if I'm going to Earth or not," I reminded her.

"Of course you're going," she said impatiently.

"Well, even if I *do* go," I said, "who would want to kill a trophy researcher?"

"Do you really want me to tell you? We'll just start fighting all over again."

"Then don't tell me." I pulled out my pocket computer. "If I go to Earth, I'll be back in twenty-nine days. Why don't you and Harold reserve us a table for three that night at the Ancient Days? It'll be my treat."

She sighed and stared at her cup of tea. "I'll think about it, Duncan."

We finished our meal in total silence. Then I got to my feet. "I hate to rush, but I've got a number of details to clear up before I go."

She remained seated and continued looking at her tea. I waited for a moment, decided that she had no intention of getting up, and turned to leave.

"Duncan?"

"Yes?" I said.

"Have a safe voyage, damn you."

We left Mandaka's ship at the only spaceport on Skyblue and took a small driverless cab into the city. Although there were rails above and below us, we actually floated through the air, an elementary demonstration of superconductivity that never ceased to delight me, since the feeling was not unlike that of flying low over the planet's surface.

This particular planet had truly earned its sobriquet, for it possessed quite the bluest sky I had ever seen, doubtless due to the freshwater ocean that covered more than eighty percent of its surface. The cab took us through a few miles of cultivated fields, where the farming communes were concentrating upon a mutated form of wheat, far larger and sturdier than that grown on most planets. The air smelled fresh and pure, and I leaned back and enjoyed the ride, though Mandaka was unable to sit still, and kept shifting his weight nervously.

At last the cab stopped at a huge square which had been designated the City Centre, and from there we received instructions on how to find the museum, and proceeded along some rather primitive slidewalks. We arrived perhaps five minutes later, and stood on the museum's stone steps, staring at the impressive structure.

"At last!" murmured Mandaka.

I looked for an escalator or an airshaft, but none had been provided, and so we trudged up the two dozen stone stairs and entered the museum. I identified myself to the door-man and asked him to direct Mandaka and myself to the Natural History wing.

"Also," I added as Mandaka headed off in the direction indicated, "would you please announce my presence to Hazel Guthridge and ask her to meet me in the fossil exhibit?"

"Certainly, Mr. Rojas," he said, and I hurried to join Mandaka.

We passed through three art galleries, plus a Science Hall devoted to a rather simplistic demonstration of quantum mechanics and Neimark's Theory, but at last we came to the Natural History exhibit, and a moment later we were in the fossil room, which was dominated by the dinosaur, but contained some fifty other skeletons as well.

"Are we getting close to the ivory?" whispered Mandaka.

"Closer than you imagine," I said. I was about to reveal the secret of its location when Hazel Guthridge entered the room.

"Mr. Rojas, I presume?" she said, walking forward and formally extending her hand.

"I am please to meet you in person," I said. "This gentleman is Bukoba Mandaka, my associate."

"Mr. Mandaka," she said, barely looking at him. "I was not aware that you were coming to Skyblue, Mr. Rojas," she added disapprovingly. "I could have prepared a proper tour for you had you given me some warning."

"Well, as I mentioned to you, I have been trying to find the tusks of a particular elephant, which I knew to be on Skyblue."

"And as *I* mentioned to you, we have no record of them here."

"I believe you," I said. "But they are here nonetheless."

"I beg your pardon!" she said severely. "I told you, Mr. Rojas, that they are not on display."

"You also told me that your specialty is bone carvings from the planet's prehistory, and that you have no Natural History Curator."

She frowned. "Are you accusing me of lying to you, Mr. Rojas?"

I shook my head. "I am accusing you of nothing more than ignorance," I replied. "The tusks are right in this room."

"Where?" said both she and Mandaka at once.

I pointed to the dinosaur. "There," I said.

"That is the reconstructed skeleton of a carnivorous dinosaur," she said.

"I know," I said. "But carnivores of this size are far more rare than you might think. There are more than two million habitable planets in the galaxy, and only twenty-seven of them have possessed carnivores of such proportions—and on only three of those planets could the carnivores be classed as dinosaurs. I had my computer analyze your planet's ecology as well as its geologic and climatic history, and it has concluded that the chances against this particular dinosaur having existed on Skyblue are approximately three hundred thousand to one."

"What are you saying, Mr. Rojas?" demanded Mandaka, staring at the dinosaur.

"I am saying that someone who knew less about Skyblue's ecological history than he thought he did found the tusks, decided that they were the remains of some enormous prehistoric animal, and extrapolated this skeleton based on a totally false assumption."

"That is not possible, Mr. Rojas!" protested Hazel Guthridge.

"Why not?" I asked. "This is a sparsely-populated colony planet. You have no paleontologists here, and as far as I can tell from your exhibits, you've never found a trace of any other oversized life form, either carnivore or prey." I stared at the skeleton. "My guess is that they're the two largest ribs, and that everything else was reconstructed based on that."

Mandaka climbed over the protecting guard rail before Hazel Guthridge could stop him and stared intently at the ribs in question.

"You're right!" he exclaimed triumphantly. "It is the ivory of the Kilimanjaro Elephant!"

"It can't be!" she said with somewhat less conviction.

"It is," I replied. "Someone made a mistake, and there were no experts to catch it. Given the circumstances, it's quite understandable."

"If you are correct, it is inexcusable," she said bitterly.

"I am correct."

"I will require independent authentication."

"That could take months," I noted.

"Possibly," she agreed.

I looked at Mandaka; he shook his head vigorously.

"Perhaps we can settle this here and now," I suggested.

"Oh?" she said, looking at me with open distrust. "How?"

"Do you have a molecular scope?" I asked. "That will tell you if they're of Earthly or Skyblue origin."

"No, we don't."

I frowned. "I thought *every* museum had—"

"We are understaffed and underfinanced," she said.

"All right," I said. "There's another way. The items in question are either ribs or tusks. If they're ribs, they'll be hollow throughout, because they had to hold marrow. If they're tusks, the bottom two-thirds of each will be solid. Any sonic analyzer should be able to give us the answer."

She nodded. "I'll subject them to analysis immediately." She paused. "If the two of you will wait in my office, I'll have the results for you within half an hour."

"That will be perfectly satisfactory," I said before Mandaka could protest.

She summoned a guard, who led us to her austerely-furnished office, and we waited in silence for forty minutes. Finally Mandaka could sit still no longer and began pacing the floor.

"She's planning some trick!" he said.

I shook my head in disagreement. "She's just been told by the Chief Researcher of Wilford Braxton's that her museum's credibility is nil, and she's trying to hide her humiliation," I said. "She found out twenty minutes ago that I was right, and now she's trying to figure out how to minimize the damage."

"If she doesn't sell them to me, I will come back tonight and take them," he said.

"She'll sell them," I answered confidently.

He was about to reply, but Hazel Guthridge entered the office just then, her face quite pale.

"Mr. Rojas, Mr. Mandaka," she said bluntly, "I owe you both an apology. You were right."

"There's been no harm done," I said. "In fact, it may

be of some benefit to your treasury. My associate still wishes to purchase the ivory."

"As I told you, it is our policy not to sell our exhibits."

"But you also told me that you exhibit only life-forms that are native to Skyblue," I said. "It would be very awkward for the museum's reputation if word of this mistake were to be circulated."

"Is that a threat, Mr. Rojas?"

"Certainly not," I said smoothly. "I was merely suggesting that the sooner the skeleton is dismantled, the sooner it will cease to be a potential source of embarrassment to you."

She stared at me, still unable to determine whether I was threatening or consoling her. Finally her shoulders sagged, and she leaned her hip against the edge of her desk.

"How much did you intend to offer for the tusks, Mr. Mandaka?" she asked.

"Three million credits," he replied.

"*Three million?*" she repeated incredulously. "I had no idea they were worth that much!"

"They aren't, except to Mr. Mandaka," I interjected.

"The Board of Directors is due to meet next month," she said. "I am quite sure that they will agree to the sale, Mr. Mandaka."

"My offer is predicated upon immediate delivery," added Mandaka.

"This is most irregular . . ." she said, trying to make up her mind.

"It is a most irregular situation," I concurred. "But if you were to agree to an immediate sale, there would be no one here to tell the board what it was that we wanted. As far as they are concerned, we might just have well have made a munificent offer for the entire artificial skeleton."

She considered my statement, and nodded her assent.

"If you will have the ivory brought to my ship," said

Mandaka, giving her his hangar and dock number, "I will have the money transferred to the museum's account." He paused. "Or to your private account, if you prefer."

"The museum's account, if you please," she said heatedly. "I may bend the rules to preserve the museum's reputation, but I am not a thief!"

"Nobody ever implied that you were," I said soothingly. "And with regard to the regrettable error that led to this meeting, I assure you that you can trust to our discretion."

"I sincerely hope so. I've devoted my life to this museum, and I will not see it become a laughingstock."

I spent a few more minutes reassuring and mollifying her, and then she ordered the tusks removed from the premises and delivered to the spaceport, and Mandaka began the process of transferring the purchase price to the museum's bank account.

Three hours later Bukoba Mandaka, standing at the cargo hatch of his ship, finally came into possession of the ivory of the Kilimanjaro Elephant. When it was safely packed away, he turned to me.

"Well, Mr. Rojas," he said, "it would seem that the moment of your decision is at hand. Shall I return you to your home, or will you complete the last step of the journey with me and observe for yourself the final chapter in the ivory's history?"

"I am not expected to participate in this ceremony in any way," I said, "but merely to dispose of your remains when it is over. Is that correct?"

He nodded.

I shrugged. "I suppose I'll come along."

"I never doubted it," he replied.

11

The Maasai
(6304 G.E.)

Alone, restless, incomplete, unable to sleep the Final Sleep for which I longed, I tested the galactic winds for the billionth time—and finally, after many false starts and eons of despair, the scent of salvation wafted across time and space to me, strong and pungent. I trumpeted silently in exultation, for it was the man, Mandaka, returning to the sacred mountain.

The New Year came and went as we flew from Skyblue to Earth, though both Mandaka and I were in Deepsleep chambers at the time. We awoke, stiff and cold and hungry—Deepsleep slows the metabolism, but it doesn't stop it, and I always wake up famished—when the ship went into orbit around Earth, and we landed at dawn the next day, perhaps two miles from the south base of Mount Kilimanjaro.

"Tradition has it that the elephant was killed on the northern side of the mountain," said Mandaka, as we carefully loaded the ivory and our supplies onto a pair of gravity sleds. "But we'll climb up the southern slope for the first nine thousand feet or so."

"Is there any particular reason for that?" I asked.

He nodded.

"The city of Nyerere was built on the southern slope, and we should have accessible roads for the first seven thousand five hundred or eight thousand feet. Otherwise we'd be faced with dense vegetation right from the outset; it thins out somewhat above eight thousand feet."

"Why didn't you radio ahead and see if they've got a spaceport?" I suggested. "It could have saved us a lot of climbing."

"They had one, but it's unusable," he replied. "The city has been deserted for more than eight centuries."

"Is there any particular reason why?"

He shrugged. "Why does anyone walk out of Eden? To see what lies beyond." He paused. "And no matter how disappointed they are, they never return."

I stood, hands on hips, and faced west, looking at the seemingly endless veldt, dotted with acacia trees, the long grasses swaying in the breeze. "It's beautiful terrain," I said at last.

"It is," he agreed. "Once, millennia ago, the Serengeti Plains held between three and four million animals. Their annual migration was a sight which, once seen, could never be forgotten." He sighed. "Now nothing remains except grass and insects—not even a bird or a mole-rat."

"What happened to the animals, I wonder?" I asked.

"*We* happened to them, Mr. Rojas," replied Mandaka grimly. "You edit the book; you know when each species became extinct."

"Seeing it in a book is one thing," I said. "But standing here on this spot, looking fifty or sixty miles off across the Serengeti, one truly realizes the enormity of what we did to this land, that there is nothing left alive." I turned to look up toward the peak of Kilimanjaro, which was hidden by clouds. "Just to realize that lions and leopards and elephants and rhinos and all manners of herbivores once dwelt on this mountain . . ."

"And *men*, Mr. Rojas," added Mandaka. "Men dwelt here too. Now only the insects remain."

"Perhaps next time we'll do it better."

He shook his head. "There won't be any next time," he said. "Not here."

"Then somewhere else."

"Perhaps," he said dubiously.

Then we were walking up the overgrown dirt track that led to the deserted city.

Nyerere began about 500 feet up the mountainside, and one could tell that it had been a carefully-planned city, with large public parks, a view over the Serengeti Plains from every home, and commercial zones carefully integrated into the residential areas. At 1200 feet we passed a small, private airport, but the buildings were crumbling and the runways had eroded down the mountain. I had seen empty cities before, but always they had been devastated by war or disease; this was the first one I had seen where the populace had simply packed up and left, and it gave me an eerie feeling. A number of the homes were still in good condition, and some of them even had their doors and windows intact, but there was a sense of desolation as we walked through the empty city that was almost tangible. It was like the plains below: once these streets had teemed with traffic and commerce, once these homes had given refuge to millions of souls; now there was only dust, and grass, and insects.

At 6,000 feet we decided to halt for the day, and we spent the night in the lobby of a once-plush hotel. The swimming pool was cracked and empty, and the casino's walls had given way to dry rot, but the steel-and-glass lobby was relatively intact, and we slept there. The temperature dropped throughout the evening, but when I awoke, shivering, I saw that Mandaka was still sleeping like a baby, completely impervious to the sudden drop in temperature.

We set off again just after the warming rays of the sun burned away the mist at the top of the mountain, and I could finally see the glacial ice cap at the summit. We passed a large public square where a number of plaques described the world-famous Waycross Sculpture, but when I asked Mandaka what the sculpture was, he shrugged and said it had been looted many centuries before his birth.

By noon we were out of the city, and now we began slowly circling the mountain, guiding our gravity sleds and carving a path through the dense vegetation with laser weapons. We slept in our heated bedrolls again, and despite the fact that I had set mine for twenty-eight degrees centigrade, I spent another uncomfortable night, as the temperature began plummeting immediately after sunset.

On the morning of the third day, I found myself short of breath, which Mandaka had warned me might happen when we topped the 8,500-foot mark in altitude. It took us about four hours to reach the northern slope, which we had been indirectly approaching for more than a day, and finally Mandaka came to a halt, his dark eyes scanning the area.

"We are getting close," he announced.

"How close?" I gasped.

He looked up the mountain.

"Another thousand feet or so."

"You're sure?"

He nodded.

"How do you know?" I persisted, trying to catch my breath. "No one took photos or measurements. Maybe he was killed right where you're standing."

"I think not," said Mandaka, starting up the mountain.

"*Why* not?"

"There's very little cover here. He would have gone higher."

"But there might have been cover here seven thousand years ago!"

"Higher, Mr. Rojas," said Mandaka, leaning forward and scrambling up the slope. "Or has all your research told you nothing about him? He was a survivor, and a survivor would have climbed higher up the mountain."

I didn't have the strength to reply, so I merely nodded my head in acquiescence and fell into step behind him.

It was late afternoon when we reached a small clearing beside a glade of thorn trees. A nearby ledge overlooked the plains below. Mandaka stopped, turned slowly in a complete circle, sniffed the air, and nodded his head.

"We have arrived," he announced softly.

"You're sure?"

"As sure as I can be," he replied. "Possibly I am wrong, but I have done my best. God will have to understand."

"And now you kill yourself?"

"Later," he said, deactivating the gravity sleds. "When the moon is full."

"Shall I fix us something to eat?" I asked, reaching into my pack for the portable kitchen.

"No," he said. "It would be sacrilegious to eat anything on this holy mountain except the milk and blood of my own cattle." He paused. "You may eat if you wish."

"Just a sandwich," I said apologetically, reaching into the kitchen pack and withdrawing one. I took a bite, and as I began chewing it I looked off into the distance.

"It's a beautiful view, isn't it?" I commented.

"Yes," he replied.

"Where did you grow up?"

"You can't see it from here," he replied. "But," he continued, pointing to the northwest, "it was about one hundred and thirty miles in that direction."

"Did you ever climb Kilimanjaro as a child?" I asked.

He shook his head. "It is a holy mountain, reserved for the act that will redeem the Maasai race."

"It must have been quite a burden over the years, knowing you would be the man to perform that act."

"It was."

"Haven't you ever been tempted to turn your back on the whole thing?" I asked. "After all, the Maasai owned the tusks for one thousand three hundred years. Any one of them could have performed the ceremony, and none of them did."

"None of them had to," said Mandaka. "I am the last; I cannot escape my destiny."

"You don't hold it against them?"

He looked directly at me. "Of course I do. I am doing this because I must; I would much rather not have to."

"Then why not just turn your back on it?" I persisted.

"I can't."

"Why? You've nothing but the word of an old witch doctor who died more than seven thousand years ago."

"And the history of the past seven thousand years," he replied. "I told you once before, Mr. Rojas: it is not necessary that you believe in what I am doing. It is enough that *I* believe it."

"I just hate to see you die for no reason," I said.

"I shall die for my beliefs," he answered. "What better reason can a man have?"

"None," I admitted.

"And what better place than here?" he continued. "This is where everything began, Mr. Rojas. Less than a day's walk from the base of the mountain is the Olduvai Gorge, where the first man took his first upright steps. This very mountain was given to my people, and from here we moved north and west and conquered everything that stood before us. Great men have climbed this mountain, Mr. Rojas— poets and *laibons*, hunters and explorers, writers and warriors. And the greatest animal of all died here." He paused, looked out across the grassland, and sighed. "No, there can be no better place for me to die."

He made me almost ashamed that I required an explanation, and I quickly asked another question to hide my embarrassment.

"Aren't you afraid?"

He considered my question for a long moment, then shook his head. "I have not enjoyed my life, Mr. Rojas," he said seriously. "The only meaningful thing I can do is to end it; I am not afraid of so doing."

"*I* would be terrified," I confessed.

"Every life forms an inevitable trajectory that ends in death," said Mandaka. "The only difference is that I have been raised to acknowledge and follow that trajectory, and you have been raised to ignore and avoid it."

"Perhaps," I agreed reluctantly, certain that there must be more differences for us to have such diverse outlooks, but unable to think of what they might be. "But even if I had been raised like you, I'm still not sure I could go through with it."

"If you knew that every person you had ever cared for, every ancestor you had ever revered, would remain damned for all eternity if you did not go through with the ritual, you would find the strength."

"I don't think I could convince myself of the truth of it."

"It is not a matter of logic, but of belief," said Mandaka.

"But if you're wrong . . ."

"Then all that will happen is that one unhappy man will go to his death a little sooner. It is neither a personal nor a cosmic tragedy."

I considered what he had said and found that I had no answer, so we sat in silence for a few minutes. Finally I remarked that I was getting cold, and Mandaka gathered some wood and lit a small fire.

"Sit closer to it, Mr. Rojas," he suggested, and I did so. "Better?"

"Yes, thank you," I said as the kindling began crackling and the pungent smell of smoke assailed my nostrils.

"You know," he said reflectively, "for untold eons men sat beside a fire such as this one, and cooked their food, and warmed their bodies, and held off the beasts of the jungle. Now we create our own environments, and manufacture food from chemical waste, and slaughter the beasts, both sentient and non-sentient, that gather around us. Our methods have changed, but have *we*, I wonder?"

"We are certainly more advanced," I said.

"That is not what I asked," he replied. "Is there really anything more important than remaining warm and dry and well-fed? And is it easier to do so up there"—he gestured to the stars that had gathered overhead—"than right here, in the cradle of the race, beside a fire such as this?"

"It must be," I replied, "or we wouldn't be there."

"Why *are* we there, I wonder?"

"The challenge."

"Has any man ever faced a greater challenge than Butamo the slave faced right here seven millennia ago?"

I thought about it, and finally came up with an answer: "Yes," I said. "You are facing a greater challenge tonight."

"If so, I did not have to go to the stars to face it."

"You had to follow the ivory," I noted.

"Then perhaps God wanted me to traverse the stars, if only to understand that all that is really important is right here."

"And about to end," I said.

"And about to end," he agreed.

I stared thoughtfully at the fire for a long moment, watching the flames flicker in the dying light. I had never sat before a fire before, and I decided that I liked it.

"What do you think lies before you?" I asked at last.

"After I die?"

"Yes."

He shrugged. "It is not for me to know yet."

"Nothingness?" I asked.

"Perhaps."

"Then perhaps nothingness is all that the other members of the Maasai found."

"Or perhaps it is all that they seek," he replied.

"If not nothingness, then what?"

He paused for a moment. "Perhaps I will find myself back before the death of the elephant, living in harmony with my surroundings."

"That doesn't sound like much of a heaven to me," I said.

"Doesn't it?" he replied. "Look around you, Mr. Rojas. For every world we conquer, we find a thousand more. For every race we befriend, we destroy a thousand more. For every disease that we cure, we succumb to a thousand new ones. For every achievement we claim, a thousand are denied to us. Perhaps your Garden of Eden was not a starting point, but an end in itself."

"You sound ready to die, I'll grant you that," I said, drawing closer to the fire as I became more aware of the cold.

"Everything dies," he said. "At least my death will mean something."

"You hope."

"I know."

"But if Sendeyo was wrong . . ."

"Then it will *still* mean something," he said with a smile. "Look at the way you try to talk me out of it." He paused. "It will have moved *you*, and I suspect nothing within your memory has ever moved you before."

"That's true," I admitted reluctantly. "But is it worth dying for?"

"I don't know," answered Mandaka. "I hope so."

"I would prefer to remain unmoved," I said after a moment's silence.

"I would prefer that a previous member of my race had done what I must do tonight," he replied. "It appears that neither of our preferences are to be fulfilled."

"It isn't fair," I said.

"Life rarely is."

"I found the ivory. I did my job. It should have ended there."

"It could never end there," he said. "Not for a man like you. It will end only when the last chapter of the ivory is written."

I paused, considering his words. "I resent it anyway," I said.

"All your professional life you have dealt with the records of dead animals," said Mandaka. "In a few hours I shall be just another of them, and then you can go back to the emotionless world of the researcher." He paused. "In the meantime, you might consider the Kilimanjaro Elephant himself."

"He's been dead for almost eight thousand years," I said. "What is there to consider?"

"If the Maasai have been doomed to wander aimlessly through the void, what limbo might he himself be in?" He paused. "Does he lie at rest, mindless and content, or does his soul cry out for that portion of him that you have rescued from the farthest reaches of the galaxy? Consider him well, Mr. Rojas—if my act does not bring eternal rest to my people, perhaps *your* act will bring eternal peace to this greatest of creatures."

"It would be comforting if I could believe that," I said.

"But you don't?"

I shook my head.

"I feel very sorry for you, Mr. Rojas," he said. "It must be tragic to believe only in what you can see, and measure, and dissect, and record."

"I feel very sorry for you, Mr. Mandaka," I said sincerely. "It must be even more tragic not to."

He chuckled deep in his throat, then looked out across the distant plains again.

"What can you possibly see there?" I asked, peering into the darkness.

"The past," he said. "The present. Perhaps even the future."

"*Your* future?" I asked, not comprehending.

He shook his head. "My future has been ordained for seven millennia, and has less than an hour's duration. You see?" he asked, pointing to the heavens. "The moon has come, fat and well-fed, to summon me before the rains come."

"I see no clouds," I said, looking up at the sky.

"The rains are coming nonetheless," he said, getting to his feet and walking over to the gravity sleds. "It is time to begin."

He maneuvered the sleds to the ledge that overlooked the plains, some forty feet away from the fire, then laid the ivory carefully on the ground, and ordered the sleds to return to their original location.

"I will perform the ritual here, overlooking the ancestral

lands of my people, where there are no overhanging branches to block God's view."

"I thought Sendeyo had instructed the Maasai to build an altar of the ivory," I noted.

"They are on the holy mountain, which was given to us by God," replied Mandaka. "They lay upon His grasses and plants, His twigs and branches. What man-made altar can compare to that?"

He pulled a net of hand-woven grasses, some ten feet long and five feet wide, out of his pack.

"This net," he said, as he affixed it between the ivory, "was made of the grasses of all the worlds that the ivory has visited. All that I could find, at any rate."

When he finished he stood back to observe his handi-work, then gathered a large amount of kindling and a dozen sturdy logs and placed them down on the net.

"After I am dead," he said, "cover my body with still more kindling and branches, and then set fire to it."

"If that's what you wish," I said.

"It is. And remember to scatter my bones."

"I will."

"I know this will be distasteful to you, but you may take comfort in the fact that I won't feel a thing."

"I said I'd do it, and I will."

"I know," replied Mandaka.

He looked up at the sky. "Another five minutes," he announced.

While I reached my hands out toward the fire, trying to absorb its warmth, he slowly took off his clothes until he stood, proud and naked, in the diffused moonlight that filtered down to us through the branches. Then he reached into his pack once again and gently withdrew a lion's-mane headdress. After he had placed it on his head, he donned a necklace made of lions' claws and spent the next few minutes painting his face a strange, chalky white.

Finally he withdrew a long, wicked-looking knife.

"This belonged to Sendeyo's brother, Lenana, the paramount chief of the Maasai," he said.

"It is very impressive," I said unenthusiastically.

"There is one last thing I must do," he said, approaching me.

"Oh?"

He nodded. "Please extend your hand to me."

"Why?"

"Just do it," he commanded.

I reached my hand out, and he grabbed it firmly with his left hand, while cutting into my thumb with the knife, which he held in his right hand.

I uttered a grunt of pain and surprise. "What the hell was *that* all about?" I demanded, pulling my hand away from him.

"The ceremony can only be performed by a Maasai," he replied as he cut his own thumb and reached out to press it against mine. "If for any reason I miss a vital area and you are required to administer a coup de grâce, you must first become a Maasai. That is why our blood must join and mingle."

He pressed his bleeding thumb against my own for another moment, then nodded and withdrew it.

"And now I am a Maasai?" I asked, placing my thumb to my lips and sucking on it.

"No," he replied earnestly. "But you are as much of a Maasai as I can make you, and God will have to understand." He stared at me for a moment. "You must help, too."

"How?"

"Take your thumb out of your mouth. The Maasai are contemptuous of all physical pain."

"Including the pain you are about to suffer?" I asked.

"I will do what must be done," he replied. "But if I prove too weak . . ."

"Yes?"

"Then you must kill me before I cry out."

"No!" I said, backing up until the fire was between us. "That wasn't part of the bargain!"

"I know," he said softly. "And I hope you won't have to do it." He paused. "But you are my only friend, and now you are my brother, and if it seems to you that I am about to cry out, then you must slit my throat before the sound can reach my lips and escape from them."

"I can't do it!" I protested.

He stared long and hard at me, and finally nodded his approval. "You are my friend and my brother, and you will do what is necessary," he said confidently.

I opened my mouth to argue, but he had already turned his back on me and was approaching the ivory. He stood before it for a long moment, muttering a chant in a language that I had never heard before, and then lay down atop the pile of logs and kindling, the tusks framing him upon the ground.

He then began a recitation of names, which I took to be the paramount chiefs and major *laibons* of the Maasai. As he did so, his hand rose, and the moonlight gleamed off Lenana's ancient knife.

"Sendeyo," he said at last, when the blade at reached its apex, "it is done! *Fezi Nyupi*, it is accomplished!"

And then he brought the knife down and plunged it into his chest.

His body stiffened, the blade fell from his hand, and his fingers locked over the two pillars of ivory. He opened his mouth, but no sound came forth.

I watched him writhe in pain for another twenty seconds. Then I could stand it no longer, and I ran over and knelt down beside him. He looked up at me, his face contorted in a terrible grimace, and tried to force a smile to his lips. I reached down and let him hold my hand, oblivious to the pain as his powerful fingers dug into my skin.

He relaxed for an instant, then tensed again, and I picked up the knife, holding it just out of his field of vision, hoping against hope that I wouldn't have to use it, but prepared, against my will, to help him fulfill his strange destiny.

His eyes ceased focusing, and I could feel his grip becoming weaker with each passing second, yet he continued to breathe, and every now and then his body arched in pain. Then, finally, he relaxed one last time.

"After seven millennia, it is done," he whispered, and died.

I fought back the urge to vomit, found that I couldn't fight back the urge to cry, and, still weeping, I covered him with kindling and a dozen stout tree limbs and then lit his pyre.

I retreated to the campfire, shuddering as I watched the blaze grow higher and higher, scorching its ivory framing. From time to time I threw more branches on it, and by dawn there was nothing left but the charred bones of Bukoba Mandaka and the charred ivory of the Kilimanjaro Elephant.

Then, at sunrise, there was a deafening clap of thunder, and suddenly the mountain was enveloped in a driving rainstorm. I donned a pair of gloves, walked over to the sizzling embers, and began scattering Mandaka's bones as he had instructed me.

The deluge became worse, and I was forced to erect a shelter to protect myself. It continued for two hours, and when it was over I stepped back out into the cold, clear air of Kilimanjaro to finish the job.

There was nothing left. The ledge on which his body

laid had broken away and washed down the mountainside, taking the bones and the ivory with it. I stood as close to the edge as I dared and looked down, searching for a sign of them, but all I could see was the verdant foliage, glistening moistly in the African sunlight.

I remained where I was for another hour, then packed the gravity sleds and began climbing down the slopes of Kilimanjaro.

Eleventh Interlude (6404 G.E.)

I returned to my office two weeks later after a brief visit to my apartment. Both felt strange to me. The office seemed especially stuffy and constricting. I ordered the computer to cool and freshen the air, and when this didn't help I had it turn the walls translucent to flood the room with sunlight.

I then took a dryshower and changed into a fresh outfit, ordered a pair of pastries and a coffee for breakfast, and then sat down on my chair.

"Computer?"

"Yes, Duncan Rojas?"

"I want to insert a footnote to the 409th Terran Edition of Braxton's *Records of Big Game*."

"Waiting . . ."

"The tusks of the Kilimanjaro Elephant no longer exist. They were on Bortai II when its sun went nova. No trace of them remains."

"Inserted."

"Send that out as an addendum to all libraries and museums."

"Working . . . done."

I spent the next few minutes catching up on my correspondence and glancing over various staff reports. Then the door opened and Hilda Dorian entered the office.

"I heard you were back," she said.

"I arrived last night."

"Thank you for calling," she said sarcastically.

"I was tired."

She shot me a look of utter disbelief.

"May I sit down?"

I shrugged. "Suit yourself."

She ordered a chair to approach her, then seated herself as it hovered just above the floor.

"Where is your mentor?" she asked.

"My mentor?"

"Mandaka."

"He's dead."

"On Earth?"

I nodded.

"Did you report it to the authorities?"

"Yes."

"What did he die of?"

"Heart failure."

"Did you bring the body back for an autopsy?"

"No," I replied. "He had no family, and his last request was that he be buried on Earth."

Hilda gave me another look of disbelief that matched her initial one, then stared at me thoughtfully. "You seem different somehow."

"Oh?"

She nodded. "You're even more wrapped up in yourself than usual."

"I hadn't noticed."

"And reticent."

"Ask me anything you want," I offered.

"Why bother?" she said. "You're just going to lie to me."

"Why should you say that?" I asked without bothering to deny it.

"Duncan, the reason I know you're back is because I saw what you ordered the computer to do."

"To freshen the air?" I asked.

"To say that the ivory was lost when Bortai went nova."

"Oh."

"I thought you told me that it was on Skyblue."

"I was mistaken," I said.

"And you went to Earth without the ivory because your friend Mandaka wanted to visit his old haunts," she concluded caustically.

"The ivory is lost," I said. "I don't want anyone ever to go looking for it again."

"Is that your decision to make?"

"There's nobody else left to make it," I replied.

"Mandaka's really dead?" she asked.

"He's really dead."

Suddenly she frowned. "You didn't kill him?" she asked sharply.

"No, I didn't kill him," I responded. "But I was prepared to."

"I don't understand."

"I know you don't."

"I thought he was your friend," she continued.

"He was," I replied sincerely.

She stared at me for a moment, and then spoke in a more compassionate tone. "Then I'm very sorry for you, Duncan," she said. "I know how difficult it is for you to feel close to someone. I hope you'll find another friend."

"I hope so too," I lied.

We spoke for a few more minutes, and I reminded her

that I owed Harold and her a night on the town, and then she went back to her office, and I was left alone, to sit and stare out at the midmorning pollution and sort out my emotions.

But emotions are not like facts, and the more I tried to order them, the less they responded. In the end I could only conclude that empathy was an emotion better left to people like Hilda, who actually considered it a virtue. I had finally tried it, found it distinctly uncomfortable, and was determined never to yield to it again.

By midafternoon I was starting to feel like myself once more. In the evening I took Hilda and Harold to the Ancient Days, which served as both dinner and theater. Then, my obligation fulfilled, I returned to the office for the night and tried to authenticate the wingspan of a recently-slain Devilowl. By the time I began weighing the conflicting testimony, all thoughts of Mandaka and the ivory had been permanently banished from my mind.

It was almost dawn when I finally fell asleep.

12

Ivory (6304 G.E.)

I watched the ivory—my ivory—as it washed down the slopes of mighty Kilimanjaro, at last to join the rest of me beneath the mud and the earth, and finally my waiting was over.

I am very old, and I have seen many things. I have seen the dimly-lit interior of a cave on Belamone XI, and the world-shaking storms that swirl around far Athenia. I have been stalked by hunters, and by thieves, and by religious zealots, by good men and bad.

Even now, though my vision grows hazy, I can still look across the tapestry of events that brought Bukoba Mandaka to the holy mountain. I can see Tembo Laibon laying his bets and taking his percentages; I can see Amin Rashid XIV striding across the silent streets of Plantagenet II, oblivious of all danger; I can see Hannibal Sloane studying me from afar, grinding dust between his fingers to test the wind. I can feel the delicate tendrils of the alien Eyes-of-Fire imprinting the history of her race upon me, and the ragged stone of Rakanja as he chopped away at the base of my ivory.

Many millennia have come and gone, and always I have waited here atop my mountain. I have whispered my unrest to Sendeyo, and to Maasai Laibon, and to Leeyo Nelion, and to Bukoba Mandaka who died, arrogant and silent, as he was meant to die. Empires have risen and fallen, planets have been discovered and colonized and deserted, generations of men have come and gone, and through it all I have persisted.

I have seen the birth of stars, and the death of worlds, and have watched as the last of my kind died the lonely death of a captive animal—and throughout it all, I have waited for the odyssey to reach its conclusion.

And now, finally, the restlessness is gone, the loneliness has vanished, the anguish has disappeared. The galactic tapestry continues, but it will continue without me, for even now the vision fades, the echoes dim, and oblivion intrudes.

I am complete again.

AUTHOR'S NOTE

Yes, he really existed. He is listed in *Rowland Ward's Records of Big Game*. His tusks are in the storage area below the British Museum of Natural History. Two photographs of his remarkable ivory are still in existence. His tusks were registered and sold at auction in Zanzibar in 1898. Though none of them ever personally encountered him, he nonetheless appears in the memoirs of such famed hunters as Karamojo Bell, Denis D. Lyell, T. Murray Smith, and Commander David Enderby Blunt.

During my two most recent trips to Africa, I discovered that almost every old-time hunter and colonist I met knew of him, and I spent many fascinating evenings listening to their wildly differing speculations concerning where he lived and how he died.

Of such stuff are legends made.

M.R.

THE BEST IN SCIENCE FICTION